Please return/renew this item by the last date shown. Books may also be renewed by phone or internet.

 www.rbwm.gov.uk/home/leisure-and-culture/libraries

☎ 01628 796969 (library hours)

☎ 0303 123 0035 (24 hours)

Royal Borough
of Windsor &
Maidenhead

www.rbwm.gov.uk

THIS IS GONNA
END IN TEARS

Also by Liza Klaussmann

Tigers in Red Weather
Villa America

THIS IS GONNA END IN TEARS

Liza Klaussmann

JOHN MURRAY

First published in Great Britain in 2022 by John Murray (Publishers)
An Hachette UK company

1

Copyright © Liza Klaussmann 2022

"I'm Going Home" by Richard O'Brien © 1983 Druidcrest Ltd PRS admin.
by Wixen Music Publishing, Inc. All Rights Reserved. Used by Permission.

"Night Moves", Words and Music by Bob Seger. Copyright © 1976
Gear Publishing Co. Copyright Renewed. All Rights Reserved. Used by
Permission. Reprinted by Permission of Hal Leonard Europe Ltd.

"Once in a Lifetime", Words and Music by Brian Eno, David Byrne,
Christopher Frantz, Jerry Harrison and Tina Weymouth. Copyright
© 1980 by EG Music Ltd., WC Music Corp. and Index Music, Inc. All
Rights for EG Music Ltd. in the United States and Canada Administered
by Universal Music - MHGB Songs. All Rights for Index Music, Inc.
administered by WC Music Corp. International Copyright Secured. All
Rights Reserved. Reprinted by Permission of Hal Leonard Europe Ltd.

A CIP catalogue record for this title is available from the British Library

Hardback ISBN 978-1-529-38936-4
Trade Paperback ISBN 978-1-529-38937-1
eBook ISBN 978-1-529-38939-5

Typeset in Sabon MT by Hewer Text UK Ltd, Edinburgh
Printed and bound in Great Britain by Clays Ltd, Elcograf S.p.A.

John Murray policy is to use papers that are natural, renewable and
recyclable products and made from wood grown in sustainable forests.
The logging and manufacturing processes are expected to conform
to the environmental regulations of the country of origin.

John Murray (Publishers)
Carmelite House
50 Victoria Embankment
London EC4Y 0DZ

www.johnmurraypress.co.uk

It is not down in any map; true places never are.

Herman Melville, *Moby-Dick*

PART I

ALL IN THE GOLDEN AFTERNOON

AUGUST, 1952

1952

The summer they'd turned nine had been particularly hot, the kind of heat where the bed sheets stick to you all night and your clothes stick to you all day.

One August Sunday, they all sat in the small meeting house in Wonderland, sweltering—the ladies fanning themselves; the men suffering, but motionless; Miller and Ash and Olly trying not to knock their heels against the back of the pine box pews.

The meetings could often pass in total silence. But on this day, several members had given vocal ministry, perhaps out of a need to do something, anything, to forget the heat.

When it was over, the three of them had gotten permission to go swimming. There was a little cove on the strip of Dune Beach between the meeting house and the high school, and they collected their suits, the boys their rods and bait, and they all made their way down the Ring Road.

An unmerciful sun beat down on them as they ambled past Wonderland's houses, painted in sugary greens and pinks and yellows, like a roll of candy buttons. When they reached the cove they stripped down to their bathing suits and sprawled in the shade of a big rock.

After a while, Olly and Ash baited their hooks and climbed atop the rock, dropping in their lines, squinting in the brightness of the day, their browned backs squared up. Miller didn't bother with fishing, instead looking for steamers and hermit crabs and periwinkles in the rock pools. From time to time, she immersed herself in the shallow water to keep off the heat, her head coming up sleek and wet. From where they were sitting the boys could see the words that she'd embroidered on her red, criss-crossed bathing suit. The lines from her father's poetry books, stitched in white thread—*Enwrought with golden and silver light; whatever a sun will always sing is you; Are you nobody, too?*—appeared and disappeared as she moved in the water.

Eventually, the boys gave up fishing and joined her.

They floated on the glassy water like three pieces of driftwood, every so often jack-knifing under the surface, before re-emerging and resuming their semi-motionless state.

When they got hungry, they ate the sandwiches packed by Miller's mother—egg salad wrapped in brown paper—and drank the colas they'd bought at the store on Main Street.

The earth rotated and the sun moved across the sky. The tide went out, revealing the sandbar that connected the tidal island to the mainland, and came back in again. They became hungry for dinner, but they were lethargic from the continuing heat, so instead they started telling ghost stories and, by sunset, they'd forgotten all about supper.

"We should go," Ash finally said.

"We should," Miller agreed.

They knew their parents would scold them for staying out so late.

"Let's go for one last swim," Olly suggested. In those days, Aunt Tassie let him get away with anything.

As they waded into the water, it began to glow with a million tiny blue-green stars. When they dove in and came up, it was all around them. They looked at each other, the three of them laughing, amazed, their skin dripping glowing dots of green light, as if they were made from light, as if they'd become the constellations in the sky.

They'd learn later, in school, that it was luminescence, the glow given off by a particular mix of unusual chemicals colliding, acting upon each other, when phytoplankton are disturbed by unexpected vibrations or sudden movements. They bloomed in warm weather.

4

PART II

AND HOME WE STEER, A MERRY CREW

LATE MAY, 1984

The Day

It was the most perfect day. The sound of sprinklers ticking away and the warble of house finches drifted lazily in through the open sash window. Outside, a technicolor scene hung suspended in time, as if waiting only for a director to yell *Action!* and put the whole thing in motion: a small footpath bordered by tightly clipped grass, a crystalline sky, and in the center of the frame, a twirly jacaranda tree just coming into its concupiscent flower. The air was light and fresh with just a whisper of humidity like only slightly damp, very clean laundry.

It was a shining day, a sparkling day. The kind of day that made you glad to be alive.

It was also the day that Olly Lane was going to kill himself.

Olly was sitting at his desk in his office at Obscura Pictures in Los Angeles, surrounded by his Philippe Starck furniture, an enormous framed poster of *The Third Man* rising behind him. Olly knew he needed to move, to get up, to leave, drive home, but he was arrested by the view outside his office window onto the lot. How strange that it could be this beautiful, this—*dazzling*—was the word for it: the day, the view, the purple jacaranda blossoms, and that it could have absolutely no connection to him. It felt like a rebuke, as if by its sheer gloriousness the day was telling him: *Yes, that's right, you've got it—you ARE insignificant. I am a marvel. I am immutable. I am eternally switched on. But YOU, Olly Lane, you're terminable. And you're getting written out of this one.*

As if he were already gone.

Well, that was the point, what he'd only recently realized: there is no point; everyone thinks they're the hero of their own story, when actually there's no story at all. Just an outline that gets filled in with nonsense and accidents and happenstance and luck. And then, well . . . and then nothing.

The day went on shining, and the finches went on warbling, and the jacaranda blossoms floated by on the air like confetti, and in the end, Olly did get up.

Ignoring the empty cardboard boxes stacked tactfully in the far corner—presumably by Gloria—he walked out of his office for the last time, taking only his car keys and his jacket.

In the waiting room-cum-lobby, Gloria, with her gray bob and oversized lavender glasses, was conspicuously absent—the first time in the two years he'd worked there that his secretary wasn't at her desk when Olly was on the lot.

He was glad to be leaving this place. The last two years had, for the most part, been a series of meaningless projects that he would rather forget.

Outside, Olly put on his Wayfarers and looked at the main building across the way, where his boss, Seymour Geist, now sat. There was no need for any further goodbyes: everything had already been said.

When Olly had first agreed to sell a controlling stake in Lay Down Records, as part of a deal that'd landed him the job at Obscura, Geist had asked him about the name of the label, where it had come from.

"It's a Quaker thing," Olly had said. "What we say when we mean we're going to stop doing something, you know, when something's come to an end."

"Fucking Quaker fuck," was how Geist had responded.

That had set the tone for their future intercourse, and yesterday had been no exception. Things had been coming to a head for some time, but when Olly refused to get on board with *Doctor Zhivago II: Doctors Zhivago*, it had been the last straw for Geist. The studio head had called him into his office and delivered the news with his usual panache: "I hired you because I needed an asshole. And you, Olly Lane, are an asshole. You fucked your friends. Everyone knows that. That's what I loved about you, Olly, you Quaker fuck. That's what I hired you to do here. Fuck your best friends, fuck the other studios, fuck the writers and the actors and fuck the assistants and the fucking gaffer, fuck the public. Now, if you won't make me a fucking *Doctor Zhivago II* with a fucking fighter pilot and some barn sex and a red-blooded American ending that sticks it to those gulag-loving, freedom-fucking motherfucking Russians, then, my friend, you're fired."

And that had been that.

Jingling his car keys in his hand, Olly walked to his white convertible Porsche Cabriolet, resplendent in the glorious afternoon sun. He sat in the car wishing he smoked—then laughed a small laugh because, Christ, there was no reason not to now.

Next to him, on the passenger seat, was the script of *Moby-Dick*, given to him for final approval. If there was one thing that he vaguely regretted leaving undone at Obscura, it was *Moby-Dick*, and that was only because of Rodrigo, the director he'd hired who'd become a friend.

Olly rolled down the window and tossed the script onto the pavement. Then he started the ignition and headed towards The Bower.

Olly had always felt that if there was one thing he'd done completely right in the last ten years, it was to buy his home in Beverly Hills. Spaces were important to him. He believed that they should be an expression of who you wanted to be, or who you imagined you could be. They brought their own magic, cast their own spell on your destiny; if the space were right, the setting done correctly, the atmosphere and the detail—if all that was pitched unerringly, then it opened up the possibility of being someone better, someone you were on the inside but maybe not yet on the outside. Someone you were only waiting to become. Well, at least that's what he used to think.

When he and Miller and Ash had first settled in L.A.—before everything had fallen apart—they'd lived in Malibu. First in a ramshackle place on the beach, the three of them sharing the house with its peeling paint, the cracked dishes Miller had found at the five-and-dime, the old couch Olly had rescued from the side of the highway. They'd loved it. He'd loved it: the caftans, and the shabby, sandy, sexy bungalows—fruit left out to overripen on the counter, overflowing shrimp pots—all that had been the perfect backdrop to his life at that moment.

Later, when there was a little more money, Ash had taken it over and Olly and Miller had moved to their own place just down the road. They hadn't wanted to be far apart, the three of them. He thought they'd never leave, that he'd never leave. And in fact he had stayed on in the house in Malibu, even after things had fallen apart with Miller.

But by the time The Bower had come on to the market in '74, things had changed; Olly had changed. And he'd needed a new stage on which to perform his next transformation.

He'd stepped on a lot of toes to secure the coveted 1940s Hollywood Regency house once owned by a famous and degenerate actor. It was basically a large one-bedroom ranch, with a pool and a guesthouse. But, like so many things, it was The Bower's perfect scale that made it one of a kind.

He remembered the first time he'd walked through the black lacquer Pullman doors, how the house had sort of unfurled before him: an octagonal foyer, highly polished floors, circular antechambers, perfectly proportioned galleries—one charm after another.

The showpiece was the living room: grand double doors opened onto an oval room with a floor-to-ceiling bow window overlooking the gardens. In the central windowpane, with columns on either side, sat a fireplace whose marble mantel seemed to float in the glass without chimney or flue. French doors led to a terrace. Below, an elliptical pool, with small waterfalls breezily spritzing the surface, and a vine-covered guesthouse, all set in a grove of eucalyptus trees, Montezuma cypress and weeping cherry.

Olly had taken one look at it and thought: *This is me. This is me now.* And he'd called his banker and packed his things. He'd seen the future, his future. He'd been just 30 years old and he'd been on top of the world, and king of his perfect castle.

Turning off North Beverly Drive, Olly drove through a copse before arriving at the wrought-iron gates. As he got out of the car, the smell of the roses planted thickly around the circular drive assaulted him, their sweetness overpowering him. At one time, he'd thought they gave the place the air of a Mediterranean villa somewhere, in the South of France, maybe. Olly winced, remembering that vanity now, how he used to say that sort of thing to the women he brought here. They'd say something like: "Oh, it's so beautiful." Then he'd say: "It always makes me feel like I'm on holiday, the South of France, maybe. Don't you think?" But casually, an off-hand remark, as if it had just popped into his head. And: "Oh, yes, yes," they'd reply enthusiastically. Perhaps they'd all seen through him, and he'd never noticed. Blue certainly had. "I don't feel like I'm on holiday," she'd said. "I just feel like you have a really expensive gardener." Not that it mattered now. Blue was gone and, as usual, her timing had been impeccable.

The shuttered French windows in the front of the house blinked at him. Oh so gently, Olly closed the car door and, shading his face from the sun, he looked up at the mansard roof, eying the spot where a leak had sprung. He remembered then that he'd booked a handyman to come in and repair it, and was struck with horror at the thought that it might be this unwitting handyman who found him.

He couldn't think about that. There was no good person to find him. There were probably worse people.

Olly walked purposefully up the front step, took out his house key, fitted it into the neat lock and walked into his cool, silent house.

It was the golden hour, the Los Angeles sky bathed a shimmering red, and Olly was sitting by the pool. Next to him on the glass table sat an Iittala Otso glass, a bottle of Smirnoff, and a bottle of Seconal—the last two items belonging to Blue.

Blue . . . He wouldn't think about her now. And if not now, he realized, never again. Also on the list of things he didn't want to think about now, or ever again: Miller and Ash, the Gordian knot tying them together; Lay Down Records; Aunt Tassie; the music. Especially the music. Because of all the things that had led him to this moment, losing that had been the one he knew he couldn't fix. He'd woken up one day, and it was just gone. His gift. The colors he saw, the flavors he tasted. All gone. And with it had gone the person he knew himself to be.

Olly had decided on a pair of Ralph Lauren salmon-colored linen swim trunks, a ridiculously impractical concept, but, he thought, better than being found completely naked. That felt indecent, presumptuous somehow.

He'd already consumed ten of the pills, washed down with five fingers of vodka, which he was drinking neat. In a little while, he'd take the next twenty, all at once, and then float himself into the swimming pool and wait for sleep.

He knew his choice of exit would confound some of the people he knew. Especially the music and movie people. Olly stood out as probably the only teetotaler in either industry. He'd never been that into drugs or booze, but at a certain point early on in his career he'd seen just what an enormous advantage his sobriety was. Being in control when everyone else was off their head was like having magic powers. Besides, he'd been afraid of dying from an overdose.

It was an appalling moment, realizing that the thing you were most afraid of happening—really, really afraid of, in a sickening, trembling kind of way—became the second thing you were most afraid of happening, next only to it not happening.

Still, he'd seen the effect of this particular cocktail before, so he could be sure that it worked, and that was the important thing. Another thing he didn't want to think about: his mother.

Olly reclined his lounger all the way back and looked up at the sky, which admittedly looked a little crazy. It was illuminated by a kind of biblical light, as if the clouds had been colored in by all the crayons in the Crayola jumbo box, the expensive one with 64 shades. Olly thought back to the meeting house in Wonderland, to the ministries of the Friends of his youth, about the glow of the inner light, how God was in all of us, was in Olly, too.

As he lay there, the light only grew stronger and there was a growing hum, which he could feel vibrating in his body. He closed his eyes, squeezing his lids together, until a kaleidoscope of green and blue and yellow paisleys swirled behind them. The colors expanded, moving in an outward circle. A dark hole appeared in the center, growing larger and larger. All at once, he could see the shockingly white face of a boy, staring as if pressed against glass, looking straight back at him. He abruptly opened his eyes.

So this is what real drugs are like, Olly thought, and wondered if the Seconal was working faster than he'd intended, and if perhaps he should get into the pool now.

Olly was thinking this, looking at the astonishing sky, when several things occurred at once. First, he heard a noise, a kind of pattering-splatting-thwacking sound, rapidly increasing in tempo. He looked at the pool: there were things floating in it, big fat bugs with wings, struggling, drowning. They were all around the lounge chair, too, and in the grass. At the same time, he could also *feel* them; they were falling on him, falling out of the eucalyptus trees, wet and new, thuddering softly against his bare skin, his face, his mouth.

Dog-day cicadas, hundreds of them. They were falling from the sky.

His brain started making erratic calculations: Was it a hallucination? Was it some kind of sign from God? He tried to remember what the plagues meant: There *were* locusts, weren't there? But were locusts the same things as cicadas? Jesus, if only he could think straight. But the things just continued dropping, dropping . . .

Who gives a shit? his brain yelled. *This is bad, bad, bad. Abort! Abort!*

Olly jumped up, but being drunk and high, he immediately fell over, scraping his hands and knees on the limestone paving, his palms pressing down on a carpet of insects. Lurching up, he staggered across the lawn, crushing their damp, fragile wings underfoot.

He leaned on the hedge with his hand, groping his way up the stairs towards the terrace and the French doors that would bring him to safety. Once inside, he shut and locked the doors.

He had just started across the living room, when it began—at first a small shifting, a light shaking beneath his feet. Then, it was as if the ground were no longer ground but was moving, sliding, like he was trying to walk on a waterbed. Olly only just managed to clutch onto the back of one of his spotless cream-colored sofas to keep from toppling over entirely. The air around him vibrated.

He was feeling violently ill when the real shock finally hit, ripping through the house like a wave. He watched in horror as the floor planks in the living room rose and fell like piano keys.

Above him, the French chandelier spun and swayed, fissures radiating from the ceiling rose like fingers loosening their grip. Then the whole business—plaster and all—came crashing to the ground, teardrops of glass skittering across the broken floor.

As Olly instinctively began to head for the front door, there was a slow cracking sound and he turned back to see one of the decorative plaster columns in the bow window rending away from the wall, falling straight towards him. He had a moment of—perhaps clarity was too strong a word—but of understanding that he would die here, and that perhaps it had been taken out of his hands as an act of mercy. Perhaps God had taken pity on him, perhaps He was with him, after all.

Before he could continue this train of thought, his perfect house began to crumble, and the column came crashing down on his head, smashing a multitude of bones in his skull and his face, felling him like a rotten tree.

FUCKING OLLY LANE

Miller Everley stood in her underwear in the kitchen of her orange house in Wonderland staring at the pea-green phone on the wall, willing herself to pick it up. The room was bathed in a kind of mossy iridescent glow that she at first thought was cast by the early morning rain on the growing leaves and grass outside, but then remembered was just the tint of her Ted Lapidus sunglasses, a gift from Ash for her fortieth birthday, earlier that year. She wore them so often now that at times she forgot the world wasn't actually green.

Miller chewed delicately on a tender part of her cuticle, weighing her options. In the end, she walked over to the fridge—marigold yellow with fake wood detailing on the handle. When they'd bought the house twelve years ago, the salesman had told her that it was *the* color to have. She'd regretted it almost immediately.

She took out a Tab and drank it down, leaning against the open fridge door, the cold air leaking out and prickling her bare skin. Then, choosing one of the twenty or so personal-sized tins of Blue Diamond almonds that lined the shelves of the cupboard, she sat down at the table, hooking her finger through the tab and pulling back the lid. The vacuum seal made a kind of click-pop, a tiny ecstatic release.

She ate the almonds deliberately, one by one, her foot propped on the edge of the battered farm table, thinking about—but refusing to make eye contact with—the telephone. She knew that once she picked it up a chain of events would be set in motion. Whether big or small, she couldn't say, but events all the same. And events were what she was trying to avoid these days.

Of the three of them, Olly had been the only one who hadn't had a phone growing up: *Telephones only carry bad news*, Aunt Tassie had always said. As if they were the carriers of viruses rather than information. Miller had to admit that Aunt Tassie might have a point: there might be something viral, something dangerous about them.

She knew she couldn't put it off any longer: she had to phone her husband. He needed to be the one to break the news to Olly. Between the two evils—calling Olly or calling Ash—calling Ash was definitely the lesser.

The thing was, she had no idea if Ash would be at the apartment. And she didn't really want to find out, either. She'd wait. Normally, he was at work by eight. It was nine. But today was Saturday. He might sleep in. She'd just wait.

No, she really couldn't wait any longer.

In an act of supreme will, she picked up the phone and dialed the number. She wasn't sure if she wanted him to be there, for the obvious reasons—or not, so that she could continue to be angry with him, and maybe get even angrier.

As it rang, Miller stretched out the long phone cord with her bare foot, poking her big toe into the coils, drawing it back and forth across the sandy linoleum floor.

On the fourth ring, Ash picked up, his voice groggy. "Hello?"

Her husband's voice sounded the same as always and Miller was faintly surprised by this, as if she'd imagined him differently somehow.

"It's me," she said. "It's Miller," she added, unnecessarily.

There was a pause and then: "Hi. I'm . . . What time is it?"

"Something's happened," she said, and quickly, so that she wouldn't have to think about the fact that Ash *was* there, but that maybe he wasn't alone, which of course hadn't entered into the first equation she'd made.

Miller heard rustling.

"Hold on, I'm turning on the light," Ash said.

She didn't want to dissect the rustling.

"What were you saying?"

She could picture the bedroom in their New York pied-à-terre, the one they'd bought after they'd left New York for good 12 years ago: the big double bed pushed up against the built-in shelves containing their books and family photos, the white ruffled bed skirt, the gray plush carpet. The curtains would be closed. He always slept with the curtains closed, a fact that had irritated her throughout their married life. Though now, maybe, he slept with them open? She hadn't seen him in three months. Any number of things could have changed.

"I got a call from the Starry Acres Nursing Home," she said.

"The . . . I'm sorry? What?"

"Starry Acres," Miller repeated. "You know, Aunt Tassie's nursing home. Over the bridge."

Ash had never visited Aunt Tassie there, but Miller had. A couple of times, anyway. She'd meant to go more. Now she was sorry she hadn't made more of an effort.

"Right . . ."

"It seems she attacked another resident? That's what they're saying, though, honestly, I can't imagine it. Anyway, they haven't been able to reach Olly. They're going to turn her over to social services if no one comes to collect her." She paused, waiting for Ash to respond. He didn't. "I'm going to have to go get her," Miller sighed. "Bring her here. At least until we can figure something out."

"Oh, right," Ash said. "I thought . . . well, never mind. Do what you think is best, of course."

Miller pulled the cord tighter around her toe. "The thing is . . ."

Ash sighed. "What's *the thing*, Miller?"

The wariness and irritation, the goddamn *long-suffering-ness* in Ash's voice made her want to scream. "Well, *Ash*, someone needs to get in touch with Olly. I don't have his number." This was a weak excuse, she knew. "But I know you do, from the last time, when we had to sign the papers . . ."

It had been four years since either of them had spoken to Olly. And an even longer time since they'd actually been friends.

"Hang on a minute," Ash said, his voice hardening in a way that Miller had always hated. She gritted her teeth. "Why does anyone have to do that? I mean, fuck Olly."

"Yes, fuck Olly. But unless you want Aunt Tassie living with us—me, actually—permanently . . ."

"Look, about that," he said, more gently. "I want to come home. Nate's going to be there soon . . ."

Their son was coming home from boarding school to spend with them what would be his last summer before college, film school. Nate's life was opening up before him, a prospect that alarmed her: she couldn't imagine him in her shoes, in Ash's shoes, at the same age.

"Well, that depends," she said. "Would you be coming alone?"

"Don't, Miller," Ash said.

She already regretted saying it, regretted the ground that had been given up. She raised her hand in assent. "Fine."

There was a pause, then Ash said: "Let me do it. I'll come down and get Aunt Tassie and sort it out. And then I'll stay. Just for a few days, to see Nate."

Miller pulled the cord so tight, she could see her toe going blue. "Hello?"

"I'm thinking."

"It'll be good for us."

When she didn't reply, Ash said: "I'm going to take that as a yes. I can be there tomorrow. We'll figure out the rest when I get there."

Miller nodded.

"Miller?"

"I'm nodding." She chewed her cuticle.

"I'm looking forward to seeing you," her husband said, softly.

When he said that, in that way, she felt badly that she hated him. And then she hated him for making her feel badly. So to punish him, she hung up abruptly.

Miller walked upstairs to their bedroom, and unhooked her bra, stepped out of her underpants. She caught her reflection in the full-length mirror on the back of the closet door. In the May morning light, her body looked long and white, like a cigarette. For some reason, it hurt her to see that body, and she looked away.

Lately, she'd found what seemed like fairly simple tasks—such as getting dressed—elusive. So, little by little, she'd stopped bothering with clothes, and taken to wearing only her underwear and sunglasses around the house. She had the sensation, as she abandoned first socks, then shoes, then pants, then shirts, that she was getting sleeker, streamlined, being made new, like a snake shedding her skin.

After changing into the black one-piece suit—racer-backed, the elastic going at the edges—Miller grabbed a towel from the basement, a couple of cans of almonds and another Tab, and headed out the kitchen door.

She settled herself in the Volvo station wagon. "All right," she said to herself, because this was always the hard part of her daily pilgrimage, getting going, and she needed encouragement. "All right. Let's go." She turned on the ignition and carefully backed the car out, tires crunching on the shell-covered driveway.

Miller drove slowly down Church Street; even this early in the morning there were always children playing about, teenagers racing around on their bikes, dogs ambling out of driveways. Wonderland was not a town you drove fast in.

The sound of the town waking up on a late spring morning— the hum of lawnmowers, the scratch of AM radio stations, the high clink of someone practicing their scales, the lower register of breakfast pans clanging in the distance—floated on the air, through open windows and into the car, along with the sweet scent of newly cut grass.

She passed the rows of brightly colored houses, little emerald squares of green shining out front, the pretty ornamental gates making tidy borders.

When she was very young, before she could remember, the town had looked like any other Quaker settlement. But a post-war "beautification" scheme had resulted in a riot of color, the once plain clapboard houses dressing themselves up in lilac, melon, sunflower yellow, lime green, robin's egg blue, like fancy ladies.

Passing the First Presbyterian church, Miller saw Dick Cross and his son Cam, sweeping the church walk. While she and Ash had never been particularly close with the minister —Dick's wife had left when Cam was still a baby—Cam and Nate had been thick as thieves growing up; they still were, she supposed. He'd been a beautiful child, Cam, all golden blond with a pretty, red mouth, but he'd always made Miller uncomfortable. No, not uncomfortable exactly—sad. He had this strange condition—he couldn't cry, or more precisely, he couldn't make actual tears. She remembered once, when he'd been about five or six, he'd skinned his knee in their driveway and as she'd held him, he'd just scrunched up his lovely face and made moaning noises. She'd been alarmed, confused, wondering if he was faking it. Of course, when his father had explained the situation, she'd understood. But it had stayed with her: the fact that without the actual tears, crying became a pantomime of pain, an act not to be trusted.

She waved at them now, and Dick waved back, his figure cut sharp against the white neo-classical church. An image came to Miller of Aunt Tassie in the meeting house, arrayed in one of her intricate lace Sunday dresses, complete with a whalebone corset from god-knows-what century, holding Olly's hand.

Thinking about Aunt Tassie, Miller found herself getting angry, murderous, in fact: she could kill Olly, she really could. He'd taken the woman who had raised him, who had loved him, who had always held his hand, who'd literally saved his stupid life, and dumped her, alone, in a place 3,000 miles from where he lived.

Miller stopped the car. "Breathe," she told herself. "Breathe."

She breathed. She put the car in drive.

Fucking Olly Lane. Fucking Olly. *Fucking* Olly.

She tried really hard never to think about fucking Olly. About what it had felt like to be with him, the taste of him, the feel of his skin beneath her fingertips, beneath her whole hand. About the way it was before Ash, before they left for L.A., before Lay Down

Records. When they were young in Wonderland, and it was all just beginning.

It had been the night after they'd all been to the carnival, after she'd almost drowned. They'd been seventeen and it had been late, and she'd been asleep. He'd climbed up the trellis of her parents' house and knocked on her window. Outside, a dark, moonless night, her parents asleep down the hall.

She'd gone to the half-open window, and looked at him through the pane. Even now, that suspended moment had a real-life weight, a density she could feel, turn over in her hand. She could remember feeling surprised and also not surprised. For so long, she'd wanted—not just something to happen to her—but for *him* to happen to her, that it felt that night as if she'd conjured him herself.

"Hey," he'd said, the word, his breath, condensing on the glass.

Silently, she pushed the window open, lifted the screen and took his hand. She followed him down the trellis, the dew from the chinaberry vine leaving her thin nightgown, the one with the strawberries on it, damp, clinging to her legs.

He led her to his car, and she went like a sleepwalker, as if under a charm. She stared at his profile as he drove: straight nose, thin, curving lips, his dark hair swept off his forehead.

They parked at Dune Beach, and he pulled her nightgown over her head and slipped his hand into her cotton underpants, saw his name written on her inner thigh. And she lifted his white T-shirt off, and felt their bare skin together, warm, then slick, no space in between, slipping like oil. Like a goddamn fire. She'd known then that her future was sealed, that she'd follow him anywhere.

But things, of course, had turned out very differently. So she tried never to think about fucking Olly Lane.

When Miller reached the long, flat Ring Road that circled Wonderland, she leaned over and popped open the glove compartment, rummaging around among the loose cassette tapes before sweeping them all onto the passenger seat. She looked up and had to swerve slightly to keep the car straight on the road. Glancing sideways again, she picked out the Talking Heads tape and slid it into the tape deck. There was white noise then the cassette clicked to the end and Miller had to eject it and turn it over, before pushing it back in.

The sound of the synthesizer drifted out of the speakers. Miller turned the volume all the way up and cranked down her window, letting the misty air fill the car.

"*You may find yourself living in a shotgun shack*," Miller shouted over the music, only then realizing that she'd been wanting to shout for hours, for years.

"*And you may find yourself in a beautiful house, with a beautiful wife, and you may ask yourself, 'Well . . .'*"—Miller shrugged—"'*how did I get here?*'"

She kept time with her hand on the steering wheel, her bare foot pushing down on the accelerator, feeling the town receding behind her, slipping away, giving way to a sense of lightness.

The post-rain glow made the shapes and colors outside slightly indistinct, like a blurry painting. The sunglasses didn't help either, interfering with her depth perception, but she'd driven this road so many times she could have done it with her eyes closed.

"*Letting the days go by, let the water hold me down . . .*" She put her left hand out the window, making waves through the passing air.

When she reached the wooden bridge that connected Wonderland to the mainland, a trailer passed from the opposite direction, swerving in and out of her lane, forcing Miller to swerve herself to avoid being sideswiped.

"Chill out. *Jesus*," she yelled over the music.

In her rearview mirror, she saw the trailer had *Superstarz Location Services* written on the back. Must be something to do with the movie they were about to shoot in Wonderland. Somebody had said *Moby-Dick*, but Miller couldn't imagine that was true. Who'd want to see that?

At the beach in Longwell, the water was cold, and gray from the rain earlier, and she walked in, then dove as the shore dropped quickly away. She resurfaced and treaded a moment, eyed her destination: the blue and white bell buoy swaying in the distance. Then she put her head down and began: her arms like scythes, water sluicing over her muscles, covering her with a silvery wet skin, salt stinging her eyes.

Maybe, she thought, today would be the day she'd make it all the way there.

VANISHING ISLAND IN THE CROOKED BAY

Ash Everley entered the building at East 88th, nodding to Bobby as he went in, feeling strangely proud that Candice Cressman's doorman knew him by sight. This was followed by the reflexive thought: What other men did the TV star's doorman know by sight?

Ash pushed the idea out of his head. What did he care anyway? He was married, he didn't need these petty jealousies.

He took the elevator up to her floor. It was the kind of set-up where the elevator opened right into the apartment. If he ever got another place in the city—well, a real place, not the pied-à-terre on the Upper East Side—this would be what he'd want. He pushed that thought out of his head, too. He was married, and besides, Candice had never said whether she'd want him. They never talked about Miller, or about divorce. They lived in the present. And if Ash were a betting man, he'd bet she'd be—at a minimum—*ambivalent* if he showed up with his suitcase at her fancy uptown apartment.

"Oh, hi," Candice said, when he walked into the living room, as if she were surprised to see him, before turning her back on him.

"Expecting someone else?" The minute he said it, Ash hated himself. It sounded weak and whiny and desperate.

"No. I'm just distracted." She took a big gulp from an over-sized glass of what he guessed to be Chardonnay. It was her drink of choice. Unless she was on a diet, then she drank spritzers.

"I can't stay long," Ash began. "I've got to go to Wonderland . . ."

"Fucking Clark Dennis. Dickweed pervert," she muttered. Then spun around to face Ash. "He's trying to push me out, I just know he is. But I'm not going down like that, not like poor dumb-dumb Susan." Pacing the chintz living room in her electric-blue aerobics gear, Candice looked like an exotic and dangerous animal.

"What?" Ash said, tearing his gaze away from her slippery Lycra, trying to focus. "He's trying to push you out? Already? You just got the job. Are you sure you're not being paranoid?"

Candice looked at him, her blue eyes hardening.

Ash held up his hands. "Sorry."

"No, I'm not being paranoid, *Ash*. How do you think I got the job in the first place; why do you think Susan got fired? She wouldn't blow him wearing a shower cap and holding a Twinkie in her cooch, or whatever that loser's into. So he pushed her out. I mean, good for her and her morals and everything, but I'm not going to be roadkill for some sicko creepo. *Goddamn it*."

Ash walked over and took her in his arms. Her hair roughed his cheek, that familiar, crunchy texture that came with the enormous amount of Aqua Net the network insisted on shellacking her with.

She let herself be held, her glass of Chardonnay pushed close to her chest. Then: "I need to come up with a game plan," she said, trying to pull away.

"Hey, hey. You'll figure it out. You're Candice Cressman, you've just landed one of the most coveted jobs in morning television. You're beautiful. You're talented." He felt, foolishly, a little breathless. "And I, for one, can't get enough." He tightened his arms around her.

"Oh, I don't know." She cocked her head, looked at him thoughtfully. "*Will* sex help?" This was rhetorical, or at least not directed at him, so Ash kept his mouth shut. "I suppose we could try," she said, sighing.

She led him to the bedroom, bathed in that blue New York May light. She made him sit on the bed while she pulled and slid and yanked off every stitch. Then she ambled over with her smooth skin and her long limbs and blonde helmet-hair, smelling like Opium and money and ambition, and spread her legs and sat on his face.

Ash didn't make it to Wonderland until the following day. But then again, he hadn't really shared Miller's sense of urgency. In his experience, places like Starry Acres were rarely anxious to get the authorities involved in their business.

So, it wasn't until around three o'clock in the afternoon that he found himself nearing home, Aunt Tassie safely strapped into the family Volvo. The car was fragrant with the once-familiar perfume of the hair powder responsible for the startling white cloud puffed out on top of her head.

Aunt Tassie had said very little from the moment he'd picked her up, only whispering once that *something was happening,* which seemed to Ash a sensible thing to say, seeing as something was indeed happening. The rest of the journey she'd just spent staring at her hands like it was the first time she was seeing them, and looking out the window.

It wasn't a great time to be undertaking this mission—work was insane at the moment, and there was Candice. But he'd offered to do it for a few reasons, all of them self-interested: the thought of Olly looming up again in their lives, even if it was from a pretty safe distance of 3,000 miles, unsettled him, and he'd wanted to see Nate. And, frankly, he'd wanted to come home; he didn't like feeling like he was banished.

But after his visit to Starry Acres, he saw that his intervention amounted to an emergency rescue, and he congratulated himself on having effected it so efficiently. After all, Aunt Tassie had saved his life once, it was only right he should return the favor.

Ash's first feeling upon arriving at Starry Acres had been one of surprise. Miller's panic had made him imagine a kind of *One Flew Over the Cuckoo's Nest*-type place, but the nursing home had looked more like a Cape Cod vacation community: clapboard bungalow-style buildings, the usual box hedge and hydrangea shrubbery, gravel pathways. Though he'd had to laugh when he saw the names given to the residential bungalows: The Shangri-La Shanty, The Nirvana Nook, Paradise Place, Canaan Corner, Elysium Escape, suggesting that the residents' imminent death would be swiftly followed by a homey, almost corny afterlife. It was genius, really, the idea that all these mysteries everyone was forced to negotiate and ponder and fear could be boiled down to a marketing ploy.

Inside, he'd been trapped into a boring argument with a woman with a face like a suburban Debbie Harry—one Carol Dinkus, judging by a brass nameplate at the reception desk—over his right to collect Aunt Tassie.

"It says here that Miss Shaw is only to be released to Mr. Lane."

"Right. But I think you said on the phone . . ."

"*I* didn't say."

"Okay. Well, someone said—the person who called my wife—they said that they were going to release Mrs. Shaw to social services if someone didn't come get her."

"Un-hunh."

"Well, as you can see: here I am—a person—come to get her." He'd smiled. At forty-two, Ash had become what people referred to as distinguished: his brown hair prematurely graying at the temples, his skinny frame filling out a bit—but not too much—and his posture ramrod straight. He'd found that in the past few years he had an effect on women that he could have only dreamed about in his twenties.

Carol Dinkus, however, had been unmoved.

But she did call for the director, who didn't share Carol Dinkus's reservations. She'd quickly delivered Aunt Tassie and one sad, battered suitcase in return for his signature, and a little spitefulness.

"You know," she'd said, "you're lucky the other resident and his family don't want to press charges."

When Ash had laughed, she'd replied: "Well, actually, Mr. Everley, it's no laughing matter. It was quite a vicious attack. Claggart Morris is a lovely man and we absolutely do not condone violence of any kind at Starry Acres. Miss Shaw has not been the easiest of residents. Despite appearances."

Ash had just shaken his head in disbelief and steered Aunt Tassie out to the car.

"Tell you what, Aunt Tassie," he'd said, hustling her into the passenger seat, "I think you've dodged a bullet there."

As they neared the bridge to Wonderland, Ash pressed play on the tape deck. The Talking Heads greeted him. He immediately shut it off. He'd never been a huge fan. His taste in music was more pedestrian, he knew that; he was unashamed. He fiddled with the radio dial until he found a perky little tune, and he hummed along. He couldn't catch all the lyrics, but he did get that nothing was gonna break the guy's stride.

The grass was green and lush around town, the trees pushing their new leaves out. But against this fresh springiness, the sky was a leaden gray, the kind of depressing sky that out-of-season beach towns always seemed to have.

By tidal-island standards, Wonderland was huge; in reality it was a small, small town. They'd been connected to the mainland since the '30s by a bridge built with federal money. Before that, though, the only way across had been either by boat or by the sandbar that appeared at very low tide, only to vanish again a few hours later.

When they were young, Aunt Tassie had told them stories about people she'd known in the olden days—generally some bad-intentioned youth, some *rapscallion*—who'd miscalculated the tide and found themselves trapped on the causeway as the water came rushing back in, picking them up and washing them out to sea, never to be seen again. Those stories had scared the living bejesus out of them. Though it hadn't stopped them from trying it once themselves.

The town had been given its unusual moniker by English settlers who'd mistranslated the Wampanoag name for the place—apparently "Vanishing Island in the Crooked Bay," or something like that—and had declared it Wonderland. Which, of course, was the name that'd stuck.

Now, in the glorious future of 1984 they had a high school, and a small airport (well, airstrip, really), an A&P, a post office, a couple of churches, three restaurants, a hotel, two bars, and a movie theater, not to mention the usual bric-a-brac: hardware store, shoe store, thrift store, library, etc. And in the summer, even a local radio station.

He passed Annie Oakley High, still the same: a red-brick building with a large central window, two stories high, revealing the staircase that he and Olly used to loiter beneath, watching the girls' young, strong legs climb upwards, the whites of their bobby socks disappearing into their two-toned saddle shoes. And their sweaters. God, those sweaters.

He'd had a promotional photo of Janet Leigh from *Jet Pilot* that he'd treasured when he was around fourteen, fifteen. In it, she had her arms over her head and was lifting her tight white sweater, revealing skin and a slice of brassiere. He'd kept it tucked into one of his Hardy Boys books, and would take it out at night and gently jerk off to it. Ash still loved a woman in a tight sweater, he couldn't lie.

When they arrived, the house was empty; a note on the kitchen counter read: *Gone swimming—M.* He hadn't seen Miller since February, the last time being an uncomfortable meeting at their place in the city where she'd confronted him about Candice and told him he couldn't come home. But he did remember that she'd looked nice: a white tank top, jeans, her curly blonde hair loose, sunglasses on, which was a bit weird since it hadn't been sunny, but hey. Anyway, Miller always looked nice. But these days, it was more like the way a painting in a museum looked nice: he could appreciate it, but it wasn't much to do with him.

Ash led Aunt Tassie upstairs to one of the back bedrooms on the second floor, the one with the big brass bed, and the rosebud wallpaper that Miller had insisted on when they'd first moved back to Wonderland from the city in '72. He could remember how happy they'd been, buying the house, doing it up. Nate, five years old, running around wildly, astonished at having stairs in his own home after the New York apartment. That kid could spend hours just running up and down them, counting them, sitting on them, playing Blind Man's Bluff at the top of them, giving his mother a heart attack.

Ash cracked the window and the room filled with the grassy smell of the back lawn. Above the privet hedge, he could see their neighbor's daughter, Suki, standing next to the Pfeiffers' swimming pool in her tennis gear, tying her red hair into a ponytail, arms reaching up high, the muscles working under the taut skin.

He turned back to Aunt Tassie. "Is this all right?"

Aunt Tassie stood stock-still in the doorway next to her suitcase, watching Ash with her startlingly pale blue eyes; she'd apparently been one of Wonderland's great beauties in her day. Eventually, she walked over and sat on the bed. She removed her shoes and lay down, closing her eyes. It seemed she was asleep in seconds.

"Right. Okay," Ash said. "Well, make yourself comfortable. I'll just . . . I'll be downstairs if you need anything."

In the kitchen, Ash realized he was hungry; he'd missed lunch. He opened the fridge. It was full of cans of Tab, a grapefruit, a couple of tomatoes, some other detritus. When he looked in the cupboard, it was almonds, as far as the eye could see, interspersed with a couple of tins of soup.

"Jesus, Miller," he said aloud to the empty kitchen.

He managed to scrounge up an old Pop-Tart, probably Nate's, which he put in the toaster, and some Folger's Crystals. He found himself humming the TV jingle as he poured boiling water over the coffee—*The best part of waking up is Folger's in your cup!*

He had to admit, it was catchy. These days he never listened to an ad without weighing it up, judging its merits, wondering if he could do better—a side-effect of working almost fifteen years in the business. After he and Miller had left L.A., left Lay Down, Ash had sort of fallen into it, parlaying his "experience" with music production into advertising. He now worked for a firm that handled political campaigns. They hadn't been tapped for Reagan's re-election, but they'd recently scooped up Walter Mondale and they were all scrambling ahead of the Democratic

30

convention in a couple of months. Still, he'd been disappointed about the Reagan campaign, though it was probably for the best. Miller had said she'd never forgive him if he got Reagan re-elected. They'd argued, half-heartedly: he'd told her she didn't understand business, she'd said he didn't understand anything.

Taking his Pop-Tart and coffee over to the table, he sat thinking about his wife, and not for the first time since that early morning phone call, Ash wondered what she was up to. She didn't need his permission to bring Aunt Tassie back to the house, so why the phone call? Did she miss him? Did she want a divorce? If there was one thing he knew about his wife it was that she could be a slippery fish. She could drown in indecision, and then one day just make some insane, snap resolution.

Ash took another bite of the Pop-Tart: strawberry, definitely the best flavor. He wasn't sorry about the affair, but it made Ash sad to think that he was hurting her. Still, things changed. And if she was being honest with herself, Miller would have been able to admit that it hadn't started with him.

He thought about Aunt Tassie upstairs, and wondered what had happened to her old place, the house on Foster Street that Olly had grown up in. The last time he'd passed by, it had been shuttered. Had Olly sold it? Or was he hanging on to it for some unfathomable reason?

Ash smiled now, thinking of how after football practice he and Olly would go back there and Aunt Tassie would feed them bologna sandwich after bologna sandwich. He'd loved those sandwiches—mayo, French's mustard, iceberg lettuce—Aunt Tassie manning a production line on the old stone counter. "I should have bought stock in Wonder Bread," she'd always say. "I'd be rich as Croesus by now."

Outside the big kitchen windows, the leaves would be changing color, orange and red burning out the gray sky. How their gear used to turn stiff when their sweat froze, how their lockers stank, how *they* stank. Even after their showers somehow their clothes still smelled faintly mildewed.

Those were the moments when Ash had been able to love Olly without reservation, without feeling like somehow Olly always got more, got the better end of the stick.

When something had happened, had changed between Olly and Miller, in the summer after the junior year in high school, Ash had known immediately. Just from one day to the next, it had gone from being the three of them, to being Olly and Miller plus Ash. All that Ash could do was to stay close, so that he didn't lose either one of them. But that had left him with a desperate, anxious feeling, like always being hungry; no matter how much he ate, he could never be full.

He could remember drinking beer with Olly and Miller on the Annie Oakley football field the night before they all left for L.A., after Aunt Tassie had made her fateful trip to the local draft board, and Olly had made up his mind that the only place far enough away from her was California.

Miller had been lying on her back, beer bottle in one hand, and he remembered watching as Olly leaned over her and—almost, but not quite, casually—kissed her. Watching Olly's hand sliding under the edge of her peasant blouse a little, touching what must have been warm skin. And he could remember that the feelings of desire and envy were so strong in him that he had to look away so that he wouldn't hate his friends.

Ash exhaled. He needed to get some air. He didn't want to think about these things. He didn't want to be reminded of the past, he only wanted to be in the present. The present was the only thing that mattered. He put his dish and cup in the sink, and stepped through the kitchen door into the warm spring day.

He took a few deep breaths, eyes closed, as Candice had taught him to do, trying to breathe from his diaphragm. On the third breath, he felt something—that pulling feeling that tells your body, but not your brain, that you're being watched—and he opened his eyes to see their neighbor, Cricket Pfeiffer, trimming the roses climbing the waist-high fence that divided their properties.

Over the years, her name—calling to mind some chirpy, lithe girl—had become increasingly incongruous with the woman before him. On the heavier side, quiet, always wearing these kind of nurse-y shoes below her muscular calves, Cricket seemed to want to be invisible. It was like crossing paths with a ghost. Her husband bullied her—they could hear the shouting, the fighting from next door. Maybe he hit her. So there was that.

He and Miller had called the cops a couple of times in the early days, anonymously of course (though in a town with a police force of four, nothing was exactly anonymous), but the police were always turned away from the Pfeiffer house, making Ash and Miller feel like they were the problem. So at some point, they'd just stopped, and turned the radio up in the house when they heard anything disturbing. It wasn't very often, but it happened.

There was no denying that Dutch Pfeiffer was a real, grade-A asshole. A rich, grade-A asshole, as it turned out, though his business affairs had always been murky. Ash had had some vague dealings with him when Dutch had been starting up Wonder Air, the small-craft airline whose route now ran between Wonderland, Boston and New York, and Ash's firm had pitched for the account. It hadn't worked out, mainly because Dutch was, of course, a grade-A asshole.

The Pfeiffers had bought the house next door and the one behind it in '75, when Dutch was still working in junk bonds on Wall Street. He'd razed both places, installed a swimming pool, and built a larger house "in-the-style," which had the effect of looking both old and wrong at the same time.

"Hey, Cricket," Ash said, walking over to the fence.

"Oh, hello, Ash," Cricket said, squinting at him, pretending she hadn't seen him breathing like a maniac. Her hair was a kind of silky dark cap on her head, parted in the middle. A kind of non-style style. "Nice to see you."

"You, too. Doing some gardening?"

She smiled.

"I saw Suki getting ready for tennis. Looking very professional."

Cricket lit up at the mention of her daughter. "Oh, she's really good, just takes my breath away." She stopped, her hand on her heart, as if to prove this point. Her hand then rose and smoothed her short cap of dark hair, as if she were checking it was tidy.

There was something about it, that small unconscious gesture that was so sexy, and for a moment he could imagine what it felt like to desire her, the surprise of her, like opening a soft, familiar brown paper bag to find a peach inside.

"I hear Nate's coming home for the summer. Suki's really looking forward to seeing him. I think it's so lovely how they still keep in touch."

This was news to him: Ash had no idea his son and Cricket's daughter were friends.

"And Nate's going to film school, Suki tells me. In Los Angeles. Gosh, that is really exciting. You must be so proud."

"Yes, I am. We are. Though, I wouldn't have minded if he'd done something boring, like accounting. Just for his poor old father's sake." This was a complete lie: Ash loved that Nate was doing something cool. He only said the accounting thing so that people would continue in their praise of his son. It was stupid, but he couldn't help himself.

"Oh, no," said Cricket, "it's wonderful. So creative."

"Ha. Well, if you say so, I'll try to be brave, then," Ash said, leaning in, touching her arm.

Cricket tilted her head, almost imperceptibly, away from Ash, and he withdrew his hand quickly, the two of them standing awkwardly for a moment.

"I think my phone is ringing," Cricket said, backing away, blurring at the edges, walking towards her front door, fading across her front lawn, into her blue house.

Ash stood looking at his street, the houses, each with their own agonizingly perfect lawn and gently swaying American flag. Wonderland had been a great place to grow up, and a great place for Nate to grow up, too. But there would always be something weird about coming back to your home town, like trying to put on shoes that no longer fit.

Many of the Quakers had left Wonderland—his own parents lived in Boca now, and Miller's mother and father had decamped for Paris after Reagan had gotten elected, in protest. Miller's dad, a professor of poetry, had legitimately been offered a post there, but Ash had always thought the Fairlines were a touch overly dramatic, and thought pretty highly of themselves. Anyway, the whole make-up of the town had changed since he was a kid.

Now, there were people like Dutch and Cricket Pfeiffer, with their big money and swimming pools looking for some fantasy of small-town life; there were the summer people, with their big money and no swimming pools; there were the people who'd always been here and didn't have a whole lot of anything, who waited the tables, did the snow-plowing, mowed the football field, cleaned the toilets at the hotel, ran the fairground, and, a lot of times, had to drive over the bridge to make a dime. And then there were the people like Ash and Miller who'd always been here, but now they had some money, they were summer people and year-rounders, they had history, but they didn't need to clean anybody's toilets. Sometimes not even their own.

Jesus. Ash had been here barely two hours and already his thoughts were getting really depressing. He needed to talk to Candice, get grounded again. Get back to what really mattered. Like the way she smelled and the soft spot on her inner thigh.

When he walked into the house, though, he realized almost immediately that there was not going to be any grounding anytime soon.

Standing in the middle of the kitchen, dressed in a sailor outfit that Nate had worn for some costume contest years ago, was Aunt Tassie.

She was smiling, the most lovely, beatific smile. The smile of a saint, the smile of the innocent.

"Aunt Tassie?"

"Oh, it's the most marvelous thing," she said to Ash, walking towards him, holding out her hands, the sailor cap at a jaunty angle. "I had a dream. A wonderful dream. And now . . . I can barely believe it . . ."

"What? What can't you believe?" Ash felt her joy in his very bones.

35

"Dearest Ash, I'm transformed."

"Who are you transformed into?" he asked, smiling, taking her small hands in his. He had a fleeting thought that maybe it was like the Folger's ad, after all, and they were all going to wake up fresh and happy and different. That she knew something they didn't.

But then she said: "Can't you see? Oh, it's a miracle. Now everything is as clear as a bell. Now everything makes sense. Can you really not see? I'm not Aunt Tassie. Oh, Ash, I'm Billy Budd."

1952

The summer they were sixteen had come after a long, hard winter in Wonderland, where the snow had built up in drifts so high children could jump out of their first story windows and land soundly in a pillowy cushion of cold, white powder. Rime ice, hoar frost and verglas had covered the town, the bare tree branches crackling and snapping under the weight of winter's glaze.

So when the days got longer and the nights warmer and the traveling carnival appeared in Longwell, Olly, Miller and Ash were more than ready to ignore the warnings from the adults in Wonderland to stay away from the fairground. In fact, the dark rumblings from the Quaker elders that such a place was a breeding ground for perverts and disease only added to their curiosity.

Olly borrowed Aunt Tassie's Oldsmobile and Miller snuck beers from her dad's fridge in the garage, and the three of them made the trip over the bridge—Olly and Ash in the front, Miller stretched out on the back seat, her feet propped up on the door handle. They'd been carrying on a debate from the afternoon about who Kennedy would choose as his running mate: Symington or Scoop Jackson. Miller put her money on Symington while the boys were betting on Scoop. When they'd fully exhausted their hypotheses, talk turned to the little boy who survived going over Niagara Falls, then finally what they might see at the carnival— whether there'd be bearded ladies, strong men or any of the other exotic freak shows they'd heard about, but never seen.

Curling her toes upwards, Miller recited: "In the circus tent of a hurricane, designed by a drunken god, my extravagant heart blows up again, in a rampage of champagne-colored rain . . ."

"Noooo . . ." groaned Ash. "No more poetry."

"Mercy," said Olly.

Miller laughed. "Oh, you used to love it when I read you poetry."

"That's when we were young and impressionable," Olly said. "We didn't know any better."

"She probably has the whole thing embroidered on her underpants," Ash said.

"I do not," Miller said, defensively.

Just then the lights of the fairground came into view, and they fell silent.

When they arrived, they stood on the midway, stunned by the neon lights, the swish of the tilt-a-whirl, the curve of the Ferris wheel. There was a band playing hoochie-coochie music, a two-headed lady, an "Electrifying Girl," and an anaconda; there was skeet shooting, a carousel with painted horses, the Tunnel of Love, and cotton candy.

There were beautiful girls with ironed hair and gold hoops in their ears leaning in tight to big men with tattoos. There were older, smaller men, furtive, ducking into tents with posted signs reading: 18 AND OVER ONLY! There were roving gangs of boys their own age, from Longwell or Cuttersville, whom they recognized vaguely, who were smoking cigarettes and sniggering behind their smiles.

"The sound and the fury," Miller said.

"Signifying S-E-X," Ash said, laughing.

And he was right: it was sex, sex made manifest in light and sound and smell. If this was disease and perversion, they were all for it.

Matt McCauliff watched his three classmates standing on the midway from his position behind the cotton candy counter. He'd told his parents that he'd taken a job at a diner in Longwell because they sure as heck wouldn't have let him work the carnival. He'd assumed, of course, that no one from Wonderland would come to the fairground—they'd all been warned against it. So he was surprised to see Miller and Ash and Olly turn up, but he knew they wouldn't rat him out.

The Three Musketeers, that was how they were known in town. At school they were well liked: they were friendly, they were good looking, the boys played the right sports, and Miller was a good student, really good at writing stories. There was a sense that they'd been marked for something special, that they were really going to make something of themselves. He didn't know why, but they all felt it, everyone at school.

Still, they weren't exactly popular; there was something about them that rubbed people the wrong way—they stuck too close together, like they were keeping a secret they refused to share.

But Matt liked them and he was glad when they spotted him and waved and they all ambled over to his stand, the two boys and Miller in between.

"Does your mother know you're here?" Miller asked, smiling.

His own smile was like an involuntary chemical reaction; she *was* pretty—pale like a scoop of vanilla ice-cream, her blonde, shoulder-length hair pinned to the side with a barrette, those tight, white pedal pushers. "Does yours?"

"I hope not," she said.

They ordered three cokes and a cotton candy from him, and the four of them chatted a bit, and then Matt watched them walk down the midway, swaying in unison, bending in towards each other, like trees growing towards the light.

As they stood in line for the Ferris wheel, Miller could feel the pull of Olly's body, like a magnet. She was experiencing that peculiar, biting kind of pleasure—the desire for everything to change and for nothing to change at all. The feeling that everything was perfect at that moment, and the feeling of wanting more and more and more.

When their turn came, the three of them crammed together in one seat. As they rose up into the night sky, Ash looked over at Miller, her blonde hair a halo, illuminated by the neon lights. He wanted to reach out and brush his hand against it, press his fingertips against her downy neck, to bury his face in it and rest there. He wanted to touch her breasts and see what they felt like, if they felt as soft as they looked.

When they reached the top, Olly looked down at the fairground glittering below. His head felt light with possibility: this was just one tiny corner of the world that was waiting for them. As they moved over the crest of the wheel, Olly watched Miller put her arms toward the sky, long white arms curved above her like crescent moons. He wasn't sure when exactly it had started, but, slowly, he'd begun to feel that they might be the only two of their species, that they were meant to be together. As he thought this, though, he found that there was a tight knot of such sadness inside of him, and he had no idea where it came from, only that maybe he was afraid that it was a mirage—the promise, the desire—and they'd never actually get the chance to see it all.

On the way back, too full of the evening to go home, they decided to go to Shell Beach and drink the beer that Miller had brought along, which had been warming in the trunk ever since. They could see the sandy causeway that connected Shell Beach to the mainland.

"Should we do it?" Olly asked after a couple of beers.

"We'd have to walk home along the bridge," Ash said.

Miller shrugged. "It's not so cold."

They all looked at each other, and it was decided without another word.

They began walking the sandbar, but soon Miller had run ahead on the causeway, disappearing into the darkness.

They hadn't been going very long when the tide started coming in fast.

Olly and Ash saw first their feet, then their ankles, then calves covered in water and the causeway felt like quicksand, sucking them down. They called out for Miller, but they were met with silence.

"You go back," Olly said. "In case we need help. I'll go get her."

Miller was farther out than the boys, and she'd known sooner that she was in trouble, but the soft silt of the wet causeway made it difficult to move at any speed at all. After struggling a few moments, she managed to lie flat on her stomach, craning her face upwards, above the coming water, and kick her feet free from the silt. Then she began to swim, first in shallow water, then deeper as the tide lifted her up until she couldn't feel land beneath her at all. She knew the vague direction of the shore, but the night was pitch-black, and she had no idea how far out she actually was. She called for the boys, but heard no reply. She considered doing the dead-man's float, but was worried the current would pull her even farther out into the dark.

She swam and swam and swam until her muscles screamed and her breath was ragged and her throat burned. And then all at once, she could feel someone grabbing her and turning her over on her back and shouting: *She's here, she's here*. She was sure it was Olly, and he pulled her ashore. But when she looked up, it was Ash's face she saw. She threw her arms around his neck, whispering, *Thank you, thank you*. And over his shoulder she saw Olly emerging from the water, his face white and stricken.

I couldn't find you. I looked and looked for you everywhere. I couldn't find you.

BALL AND CHAIN

Miller pulled the Volvo into the driveway, her wet suit sticking to the Naugahyde, and switched off the engine.

Through the open windows of the house she could hear Crosby, Stills & Nash, "Southern Cross." She sat for a moment listening to the music. Very much Ash's taste, their latest album. A song about a guy whose dreams haven't panned out taking off on a sailboat in search of a woman (or girl? Or woman-girl? The lyrics were unclear) who believes in true love.

Is that how he thinks about Candice? she thought, then hated herself for even thinking about it. She hated how everything had become about that, about how Ash felt about Candice. What about her? What about how *she* felt? Why did she care so little about herself?

She didn't even like that stupid song. She got out of the car and slammed the door.

As she opened the screen door to the kitchen, she saw the counters strewn with evidence of chopping and cooking. The candles on the bar were lit and someone had cut flowers from the garden— peonies and Queen Anne's lace—and put them in the mustard-colored vase in the center of the table. They were somewhat past their bloom, and pale pink petals, yellow and white pollen, dusted the table.

Aunt Tassie, wearing a strange yet vaguely familiar sailor suit, sat in one of the two slipper chairs Miller had rescued from a yard sale a few years back and re-covered in a blue and white Laura Ashley pattern, nodding along to the music. Ash was at the stove, stirring pots and saucepans.

Staring from one to the other, Miller had a sense of dislocation, as if she'd walked into a dream.

"Hello, Miller, dear," Aunt Tassie said.

"Hi," Ash said, not turning, as if it were the most natural thing in the world that he should be there, in their kitchen, after all this time. "That was a long swim. Must be cold out there."

Miller kissed Aunt Tassie on the top of her head. "Hi," she said. Then she walked over to where Ash was standing.

"I'm making my famous Bolognese," he said. Ash's "famous" Bolognese was only famous because it was all he knew how to make.

"Hey," she whispered. "Do you want to tell me what's going on here?"

He looked up. "What?"

Miller inclined her head towards Aunt Tassie.

"Oh, right, that," he said, grimacing a little, keeping his voice low. "So, well . . . she thinks she's Billy Budd?" He shrugged his shoulders.

"Sorry, what?"

"I don't know. She said she had a dream and then woke up and realized she was Billy Budd."

"What, like from the book?"

Ash nodded.

"And the sailor outfit?"

"I guess she found it. I think it was Nate's?"

"Right," Miller said, looking back at Aunt Tassie. "Well, that's not good." When she looked back at Ash, he was smiling at her.

"It's nice to see you."

He leaned in, as if to embrace her.

"Jesus, Ash." Miller turned her back on him and walked over to the yellow fridge.

She took a Tab out of the fridge, grabbed a tin of almonds from the cupboard, and sat down on one of the yellow-painted chairs at the kitchen table.

Ash watched her. "Oh, Christ, Miller." He set the wooden stirring spoon down on the stove, a red stain blooming on the white metal. "You can't live on almonds and Tab. Seriously. It's not healthy."

"Ash is right, dear," Aunt Tassie piped up. "You need sustenance. You never know what lean times might come in inclement weather. "

"Well," Miller said, putting down the almonds with exaggerated carefulness. "Since you put it that way."

"Good girl," Aunt Tassie said. "You were always a good girl. And so clever."

Ash had gone back to stirring the sauce. Miller watched him as he tested it, bobbing his head from side to side, deciding. She wanted to smash the pan over that head.

She hadn't known exactly how was she was going to feel seeing him again, but she hadn't expected it to feel like an out-of-body experience. Then again, when she'd imagined it over the past three months, she hadn't counted on Aunt Tassie being there, let alone believing herself a character in a Herman Melville novella.

Miller had gotten used to being on her own in the house, and the effect of all this sudden life was disorienting. All the ordinary, everyday objects that lined the walls, or were crammed into the kitchen shelves—framed pencil drawings by forgotten relatives; photographs of her, of Ash in younger, more glamorous times; glass boat lights resurrected from her parents' basement; Dutch painted plates from some long-ago family trip to Europe; shells and striped stones collected indiscriminately over the years—all these things suddenly seemed to jump out at her, like she was seeing them for the first time.

It hadn't been that long ago that this house had been the scene of children's birthday parties and cookouts with burned burgers and dinners where too much wine was drunk and bad poetry was read aloud. It had been a relaxed house, where everything went on too late, and the children were bundled, unbathed, together in heaps of coats on the bed to sleep, while the adults gossiped and cut themselves on the cheese knife and scratched the records and went skinny-dipping at Pebble Beach.

44

But maybe, she thought now, it hadn't been relaxed at all. Maybe that's just how they'd all gotten through. Thinking their own secret thoughts, harboring their own secret desires.

She knew it wasn't just Candice. This thing in their marriage had been going on for a long time. Not a deterioration exactly, but a disappearing. When she'd first decided to be with Ash, to have a family with him, to *be* family with him, it had been a conscious decision to try for a smooth kind of happiness that had been eluding her. And she'd liked being married in those early years: it had been a protection, not against loneliness, but against *alone*ness. But somewhere along the line the novelty had worn off, or maybe she didn't want the armor anymore.

Or maybe none of that was true. She supposed she had loved him. Hadn't she? It was hard to remember exactly, like trying to pick out one distinct flavor from a complicated dish. Anyway, he'd certainly been dissatisfied, that was now clear.

The affair with Candice had been a concrete act; as if a rotting board had suddenly given way without warning and she found herself in a life with no underpinnings. And suddenly here he was, back, after three months, cooking and acting as if nothing had ever happened. And it was this last part that made her feel impotent with rage.

"Dinner's ready," Ash announced, loudly. He looked at Miller. "Unless you want to change out of your suit first."

Miller busied herself, pulling cutlery out of the drawer.

"Or at least take off your sunglasses."

"Nope," she said, getting the plates.

At the table, Aunt Tassie said: "Who shall say grace?"

"Please, by all means," Ash said, gesturing towards Aunt Tassie.

She closed her eyes, hand over her heart. "God save the Queen. Bless our victuals and make us thankful. Amen."

Miller could remember, growing up, the little silence left before the beginning of a meal, the Quaker grace. In her head, during that moment of quiet, she'd always said to herself: *On your mark, get set, go!*

"Amen," Ash said, and they began eating.

"Delightful, delightful," Aunt Tassie said, tasting the food with a delicate kind of reverence.

Miller looked at her, at her little, bird-like frame, her powdered hair, tiny wrists protruding from the cuffs of the polyester sailor suit. She could remember the hundred and one ways Aunt Tassie had been good to them when they were young. And they'd repaid her with carelessness.

When they'd first returned to Wonderland, and Nate was little, they'd visited with her, had her over for dinner. But as the years went by, life had seemed to get in the way and even those small kindnesses had fallen by the wayside. It wasn't only Olly's fault Aunt Tassie was like this now; they were all responsible for abandoning her to this fate.

Miller reached out and squeezed Aunt Tassie's hand. "We're so glad you're here," she said.

Aunt Tassie looked into her eyes, put her hand to Miller's cheek. "Such a sad face," Aunt Tassie said, then patted her gently. "Don't worry." She turned back to her meal. "It will all be all right, in the end."

"Yes, of course," Miller said, and felt something crack inside her heart.

After showering, Miller slipped into the Violent Femmes T-shirt that she'd found abandoned in the washing machine on Nate's last visit. She brushed her teeth, and half-heartedly combed her hair in the bathroom mirror, before heading to the bedroom.

Their bedroom, like much of the house, was filled with various pieces of furniture from small-town flea markets and bric-a-brac shops that Miller had picked up during their first years back in Wonderland, then lovingly restored: the intricate bamboo bed frame she'd lacquered, the blue hooked rug she'd mended, the Victorian dresser with the clouded mirror. Antiquing, her parents used to call it. *More like collecting strays*, Ash had said. But, in actual fact, it was more prosaic than any of that: she'd needed something to do with her days, other than looking after their child and waiting for Ash to come back from the city.

Standing there now, she knew immediately that the air had changed, that something had shifted, like walking into a house that's been burgled. She looked around and saw his book arranged neatly on what had been his bedside table, a mirror image of her own on the opposite end.

Her: Kundera's *The Unbearable Lightness of Being*. Him: *The Kennedys: An American Drama*.

She opened the closet and saw his city clothes hanging there, silent intruders. In the top drawer of the bureau, new underwear. For *her*, no doubt.

Miller got into bed and picked up her book. Downstairs, she heard the hum of the television go silent. Then the sound of Ash's footsteps ascending.

Over the top of her book, Miller watched Ash undress then re-dress in a pair of crisp, striped pyjamas. His body was the same as she remembered: good posture, no belly, the muscles of a man who worked in an office. He was handsome, she could still see that. But she wasn't sure if she cared about bodies anymore, including her own. What difference did shape, or smoothness, or roughness, or muscles or breasts or anything make? They were only what was inside their heads, in the end, anyway.

She watched Ash regard himself in the mirror, brush a stray hair back into place, before getting into bed beside her.

She didn't know why she wasn't protesting his assumption that he would be sleeping in her bed. Maybe she didn't have the energy to protest, or maybe she wanted to see what it felt like to sleep beside him again. It didn't feel like much, she admitted to herself, as he lay there now. She felt no desire for him. And yet, strangely, lying this close to him, their bodies almost touching, some part of her wanted him to want her.

"So . . . Aunt Tassie . . ." she began.

"Mmmm." Ash switched on his lamp. He began fiddling with the pillows, adjusting the sheet.

"Well, what are your thoughts?"

"Honestly, I don't know," Ash said, leaning back. "Maybe a private nurse? We could find a place for her?"

"And who's going to pay for that?"

"Well," he shrugged, "we could get it started and then . . . I don't know, send the bill to Olly."

"All this to avoid calling him?"

He looked at her. "What do you want me to say? You know how to use directory assistance. Why don't you call him?"

"I have," she said, allowing just the faintest of smiles.

"What?"

"Well," she picked up her book, "it was clear you weren't going to."

"What did he say?"

Miller was quiet, pretending to read. She had to admit she was enjoying this moment. She'd been waiting all day for it.

"*Miller?*"

"I didn't speak to him," she said finally, laying the book on her chest. "I called the studio. He doesn't work there anymore." She chewed her cuticle. "Fired, I think."

"Right." Miller could detect the relief in his voice. "Well, there you go." Ash opened his book.

"You have heard they had an earthquake in L.A.? Right through Olly's neighborhood?"

"Olly's fine. He could survive a nuclear meltdown."

"That's true."

"And if not, good riddance."

"Ash . . ."

He put his book down. "Well, I don't want him back in our lives. Do you?" It was not a question, it was an accusation, she knew well. "Because, you know what, Miller? I'm beginning to get the feeling you do."

"Don't be ridiculous," she said. "He was in our lives for years, we were in business together. He never tried to interfere."

"Are you seriously saying that to me?"

"I mean afterwards."

Ash sighed. "Look, Olly's the last person in the world who's going to be jumping at responsibility. I know that," he said. "But I just don't see why we should tempt fate. Everything's fine, just rolling along. We don't need to muddy the waters."

"Of course." Miller picked up her book. "Everything's peachy."

"Let's just see how things play out. Okay? Nate's coming home. That's going to be nice. For both of us. Let's not make any snap decisions. We can deal with the Aunt Tassie situation ourselves. For a little while longer, anyway. Then, after Nate goes to college, well, then we can see about Olly."

Miller said nothing. Because she didn't yet know what she wanted to say, or how to say it. So instead, she closed her eyes, and lay very still, and quieted her brain, until she tricked herself into falling into a dreamless sleep.

1980

Olly sat waiting at a small, polished cocktail table near the stage of the Eidolon Lounge. The show hadn't yet begun and the supper club was full of cocktail-hour buzz: men smoking cigarettes and sipping Scotch, stylish women, their diamond tennis bracelets hanging nonchalantly from their wrists, leaning across their partners to make themselves heard.

There was a hum in Olly's head, as well, as he waited. Miller and Ash had flown all the way from the East Coast to wrap up the sale of Lay Down Records. Well, that's what they thought—that they were coming for a last-minute business meeting. Which in a way it was. Unfinished business. He'd actually invited them out that evening to announce to them that they'd lost. He'd invited them out to watch them go down.

Olly had positioned himself with a view to the entrance, and after about ten minutes he saw Miller come in, wearing some white silk pantsuit, her lovely, long, rangy limbs striding across the floor of the Eidolon Lounge, her blonde hair curling around her face. And as much as he hated to admit it, Olly felt it again, something from a long time ago, something that had never left, maybe never would. He barely clocked Ash.

And then they were upon him, seating themselves around the cocktail table, their faces open, expectant. He hadn't seen them in a few years, not since a meeting in New York in '77. Ash and Miller had fled L.A. ten years ago and, in all that time, the contact between the three of them had been limited to phone calls and a handful of meetings, all regarding Lay Down.

He'd tried to buy them out several times over the last few years, but they'd refused to sell. Why should they? They were making money. But it was something that Olly hadn't been able to get over, something that ate away at him. They'd walked away with everything—a marriage, a child, their share in the business, a business *he'd* created—they were unscathed, and he'd been left to pick up the pieces. Now it was his turn to mete out a little pain.

"So," Ash said, "this is it, hunh? The end of an era. But we did it. Built a business, and sold it to the big guns. I never thought we'd make this kind of money."

Olly just stared at him.

"Well," Ash said, "what do we need to sign to get this sale done and get on to celebrating?"

"Nothing," Olly said, sipping his water. "You've signed everything you need to. The papers your lawyer sent over were sufficient."

Ash looked perplexed. "I don't understand. You said we needed to come out here to rubber-stamp some last-minute paperwork."

Miller was silent, perhaps sensing something was about to go very wrong.

"I did say that," Olly said, nodding. "But, as it turns out, it wasn't true. You see, I *just* wanted to see your faces when I told you."

"What the hell are you talking about?"

Miller put her hand on Ash's arm, as if to still him. Olly could see her diamond wedding band winking in the low light. He felt bolstered.

"Well, the sale went through. To Seymour Geist, as planned." Olly stretched his legs out. "And then he gave me a 30 per cent stake back. A finder's fee, let's call it. And the option to buy back more, based on performance, of course."

"What?" Ash's face was getting flushed.

"It's complicated, I know." Olly patted Ash's hand. Ash looked like he was going to clock him. "So, I got the buyout money, and I got the stake. Seymour and I are going into business together. And I'm going to work for him, in movies." Olly looked from one to the other, not bothering to suppress his smile. When neither of them said anything, Olly let out an exaggerated sigh. "Look," he spread his hands out, "to put it simply: I'm in, and you're out."

"What the fuck?" Ash turned to Miller. "Do you understand what's going on here? Because I sure as hell don't."

Miller looked at Olly, then back at Ash. "He swindled us. This Geist guy, they were in it together. All that crap about having inside information, about the industry facing a downturn, that we should get ahead of it—that was just to scare us into selling, wasn't it?"

"Well, you wouldn't sell if you thought it was going to me, would you? Because you're petty or greedy or whatever. So I had to get creative," Olly said, evenly.

"It wasn't *your* business, Olly, it was *ours*. All three of us. We built it together." Ash looked up at the ceiling, exhaling. Finally, he shook his head and looked at Olly. "Why? Why would you do this to us?"

Olly raised his eyebrows. "Really?"

"Never mind, sweetheart," Miller said. "He's done us a favor. We're free." Then standing and staring down at him like an avenging angel delivering some dark prophecy, she said: "Congratulations, Olly. Now you're fully alone. That's your reward. And you're going to be alone for the rest of your life. Enjoy it."

Olly didn't feel cursed, though, he felt triumphant, vindicated, revenge like hot syrup in his blood.

SLEEPERS, AWAKE

When Olly first woke up at Cedars-Sinai, it was like rising slowly out of a warm bath. They were kind and gentle—changing dressings, bringing him sweet, cold drinks, speaking in low, soothing tones—and he bobbed in and out of sleep.

His dreams, when they came, were fragments, strands he struggled to follow, eluding him when he woke. He could remember colors, like crayons, paisley shapes, a tender-faced young boy staring at him, his mouth moving but making no sound, as if he were behind a window or a wall of water. They didn't upset him, these dreams, only hovered around him like a cloud or a perfume.

On the second day, he met his doctor—*Call me Dr. Frank*—who explained to him that he'd been very lucky, that his injuries—concussion, broken nose, cheek fractures—were basically superficial, would heal, with no real lasting damage.

"You gave us a scare, Mr. Lane. We thought it was much, much worse when you were brought in—your vitals were pretty low. Blood tests got to the bottom of it." He looked at Olly out of the corner of his eye.

On the third day, he was well enough to watch television—the news, *General Hospital*, *The Jeffersons*, *The A-Team*—and eat three, surprisingly decent meals.

On the fourth day, Dr. Frank—so very young, a smile so white it almost looked blue, and a full head of overly coifed black hair—appeared with the hospital psychiatrist, Dr. Bob.

"Dr. Bob and I thought it might be a good idea for you two to have a chat," Dr. Frank said.

The blue, pleated curtains had been pushed aside and the late afternoon southern California sun was streaming through the windows, bouncing off the linoleum floor and the metal frame of the bed where Olly lay.

"I'm all right," Olly said. "I feel good."

"You're definitely healing," Dr. Frank said. "And we'd love for you to be able to go home."

"Great," Olly said.

"Once you've had a chat with Dr. Bob here."

"No, I'm okay," Olly said, looking from one man to the other. "I'm good."

"Well, you see, Mr. Lane, there's the issue of the secobarbital." Dr. Frank wrinkled his perfect nose. "We can't just ignore that, can we?"

There was something incongruous, Olly felt, about being patronized by someone who looked like he'd walked off the pages of *Tiger Beat*. "What? What do you mean?"

"The high level of barbiturates in your system? Seconal, most likely?"

"Oh," Olly said. "Oh." He rubbed his hands over his eyes, as if trying to remember. "I don't know. I get bad migraines . . . Maybe I mistook my girlfriend's Seconal for aspirin? You know, now that I think about it, that's probably what it was."

"Okay, I get it," Dr. Frank said. "Still, that would be a whole heck of a lot of aspirin." He inclined his head.

Olly's first clear thought upon waking up had been that it was a miracle he was alive. His second had been: *Now what?* He found himself in a strange state, somewhere between the man who'd taken the Seconal, so certain of what he'd been doing, and the man who could now see the potential in weightlessness.

But these were not things he intended to talk to Dr. Bob about, now or ever.

"I'm pretty tired," he said, opening and closing his eyes as if he could barely stay awake. "Maybe tomorrow?"

The two men looked at each other.

"Mr. Lane . . ." Dr. Frank began again.

"It's all right," Dr. Bob said. "I can come back tomorrow."

Dr. Frank seemed to take a minute to consider this, then smiled. "You're off the hook. For now. Get some rest, Mr. Lane." He made to leave, then turned back. "You know, Mr. Lane, we're all big fans of yours here."

"Well . . . thank you, Dr. Frank." He stopped. "Sorry—is it Dr. Frank, like Dr. Frank Something, or is Frank your last name or . . .?"

"You have a rare talent and we all think you're pretty special. So it's our duty to take the very best care of you."

"Yeah. No, yeah. Great. Thanks."

"Besides, my wife's a big fan of Blue, and she'd never forgive me if I let her down." Dr. Frank winked.

Olly winked back for some unfathomable reason. Probably because he hadn't been called special in a long time, not since he'd left the music business for his now apparently disastrous career in movies. It was pathetic, really.

When he'd still controlled Lay Down Records, people used to treat him like that, used to jump to do his bidding. He'd once overheard someone in a men's room at an awards show say: "Olly Lane, man. If he likes you, he's the best friend you could ever have. But if he doesn't, well, you might as well kill yourself." And he'd liked that. Liked that he was thought of as ruthless, as that powerful.

In those days, he'd listened to music all the time, a lot of it good, not all of it sellable, and a whole swath of it beyond dreadful, of course. Olly had been good at telling the difference. That was his gift. A golden ear, someone had once called it. And this talent had made them—him and Miller and Ash, all of them at Lay Down Records—a lot of money.

All his life, Olly'd had a strange, extra-sensory reaction to music: each note lived as a different color to him; each word sung, a different flavor—bacon, rubber, meringue. When Olly heard a song, he entered a particular landscape, walked in it, felt its contours, sensed its mood—sometimes bright and vivid, sometimes soft and pale, like a rain-washed city. It could be painfully beautiful. Or painfully ugly. He experienced harmony and dissonance differently to other people. When it came to music, for Olly, good and bad was like the difference between sick and well.

But it was rare that he heard something that really and truly moved him. Not just something he knew was great and would work and could dominate the charts. But something more profound, that had the feeling of church to it. Blue's music had that.

He'd known about Blue before he'd actually seen her. It was hard *not* to know about her; the world knew about her. And when he finally *did* see her in the flesh—an intimate show at a supper club four years ago, the same night he'd delivered his *coup de grâce* to Miller and Ash, just before he began to crack up—he'd realized just why she was a superstar.

That evening at the Eidolon Lounge she'd stood on stage in a gown sewn with thousands of beads or rhinestones or something that sparkled in the light, a slit riding all the way up her left side, above where the top of her prosthetic seemed to flow seamlessly into her knee. Bone-white and corkscrew-shaped, it, too, was encrusted with some diamanté ornamentation. Her black, straight hair, like a Cherokee's, hung smooth: dark water down her back. There was only one hot spotlight trained on her, casting the rest of the room and the corners of the stage in darkness.

She was looking downwards, her face hidden in shadow. Everyone had gone completely silent, then came the sharp intake of breath caught in the microphone, a sound like sudden pain. She raised her face to all of them and began to sing. One clear, pure note. And, Jesus Christ, that voice, that face. The hair on Olly's arms had risen. The aura was gold and the taste was of crisp, bright fruit and also salt, like salt-encrusted cherries, maybe.

Afterwards, Blue's husband and manager, Slade Winters, had been all too happy to arrange an introduction, sensing a potential angle with Olly. Olly hadn't cared one way or another. He'd felt empowered by his meeting with Ash and Miller, bolstered by his righteous betrayal of them. When he'd entered her dressing room, he'd turned to Slade and said: "Shut the door." When Slade did and then stood leaning idly against the frame, Olly had smiled and added: "I meant with you on the other side of it."

Blue had been sitting at her dressing table, her sparkling corkscrew prosthetic propped up next to her. She was wearing an ivory silk kimono opened slightly between her breasts. The robe trailed down her body, pooling in her lap and opening again above her left leg. She was lifting the stump—which he saw now ended at the middle of her calf, not the knee—up and down from the knee joint, in some kind of exercise. At the same time, she was brushing her hair, her face in profile. She didn't turn to look at him.

"Olly Lane," she said.

"May I?" he asked, gesturing to a chair abandoned in the corner, shimmering, colored costumes on a rack next to it.

Blue just kept on brushing her hair. "I'm married," she said.

"I know," he said, smiling. "My condolences."

She laughed, a row of perfectly veneered teeth flashing between her curved lips.

"How do you know I'm not here to offer you a contract?"

Blue shrugged. "Because I know your label, I know what you like. And it's not what I do."

"Listen," Olly said, leaning forward, forcing a small intimacy with her. "I don't know what it is you do exactly, because I've just seen you this one time. You're fucking moving, though, I'll tell you that. I'd give you a contract tomorrow, if that's what you want. But that's not the reason I'm here, in your dressing room, talking to the side of your face. I want to know you. I want you to know me. I know you're married, and I don't care. He's an asshole, everyone knows that. Including you, I assume, because you seem extremely intelligent. Maybe you need some help, maybe you don't. Either way, here's my phone number. Call me whenever you want to, whenever the spirit moves you."

She was looking at Olly now and he smiled at her; he noticed that her eyes were the color of black dates, so dark they had no depth, just a shiny surface. She tilted her head and looked at him for a moment longer, then turned back to the mirror and resumed brushing her hair. "I see why your artists like you so much," she said in profile. "You're just so very winsome, aren't you Olly Lane?"

"I'm being sincere," he said.

"I know," she said, smiling. "That's why it's so appealing. Listen, seriously, Olly, thank you. That was charming. But I really do have to get changed now."

A month later, he'd gotten her out of her contract with Slade, moved into The Bower, signed to his label, and on her way to a divorce.

That. That was the man Olly Lane used to be.

But what that man hadn't known was that he'd been cursed that night. Miller's prophecy had come true; not too much later, a month or two, it had had happened. It'd started gradually— songs he thought would work bombed, just one or two here and there. A blip. Then whole albums. Then the color and flavor went—they all looked gray, they all tasted gray, like water left standing too long. Then one morning he woke up, lying next to Blue, in his beautiful house, in his town, and it hit him: he'd lost it. Lost his only gift. He was truly alone.

And all that was left was the space where it had once been. And, most punishing of all, the memory of it, and the memory ate everything else that was good.

And Blue? Well, he supposed it was a wonder that it had lasted as long as did, given the hole where his heart should have been.

As the morning turned to afternoon, as nurses came and went, opening and shutting the curtains, bringing pain relief (though nothing prescription, sadly), Olly considered his predicament.

The situation, as far as he could tell, was this: he'd tried to kill himself and he'd been stopped by a fucking biblical intervention. It must mean something. Of course, he'd lost everything in the process. But having nothing left might mean being free. There were no obligations now to be the man he was before, to have the problems, the baggage he had before. He could reinvent himself. But reinvent himself as what, exactly?

A nurse came in and switched on the TV, the screen blinking to life in the middle of a Reagan re-election commercial, one that seemed to have been playing on a loop since Olly's arrival. The old Gipper certainly was eking out his third act, from Hollywood B-list to FBI informant, to president of the United States.

Olly's eyes flickered over the images in the ad: a little girl running into her father's arms, an old woman holding out a pie. The voice-over was intoning gently, manfully, about the economy, about family.

He thought about Aunt Tassie. There'd been a couple of calls shortly before the earthquake from the Starry Acres Nursing Home, some garbled nonsense about how she'd attacked another resident, about how he needed to find somewhere else for her.

How long ago had that been? A week? Longer? That was something that needed to be set right.

He turned his eyes away from the television and looked at the nurse: "I need to make a long-distance call," he said.

After he'd hung up with Starry Acres, Olly leaned back in his bed. The conversation with one Carol Dinkus had been surprising, to say the least.

The Reagan ad played again in his mind: an old woman holding out a pie, a child running into its father's arms. An ancient longing for something almost forgotten, lost.

A thought, unbidden, unlooked for, unbelievable, began skittering around his head, just at the edges, out of his sightline, forcing him to follow it, to find it, catch it, try to hold it in his hands. Was it possible?

No.

Yes.

Yes, it was possible. More than possible. If he thought it through, it was so simple, so obvious, he could have wept. How could he have forgotten this very basic dramatic rule? Redemption was always possible in the third act. He'd been saved for a purpose, he could see that now.

Olly told Dr. Frank he was checking himself out. Dr. Frank was skeptical, though in the end, he agreed to his request after Olly promised to come back in two days for a thorough check-up and attend a minimum of four appointments with Dr. Bob on an out-patient basis.

"This is also on the understanding that someone will be looking after you," Dr. Frank said, as he scribbled on Olly's chart. "Blue, I assume?"

"She's on tour."

"Shame," said Dr. Frank. "Anyway, we can arrange a private nurse. Do you know where you'll be?"

"Home," Olly said. "I'm going home."

CAM

He was lying in the tall switchgrass, his arms by his sides, palms flat against the humid earth, legs outstretched and Adidas pointed toe-up. Above him, all he could see was blue sky framed by the swaying stalks, the seed heads like clusters of tiny stars the color of baby aliens. He squinted on and off, making the sky and the grass move side to side, fractionally, like slides. Then he closed his eyes and lay very, very still, pretending to be dead. Or trying to see what it might feel like to be dead. But dead wasn't a feeling, was it? Then again, what did he know about being dead? Maybe it was a feeling. Maybe the state of being dead hurt. Well, whatever it was he was trying to be it, to feel it.

He was in the old cemetery, the one the town had stopped using because it had run out of space. Eventually, he guessed, all the people who knew someone in the old cemetery, who had any reason to visit those graves, would be dead, too, and he wondered what happened to the ghosts when no one came by to be haunted anymore.

They'd built a new cemetery over the bridge. It didn't have a view of the sea, and even though it wasn't technically *in* Wonderland, it still had a shiny new sign that read: Wonderland Cemetery. Well, not anymore: last year someone had graffitied it, crossing out "Wonderland" and writing "Pet" above it in red paint. Because of the Stephen King book. They'd all thought that was funny.

Cam put on his Walkman and pressed play. Through the orange foam of his headphones came the sounds of Pachelbel's "Canon". He'd taped it off the radio after he'd seen *Ordinary People*. When his father had heard him playing it, he'd laughed, saying that these days it was every bride's favorite opener, and that he'd probably heard that darn piece more times than he'd heard the Lord's Prayer.

He didn't care. Listening to it made everything—the switchgrass, the sky, his palms touching the ground, the smell of the sea—seem as if it were all part of one thing.

As the third violin came in, he could feel the ground vibrating slightly, and then a pair of bicycle wheels passed slowly next to him.

She was completely unaware of him lying beneath her, hidden in the tall grass. He could see everything: the white-walled tire cutting through the grass; her blue Candies pushing the pedals, a flash of hot pink toenail polish; her yellow cotton dress fanning out from those tan, lovely legs; and up, up, all the way up to her white underpants.

He wasn't surprised to see her: she came this route every Thursday on her way from the high school to the thrift shop, where her mom volunteered. And every Thursday he lay here, watching.

She was the only thing that felt truthful and honest and real. She was the only thing in this town that didn't make him want to be dead.

And seeing her gave him the rush he was expecting. But very quickly it was replaced by that same sick, empty feeling he always got, the kind when you feel hungry but really you've got the stomach flu. He waited, trying to control his breathing, until he knew she'd have cleared the field. Then he pushed the headphones off and sat up.

Part of him thought it was possible: a life beyond this place; part of him thought maybe not. And if not, what would happen to him?

Well, he supposed, either way, he wasn't going to cry about it.

THE STORY OF US

Olly was sitting in the hospitality wheelchair at a table in the Pan Am first-class lounge in LAX, drinking a Jack and Coke and wondering why he'd ever given up on drugs and booze. The TV was full of reports on the earthquake, which the news stations were calling the Newport–Inglewood quake, after the fault line that ran through that area into Beverly Hills.

He thought about his beautiful house, in ruins, and took another sip of his drink. It didn't matter anymore. It couldn't matter anymore.

One of the waitresses, young, pretty, brought over a selection of the day's papers and magazines on a tray. Next to the nationals with their headlines about Reagan meeting the pope and Syria taking three Israeli officials captive in Lebanon, sat *Variety,* whose headline read in all its usual incomprehensibleness: *Lane Ankles Prexy Post at Obscura; Moby-Dick Still Afloat.*

At the top of the article was the studio headshot of Olly: blue blazer, crisp white shirt open at the collar, dark hair slicked back. He looked strangely sinister and weirdly varnished.

He was definitely sporting a new look now (he was surprised they'd let him into first class). He'd caught a glimpse of himself in the hospital elevator on his way out: his head bandaged, disheveled hair sprouting out around it, broken nose, white padding and gauze across one eye; under the other the swelling and bruising rose like a miniature mountain range, the color of dusk. And his clothes: a pair of chinos and a *Splash* T-shirt with a Daryl Hannah decal he'd bought at the hospital gift shop. A new look for a new life.

He picked up the magazine and scanned the story. The article strongly suggested that Olly had been fired, though it didn't say so outright. It did mention that Obscura was going ahead with *Doctor Zhivago II: Doctors Zhivago (Working Title)*. He laughed. Anyway, no one was ever fired in Hollywood: they moved on or took some time out to be with their families etc., etc. It also said that Geist would keep the controlling stake in Lay Down Records, as part of their original deal.

"You can take it away, I don't want it," Olly said, handing the magazine back to her.

"Okay, sure," she said.

"Can I get another one of these?" He held up his glass.

He watched the waitress navigate her way to the bar between the plush red and royal-blue club chairs, her low black pumps sinking into the carpet, ankles buckling slightly as she walked.

It was quite a different journey returning to Wonderland than it had been leaving all those years ago. When they'd first arrived in L.A. in '63 they hadn't had the money for a flight, let alone a first-class ticket. They'd come cross-country in Miller's father's car, a white Mercury Comet with red interior; Mr. Fairline hadn't wanted his daughter to go at all, but if she was going, he'd said, she was going in a car he could trust not to break down. God, they'd felt like they'd won the lottery with that car.

They'd driven through Pennsylvania, Ohio, Indiana, Iowa. The Vietnam war was just beginning to bleed into the collective consciousness, but by silent pact they never spoke of it, not after what Aunt Tassie had done, not even when that photograph of the Buddhist monk burning himself alive in protest was on the front of every newspaper in every town they drove through. They'd headed north to the Dakotas because Ash's parents had friends there—Quakers who'd offered to put them up—and also they'd wanted to see that part of the country. Then through Wyoming into Colorado and across the South West. When there were no friends to stay with, they'd camped, or sometimes stayed in small motels.

Olly's overwhelming memory of Miller from that trip was a blue sleeveless gingham dress, fitted at the top, full skirt on the bottom, which she'd wash out every other day and hang over the hood of the car to dry. And that her hair always seemed to be wet, because she'd swim wherever there was water.

Ever since that night she'd almost drowned in the cut, Miller had worked tirelessly to become a fierce and capable swimmer.

Another obsession that had come out of her near-death experience had been a sudden and strange penchant for writing on her body. He and Ash had both noticed it: she'd ink words, sentences, advertising slogans—almost anything—on her skin, often in places where it could be hidden by clothes. But by the time they'd left for California, it seemed to have almost stopped completely.

Instead, she took Polaroids of them: Ash, his blue jeans rolled at the cuffs, white T-shirt tucked in; Olly in his shorts and white button-down, frayed at the edges; arms clasped around each other, squinting into the sun. Photographs of donkeys and black bears by the side of the road, lakes and geysers, and snow, and fields of yellow and white flowers. Beautiful cars passing them on the highway, dude ranches, Bethlehem Steel, American Indians at the Four Corners selling beads and feathers.

She'd paste the pictures into a journal she kept with her, scribbling notes next to them instead of on her skin. Once, when Olly had complained, told her he was getting fed up with all the picture-taking, she'd replied: "Well, you can't get fed up. It's the story of us."

When they'd finally made it to L.A., it had been like stumbling into a neon dream: the sunshine, the palm trees, the colors of the Venice Pier, the lights on Sunset Boulevard, all the young people, the hundreds of cars and fluorescent signs, and noise and winds and ocean. And for Olly, all the music, lighting up before his eyes, exploding on his tongue.

They'd started Lay Down Records out of the motel room they were living in, a cheap joint in West Hollywood called The Coconut. They'd take meetings by the swimming pool, sitting on the blue plastic sun loungers, speaking loudly over the sounds of kids doing cannonballs into the overly chlorinated water. At night, while Miller slept, Ash and Olly would stay up late, talking, making plans. Ash wanted to get rich, Olly wanted to get power- ful. They'd seemed like the same thing.

During the day, Olly and Miller tried to devise errands to send Ash on so they could have the room to themselves for an hour or so, lying on the bed, the cheap quilted cover turning slippery, the sound of the striped awnings outside snapping in the breeze.

The motel had been nothing when they'd moved in, but by the end of the '60s, Lay Down—the deals that had been done there, the musicians who'd passed through—had made the place famous, even though they hadn't stayed very long. Six months into their time in L.A., they'd been able to afford real digs—a shared house in Malibu, and the office off of Sunset, where things had really begun to happen. They'd had luck, they'd had each other, and they'd had time on their side. It had taken them all of three years to start tearing it down.

The waitress returned with his drink, wiping his table, putting down a fresh coaster. "You're lucky to have gotten a flight out tonight," the waitress said, nodding to the TV. "You must be someone pretty important."

Olly looked to the TV screen over the bar: fissures like asphalt riverbeds wending through the highway; sidewalks sheared off completely; signs for pawn shops and cheap loan shops and arcades and surplus furniture stores scattered and twisted and jumbled around like confetti; buildings without parts—a roof, an entrance, a side—like bodies missing a limb.

"No," he said. "Not anymore."

BILLY BUDD, THE HANDSOME SAILOR

Billy had decided to go for a walk. There had been no one at home when she'd come downstairs after her afternoon nap, and the day outside had beckoned. She set off without a plan, but found her path led her to her old house on Foster Street.

From the front, it didn't look like anyone was living there so Billy used the spare key that had always been kept hidden under the planter and let herself in.

It had a cool white feel inside—the furniture covered with sheets, the muslin curtains drawn to keep out the sun. But the smell, the smell was exactly the same. In the front parlor, on the bookshelves, all the same old beloved books were there, and Tassie's father's portrait hung over the mantle, his eyes now regarding Billy.

The books were, strictly speaking, Tassie's father's, added to over the years, of course, but the bulk came from him. He'd loved books, and so had Tassie and so now, did Billy, though Billy had no formal education. She sat down on the sofa, took off her sailor's cap and breathed a sigh of relief. She was glad about the change. Things had been bad when Tassie was just Tassie. Things had been bad at Starry Acres.

It had started with her being accused of numerous infractions that she *knew* she hadn't committed, but somehow the evidence was always against her. It was only recently that she'd realized why, and then, well, then she'd had to do something about it. She could still remember the feeling of Claggart's hand on Tassie's mouth in the dark of her bedroom in Nirvana Nook.

But that was over now.

She didn't know how it had happened exactly, this conversion. She couldn't say which of the Tassie molecules had mutated into Billy Budd, and which had stayed the same. It was like that image of a double helix she'd seen once on television—two different-colored strands coiling around each other, connected by intricate pathways. In her new state, she *was* Billy, but somehow she was also Tassie. Because Billy held Tassie's memories for her, unaltered. So she could be without fear—fear of disappearing, fear of being silenced, erased.

She'd sensed the change coming on; she'd tried to tell Ash when he'd rescued her from Starry Acres, but he hadn't understood what she was saying, and Billy supposed she hadn't really understood either. But when she'd awoken, and become fully aware of the situation, she'd quickly realized that it would be difficult to explain. It would be much easier just to say she was now Billy Budd. People never liked gray areas.

She knew Billy's story well: Melville was Tassie's father's favorite and they'd discussed the work many times. Billy Budd was a hail-fellow-well-met; he was young and innocent and beautiful and strong. But he was also targeted, and martyred—killed to serve a greater good. And he had a fatal flaw, a mute seed within him that led to his destruction.

The thing she couldn't figure yet was how Billy's story and Tassie's story intersected. She would have to look closely for the signs. Though possibly they were already beginning to make themselves known: there was Ash's unexpected reappearance in her life, for one. Ash who had long ago played a part, unwittingly, in her effort to save Olly.

Billy sighed. She could remember them all so differently. The Three Musketeers. So full of promise. And then there was that lovely boy that Miller and Ash had brought back to Wonderland. For reasons of her own, Tassie had followed his progress closely, taking pride in his accomplishments, albeit silently.

She rose and looked at her reflection in the mirror hanging over the sofa: it was Billy's face she saw looking back. Billy knew she'd have to pay for it, for what Tassie had done, in the end. She would have to face her judgment. But for now, she needn't worry about that. She'd been given a reprieve, temporary to be sure, but she knew it had a purpose that had yet to be revealed to her.

In the meantime, she was here, in the light—free, young, beautiful, innocent. Everything was before her and she planned on doing some living.

SAY HELLO, WAVE GOODBYE

After a long journey, Olly found himself standing outside the house he grew up in. He smiled at the sight of the big yellow Victorian "cottage," with its turret and peaked roof, its green shutters, the old wrought-iron gate whose latch was still broken. The curtains were drawn against the sun—had been, he assumed, since he'd had Aunt Tassie moved to the nursing home.

It hadn't been as heartless an act as some might think, sending her there. It'd started slowly, with Aunt Tassie forgetting to pay her bills, and crescendoed when she'd accidentally left the gas lit on the old stove and nearly died of carbon monoxide poisoning. It was then that Olly had made the decision to send her to Starry Acres. She hadn't protested.

"Whatever you think is best, Olly, dear," she'd said over the phone, although he couldn't deny the sadness he'd heard in her voice. His secretary had found the place, promised him it was a good one, close by to Wonderland, so it would be easy for her friends to visit.

Olly made his way up the front walk, past the overgrown front lawn and tangle of once well-tended plantings, and onto the porch. The front door was slightly ajar and he walked right in.

It was still the same, if slightly dusty: the old, worn Oriental runner in the hall; the marble-topped plant stand where a now-dead fern sat; the portrait of Olly and his mother, painted when he'd been around three years old: she with a pink ribbon in her jet-black hair, he in blue pajamas, a once beloved teddy bear dangling from his left hand. Like all houses, it had its own particular smell: wool rugs and old paper and hot air heating and the faint, sweet odor of leftover baking. Olly had a sense of being enveloped by it, almost suffocated by it.

He could remember a time when the house had felt terrifying. When he would stay away as much as possible, playing at Ash's or Miller's house, trying to avoid the pity he saw in their parents' eyes.

Peering into the front parlor, he saw the Sheraton sofa, the upright, unaccommodating Paul Revere chairs, the shelves lined with old books, including a whole two rows of a rare collection of *Encyclopedia Britannica*. The 1911 edition was the longest ever to be published and had been his only inheritance from his father, a traveling salesman who hawked *Encyclopedia Britannica* door-to-door. Olly had never known his father: he'd died in a car accident when Olly was a baby.

"I didn't know him very long, but he was a nice man," his mother had told him.

"No one thought it would last, but they seemed happy," Aunt Tassie had said.

These types of vague and uninspiring comments had been an advantage: Olly had never fantasized about his father, was never particularly curious about what his life would have been like if he'd been around. He was a footnote in Olly's existence, like a long-dead ancestor.

His mother was a different story.

He could still see her lovely face ravaged by the cancer. He could hear her explaining it to him, how she loved him so much, how she wanted to choose her time for herself. Explaining that what he saw now, this stranger's body, would only get worse, and she didn't want him to see that, to remember her that way. How choosing for oneself was the greatest gift God had given them.

He could see himself nodding, telling her he understood—because her eyes pleaded with him to say that—but in his heart, saying: *Please, please, please don't leave me. You don't know everything, you don't know you can't get better. Don't leave me.*

He opened the curtains drawn against the bay window, to let in the light. A layer of dust lay on the card table where Aunt Tassie had always played bridge. She'd been a mean bridge player in her day. So had her sister—his grandmother—before she'd died of cancer (dying of cancer was a family habit, it seemed).

Olly's great-grandfather, a man who practiced the traditional Quaker plain speech, all *thees* and *thous*, had forbidden his girls to play any games of chance. It was immoral, he'd told them. But they'd somehow managed not only to learn bridge, but to excel at it. "If God hadn't intended us to play, he wouldn't have given us mathematical minds," Aunt Tassie always said, though they never played for money.

In the end, he supposed, it had saved her life—it had been a member of her bridge club who had found her in the nick of time, that fateful day.

At the end of the hall, the house opened up into a big, bright kitchen, white enameled walls. The old stone counter. He could remember the cold feel of that counter under his hands. A slice of memory came into his mind, a shuffle of images. Spring, '63, the Vietnam War all over the evening news, her betrayal. Standing there now, he could remember exactly how he'd felt all those years ago.

I'll never forgive you.

Olly felt his chest tighten; it was dawning on him in that moment that, perhaps, effecting this third act that he'd put all his faith in might be a more perilous journey than he'd first imagined. Like those heroes' quests, where all sorts of unforeseen dangers lurked at every turn. Not least of all the danger that the hero, too weak, too fragile, was not up to the task. *Here be dragons.*

"Hello, Olly dear."

He turned and there was Aunt Tassie in the doorway, wearing a sailor costume. Somehow this didn't surprise him: there was a logic to it, a kind of symmetry. Because, of course, there were also helpers on those journeys, bearers of magical gifts. You just had to be able to figure out who was friend and who was foe.

"Hello," Olly said. "I've come home."

1952

Olly held Aunt Tassie's hand in the stillness of the meeting house, his palm clammy. Olly didn't mind the heat, it kept him from thinking about anything else. Mainly, from thinking about his mother.

Next to him, he could feel Miller twitching, picking at her dress; he could hear her laugh as Ash kicked the back of the seat behind them.

Olly closed his eyes, tried to fill his mind with the silence. Then Miller's father started speaking, breaking his concentration. Mr. Fairline was talking about Walt Whitman. Olly had heard Miller's father talk about Walt Whitman before, calling him "the almost-Quaker poet," in a way that made Olly think he agreed with him, whatever that meant.

Mr. Fairline was talking about a great city, and something about love and about doubting men. But it wasn't vocal ministry: he had no message for the congregation, and Olly could feel the air in the meeting house shift, because this wasn't how it was done. This wasn't God speaking through Miller's father. This was Mr. Fairline worrying about himself, not them.

Olly felt anxious for Miller's father. Then he felt Aunt Tassie let go of his hand. And she stood and started speaking, trying to make it all right, trying to smooth it all out, to take away the anger. She was always doing that, he thought, trying to save people.

After the meeting, they all went to the cove. Olly lay on his bare stomach on the warm planks of the dock, his shoulder touching Ash's as they lowered the hooks and lines into the water. He could see minnows just below the mossy-green surface of the water, small black arrows shooting one way, before quickly darting in another direction, disturbed by some unseen movement. Ash turned to him and smiled, clapped him on the back, as if he'd done something great when he hadn't done anything at all.

When he was with them, with Ash and Miller, he was somebody different. He was a musketeer, not a fatherless boy whose mother was dying in a dark room.

He tried not to think of his mother. He was both frightened of her and frightened to be away from her. On the good days, when she had enough strength, they would listen to the radio, and in those moments, they escaped, in his mind, to far-off lands, with colors and tastes so fresh and bright, so far from the room that seemed constantly filled with shadows. On the bad days, she talked about things that he didn't want to hear.

As it began to get dark, Olly did everything he could think of to keep his friends there with him a little longer, so he wouldn't have to go home. When they agreed to go for one last swim, and they walked into the water and it lit up, he could have laughed with joy. "It's like the music," he whispered, but his friends didn't hear him.

On the way home, they walked together, he and Ash one on each side, and Miller in between, to the end of Vere Street. On the corner of Foster Street, Olly turned and looked at Miller and Ash, and knew that what had happened at the cove that night would bind them forever in its mystery, and he ran all the way home because this was something he could tell his mother, that would make her happy, that would keep her thinking about the world.

When he got inside the house, Aunt Tassie was listening to her radio program in the parlor, and he made his way quietly up the stairs. But when he opened the door to his mother's bedroom, he knew immediately something was wrong.

She was lying on her side, her back to him. It wasn't unusual for her to be sleeping, but there was just something about it, about her body, that didn't look right. He moved around the bed and saw her face, puckered, like a plant someone had forgotten to water, or an old apricot. Her mouth was open, and there was a trail of vomit on the pillow. On the bedside table there was an open decanter and note with his name on it. A bottle of pills was clutched in her hand. Squeezed tight, as if for luck. The strangest part was that her hair, which he'd always thought was so beautiful, looked suddenly too big, too much for her head.

Olly backed away slowly, afraid that this monster that had once been his mother might rear up at any moment. Then he took off running, down the stairs and out the front door. As he flew down Foster Street, he could hear Aunt Tassie calling his name.

He ran all the way to Miller's house. He didn't know why he chose Miller in that instant instead of Ash, but when he arrived at the Fairlines' house, he could see the lights burning in the living room windows, reminding him of a lighthouse on a dark ocean. He moved towards it, towards the light, and put his face close to the glass. He could see them—Mr. and Mrs. Fairline and Miller— curled up together on the sofa, Mr. Fairline reading from a book.

He felt such an ache watching them, a sick, empty, gray feeling, like when he'd fall off his bike and get the wind knocked out of him. It was the way they were close, touching each other, so complete—no broken parts, no missing bits, or strangeness or dead mothers who looked like monsters, who had left and gone away and were never coming back to kiss him or hold him or touch him.

Olly tried to call out for Miller, his mouth opening in a perfect circle, but nothing came out. He was about to start banging on the glass, to tell them he was drowning, or dying, or suffocating, when he felt a hand on his shoulder and he turned around and there was Aunt Tassie.

She put her arm around him, her palm on his chest, pulling him gently. "Come away now, Olly. Come away, my love," she said.

And all the way home, she held him tight to her, like she would never let him go.

YOU'VE COME A LONG WAY, BABY

By the time Nate Everley reached the Wonderland bridge, the radio station had cut out, silencing Culture Club mid-"Karma Chameleon." But he was just relieved his old VW Bug had made it, survived the five-hour journey between Leighton Hall and Wonderland without breaking down or just dying completely. He loved his car, but it was never clear whether it would actually get to its destination.

He could hear his stuff rattling in the back as he crossed the bridge. Four years' worth of accumulated chattels: his Indian tapestry, some books, his boom box, his bong with a picture of Reagan's face scotch-taped to the tube, his T-shirt collection, a few pairs of jeans, a whole lot of random socks, his brand-new all-in-one JVC video recorder, and his prized library of bootlegs. He'd chucked out a bunch of other crap before he'd left: posters, old underwear, half-used pencils and notebooks, some text-books—pre-calculus and an enormous tome on the history of taxes.

He felt good, crossing that bridge.

While the rest of his class was playing hacky sack or drinking beer in the woods, preparing for graduation, Nate was beginning the rest of his life. When he'd told his parents that he wouldn't be attending his graduation, they hadn't seemed particularly surprised. At least not his mom: his mom had grown up in an "arty" household and was big on people doing what they wanted, making their own choices, forging their own path, all that jazz. His dad, on the other hand, had been a little disappointed. But his dad was more of a regular guy—he just wanted to know Nate was okay, that he was comfortable, that he had enough quarters for his laundry.

It wasn't that he had anything against his school or that he didn't have great memories, but he had more important things to do. When he'd found out that they were shooting *Moby-Dick* in his hometown, he knew this was a chance he couldn't pass up. If he could get a job on the film set, he'd be heading into film school with real experience, something that would set him apart from his classmates. Also, when something was done it was done: the future was much more interesting than the past.

He was still tinkering with the short film he'd been working on in his senior year, the one that had gotten him into UCS, and he hoped a change of scenery would help him finally finish it.

He'd watched it again last night, after a strange dream had woken him up, dry-mouthed and unsettled in his dorm room. The dream had been some kind of after-effect of taking bong hits with his roommate and watching a weird Mexican movie about a video camera that falls in love with a woman. When he couldn't get back to sleep, he'd turned on his contraband TV and the VHS player hidden in his closet and pressed play on the tape in the machine—the most recent edit of his project. He'd fast-forwarded the tape a few minutes, until his interview with Cam, or one of them, came on: *Cam, 18*.

"So, I'm going to play a song that you know," Nate's voice said.

"Okay." Cam was looking straight at the viewer, his face expressionless.

Suddenly, blasting out came the *Star Wars* theme song, and immediately Cam's face was transformed into a huge smile, a look of surprise. His face turned toward where the music was coming from, grinning, then looked back at the camera.

"Can you see anything in particular when you hear this?" Nate asked, when the music was over.

"No." Cam shook his head.

"Can you say how it makes you feel?"

In the close-up, the viewer could see Cam struggle to find the right words: "Good. Strong," he said.

"Do you have a memory attached to that?"

"Going to see it with you," Cam said. "Summer. I just remember . . . Going to see it with my best friend."

He'd called Cam from a payphone on the road that morning, letting him know when he'd be arriving. The conversation, as usual, had been short. Cam wasn't much of a talker, but that didn't matter. Whenever Nate was in Wonderland he was with Cam. And if he wasn't, it wouldn't have felt right, it wouldn't have felt like home.

The last time that he'd brought a few friends up from Leighton Hall for the weekend, in his sophomore year, Nate had invited Cam over to hang out, but it was clear pretty quickly that it wasn't going to work. These guys had a certain way about them, the sharp way they spoke, the sarcasm, the music they listened to. They were okay guys when they were all at Leighton Hall together, but they didn't get Cam, they made fun of him a bit, under their breath, in side-laughter. They'd mocked the songs Cam talked about. It had pained Nate to watch. That was when he'd decided not to bring anyone home again. Wonderland was him and Cam, and Leighton Hall was Leighton Hall. And that was that.

It had been different when they were younger: Cam had always been bigger and better looking than Nate, and the other kids in their elementary school had respected this—his strength, his looks. Cam had kept Nate from getting beaten up more times than he'd like to admit.

"Don't be a smart aleck," his fifth-grade teacher Mrs. C was always telling him. "It's that smart mouth that gets you into all that trouble."

Cam didn't have a smart mouth. And he didn't get into trouble. But things shifted as they got older. Some of the stuff about Cam that had just been accepted when they were kids became liabilities, points of difference as they hit middle school. His friend's condition became seen as weird, and freakish by some of the kids in town. To make things worse, kids made up stories about Cam's mom—what had happened to her, and so on. Not nice ones.

These small cruelties probably felt even harder for Cam because then, of course, he wasn't even able to cry about it to anyone. There was no release for him. He could make crying-faces, but Nate knew he was ashamed of those, thought they made him look like even more of a freak, and he'd stopped doing it some-time when they were around twelve.

Still, Cam's enforced stoicism meant he never looked weak, and that's probably, ironically, what had saved him from being complete social napalm.

By the time he reached high school he wasn't an outcast, exactly. He played on the football team because of his size and his strength, and he was included in stuff, and the other guys at Annie Oakley didn't mind him. But that seemed to be as good as it got, not being *minded*. Nate wasn't sure exactly how things stacked up at Annie Oakley High, but what he did know was that, as time had gone on, Nate had ended up on the inside of life, and Cam . . . well, Cam was on the outside.

As Nate turned off the bridge, he passed a trailer with *Superstarz Location Services* written on it. He thought again about the film he'd watched the night before, *Lente del Amor,* the one that had gotten into his dreams. It was directed by Rodrigo Rodrigo, the same guy now in charge of *Moby-Dick,* which, of course, had been his reason for watching it in the first place.

In the movie, the camera only worked properly when it was filming the object of its desire, a mousy woman who bloomed under its gaze. Eventually, the camera turned her into a great actress. But the price she had to pay was trying to keep the secret of why only that camera could be used to film her. In the end, she went mad and the movie closed with the camera filming her in an asylum.

He'd liked it, liked what it said about love: how love was every-where, how it touched and altered everything in the universe. Even inanimate objects were changed by love.

Nate fiddled with the radio dial, looking for WNDR, but it was just dead air. Too early in the season for Wonderland's local station, he guessed; it wasn't even Memorial Day yet. He spun though the dial, snatches of songs crackling quickly out of the speakers, making a kind of syncopated jerking noise, until something familiar caught his ear and he stopped. Steely Dan, "My Old School."

Nate smiled and accelerated towards home.

The house looked the same as it always did: orange with white shutters, hydrangeas planted on either side of the front door that no one ever used—they all used the kitchen door in the one-story side-extension to come and go.

Inside he knew it would also look the same: the big kitchen with all the knick-knacks, the old wooden table and painted yellow chairs; the red and green den, where they watched TV, pictures of hunting scenes hanging on the wall; the dining room no one ever used; his bedroom on the top floor, under the sloping roof, with windows that overlooked the street and the Pfeiffers next door.

Home was like that: always the same, his parents always the same. If Nate was being honest, he thought they'd abandoned a really interesting life for a pretty dull one. He could have grown up in L.A. around artists and musicians. It was unbelievable, sometimes, what they'd given up. But maybe his parents just hadn't been cut out for it.

After he parked behind the Volvo, Nate left his boxes in the back of the Bug, carrying only his duffel bag full of dirty laundry into the house, the screen door banging behind him.

He was surprised to find the house empty: his parents knew he was coming home. He dropped the duffel bag by the kitchen table and opened the fridge. Tab, as far as the eye could see, some old spaghetti, and a rotting lettuce leaf. He wondered momentarily if he'd walked into a hostage situation.

He grabbed a Tab and headed out of the kitchen into the front hall.

"Hello?" he called up the stairs, but there was no answer.

He looked at the "Fuck" painting hanging on the wall next to the stairs and smiled. He used to be so embarrassed by it, embarrassed his friends would see it and think his parents were weird and perverted.

But now he found it comforting. His parents *were* weird, but everyone's parents were weird, just weird in their own particular way.

He knew his house was considered bohemian or hippy or something compared to some of the families of his friends at Leighton Hall. His parents were *cool*. Not cool in the way they'd buy you a keg and leave you to it, but cool in the way they offered your friends wine at dinner.

The one or two times he'd brought kids from Leighton Hall home for the weekend, they'd been both impressed and disdainful, their eyes—practiced in cataloguing wealth and hierarchy—slipping over the large framed black and white photographs of his mother, young and beautiful, leaning in against Joni Mitchell; of his father in a tux at the Grammy Awards; narrowing at the huge painting of a dick and vagina ("A 'Fuck' painting," he'd become adept at saying nonchalantly, "by an artist named Betty Tompkins"); their hands carelessly flipping through the copy of Frank O'Hara's *Lunch Poems* with the personal dedication to Nate's grandfather.

These kids knew money. They knew what it was supposed to be used for: cars, swimming pools, ski vacations, Brooks Brothers' suits. But they were also fluent in the language of power, their mother tongue so to speak, and in this regard Nate passed the test.

"Hello?" He heard his dad call out from the kitchen. "Nate?"

Nate walked back through the door that led into the kitchen.

"Hey, you," said his father, raising his eyebrows and smiling at him. "Saw your car parked there. I'd just gone to the A&P. Sorry I wasn't here to give you full the welcoming committee."

"Hey, Dad," Nate said, going to give his father a hug.

His father looked at him. Squeezed his shoulders. "How 'bout a beer? I picked up some Heineken at the market."

"Heineken." Nate smiled at his dad. "Fancy."

"What? What's wrong with Heineken?"

"Nothing, Dad. I'm just kidding you. It's great. Thanks."

They sat at the kitchen table drinking the cold beer, Nate peeling the foil off of the neck. "So where's Mom?"

His dad squinted at Nate, then pointed to his T-shirt. "Air Supply. I like those guys."

Nate just looked at him.

"Really. I've seen them on *Solid Gold*."

"*Solid Gold*, Dad?" Nate took another swig of his beer, eying his father more closely now. "So, what, you're not going to tell me where Mom is? Are you guys getting a divorce or something?"

"What? No . . ." His dad looked really flustered. "Why would you say that?"

"People do it." Nate shrugged. "Okay, sorry. You're just acting a little weird, changing the subject."

"No. No. There's nothing weird going on." His dad stopped. "Well . . . we do have a house guest. Do you remember Aunt Tassie?"

"Aunt Tassie?"

"Olly Lane's great-aunt."

"Oh, yeah." Nate vaguely remembered her—she'd given him presents on his birthday, once a basketball. But he couldn't remember the last time he'd seen her.

He did know who Olly Lane was. He'd heard the stories about the three of them, though he'd guessed they'd been whitewashed for his benefit. He knew they'd all grown up together, that they'd started a record label, Lay Down Records, which ended getting sold, that Olly had been his mom's boyfriend before she'd chosen his dad, and that they'd fallen out over one or more of those things. Your basic crazy '60s shit.

He also knew about Olly Lane because anyone who was interested in Hollywood, where he was considered a kind of Renaissance-man-about-town, knew who he was. Nate had read more than a few articles about him in *Variety*, which he'd started subscribing to in his sophomore year: he had a golden ear for hits, he'd discovered tons of successful bands, and in the last few years, he'd made a transition into movies. That's also how he knew it was Olly Lane who was producing *Moby-Dick*.

"Anyway," his dad continued, "your mom and I grew up with her, around her. Olly lived with her, and she was sort of . . . a kind of mother to him, you know, after his mom died."

"Okay," Nate said.

82

"She was having a hard time at her nursing home, so . . ." His dad shrugged. "So we brought her here."

Nate nodded.

"She's really sweet, Nate. You have nothing to worry about."

"Why would I be worried, Dad?"

"Well, I think she must have had a shock or something, because now . . . well, it seems she thinks she's Billy Budd." His dad said this as if it were somehow good news.

"Really?"

"And she's taken to wearing your old sailor costume."

"The one from the Pearl Harbor dance?"

"I guess . . . I mean, I don't know about that dance."

"So, wait," Nate said, "where's Mom, again?"

"What? Oh, your mom's out. Swimming, I think."

"Listen, Dad. This is all really extraordinary information"— Nate finished his beer in one swig—"and I'm not being facetious . . ."

"Facetious?"

"Yeah, I'm not making fun of you . . ."

"I know what facetious means, Nate."

"Oh, good. I was a little worried there for a second . . ." He stopped. "'Cause, you know, Dad, you're acting weird—about Mom, and *Solid Gold* and I don't know. But I do actually have to meet some people right now . . ."

"What do you mean, weird? What people? You just got here."

"Dad . . ."

"You're home." His mother's voice floated into the kitchen. She was half-in, half-out of the door, sunglasses on, hair wet, in some old bathing suit and his Violent Femmes T-shirt.

He'd wondered what had happened to that shirt.

His mother crossed the room and enfolded Nate in her arms, her sunglasses cutting into the side of his head a little. "Oh, you look wonderful, baby. When did you get here?"

"Just now," his dad said. "I was telling him about Aunt Tassie."

"Right," his mom said, sitting down. "You have missed a few mini-dramas."

"I can see that."

"Well." His mom shrugged.

"We studied it in school, actually," Nate said. "*Billy Budd*. They made a gay opera out of it."

"Honey, I don't think it was exactly a gay opera . . ." his mom said, wrinkling her brow above her sunglasses.

"No, it was definitely a gay opera," he said. "Benjamin Britten. You know, Billy Budd's really good looking and the reason that guy Claggart hates him is because he wants to have sex with him. But Billy's got that speech impediment, so when he's confronted he kills Claggart and then he's hanged for it." Nate looked from one of his parents to the other for any flicker of recognition. "It's a commentary on homosexual persecution."

"Ummm," his mother said.

"It was her father's favorite book."

The three of them turned at the sound of the voice.

If Nate had been writing this scene, he would have used a dolly shot, where the camera moved slowly backwards to reveal a man behind them with a broken face and bandaged head, wearing a *Splash* T-shirt and smoking a long white cigarette, opening their screen door.

"*Billy Budd*," the man repeated. "It was her father's favorite book."

"Jesus Christ," his father said, after a beat.

Nate looked more closely. Though he didn't look like the guy in the *Variety* photos, Nate could see that it was him: older, looked like crap, but it was definitely Olly Lane.

Nate's dad turned to his mom: "Miller?"

"Not me," his mom said, holding up her hands. "I didn't know."

Olly exhaled, smiled slowly at them, a broken kind of smile. "I see the gang's all here."

When no one said anything, Olly crossed the kitchen. "You must be Nate," he said, holding out his hand. "I'm Olly."

"Yeah." Nate shook his hand, smiled. Then: "Virginia Slims," he said, nodding at Olly's cigarette. "Choice."

Olly looked at the cigarette in his hand. "It was all they had on the plane. And it was a long flight, I'm not going to lie."

"What are you doing here, Olly?" His dad crossed his arms.

"I've come to see about Aunt Tassie," he said. "Or Billy Budd, as she's going by these days."

"She's not well," his mom said, giving Olly a level stare. "That's something you might have known if you'd been looking after her. Charming place you put her in, by all accounts."

"Well, she and I have had a little chat and now she wants to go home. So I've come to collect her things." Olly turned to Nate. "So, how old are you now? Sixteen, seventeen?"

"Seventeen. I just graduated."

"Aren't you a little young?"

"I skipped a grade. When I was twelve, so it's not really that impressive."

"The last time I saw you, you must have been two or three."

Nate could feel his parents watching their exchange like they were watching a tennis match, but he wasn't going to let a little awkwardness get in the way of a perfect opportunity. "I'm going to film school in the fall," he said.

"Great."

"You're producing *Moby-Dick*, right?"

"Not anymore," Olly said. "But the director's a friend."

"Do you think they might be looking for someone to help out? I can do anything."

Olly smiled. "Possibly." He looked at Nate's parents. "So, Aunt Tassie's things?"

"Well, they're not packed," his mother said, smoothly.

"I can wait."

"I could pack them up for you," Nate said, "bring them over, if you want."

"Perfect," Olly said. "Bring them by tomorrow and we can have a chat about that job."

ENTERTAINMENT TONIGHT

After Nate had left to meet his friends, Miller and Ash sat at the kitchen table.

"He's got to go," Ash said.

Miller chewed her cuticle, thinking. Events, it seemed, were catching up with her, no matter how hard she'd been trying to avoid them.

"*Miller.*"

Outside the French doors, she could see the spring flowers were coming to their end. In June, there'd be roses and larkspur and sweet peas.

"*Hello? Can you hear me?*" Ash waved his hand back and forth in front of her face.

Miller got up and walked out of the kitchen. She went through the foyer and headed up the stairs.

Ash followed her, watching her from below. "Miller, now is not the time to be indecisive."

At the top, Miller hesitated, then headed towards their bathroom. She stood at the sink, looking at herself in the mirror, as if to see if she looked the same as she had an hour ago.

Ash appeared in the doorway, frowning. "Are you listening to me?"

She tore herself away from her reflection. "Look," she said, finally, "we don't know what his plans are. Maybe he's just going to get Aunt Tassie settled and taken care of, and then go back to his life in L.A." The thing about Ash, which she knew well, was that he had no desire to rock the boat, any boat. He didn't like confrontation, and would rather persuade himself of the most advantageous outcome. So she said: "I'll go talk to him."

Ash studied her a moment. "Okay." His voice sounded wary. "But I need to know we're on the same page. Make it clear that he shouldn't hang around here. This is not a good situation, Miller."

She looked back at herself, nodded.

"Fucking Olly," Ash said.

"I'll talk to him," she said.

"You might want to put some clothes on first."

Miller looked down at her bathing suit and T-shirt.

"Just a suggestion."

Miller walked over to where he was standing and looked at him a moment. "Mmm." Then she shut the door in his face.

In the shower, she watched the water running down her body, watched the droplets cling to the fine, light hair on her forearms. She brushed them away with her fingertips. Cool air pricked her skin, and the hair rose, tiny antennae.

She supposed she'd always known he would show up, at some point. She just hadn't known how it would make her feel: like a filament in a light bulb suddenly crackling on.

In their bedroom, she sat down on her bed, undid her towel and looked at the expanse of white skin covering her body. It was smooth and blank and vulnerable. A desire—needy, itchy, insistent—crawled through her blood, her whole circulatory system, until it reached her fingertips and she grabbed a pen from the bedside table and pressed the tip into the flesh just below her hipbone. *Spiders, Billy Budd, Gay Opera, Cigarettes, Husband*, she wrote, her breath catching in her throat as the words spilled out. *Candice, Sex, Home, Prison, Body. Nothing. Olly. Nothing.*

She stopped, willed herself to put the pen down. She looked at what she'd written, the small script curling around itself like a seashell, the black ink ragged at the edges where it met her wet skin. Then she licked her fingertips, and rubbed at it, leaving a smeared, black trail down her thigh.

*   *   *

After Miller had dressed, she left the house and made her way to Aunt Tassie's old place on Foster Street; above her, a dome of periwinkle blue that marked the evening sky at that time of year. The front rooms of the houses she passed were burnished by the golden-pink glow of lamplight, and the air had the smell of humidity, of salt and soil and plant life clinging to it, a familiar smell that always gave her an empty, aching feeling.

When she arrived at Aunt Tassie's, she opened the gate and went up the porch steps. She couldn't remember the last time she'd climbed those steps. Years ago, anyway. Through the window, she could see the television was on in the parlor, casting a blue flickering light over Aunt Tassie and Olly sitting on the old upright Sheraton sofa, drinking something from silver mugs.

She didn't bother to ring the bell, but instead went straight in. She stood in the doorway of the parlor. Olly looked up briefly, nodding at her, before turning his attention back to the TV.

Even damaged as he was, he was still handsome. All the parts of his body known to her: the shallow dip of his top lip, the shape of his hand, the twist of his forearm. They'd all belonged to her, once. All of it, all of him.

The familiar theme tune from *Entertainment Tonight* filled the room and Miller leaned against the door jamb, waiting.

"*They say love conquers all and while this doesn't always ring true, especially in Hollywood, it seems it has in the case of two very different musicians, with the recent elopement of Blue and Felix Farrow. Our very own Mary Hart sat down with the pop star and her rock star husband to discuss their whirlwind romance and their very private wedding.*"

Miller looked sharply over at Olly, but he kept on staring straight at the screen.

"*First of all congratulations . . .*"

Blue looked beautiful, as usual, her long dark hair in glossy curls, swept to one side, a dark, sequined top glittering in the camera lights. The shot stayed tastefully above her waist, avoiding her prosthetic leg, and Miller wondered how she felt about that sort of thing. Felix Farrow looked like shit, but sexy bad-boy, naughty-but-you-want-to-do-it kind of shit, all blond and craggy and stubbly and cigarette-y.

"*Thank you, Mary,*" Blue said, evenly. "*It's been, um . . .*" Then she laughed, looking over at Felix and smiling. "*It's been something else . . .*"

Miller looked back at Olly's shattered, shattered face and for a moment she could imagine that his heart was in the same shape, and she could feel something close to empathy.

His one good eye met hers, and she saw the blue darken slightly, or retract or something with the pain.

"I'm sorry," she said. "I didn't know."

"Yeah," was all he said.

Aunt Tassie, hearing Miller's voice, looked up. "Hello, Miller, dear. Come in. Join us. Would you like a hot toddy?"

"Sure," she said. "Thanks." She eyed Olly; so he was drinking now.

Aunt Tassie rose, leaving them alone in the room. Miller sat down on a slipper chair next to the sofa.

"*When did you know Felix was the one?*" Mary Hart smiled her bright, hard TV-presenter smile, and Miller was reminded of Candice Cressman, which made Miller hate Mary Hart more than she thought possible. "*Because you've both been married before . . .*"

"Which one of their publicists insisted on this, do you think? Hers or his?"

"Hers, definitely," Olly said. "It's her reputation at risk."

"Surely, even a bad reputation needs some nurturing," Miller said.

Olly inclined his head. "Yeah, but all he has to do is break her heart to restore that. That's easy. She has to keep him on the straight and narrow to keep hers. And he is very serious about his heroin, a real prodigy."

"Maybe she doesn't care about her reputation. Some people are like that." Miller noticed Olly's drink was untouched.

"Those people don't go on *Entertainment Tonight*."

"Everyone's got a keeper."

Olly looked at her.

"What?"

"You look good," he said, an expression on his face she knew from long ago, a sort of hunger mixed with sadness. "Really good."

"Don't do that," she said.

"What?" He turned back to the television.

"Don't do that. Don't flirt with me. Don't flirt with me and then pretend you're not flirting with me. Don't fuck with me, Olly."

"You know what, Miller? You're really hard to get close to." He shook his head. "It's sad, actually."

"Oh, please . . ."

"I mean, after all that *therapy* . . ."

"Oh, does that still sting?"

Aunt Tassie returned at that moment, handing Miller a warm, strong drink. "Would you like to stay for supper?"

"No." She smiled. "I have to get home." She took a sip of her drink, then another, then got up. "Thank you, though."

"I'll walk you out," Olly said.

"No need," Miller said.

"I insist."

"So," Miller said when they found themselves alone on the porch, "what? You're going to take care of her now?"

"That's the plan." He was standing in front of the steps, facing her, arms crossed.

"*Is* that the plan?"

They stared at each other.

"No other plans?"

"Nope."

"Because," Miller said, "we've had her for days now. And we never heard from you."

"What can I say? I was a bit busy, Miller." His voice was brittle. "Anyway, she was fine in the end. No lasting damage."

"*Jesus*, Olly." Miller looked at him, a sense of vertigo overcoming her. "When did you become such an asshole? I mean, I knew you blamed me, blamed Ash for . . . I don't know, us? But Aunt Tassie? You can't be such a child that you're still punishing her, too. What's *happened* to you?"

"I take it back," he said. "You don't look good. You look pretty fucking sad, actually. So tell me: What's happened to *you?*"

"Oh, drop dead," she said, stalking by him down the steps into the tangled, overgrown front garden.

"Don't worry," he called out after her, "I've already tried that."

After she left, Olly stood on the porch for a few minutes until some unknown force compelled him to follow her. He hadn't expected to feel so angry with her, with them. It had caught him off guard.

When he reached Church Street, he ended up standing across the street from their house in the shadow of a privet hedge. This is what privet hedges were probably invented for, he thought. He smoked a cigarette, marveling at how quickly he'd taken to them. After a while, a light came on in the kitchen and Olly moved closer to get a better view.

Miller stood framed in the window. Her hair was pulled back, and he could see the line of her jaw, her cheekbones. He watched as she filled a glass of water from the tap, and lifted it to her mouth, her lips closing around the rim, her pale throat extended, pulsating slightly as she drank.

Moments later Ash appeared, his face over her shoulder. She put the glass down, and turned to him.

Olly crushed out his cigarette, shoved his hands in his pockets and walked quickly away. He couldn't stomach that scene of marital complicity, the contentment, the easiness between the two of them.

To console himself on his way home, he thought about Nate. He seemed happy and smart and ambitious, and Olly liked him a lot, though it had never occurred to him that he wouldn't. He'd been startled at first by how much the boy looked like Miller—he thought he'd be darker. But the biggest surprise of all was how easy Nate had made it for him. It would all begin tomorrow, he thought. And for the first time in a long time, he felt a tiny sliver of happiness lodge in his heart.

By the time Miller returned home, Ash had consumed more than a few beers and had started in on a whiskey. He rarely got drunk anymore, but now seemed like a good time to restart the habit.

"He's just here to look after Aunt Tassie. He won't stay long," Miller said, when she walked back through the door. She looked tired, sad.

She walked over to the sink and filled a glass of water from the tap.

Ash followed. "Are you sure?" He was unconvinced. "What did he say exactly?"

"He made it clear he has no interest in any of us. He told me to drop dead."

"Sounds like Olly." Ash felt somewhat relieved.

"Anyway," she said, slipping off her shoes, "I think he's just lost . . . and pathetic."

Ash eyed her, wondering what she was actually thinking. "Well, whatever," he said. "As long he stays in his lane."

"I'm tired. I'm going to go to bed."

After she'd gone upstairs, Ash refilled his glass and took it out into the backyard. He could hear Cricket Pfeiffer and her daughter Suki over the fence, an indistinct hum, recognizable only by the pitch. He heard the sound of their sliding glass door opening and their voices trailing back inside, snuffing them out.

He stood looking at the stars, cold and hard in the night sky. It was strange how the stars always looked brighter, meaner when the air was sharper. His feet were chilled and his suede loafers were turning dark at the edges from the dew.

Ash lay down on one of the plastic sun loungers and closed his eyes. Events were definitely spiraling out of control. Candice and Miller and Nate and now fucking Olly. The question, of course, was what would he actually do if Olly was here to put up a fight?

This was not his strong suit. He wasn't the sort of man who rode around on his steed righting wrongs and rescuing damsels in distress. No, he waited for opportunities to present themselves, he didn't make them. He'd always been like that, he supposed. He couldn't remember a time when he'd been any different. So, this current situation was a conundrum. He guessed he'd just have to see how it played out. He sighed. Well, he decided, waiting had always served him well. Besides, what choice did he have?

He finished his whiskey and went inside for a refill.

CLEANING UP AFTER THE PARTY'S OVER

The next morning, Miller arrived early at the beach in Longwell, her body slicing through the cold May water. She swam, her breathing in perfect time with her stroke. She made it halfway to the buoy and found herself winded. She treaded water for a while, catching her breath, then turned and began her journey back to the shore. The sky was gun-metal gray, and the water reflected the color back. A change in the tide or the current had brought a yellowish foam that skimmed the waves. On the beach, nests of fine, brown, dried-out seagrass collected near the tideline. She grabbed her towel and wrapped herself, shivering.

In the parking lot, she realized she'd stepped on some beach tar. She sat in the car and rummaged through the glove compartment until she found a pen. With her leg propped up on her knee, she worked at the tar with the edge of the tip of the pen, digging the soft, black petroleum out of her foot.

When she'd gotten most of it off, she wiped the tip clean on her towel. She shut the car door and put the key in the ignition to get the heat running. The radio switched on. Simon and Garfunkel were singing that saddest of songs, "The Sound of Silence." That song had followed the three of them everywhere that first, crazy year in L.A.

Miller stared hard at the pen in her hand. She twisted it open, then closed it. Then twisted it open again. Then she pulled a small notepad out of the glove compartment and started writing, the tip leaving minute traces of beach tar on the soft lined paper.

After they'd arrived in California in '63, they'd thrown themselves into meeting people, into integrating into the lifestyle—haunting parties in Laurel Canyon that went from dusk till dawn, when they'd wearily make their way back to Malibu to sleep for a few hours and get up and do it all over again.

They'd been a novelty on the scene, at first, these three small-town, East Coast, Quaker kids. A charming joke. But when people met Olly, got to know him, they changed their minds.

She could remember the first big party they'd gone to. A girl they'd met at the Whiskey, with a curtain of hair parted down the middle, had invited them along, in exchange for a ride out to Laurel Canyon.

They'd never seen anything like it: beatniks, and folk singers, and druggies. A haze of dope smoke and cigarette smoke. Cushions had been taken off one of the sofas and laid on the floor, where girls and boys lolled around together. People were everywhere: the living room, the kitchen, the bathrooms. And the music—the radio was on in one room, a record player was going in another, and then people just doing their own thing with their voices and a guitar.

Miller and Olly and Ash had stood around watching on the outskirts for a while. Then someone, a musician wearing a broad hat and cape, offered Olly a hit from his joint. Olly had shaken his head, and the guy had laughed at him, mocked him.

"You're an artist," Olly had said. "You need to expand your mind. Mine's just fine for what I want to do."

And the man had been taken with him, flattered, as they all were. And they'd gone off into a corner, where they'd stayed talking all night. And that's how it had started.

First there was The Coconut, then the house in Malibu, which quickly became a hang-out joint, with an office in a spare bedroom, rather than a real home. And, as time went on, Olly always seemed to be in that office. He was fascinated, obsessed with the music, with the relationships with the artists who surrounded him, with what he could do for them.

It was Olly's gift that had been the instrument of their success. He'd had the ability ever since they were children: something happened in his brain when he listened to music and he just *knew* what would work. That—along with his charm, his conviction in the musicians' inherent gifts, the sense he gave of being a killer—had been the overriding factor in their success.

Ash had brought up the rear: he was the go-to guy when it came to securing drugs, and places to stay for the itinerant among them, or smoothing over problems with recording studios, managers, nightclub owners.

And Miller—what had she done? She couldn't say, really. Those were the days she still thought that she'd write a novel. Instead, she'd smiled, she'd poured drinks, she'd listened to break-up stories, and lit cigarettes, and cleaned up when the party was over. (She'd always known that being a woman was an impediment, she just hadn't yet realized it was a life sentence.)

And somehow, as if by magic, before they knew it, they had a small stable of hot, bankable new voices. They had Lay Down.

When they knew they were going to the Grammys, in '65, Miller had panicked. They might have been Young Turks, but they were Young Turks with no money. So Miller had bought a roll of smooth, white fabric in a dinky shop in Venice, the air perfumed with pot, and paid the dry cleaner to make up a dress, praying no one would find her out. She could still picture it now in her mind's eye: a white, one shoulder design ending in a long straight column.

She could remember Olly pressing his mouth against her single bare shoulder before they'd left their place in Malibu, telling her: "That shoulder is the sexiest thing I've ever seen. Like Victorian ladies showing a glimpse of ankle."

And she'd been grateful for that kiss, for that line from him, because things had already started to change by then. It had been the oddest feeling to be *so* seen, like having a white-hot spotlight shone upon her, and then to slowly feel it dim, until it felt like no one ever looked at her at all. Because, in the end, his gaze had been the only one that mattered.

Staring down at the notebook, at the pages she'd filled, at the neat, tight writing, Miller felt startled by it, almost afraid of it.

This was a dangerous business, this remembering, this committing to paper. But maybe, just maybe, this was her way out of the mess they'd made. She shoved the notebook back in the glove compartment and closed it with a snap.

She put the car in reverse, backed out, and started the drive home.

She'd always been impulsive. And she'd found out too late that it was a trait that had determined much of her life. Not a well-formed plan, or a logical pattern or even a consistent philosophy. Just inaction then some unprepared act in the heat of the moment, and *poof*: it was all gone.

But, as she drove home now, she wondered: Could it work the other way? Could it go *poof*, and something be regained?

PART III

SO YOU THINK YOU'RE CHANGED, DO YOU?

MIDDLE OF JUNE, 1984

SUNDAY

"Gin," Rodrigo Rodrigo said, slapping his hand down on the pile of cards.

"Jesus. Again?" Olly had taught Rodrigo how to play gin rummy a week ago and already his friend was obsessed, beating him soundly in their running tally.

"What can I say? I'm a natural."

Olly shook his head, stretched out his legs against the boards of the tree house. Outside, the light purple sky was turning molten blue at the edges. Lately—for the first time in he couldn't remember how long—he'd found himself admiring things like this, the sky, the smell of the air. Like his conversations with Nate, these ambassadors of the natural world stirred something in him, some part of his stupid heart remembered what these things were for.

Olly had moved into his old childhood hideaway a week or so after he'd arrived in Wonderland, when he could physically manage to climb the ladder and bring up the cot bed.

His bedroom had begun to feel oppressive, all the once-precious possessions haunting him. The tree house, on the other hand, felt like its own world. One set of windows looked towards the house and the other set gave him a view out over the untended back garden. Beyond that: the hedge, the Ring Road, Dune Beach, and finally, the ocean. The water, the slice near the horizon that he could see, changed depending on the day—alternating shades of unpolished pewter, milky green, and a bright, hard blue.

It had been dusty and dirty, when he'd first arrived, the boards worn and green from years of weathering. But he'd paid a couple of girls to deep-clean Aunt Tassie's house and give the tree house a once-over, as well. Then he'd kitted it out with sheets and a pillow and a scratchy wool camp blanket from the linen closet, a kerosene lamp, a small table, a mirror, an ashtray, and an old foot-locker where he kept his clothes and other personal items. It had a clean emptiness to it, despite its small dimensions, and it suited him.

"Another hand?'

"Your deal," Olly said.

One of the first things Olly had done upon his return to Wonderland had been to pay a visit to Rodrigo on set. He'd heard that his former classmate, Matt McCauliff, had taken over the old bar on Cutter Road, the one once favored by lobster fishermen and the old guys that dug for steamers on the tidal flats, and was now letting the film crew use it for interior shots. (He'd been glad, but surprised, to know Matt was still alive: While he and Ash and Miller had gone to California, Matt had gone to Vietnam, and he'd been setting out on his second combat tour the last Olly had heard.)

When he'd arrived at *Matt's,* though, instead of the plain clap-board building he was expecting, there stood some strange, dilapi-dated structure with an old-fashioned lantern swinging from one side of the door and a creaky sign hanging above that read: "The Spouter-Inn:—Peter Coffin."

Looking more closely, he could see the worn boards were hastily applied and the cracked sign looked just a little too perfectly cracked. Movie magic. He'd smiled; he'd missed it, a little.

And when he'd pushed open the door, he'd had to laugh: scat-tered about on the now soot-darkened walls were various shrunken heads, clubs with teeth and tufts of mangy hair sticking out, lances and spears and harpoons. Clam shells covered the floor and, at the far end of the room, a bar had been fashioned from the giant jawbones of a whale. He could almost smell the burning oil and sickly grog and fishy chowder, hear the Quaker plain speech. A line from *Moby-Dick,* one that had secretly thrilled them as children, came to him: "*For some of these same Quakers are the most sanguinary of all sailors and whale hunters. They are fighting Quakers; they are Quakers with a vengeance.*" They'd loved that one.

Billy Joel's "Piano Man" was playing on the stereo and the crew of *Moby-Dick* had obviously knocked off for the day and were in the process of getting drunk on their own set; they were unmistakable, these skinny young men with broad shoulders and scruffy hair, with their worn T-shirts and sense of jocular entitlement.

As Olly stood near the whale's mouth looking at them, he'd felt a hand on his shoulder and turned to see a large, dark man behind him.

"Olly," Rodrigo had said, enfolding him in a powerful embrace. "My friend."

Olly had felt strangely emotional, then realized that the hospital was probably the last time anyone had touched him. And, perhaps, the last time anyone had been truly glad to see him.

"I love what you've done with the place," Olly said.

"This is one weird fucking town you grew up in, man." Rodrigo shook his head.

Olly laughed. "Where weird is normal and normal is weird."

"I'm very glad to see you. Wasn't sure you were still alive, between Geist and that earthquake . . ."

"I'm glad you're glad, because I have a favor to ask. There's a kid I want you to hire."

And, just like that, Nate had gotten the job, and Olly was one step further along his journey to a new life.

"So," Rodrigo said now, picking up a card Olly had discarded, "I'm having a little get-together for the crew tomorrow at my place. You know, some *gorditas*, a few *tacos al pastor*, a little beer. You in?"

"Can't." Olly picked a card from the stock pile. "Nate's coming over." Olly smiled. "Gin."

"Shit," Rodrigo said, whistling softly. "I was *this* close, man. One more hand."

It was Olly's turn to grin. "Sure you can take it?"

"Your deal," Rodrigo said.

Olly shuffled the deck.

"So this kid, what do you guys talk about? I always see you coming with your little sandwiches to set, having your little conversations."

They spoke about important things, about music they liked, about the films they thought were iconic. About who was influenced by whom, who had been underrated, who had been overrated. They agreed, they disagreed. They spoke about the landscape of Ingrid Bergman's face, of Eli Wallach's face. About Monroe singing "Kiss" in *Niagara*, De Niro practicing his speech in front of the mirror in *Raging Bull*, Diana Sands dancing in *Raisin in the Sun*. About the zipper on the cover of *Sticky Fingers* and Janis Joplin's glasses. Nate loved the French New Wave and Frederick Wiseman and Scorsese and Jack Hazan and Sergio Leone and Billy Wilder and Fellini. He loved the Violent Femmes and the Talking Heads and The Police and Patti Smith and Cyndi Lauper and The Rolling Stones and Curtis Mayfield and Joan Jett and Roberta Flack and Fleetwood Mac. Actually, it seemed there was very little music he didn't like. And Olly, well, Olly loved listening to him.

"This and that," Olly said.

"This and that, hunh?" Rodrigo discarded an eight of clubs and picked up a card from the stock pile. "Don't piss in my face and tell me it's raining."

"I don't know . . . we talk about working in the industry, how tough it is. How you have to be a genius like you to get very far."

Rodrigo laughed.

"He's making a short film." Olly discarded the jack of hearts, reluctantly. "He's asked me to look at it."

Rodrigo rubbed his hand through the thick pelt covering his head, a small smile on lips and picked up the jack Olly had discarded. "Gin," he said, putting down a nine, ten, jack, queen, king—all hearts—plus four sixes. "Eat that, *cabrón*."

"Jesus, you're a killer." Leaning back, Olly eyed his friend. "And you? How are things in Wonderland?"

"Well, I've been getting a lot of invitations, I can say that, my friend. And some of them smell very nice."

Olly laughed. Rodrigo had always been very easy, very natural with his appetites, something Olly envied.

Rodrigo raised an eyebrow, shrugged. "Another?"

"I surrender," Olly said, hands up. "I can only take so much defeat in one night."

As they walked across the lawn to the side gate that led to the street, the stars were beginning to show.

"So," Olly said, opening the gate so Rodrigo could pass through, "heard anything about your whale?"

"Oh, you know, man, this and that." Rodrigo stopped a moment. "I like this expression of yours." Then he walked through the gate, putting his hands in his pockets. "This and fucking that," he said to the sky, as he walked away.

After he'd gone, Olly went into the big house, as he'd begun to refer to it in his head. Most nights, when he found himself lonely or bored, he would seek out Aunt Tassie, or Billy Budd, as she'd delicately asked to be called. He found her, as usual, sitting on the Sheraton sofa in the parlor watching her program, *The Price Is Right*.

On the television, the contestants were trying to guess the price of a fancy aquarium. It even came with its own small pedestal.

Olly had to admit, Billy was actually a pretty good roommate: always cheerful, never complained about him leaving dirty dishes in the sink or smoking in the house, never gave him grief about living in her backyard. And the change, it seemed, hadn't wiped out Aunt Tassie's memory of the twentieth century, which made things a hell of a lot easier.

Billy did have a habit of wandering, which had alarmed Olly at first, and he'd followed her to see what kind of trouble she might be getting into. But all she really did was take a tour around the tidal island—she seemed to love to visit the film set—before returning home, so after the first few times, Olly had stopped worrying.

When all the contestants had put in their bids, Bob Barker revealed that the actual retail price was $625.

Sure, it was weird, her *transformation*, as she called it, but then again, why not? If she didn't want to be Aunt Tassie anymore, who was he to judge? In fact, he sympathized profoundly with wanting to be someone else. He had begun to think that perhaps she was the sanest person he knew.

A young girl named Wendy had won and was going crazy. The crowd was going crazy with her.

But sometimes, like tonight, as he sat down beside her and she lay her hand, warm, on his back, Olly wished that, just for a moment, just for a few minutes, she could be *his* Aunt Tassie again. It had been so long since she'd been that person to him, in his mind. So long since he'd left her behind, since he'd left Wonderland behind. It seemed strange to him now, that he could have held on to that anger for so long.

"Six hundred and twenty-five dollars for a fish tank," Olly said. "That's insane. I mean maybe if you're Phil Spector or something."

"Everything has a price," Billy said.

And Olly wondered about this, and then stopped because he didn't want to start thinking about what he was going to owe, what any of them owed, to each other.

1963

Olly was standing in the bright kitchen, sunlight bouncing off the white enameled walls and warming the pots of herbs on the window sills. The windows were open and the smell of late spring—damp earth, small growing things mixed with the salty air—surrounded him. He was looking at Aunt Tassie's face, hard, set.

"I can't believe you did this to me," he said. In his hand, the letter from the draft board stating his "unfitness to serve" due to "sexual perversion."

"I had to," she said. "You wouldn't listen." She'd been drying plates at the old Victorian sink—freestanding, bulky porcelain—when he'd stormed in to confront her. She was still holding one now, yellow with bluebirds on it.

"Listen to what? You think you found clearness, that you're the one on the side of right. But you're not. Look what you've done—lying, sneaking around. Is that God's will?" It was taking everything in him to be still. Not to overturn chairs, or smash all the glasses in the cupboard.

"I don't know," she said, quietly. "Their hands were tied by their own bigotry. I see a bit of God's plan in that."

Olly shook his head, staring at her. "Unbelievable."

"We're conscientious objectors, Olly. We don't send our children to kill other children. We work for peace." She stopped, put the plate down, carefully. "You could have been a medic," she said, her face softening. "Or worked in a hospital. But you wouldn't listen. You're *young*. This is only going to get worse. You don't understand. You might survive the first year, the second year, but you won't make it all the way. You'd die there."

"That's not the point," he said, slamming his hand upon the old stone counter. "It was *my* choice. I can't be the person who's hiding and waiting for my number to come up. Who's pretending there aren't other people, just like me, over there dying. I can't pretend I'm not involved."

"It is the point. It's the point to me. You being alive is the point." She looked at him; there were tears in her eyes, but he could tell she, too, was willing herself to be still.

He shook his head. "I'll never forgive you," he said.

"You don't have to. You can hate me for the rest of your life. But you will have a life, Olly. And that's what matters to me." She turned her back on him. "I have to finish these dishes, dear."

He tried to explain to the head of the local draft board that they were lying, all of them—Aunt Tassie, the ministry elders. That they were all conspiring to stop him from enlisting. That they were Quakers, pacifists, that they didn't understand what was happening. But the man hadn't believed him. His eyes had been venomous, telling him *ho-mo-sex-uals* were not welcome in the U.S. army. And he could tell it to his boyfriend, too.

And when he did tell it to Ash, after finding him tinkering with his car in his parents' garage, Ash seemed delighted by his newfound status, delighted to be out of it. Ash was getting ready to finish his last semester at Longwell Community College and was thinking about business school applications.

"One less thing to worry about," he said. "Though it might complicate our dating life."

Olly just stared at him. Was everyone crazy?

"Oh, come on," Ash said. "I know it was important to you, but really, Ol, I don't think you would have liked being shot at. Anyway, I'm sure Brooks will let you re-enroll."

Olly had dropped out of the small private college he and Miller attended, to enlist.

He had to leave Ash's presence, for fear he'd sock his friend in the mouth. So he went to the person he always went to. He went to Miller.

Miller whose skin was golden, whose limbs were long, who smelled like heaven. Who was as much a part of him as his blood, his bones, his teeth. Miller, who, when he touched her, was like touching a hot stove. It was always the same for both of them, always the best thing he could think of.

And when he told her—*they convened a fucking clearness committee behind my back*—she said: "Oh, Olly." And she'd just held him, until his lips found hers, and there were too many clothes between them, and then there were none, and they were lying, wrapped around each other in her twin bed in the bedroom of her parents' house.

But afterwards, she said quietly: "I'm not sorry you're not going over there. I'm not sorry that you're not going to die and leave me. I could have stood it, but I'm not sorry I don't have to."

Olly was quiet. Then he said: "They took something from me."

She put her hand to his face.

"She was supposed to love me and protect me."

Miller sat up. "But, Olly. That's what she's doing."

"Don't say that." He couldn't bear it, that no one was really with him. Not even Miller.

And he'd never forget she'd said that, never forget that when the chips were down, she hadn't sided with him.

Later, he was watching Miller's pink and blue ruffled curtains blow in and out with the cool breeze. Miller had turned on the radio. Whatever was playing sounded like a dirge, dark and clouded and swelling, and he'd felt like crying. And then the music changed, and he could hear surf music, beach music, the music of sunshine. Yellow, tasting of salt and suntan lotion and popcorn.

Finally, he turned to her: "I'm not going back to Brooks."

"What are you going to do?" She didn't seem the least bit surprised.

"I think," he said, "I think I'm going to go to California. I've always wanted to see it. One thing's for sure: I'm laying down Wonderland."

MONDAY

Ash parked at the marina and popped the trunk. Miller got out and went round the back. Lifting the tray out, she was surprised by its weight.

"Jesus, Ash," she said, "what's in here?"

"Seven layer dip," he said, taking it from her.

Ash had been cooking up a storm since he'd been back, going particularly berserk on the Crockpot, stuffing their fridge with various Tupperware containers full of meatloaf, stroganoff, and something he called "Livin' Easy Lamb Stew," which Miller suspected came from the recipe booklet included with the cooker.

So, she hadn't been entirely surprised when he informed her that he'd offered to make something for the small cocktail party the Gunthersons had organized to show off their new sailboat.

"I'm just tired of trying to eat tri-color pasta salad on a moving vessel," he said.

"Fair enough," Miller said, grabbing the bag of corn chips and placing them on top of the tray in Ash's arms. "Which one is it?"

"That thirty-footer out there," he said, using his chin to indicate a large catboat moored beyond the docks. "*Mad Hatter.*"

"Original," Miller said.

Ash didn't respond, just walked ahead of her toward Kip Guntherson, waiting in his Zodiac to ferry them out.

"You're the last ones," Kip said, taking the tray from Ash. "Can't wait to show you this beauty."

"Careful," Miller said, "you can probably drop anchor with Ash's dip."

"Can't wait to see it," Ash said.

Mary Guntherson was there to greet them when they pulled up, taking Miller's hand to help her aboard and introduce her around: there were two couples Miller had never met—houseguests of Mary's—and the Pfeiffers, all crammed in the small cockpit.

"But you know Cricket and Dutch, of course," Mary said. "You're neighbors."

It was rare to see Dutch Pfeiffer out and about: he was either working in the city or "resting," as Cricket called it, whatever that meant.

"Come," Mary said. "A glass of wine."

The cockpit was getting crowded and some of the guests had already moved toward the bow, perching on the cabin top.

"A Nonsuch 30 Ultra," Kip was telling Ash. "You gotta see the cabin, it's a feat of engineering. I mean, you won't believe what they managed to get into the space . . ."

Mary shook her head, saying to no one in particular: "I should have insisted on children. He'd be much less sentimental about children."

Ash was unveiling his seven layer dip, which seemed right at home with the spinach and artichoke dip in a bread bowl, and the Ambrosia salad in small plastic cups already laid out.

"I keep telling Mary we should just sell the house and move in here."

"And I keep telling Kip that unless he's the one doing the cooking, I prefer my human-sized kitchen, thank you very much."

"Can't imagine firing up the ol' crock pot in there," Ash agreed, peering through the hatch at the galley.

Miller stared at him—this man, her husband, improbably, it suddenly seemed—then silently took her wine and made her way toward the bow. The sun was setting over the mainland, throwing a ladder of glowing orange across the water. She hadn't wanted to come tonight, and she was already finding the performance tiresome. But she knew that if she and Ash kept refusing social invitations there'd be talk.

She sat down on the cabin top next to one of the couples whose names she'd already somehow forgotten—a blonde with silky hair like a curtain, large hoop earrings and a frog print shirt, and her nondescript husband.

"What do you think of the movie?" the blonde asked.

"Oh, *Moby-Dick*? Very exciting," Miller said. "My son's actually working on it."

"Mary says she and Kip take their lunch down to the set everyday to watch them filming."

Miller laughed. "It is strange, isn't it? How fascinated we are with how they get made. Like with magic tricks: we always want to know how we're being fooled. But then knowing would ruin it, wouldn't it?"

"Well," the husband said, "I, for one, am just sorry we haven't seen the beast itself. That's going to be a sight."

"Oh, yes, the whale," the woman said. "Mary said she'd take pictures for us, though."

"It's all smoke and mirrors."

The three of them turned at the sound of Dutch Pfeiffer's voice; he and Cricket were sitting behind them on the cabin top, facing the other direction. Dutch had to crane his neck around to deliver this piece of information, while Cricket looked into her drink.

"Well," the blonde said, "I think . . ."

"*Ribbit*," Dutch said, grinning at the woman.

"I'm sorry?"

"Your shirt," he said.

"Oh."

The husband looked like he wasn't sure if he should laugh or stand up for his wife.

"At least it's better than this one," Dutch said, nodding at Cricket. "What do you call that, honey?"

"A muumuu," Cricket said.

"Looks like something we took camping last year."

"I think it's very nice," the blonde said.

"Me too," Miller said.

"Well, what do I know about fashion? Right?" Dutch directed this towards the husband, who shrugged warily. "You know what was a good movie? *Deliverance*. Now that's a movie about real life."

117

"Excuse me," Miller said, getting up.

She made her way back to the cockpit, squeezing past the others to get down to the mercifully empty cabin. Down below, the space was compact, a place for everything. Towards the bow, there were three narrow doors, one of which, she assumed, must be the bathroom. Picking the middle one, she found herself inside the shower, a plastic curtain on one side, wall on the other. It was quiet in the shower, so she sat down on the little wooden bench in front of her, and leaned her head against the wall.

After a while, she looked down at her pale legs stretching out from her light blue cotton skirt, and she began to inch it up over her thighs. She closed her eyes and an image, unbidden, of Olly's neck rose in her mind's eye. She couldn't stop herself: she took a pen out of her purse and wrote: *I can still smell him, sweet and hot and close, like the inside of my riding hat.*

She'd written that line, about the inside of her riding hat, in a poem in college that her professor had read out in class, praising it. She could remember how pleased she'd been, how special she'd felt. Those were days when she was going to write poems, novels, when she'd quit writing on her body and had started writing, seriously, on paper, endless streams about longing, and desire, about escaping small-town life, about freedom and danger. All the things that had been important to her then, before she'd followed the boys to Los Angeles, and lost her way, and come back home again.

She could remember the night in L.A. when she'd realized it had been three years since she'd put a pen to anything, except a grocery list. It had shocked her, frightened her, how very far from the center of her own life she'd become. She'd gone to the spare bedroom in the Malibu house, Olly's office, and knocked on the door. But he'd been too busy to see her. Some deal or other. And she'd decided right then and there that things had to change. She'd taken the car keys and driven to Ash's house. And the rest was history.

From up on deck, the sound of cocktail music—muffled voices, rising and falling, punctuated by loud bursts of laughter and interruptions, the sound of ice hitting glass—trailed down into the cabin. Miller heard a door open and shut and then two distinct women's voices—Mary's and another woman's she didn't recognize, her second houseguest most likely—just next to her. She realized then that the plastic curtain next to her must separate the shower from the toilet, with an outside door for each.

Miller held her breath.

There was a light tapping sound, then a loud sniff. Miller had to keep from laughing; she'd had no idea Mary was such a dark horse.

"I haven't done this in ages," Mary's voice said. "Corrupting me with your city ways."

"The old Bolivian marching powder?" the other voice said with a giggle. "I would have thought with all the Hollywood types floating around here these days it would be *de rigueur,* darling."

"Well, it has gotten very starry around here," Mary said. "Lots of very handsome men walking the streets."

"Yes," the other woman said. "I think I saw that"—she inhaled—"that music mogul guy. Nathan Lane? No, that's that not right . . ."

"Olly Lane?"

"*Olly* Lane, that's the one."

"You know," Mary said, the sound of the tap running, "he comes from Wonderland. Used to go out with Miller Everley. The tall blonde I introduced you to up there?"

"Really. Well, her husband's not so bad, either."

"Ash? I suppose. Word on the street is that he's having an affair with that morning talk show host, the plastic-looking one, Candice Cressman."

"Ugh," the other woman said.

"Men," Mary said.

Olly was on the front porch drinking a beer when Nate arrived, carrying the VCR in his arms. Olly strolled down the front steps and took the machine out of his arms and carried it into the house.

"Thanks for doing this," Nate said.

"Of course," Olly said. "Happy to do it. And I'm curious, anyway, about this big project of yours."

"No, no, it's just like a first attempt." He brushed his hair back from his face, a gesture Olly had come to recognize as a physical Nate-ism. "I just want to see if, you know, you think it has something. Or maybe . . . not."

"Well, let's have a look."

After a little fumbling they managed to hook the VCR up to Aunt Tassie's TV, Nate popped the tape in, and they sat down— Olly on the sofa, Nate perched on the edge of the slipper chair, his knee jumping up and down.

Olly watched the film unroll—it was a series of short interviews with seemingly random subjects, identified only by their name and age. They were each played a song and the camera filmed their physical response, then they answered a couple of questions about the music. It wasn't particularly complicated or flashy as a piece, but it was the responses to the songs that were enthralling: you could see how the music changed them, how these people were physically altered, were transfigured by it. The expressions—of pain and of joy and of fear—all played out on camera.

And as Olly watched their expectant faces just before and then just after the music was played for them, his own heart tightened as if a beefy hand had reached into his chest cavity and began manually pumping it, pushing blood through it. Envy bit at him. Then grief, for what he had lost when he lost his ear, his shining, sparkly gift.

In some ways, the most painful part had been knowing what life had been like before. Like losing one's sense of taste and smell—it was better never to have had it at all. That day at The Bower, the sky like a crazy painting, the hole in the roof, the vodka, the pills, the pool—it had all been because he had known what life was like before it had turned gray, flat, turned to nothing. He had known what life was like in technicolor.

The film came to an end.

Olly looked over at Nate who was staring at him intently. "I like it," he said.

"Okay . . ."

"No, it's really original." He smoothed his hair back, collecting himself. "Where did the idea come from?"

"Just something in my head, I guess," Nate said.

"Well, it's good. I like the tight shots on their faces. It's really moving."

"Ahhh, that's . . . that's a relief." Nate grinned. "You looked really serious there for a minute; I thought you hated it."

"No, of course not," Olly said. "So why documentaries? Why not features?"

Nate shrugged. "I like the surprise of them."

And, just like that, Olly felt the darkness lift. *Yes*, he thought, *yes, of course, the surprise of things*. And he felt like laughing. When was the last time he'd thought about that? About just being delighted by the unexpected, about the fact that maybe what was waiting around the corner was better than what had come before?

"Do you want a beer?" he offered.

"Thanks, I can't. I'm meeting up with some people." The hand brushed the hair away again.

Olly smiled, leaned back. "A girl."

"Yeah, I think so. I hope so. I don't know." Nate seemed to be considering whether to say more. Then he said: "I think it's going to happen, but then every time I think that, she just seems to . . . I don't know . . ." Nate was quiet for a moment, then he said: "Can I ask you a question?"

"Shoot."

"What happened between you and my mom and dad?"

Olly looked at him. "We were really close," he said, finally. "Things happen when you're that close to people."

"Like what things?"

"Things. Maybe . . . maybe we just expected too much from it. You know, from each other."

"But in what way?"

"I don't know." Olly shook his head. "The real answer is I don't know," he lied.

"I think it's the most exciting thing that's ever happened to this town," Suki said.

Nate and Cam and Suki were sitting in Cam's backyard in the semi-darkness drinking beer Nate had pilfered from his dad's stash, the three of them gathered around the plastic picnic table under the crabapple tree. In a couple of months, it would start dropping hard, bitter fruit. But for now, it only sprinkled the last of its petals down upon them.

"Of course it is," Nate said. "I mean, the last exciting thing to happen here was that bridge. And that was like, what? Fifty years ago?"

The movie had begun to overtake the town. Bright lights lit the beaches when they shot at night, and on the eastern edge of the island, where Wonderland's causeway connected the mainland, a square-rigged ship stood anchored.

There was a sense in the air that something important was happening. That *they* were important. The shop windows looked cleaner, people seemed to sweep their front walks with more care. They even spoke about it as if it belonged to them. Every sentence seemed to begin with: "Well, because we're filming . . ."

And then there was the whale. A beast that, by definition, would be far larger and more ferocious than the shark in *Jaws*. In a place where the first and last stroke of imagination had manifested itself in the town's name, a place where everything's proper name was a direct description—Dune Beach, Shell Beach, Pebble Beach, the Ring Road—the idea that they, the people of Wonderland, could actually become interesting, *known* for something, something bigger than themselves, something dangerous and wonderful, was turning into a kind of collective obsession.

Not to mention the tourism dollars it would bring in.

The movie people needed the locals, too. They needed extras, needed information about the movement of the tides, they needed help building parts of the set, keeping people quiet when they were filming, and so on. Whatever the Teamsters agreed to. Even Cam's new job—lifeguarding on Dune Beach—was down to the movie; the town had been forced to deal with the increasing crowds attracted by the promise of rubbing shoulders with movie stars.

"They say Patty Tithe's in town." Suki took a small sip of her beer.

Suki. Looking at her left Nate with a familiar ache inside—hair the color of a sunset, or a Creamsicle, and her skin a kind of tawny brown, freckled by the sun; she wasn't one of those redheads that burned at the first suggestion of sunlight. She was wearing some peachy, blousy thing that had ties at the shoulder and a denim skirt that fell away from her thighs, just a little, when she shifted her legs. He wanted to run his hands against the smoothness of those legs, all the way up that skirt.

"Patty Tithe," Nate said. "Almost every guy at Leighton Hall had a poster of her over their beds." The most popular one had been the still from *Slick Bodies*, where she was standing on a beach in a blue lamé one-piece bathing suit, tossing her wet blonde hair. Patty Tithe was the stuff Leighton Hall's wet dreams were made of.

Nate was about to mention that it was Olly who'd produced *Slick Bodies*, but he stopped himself. He'd already gotten crap from Suki and Cam about his "obsession" with Olly Lane. It was true, he had been spending a lot of time with him lately—after all, Olly'd been the one to get him the job gofering for Rodrigo. But it was more than that: Olly talked about things in a way that felt like a revelation to Nate, about the way people really were, and about Nate's work, like it was something important, like *he* was important.

"Imagine," Suki said, "being frozen like that. Stuck in one pose, tacked up on somebody's wall." Her face looked flushed in the dim light, violent almost. "And that's it, that's you forever."

"Like those flies stuck in amber," Cam said. "Like purgatory." Cam's legs were stretched out and he was tipping his plastic chair back, looking up at the sky, which was a kind of purple color, and the stars were beginning to show. It was a soft June evening, just a bit of bite to the air.

"But that's movies," Nate said, looking from one to the other. "I mean, that's the beauty of them: they're indelible."

"No," Suki said, looking at Nate sharply. "No, Cam's right. It *is* a kind of hell, never being able to change."

The outline of a smile formed on Cam's lips.

Nate stared at Suki; he couldn't figure her out.

It had started over winter break. They'd stood in the snow near the Wonderland Christmas tree after everyone had left, and she'd been wearing this blue coat, like a deep blue, almost a purple, and she'd had red lipstick on, and he'd kissed her for the first time, in the falling snow. And he hadn't been able to stop thinking about it since.

So he began to call her, every week from the payphone in the hall of his dorm, and they'd talk about their lives, their friends, their parents, what they were studying at school, and he'd listen to her, and try to read between the lines of every answer she gave him, looking for clues about who she was and what she thought, and how she felt about him.

And while he would always hang up feeling good, a few hours later, a sense of unease would set in. He hadn't been able to put his finger on it exactly. Only that, in the past, he'd never had to work very hard for this kind of thing.

The weird thing was, he'd liked it. He'd liked the longing he felt, a kind of hollow feeling that was part fear and part possibility. As spring had come on, and the classrooms at Leighton Hall had gotten that airy, empty feeling to them, as the sky had stayed lighter at night, and he'd spent his time smoking weed on the fire escape of the dorm with his buddies, or skipping class to go swim in the ponds, or sneaking off campus to the diner, dropping his laundry quarters into the jukebox to hear Duran Duran one more time, he'd felt it: the longing. Like a beat punctuating everything he did.

She was different from any other girl he'd ever met. Not because she was more beautiful, or smarter or cooler. It was because she was indefinable. She was very serious, and she had this certain sideways way of thinking about things. Like a prize-fighter, always bobbing and weaving, you couldn't pin her down. And he couldn't take his eyes off her.

There were times since he'd been back that it'd seemed like she was just on the edge, just about to fall. Then the next moment, she'd shy away, close up, move out of his reach, like they were strangers. Or worse, like now, when she seemed angry, almost furious with him.

"Well, at least you know what you want, I guess," she said, breathing out softly, the sharpness in her voice gone. "I have no idea what I'm going to do with my life." She turned to Cam, tucking her hair behind her ears. "Do you?"

Cam put his beer carefully on the picnic table and stood up. "Does anyone want another?" Then he walked across the lawn toward the house without waiting for an answer.

Nate looked at Suki. "Do you really not know what you want to do?"

She laughed. "You're just like Jess."

"What?"

Suki gathered her loose hair in her hands and pulled it over her shoulder. "I don't know, you with your films and Jess with her acting, you're both so sure of everything, of where you fit. For me, it's like . . ." She trailed off.

Tell me. Tell me anything.

". . . life." She held out her hands, as if to catch the space between them. "There's just so much of it. What are you supposed to do with it all?"

Cam returned with the beers, Jess James trailing in his wake.

"Look what the cat dragged in," Jess said, seeing Nate.

"Who, me or you?" Nate said.

"Ha ha. No." Jess folded herself into one of the seats and took a beer from Cam. "I'm always the cat, never the old dragged thing. So, Nate, congratulations on getting into USC."

"Congratulations on AADA."

"Look at us," she said, clinking her beer against his. "Though . . . documentaries? Really? Kind of dull. And you'll always be poor." She cocked a very groomed Brooke-Shields eyebrow at him, taking a long drink, then turned to Cam. "Are we all set on the bonfire situation for next week?"

"The kegs, anyway," Cam said.

"Cam's got the best fake I.D.," Jess said. "Probably because he made it himself."

It was a tradition, the bonfire—every year after graduation, the seniors from Annie Oakley held a party on Pebble Beach. The whole school went, or at least all the juniors and seniors, and whatever sophomores and freshmen could sneak away. Over the years, it had gained a kind of local notoriety, and a lot of kids from over the bridge in Longwell also showed up, though that usually meant fights and the local cops coming to break it up, which added an extra spice to the whole proceeding.

The town had done what it could, including moving graduation to the middle of the week, in hopes of discouraging a weekend bender, but the kids just waited a couple of days and held it on Friday anyway. Not wanting to draw attention to it by an outright ban, the mayor had finally instructed the small police force of four to keep an eye on it and shut it down the minute they spied trouble.

"Are you going?" Nate looked at Suki.

"I don't know," she said. "My mom . . . you know how she is."

Suki's mom was a champion worrier. She seemed to worry about everything: her roses, the swimming pool, burglars, the china, stray cats, the cold, the heat, and most of all Suki.

"She's going," Jess said, firmly.

"I could pick you up . . ." Nate said.

Jess rolled her eyes. "What? From next door?"

"Definitely." He looked at Suki. "From anywhere you want."

Suki said nothing, only bit the inside of her lip.

"Cam, do you think we could have some music?" Jess said. "And maybe just another teensy beer?" She twirled her bottle at him.

Nate stood up. "I'll get it," he said. "Have to make a pit-stop anyway."

"Stereo's in my room," Cam called after him.

The rectory house wasn't fancy; it was old-fashioned in a lot of ways—the mammoth ice-box with the latches instead of handles, the brass chandeliers, the muddy-colored wallpaper—but it was big and had an easy feeling to it. It was like Nate's second home; he and Cam had grown up a block away from each other on Church Street, lived at each other's houses as kids.

He climbed the stairs to the second floor and switched on the bathroom light. The Crosses' bathroom was a reminder that this was a bachelors' house—a razor left in the sink, tiny hairs clogging the blade. Two cans of shaving cream, toothpaste stuck to the edge of the faucet, the bathmat left damp on the floor.

After flushing, Nate made his way into Cam's room, which was pretty tidy by comparison. His brown, plaid blanket was folded neatly at the end of his bed, and two books had been carefully arranged on his bedside table next to the brown glass lamp: *The Plot to Kill the President* and *Huckleberry Finn*.

Nate flipped through the copy of *Huckleberry Finn*. Cam had underlined certain passages:

And I about made up my mind to pray; and see if I couldn't try and quit being the kind of boy I was, and be better. So I kneeled down. But the words wouldn't come. Why wouldn't they? It warn't no use to try and hide it from Him. Nor from me, neither. I knowed very well why they wouldn't come. It was because my heart warn't right . . .

On Cam's desk, textbooks were stacked neatly next to the black and white composition books. There was a typed letter lying open next to them from Longwell Community College. Nate had just assumed Cam might get a football scholarship somewhere, though thinking about it now, he didn't know why he'd thought that. He didn't even know if Cam was that good.

There was a bulletin board above his friend's desk, with a bunch of stuff tacked to it: a red ticket stub for *Ordinary People* at the Wonderland town hall; a flyer for Annie Oakley's homecoming this year (theme: Drive-Thru); an assortment of photos (Nate and Cam in third grade, arms around each other's shoulders, hair wet—at the beach, Nate guessed; Cam and his dad outside Sunday service; a picture of Cam in his football uniform).

Behind these was another, its corner just peeking out. Nate picked it out. It was a snapshot of Suki, taken from outside the thrift shop on Main Street where her mom volunteered. Suki was standing in the window, looking out through the glass, obviously unaware she was being photographed. Her expression was unreadable, but neutral. Like something had caught her eye and she was thinking about it. Or maybe she was looking at nothing, thinking about something completely removed from where she was. Carefully, Nate replaced it.

He thought about his friend, the things he didn't know: his secret pictures, his fake I.D., his community college. It seemed Cam had suddenly grown older without him realizing it. It left him slightly unsettled.

Cam's boom box was next to the closet in the corner on the floor. Nate grabbed it and headed back downstairs, where he positioned it facing out of the kitchen windows toward the yard, plugging it into the socket next to the sink.

He turned on the radio and fiddled with the dial. Blue Oyster Cult's "(Don't Fear) The Reaper" came through the speakers. Nate grabbed some beers from the fridge and walked back out into the night. It was dark now, and there were fireflies blinking on and off like tiny traffic lights. He could make out the outline of his friends at the table, as the music drifted through the window.

Jess and Cam were laughing at something Suki had just said, and Nate had a sense of real well-being, coming upon them like that in this early summer night. As he moved slowly across the grass, his eyes watched them, like a tracking shot in the film of his life: the low hum of their voices, the sound of that '70s music swelling in the damp yard, condensation collecting on the scattered beer bottles, the moon hanging low.

That was the Blue Oyster Cult with "(Don't Fear) The Reaper." You're listening to Johnny Appleseed's Timeless Classics on

WLBO, Longwell. Don't touch that dial 'cause we've got a whole hour of timeless classics coming up.

Nate looked at them. "What does that mean?" He laughed. "What the hell are 'Timeless Classics'?"

"Oh, it's great," Jess said. "He does this mix of the best songs, you know: old ones and new ones. Like Top 40 and other stuff."

Next up, a little Bob Seger for all you out there practicing your "Night Moves" . . .

The guitar thrummed, warm and low.

"I love this song," Suki said.

"Me too," Cam said, smiling at her.

"You do?" She sounded surprised.

"Yeah." He shrugged. "It's moving."

Something about the way he said it, none of them wanted to laugh, it meant something. So they were all quiet as Bob Seger's raspy tones began playing out into the yard. As the song grew, picked up pace, they all began to sway a little to the music. Then they were humming along. The background vocals made it deeper, richer, and they were carried away by it.

"*We weren't in love, oh no, far from it . . . We weren't searching for some pie in the sky summit,*" Jess sang out loudly, throatily.

Suki followed, her voice thinner, slightly sweeter, a little higher. "*We were just young and restless and bored . . .*" Her head was thrown back slightly, her white throat vibrating.

Nate wanted to reach out, touch that spot, press against it, feel the quiver beneath his fingertip. He could imagine himself doing it, gently, like taking a pulse. Instead, he kept time with his hand on the table, then joining in: "*Working on our night moves. Tryin' to lose those awkward teenage blues . . .*"

Cam broke in with a falsetto, playing an air guitar.

They laughed, looking from one to the other.

"*We felt the lightning . . . And we waited on the thunder . . .*" They were shouting in unison now. "*WAITED ON THE THUNDER!*"

In that moment, it was like they were all in something together, untouchable, rising above it all, above Wonderland, above the night, and all the ways they might be different.

"Are the Beatles getting back together?" Cam's dad was coming across the lawn towards them, his voice breaking the illusion, like a glass shattering.

"Hey, Dad," Cam said, almost wearily.

"What are you guys doing out here in the dark?" He eyed the beer bottles on the table, but said nothing. Instead, he looked at Nate, ruffled his hair. "You've grown your hair. Reminds me a little of my youth. Robert Plant, and those guys. Is that back in fashion now?"

"Oh, I don't know, maybe," Nate said, trying—and failing—to imagine Reverend Cross ever having long hair or jamming hard to Led Zeppelin.

Cam's dad turned to Suki. "How are your parents, Suki?"

"They're good, Reverend Cross. You know, the same."

"The same?" He seemed surprised.

Suki laughed. "Exactly the same."

"No, of course," he said. "Will you tell your mom . . . could you tell her I'm hoping she might have some ideas for the church rummage sale? Maybe she could stop by my office." Then he clapped his hands together. "Well, girls, I think it's getting a little late. I'm sure these gentleman would be happy to walk you home."

They nodded, said nothing.

"Okay." Reverend Cross put his hand on Cam's shoulder and smiled at his son. "'Night guys," he said. He walked back to the house, whistling the Bob Seger tune as he went.

Through the kitchen window Nate could see him turning off the radio and unplugging the boom box. Then he moved out of Nate's sightline.

"I can walk you home," Cam said to Suki.

"I should probably head myself," Nate said. "I'll do it."

"Cool it, Romeo," Jess said. "I'll walk her home. I'm staying at her house. And besides"—she punched first Cam, then Nate, in the arm—"what am I? Chopped liver?"

"Jess. You know, I'd be honored to walk you home anytime," Nate said, hand to heart.

"Forgiven," she said, emptying her beer bottle. "Come on, Sukes."

Jess linked her arm through Suki's, and he and Cam watched as the girls walked back towards the house, their heads inclined towards each other, already sharing confidences they'd never know.

Nate sighed. "One more?"

"Inside," Cam said.

The kitchen was warm and bright after having been out in the dark so long. Nate thought of his mom, her new weird habit of wearing her sunglasses all the time, and he wondered briefly if this was what the world felt like to her.

Nate sat down at the Formica kitchen table, while Cam opened the fridge.

"So," Nate said, "Longwell Community College, hunh?"

Cam looked over his shoulder. "I knew you'd go through my stuff."

"Sorry." He wasn't, really. "I don't know, though . . . I just thought you'd do something with football."

"No," Cam said, bringing the beers back. "That's over."

"Oh."

"It's not a big deal . . . it's my eyes. They get really dry and my vision's just not . . . not dependable, anyway."

When they were younger, much younger, Nate had had this weird notion that if he could play Cam the saddest song in the world, Cam would be able to cry. Never mind that his condition had been diagnosed medically, something named after a Swedish guy, that he had a problem with his tear ducts, that he was constantly using eye drops; Nate had been convinced that music could cure him. Cam had agreed it was possible.

They'd spent hours in the rectory house or in Nate's bedroom, playing music on the record player, or listening to the radio. Nate would choose the song, and then play it and watch Cam, faithfully taking notes on his responses in a black and white composition book. Nothing ever happened. Well, no tears anyway. Of course, sometimes Cam looked pretty sad, but hey, they were pretty sad songs.

"Shit," Nate said. "I'm sorry."

"It's okay. Coach was cool, kept me playing a bit last fall, you know. But I wasn't really adding much. Anyway."

"Well, Longwell's cool," Nate said. "My dad went there," he added, lamely.

Cam eyed him. "No, it's not. You don't have to lie."

"Yeah, no," Nate said, "I guess it's not."

"No, it pretty much sucks."

They laughed, both of them knowing it wasn't actually funny, until the laugh turned to silence.

"I'm not going to go, you know," Cam said, finally.

Nate looked at him. His friend was staring into the depths of his beer bottle.

"What are you going to do?"

Cam spread his hands out in front of him, as if he was seeing them for the first time. "Something else."

Suki and Jess lay in their pajamas on Suki's bed, listening to Madonna.

"Which is your favorite?" Jess asked, rolling over onto her stomach, shifting Suki's Laura Ashley sheets beneath her.

"Definitely 'Borderline,'" Suki said.

"For me, it's gotta be 'Holiday.' 'Borderline' is a little *desperate*. 'Holiday' is much more, I don't know, sparkly. Fun."

"Oh, like you?" Suki said, laughing.

"*Exactly* like me," Jess said. "*God*, I'm not tired. Let's smoke a joint and watch *Late Night*."

"If my mom catches us, she'll kill me."

"You say that every time."

"And she never does."

"And she never does."

Suki pressed stop on her tape deck and got up. While Jess rolled, she took a towel from her closet and pushed it up against the threshold of her bedroom door, before turning her fan around so that it drew the air out the window. Then she switched on the television on top of her dresser, clicking the dial over until David Letterman appeared.

My next guest has a new album coming out—and a brand-new husband to boot. A true star in every sense of the word, please welcome Blue.

"Oh, good, I love her," Jess said, lighting the joint.

"Yeah, she's so cool," Suki agreed. She loved how beautiful she was, and how she always showed off her prosthetic. Blue had a sense of confidence that Suki would have killed for. It must feel so good, she thought, to feel so much like yourself.

"Apparently, she lost her leg when she was a teenager. Can you imagine?" Jess was talking at the same time that she was inhaling, and her words vibrated from deep and low in her throat.

"I feel like surviving high school is hard enough with two legs," Suki said, taking the joint.

"High school's the worst," Jess agreed.

"What am I going to do without you next year?" That Jess was a senior had been causing Suki anxiety all year. She was leaving for drama school in New York and Suki was forced to stay behind in Wonderland.

"Well, you'll be bored, but you can hang out with the Barbie crew. And then next year you can come to school in New York and we'll share an apartment together, and drink red wine and get guys to take us out to fancy restaurants."

"I don't care about that stuff," Suki said, feeling the pot in her blood stream now, sweet and soft.

"You're high."

"I *am* high. It's just . . . when I was talking with Nate tonight . . . I really don't know what I'm going to do with my life which means . . ." She shoved Jess a little to get her attention. "*Which means*, J, I don't really know who I am. I mean, I can't go through life not knowing who I am."

"Jesus, I always forget how much you talk when you're high. How come I always forget that?"

"I don't know. But it's the best part. The talking part."

"It *is* the best part," Jess agreed. "So, let's talk about Nate. Do you want to have his babies?"

"Have you been listening to me at all? I can't have anyone's babies if I don't even know who I am."

"Sure you can. People do it all the time. Anyway, you know what I mean. Are you *totally smitten*?"

"I don't know what I think about anything," Suki said.

"Mmm, Nate," Jess said, leaning back. "I think he's got this tall, wiry, blondy thing going. Nice lips. Sexy. *Loads* of sexual energy." Jess waggled her eyebrows at Suki. "You know who I think is hot? Cam."

"Really? I mean . . . really?"

"Yes. He's all quiet and brooding and beautiful."

"*Really?*"

"Oh, my god, Suki, he's like Marlon Brando. You know, before he got all fat and bloated and crazy."

"Wow, okay. I never looked at him like that. He's always seemed more quiet and quiet and quiet to me."

"No, no. You're missing the smoldering inner . . . whatever. Still waters run deep. Plus, he's got good genes—I mean, Reverend Cross is no slouch."

"If you say so." Suki lay back.

"Just for a summer fling. You know, now that we won't have to see each other at school every day and die of embarrassment afterwards."

So, Blue, what would you say to all the young girls out there who want to do what you do? I mean, it's a rough business, right?

Well, David . . . I don't know. Listen to your parents, drink your milk?

No, I'm serious, you had to work pretty hard.

Look, it is tough. Life is tough. What can I say? . . . Okay: Until you know who you want to be, be a queen.

"Jess . . ."

"What?" Jess looked at Suki.

"Jess, what do you think is going to happen to us? Not like this year, but next year, and the year after? What's the story of our life going to be?"

"Oh, god, Suki. I don't know." Jess turned and dropped the end of the joint into a can of Fresca on the bedside table. "Why? What do you think?"

"I don't know, either." Suki tucked her hands behind her head, sighing. "I just don't want it always to be like this. Just lying here, waiting for something to happen. I feel like I'm always lying in this bed, waiting for something, or someone, to happen to me. I don't want it to be like that. I want it to *actually start happening*."

Cam was lying in his bed, the light out. Through his window the street lamp glowed. He could hear crickets, and the occasional footsteps of one of their neighbors making their way home.

He thought if he lay still enough he might hear Suki. Maybe hear the music she was playing or what she was saying to Jess. But she was too far away.

Sometimes, if he passed by her house, he could hear her playing Madonna or Men at Work on her tape player. He liked imagining her doing stuff, as he lay here at night. Maybe brushing her hair or talking on the phone. He wondered sometimes what would happen if he got out of his bed, walked out of the house, down the street, knocked on her door and asked her to run away with him—he wondered if, maybe, she would? It was crazy. A crazy thought. He knew that.

But what was so crazy about it, really? They were the same: neither one had a plan, neither one knew what came next. They could do it together. They could just take off and see what happened. They'd be free.

There'd been a girl a few years ahead of them in school, Danielle. In her senior year she'd decided to hitchhike to California, to be a star, maybe. That's what she'd told her girl-friends. She'd packed a bag and left a note and then she was just gone. Just like that.

He knew a lot of people thought she'd been picked up, killed maybe, or kidnapped into a cult or something. Because no one ever heard from her again. Her parents had moved away. But what if, maybe, she'd just gone to California and was making it? What if she'd just wanted to start again? Be someone new? Was that so crazy? Maybe to people around here. But Cam could understand it. He really could.

Miller was in bed reading *Heartburn*; Ash was next to her also reading—*Living, Loving and Learning*.

Their bedside lamps—large clear jars that years ago she'd filled with sea glass, fitted with cream linen shades—were lit, filling their bedroom with a cozy glow that was at once disorienting and infuriating to Miller.

She could hear the bite of the screen door closing downstairs, the thud of footsteps: Nate returning home from wherever he'd been—seeing friends, kissing girls, smoking pot. Whatever it was he got up to. It was funny how children just started to slip away, little by little. Even their bodies—or especially their bodies—once the private dominion of the mother, became hidden, unknowable, unthinkable.

They'd had an unspoken agreement ever since Ash had arrived to keep their problems to themselves. Well, at least to hide them from Nate. But Miller hadn't expected Ash to stay in Wonderland so long; she really didn't know why he was still here.

She was reading and rereading a line from the novel, but her mind kept going back to the Gunthersons' boat. Her cheeks still stung from the humiliation of discovering that everyone knew about Ash, about her. All these weeks she'd been going to these cocktail parties, putting on a brave face, pretending everything was fine, like a fool.

She closed her book with a sharp snap and looked over at Ash. He didn't look up. She sighed, quite loudly.

"Ash," she said, finally.

"Mmmm?" He didn't take his eyes off the page.

"Ash, we have to talk."

Now it was Ash's turn to sigh. "Okay." He slowly closed his book.

"Well, don't you think we have to talk?"

"I guess we do," he said, half-heartedly.

"I think we at least need to make a plan. I mean, how do you envision things going?"

"I honestly don't know."

He looked at her; Miller looked away.

"Are you still seeing her?"

He was silent, fiddling with the edge of the sheet.

"*Ash.*"

"Yes, I'm still seeing her."

Miller wanted to cry, but also wanted it to go away, and also wanted to kill him, and also wanted him very much not to be in her bed.

"Are you going to keep seeing her?" Ash didn't respond. "Jesus, Ash, don't make me do all the work here."

Ash leaned back against the pillows, looked up at the ceiling. "Do you really want a divorce?" he asked.

She threw her hands up. "I don't know—no. I don't know. But I can't be married to you if you go on seeing her."

"No, I know. You're right."

She nodded.

He nodded.

"So, what does that mean?" She wanted to shake him.

"I don't know."

"So, basically, you want to stay married and you want to keep on seeing *her.*" She couldn't bring herself to say her name out loud.

"Look, I know it's unfair. But, yes, I mean, yes, that's what I'd want."

"Until when? Until forever? Until she dumps you? I mean, *fuck you*, Ash, seriously."

"Keep your voice down," he said.

Don't let our son know I'm fucking someone else.

"Maybe," Ash said, slowly, carefully, "maybe we should go back and see Ron and Judy. See what they say."

Miller knew he was just buying time. "See what Ron and Judy say? About what? About the fact that you're a coward and a cheat?"

"Oh, get off your high horse, Miller. That was your suggestion when you cheated on me."

"That was very different." She put her hands over her eyes. She couldn't face Ron and Judy again—all that therapy, all that talking. God, and that letter they'd made her write. Olly had been right about that. It had been a fucked-up, shitty thing to do, something she was still deeply ashamed of.

"Why was that different?" Ash crossed his arms.

Miller sat up and turned to her husband. "Because everything was so complicated between the three of us. And, let's face it Ash, you stole me from Olly. So it wasn't exactly cheating when I slept with him."

"I *stole* you from Olly? Oh, that's rich. You ran to me. You made me believe you loved me. And I loved you so much that I betrayed my best friend for you."

"Okay, now who's rewriting the story? You were happy to do it to get one over on Olly." She suddenly felt exhausted. "Anyway, I thought we said we were never going back to Ron and Judy. That they'd brainwashed us."

"Oh, I don't know. We were probably just over-reacting. All our friends see them."

"That's the point," Miller said, slapping her book. "It was a cult. To make us all think alike. We were all *therapized* by the same two people. You don't think that's fucked up?"

"Forget it," Ash said. "It was just a suggestion."

Miller shook her head. "But seriously, Ash, how *can* you? How can you *want* to be married to me and fuck somebody else?"

"Because they're not the same thing."

"What, so you have some kind of madonna–whore complex?"

"I guess you're right: why go see Ron and Judy? You can just analyze me from our bedroom."

"Well, what does that mean, then: 'they're not the same thing'?"

"It means . . . Christ, I don't know. It means being married to you feels one way, and it feels good, and being with Candice feels another way, and it also feels good."

"I hate you."

They sat in silence for a while. Miller could hear moths thudding against the bedroom screens, trying to bump their way in to be close to the light.

"Do you want to keep talking?" Ash finally asked.

"Not really," Miller said. She picked up her book again, then changed her mind and put it down. "Have you heard from Olly?"

"No." Ash looked at her warily. "Have you?"

"No. It's weird, though." She kept half expecting him to come walking through their door at any moment. "I wonder what they talk about," Miller said.

"Who?"

"Aunt Tassie and Olly."

"Who knows? The joys of Melville's literature?"

"No, seriously. Do you think they talk about *it*?"

"*It?*"

"*It.* The war . . . the draft thing . . ."

Ash shrugged. "I don't know. No, I doubt it. Not everyone has to talk about everything."

Miller rolled her eyes. Then: "You know what I think? I think the reason Olly stuck her in that place was to punish her for it."

"Maybe. But she was only doing what she thought was right."

"Of course she was, *Ash*. You don't have to explain it to me."

"Well, I'm just saying, *Miller*, that Olly probably knows that, too."

"Olly's not big on forgiveness."

"God, I don't know, it was a long time ago, anyway."

"Right, and it's very clear that things that happened a long time ago don't bother you at all."

"Whatever, Miller. You win. Whatever you say."

She was suddenly so very tired of playing by the rules. Rules she'd adhered to over the last eighteen years, but ones she'd never believed in. "I'm going to have a dinner party." She'd only just decided right that instant, that second. "And I'm going to invite Olly."

"What?"

She picked up her book nonchalantly. "It's been weeks. We can't keep waiting for him to make the first move."

"What about, 'Don't worry, Ash, he's only coming here to get Aunt Tassie settled'?"

She shrugged. "I guess we'll find out. Anyway, you don't have to come."

"Yeah, okay, but I live here."

"Whatever you want," she said, breezily.

"Christ." Ash put his own book on the bedside table and switched off the light.

After rereading the same paragraph three times, Miller did the same. She lay in the darkness. Thinking about Olly and Ash and herself. About the letter she'd written Olly, the one Ron and Judy—and Ash—had made her write. In front of them, like she was an untrustworthy child.

How they'd read it after she'd written it, made suggestions, edited it: *This was too misleading, that was too kind. She had to think of Ash. All he was trying to get over for her sake. And what about the baby? It wasn't her responsibility to make Olly feel better. Blah, blah, blah.*

And how she'd done it. She couldn't deny she'd done it. And she'd sent it.

She remembered hearing his tires screeching outside the Malibu bungalow she was then sharing with Ash, how he'd left the motor running and barged in, waving the letter in the air.

"Really?" He'd yelled. "*This?* This is what you have to say to me? After months of silence? After telling me you loved me more than you'd ever loved anyone? That we were destined to be together? You tell me that it was the wrong *path*? That you'd betrayed Ash in a way you couldn't *understand*? What the fuck does that even mean? You understood, Miller. Don't tell me you didn't understand what it felt like to be us."

"Olly . . ." The last time she'd seen him, she'd told him she'd just needed time, to clear her head, to figure out how to let Ash down gently, that she'd gotten confused, and needed to get unconfused. And then, well, then she'd been too afraid to tell him anything.

"And what? This is an explanation? All this shit about trying to get Ash to forgive you and trust you? Your 'failure to understand allowed you to make promises'? *You didn't even write this, Miller.* I know what your writing looks like—it's written all over your body. You let them write this to me. You didn't even give enough of a shit to tell me the truth, to tell me how you really feel. Jesus Christ. Who the fuck are you?"

"Olly . . ."

"You know what? Fuck it. I don't even care who you are. You're a stranger to me. You're nothing."

And then he was gone. Miller had just been thankful at that moment that she hadn't yet bothered to get dressed, that she was still wearing a loose bathrobe. That he couldn't see the swell of her belly.

In the darkness of her bedroom, eighteen years later, Miller rolled over and looked at Ash. His eyes were closed, his breathing maddeningly even.

"Why are you still here?" she asked.

But there was no answer.

TUESDAY

It was eleven o'clock. Olly had been up for hours. He'd risen early, showered at the big house, breakfasted with Aunt Tassie, and then found himself at loose ends. So he'd taken one of his father's 1911 Encyclopedia Britannicas—*Vol. 1 A to Androphagi*—and read that until it was time to fill a Thermos with hot, black coffee, pick up the cooler and make his way down to Shell Beach.

The day was close, the sun a hazy ball. He could have whistled a tune as he went. He didn't, but it was that kind of day.

When he arrived at the small harbor, filming was well underway. The harbor had been built sometime in the '70s, using a single L-shaped breakwater, in order to accommodate the growing taste of the town's residents for pleasure boating. A small boardwalk and a string of docks had followed, and the result was a marina in miniature.

Currently, the side of a ship—or a shell of one—had been erected to appear as if the *Pequod,* the ship that hunted Moby-Dick, was docked at the boardwalk. There was a trailer parked down the beach a ways, where the actors were getting their hair and make-up done. Movie-shooting was a dull business, as Olly had learned, with the real action taking up so little of the actual time.

He sat himself down on one of the docks and watched the scene from a short distance. Assistants and assistants-to-the-assistants scurried around, checking marks and lighting, touching up paint, organizing various and sundry devices necessary to make the magic happen. He was looking for Nate, but there was no sign of him. Olly opened his Thermos and poured coffee into the cap. He removed his shoes, rolled up his khakis and let his bare feet dangle above the water.

By noon, the docks were full of townspeople, who came every day to eat their lunch and watch the filming. They were curious about how it all worked, how what they could see in front of them—a bunch of raggedy humans with cameras on a hot dock—transformed into the stories they saw on the big screen. Because these were the stories that had moved them, that had defined them, that had taught them how to kiss, how to love, how to break up, the ones they watched in the dark, with their popcorn or Junior Mints or Milk Duds or Good & Plenty.

They were also curious about the whale. The tales about the mechanical shark in *Jaws* were well-known lore: how it had been impossible to make, how it kept breaking, how the cast and crew worked heroically to find clever ways to shoot around it. The people of Wonderland wanted their own lore to trade in, they wanted their mechanical Moby-Dick. And, yet, he was nowhere to be seen. It was all Olly heard them talking about.

Every time a big truck rumbled over the bridge, people congregated to watch its contents be unpacked, thinking that maybe the whale had finally arrived. But they were continually disappointed, and it had become a talking point at the drugstore, at the A&P, at the diner.

At one o'clock, the cast and crew broke for lunch, and Olly made his way over to the boardwalk, where he found Rodrigo sitting on the edge, a red plastic basket of fried clams in his lap.

"Hey," he said.

Rodrigo nodded, picked a clam out of the pile.

"You know that there's going to be a revolution around here if you don't give these people their whale." When Rodrigo didn't answer Olly said: "I'm looking for Nate. Where is he?"

Rodrigo ate another clam, macerating it slowly between his teeth. "He went early to get some recording equipment for me and I gave him the afternoon off. What's in there?" He said, indicating Olly's cooler with his chin.

Olly looked down. "Some sandwiches, sodas."

Rodrigo smiled. "You're a very good little mother hen."

"Very funny." Olly looked around. "Well, I guess I won't be needing this. It's yours if you want it," he said, setting the cooler down next to Rodrigo.

Rodrigo looked at it, shrugged. "Thanks."

As Olly walked along the boardwalk and turned onto Main Street, he felt oddly deflated. Still, it wasn't like they had made a plan or anything. And Nate was a teenager after all; he probably had better things to do than hang out with him. Olly wandered a bit, looking into shop windows without much conviction, then stopped at the corner store to buy a newspaper. Inside, the girl who worked the till was debating with a delivery guy the various reasons for the white whale's absence.

"They'll probably bring it in at night, so people don't mess with it," the guy was saying.

The girl shook her head "Nah. I read they do a lot of that kind of stuff, the special effects, at the studios, you know, in California."

Half listening, Olly scanned the paper: Senator Ted Kennedy had endorsed Mondale as the democratic presidential nominee, the Senate had cut aid to Nicaraguan rebels, and there were changes coming to trans-Atlantic flights. A small sidebar to that article mentioned that Wonder Air was under investigation by the Securities and Exchange Commission.

"You one of the movie guys?" the girl said to Olly, as he brought his paper up to the counter to pay.

"Nope," Olly said, though even he knew the whale should have arrived by now. At least, if Rodrigo planned on sticking to his shooting schedule.

Olly had just put down his change and was turning to leave when he saw Miller walking towards him from the back of the store, an ice cream sandwich in her hand. Her head was down and she hadn't caught sight of him yet. He walked out quickly.

Through the plate glass, he could see her pay for her sandwich, before carefully removing the wrapper and licking the ice cream at the side between the two pieces of chocolate biscuit. Then she took a small bite out of the edge, before brushing her mouth with the back of her hand.

As she did, she exposed her wrist and he could see words inked into her skin, tiny black cursive that wound all the way up to her elbow, like some ancient manuscript, or intricate tattoo.

So she'd started that again.

When they were children, she'd been crazy about sewing words onto her clothes, embroidering them on pillows, writing in her diary. After she'd nearly drowned in the cut, though, it was like some switch had been flipped in her brain and she'd begun writing on her skin. He'd first seen it the night he came for her in her bedroom, the words written on her upper thigh.

Slowly, it seemed to become an obsession, one that he and Ash had both noticed, though she'd laughed it off. But afterwards she became more careful about inking herself in places where her clothes covered her, as if she were ashamed.

There was an image, though, one imprinted on his brain that he carried around like a photograph. It was the night of their senior prom, and they were in his bedroom. Her pale pink dress lay in a pool on the floor, the crinoline underskirt splayed out.

He stood watching her.

Miller was sitting on the edge of his bed in her white half-slip and brassiere, her head slightly bent over, her hair spilling across her face, as she unhooked her stockings. And in all the secret places that before had been hidden by her dress, were words, written all over her skin, like she was a book, a riddle of a woman. Like she was someone who, once she started, was unable to stop. And Olly knew, in that moment, that she was singular in the world, that he'd never meet anyone like her again.

She'd tried to explain it to him once, her compulsion. It wasn't self-punishment, she'd said, like some kind of religious mortification. It was that she was so full of words, and they needed to get out, were forcing their way out—and when the pen finally touched her skin: ecstatic release. Then she'd become empty for a while, before it all started again.

In college, it had stopped. She'd grown up, she'd told him. She was studying writing under a well-known academic, and had begun a novel that she never showed anyone. After L.A., all the writing—on skin, on paper—had seemed to just disappear altogether.

He wondered if she'd missed it, the way he missed the music, the landscape of it all, the physicality. He'd never thought about how it might have been for her, to lose that, or give it up, how it might have hurt her. Still, if gifts like that, like hers, could come and go, could his come back, as well? He wished he could ask her about that.

Standing there watching her, now, he could remember the first time they were together, lifting off her nightgown in the darkness of his car to see it written there, over and over, on the white of her inner thigh: *Olly, Olly, Olly*.

The church bell chimed eleven o'clock. Nate was lying on one of the plastic lounge chairs in his backyard working on his tan. He'd been up early to run an errand for Rodrigo, some recording equipment "for a VIP," the director had told him.

Afterwards, with the afternoon off, he'd thought about maybe catching a matinee, but once he'd lain down, the sun felt so warm against his skin that he couldn't seem to rouse himself.

He sighed and rolled over on his stomach, pushing his Ray-Bans on top of his head, laying his cheek on the plastic bands of the chair. Against his closed eyelids, he could see small, dark dots against glowing red. He could hear birds in the trees, and the church bell chiming, and through the open French doors, the sound of his father moving in the house.

Then he felt a warm palm laid flat against his back. He opened his eyes, shading them with his hand, and saw Jess James bending over him, her form blurry at the edges from the brightness of the sun.

"Hey, sunshine," she said, her teeth blindingly white. "What are you doing here all by your lonesome?"

Nate closed his eyes again. "Dancing with myself."

"Well, come dance with us."

Nate sat up, pulled his sunglasses down. "Who's us?"

"Me and Cam and Suki." She sat down next to him, shoving him a little to make space. She was wearing a blue bikini with a kind of strapless top that tied in the middle. Her mascara had fallen underneath her eyes, giving her a French look. "We're having a pool party. It's a very exclusive party of three . . . well, four now."

"You don't have to ask me twice," he said, getting up and throwing his towel over his shoulder. He'd reached the French doors when he realized Jess was still sitting on the lounger, watching him.

"Are you coming?"

She stood, still regarding him with narrowed eyes, curled mouth. "You are a tall drink of water, aren't you?" she said.

Nate laughed. "Jesus, Jess, who talks like that?"

"I do," she said, joining him.

They walked together into the kitchen and Nate stopped at the fridge and pulled out two cans of Fresca, holding one out to Jess.

"So," she said, taking the can from him, "what's the deal with Suki?"

"What deal?" Nate cracked the Fresca open, took a sip, eyed her over the rim.

"Do you like her?"

Nate shrugged.

"Of course you do," Jess said, laughing. "Well, you should do something about it."

Nate started walking towards the screen door, held it open for her. "What would you suggest?"

"I don't know, *Nate*. Kiss her?" Jess shoved him a little as she passed through.

"I have. I did. Once. A while back, but now . . ." he stopped. "Do you think she wants . . . I don't know . . . something like that?"

Now it was Jess who shrugged. "Honestly, Sukes is a mystery, even to me. Maybe. Probably."

150

They walked down the shell-covered driveway out to the sidewalk.

"I do like her," Nate said. "I like her a lot. I just . . . I don't know . . ."

They stopped at Suki's front gate.

Jess shook her head. "Nate, Nate, Nate."

"What?" Nate watched her saunter down the front walk to Suki's door.

She turned and looked over her shoulder at him. "You know what girls want? Girls want words. Good words. Great fucking words, words that make them want to die and melt and be madly in love."

Nate followed Jess through the house and out to the Pfeiffers' backyard. Suki was nowhere to be seen, but Cam was doing laps, his body almost shimmering as it rose and fell in the water. On a long glass table at the end of the pool, bowls had been neatly laid out with Ruffles and Fritos and Wheat Thins; next to it, a cooler full of Coke and Tab and Fresca.

"*Thank you, Mrs. Pfeiffer,*" Jess said, taking a small bowl and filling it with snacks.

He stood watching Cam swim and Jess arrange herself in the deep yellow cushions on one of the Pfeiffers' fancy loungers. Music floated in from somewhere behind him. Genesis. Phil Collins' voice singing "Taking It All Too Hard" growing louder. He turned his head.

And there she was. Suki, her browned legs, her white swimsuit, red hair falling down one shoulder, holding a boom box. She was walking towards him; one foot in front of the other, the arches shockingly white compared with the rest of her skin; her breasts, her thigh muscles, moving, and it seemed like it was happening in slow motion, like he was seeing it from underwater, and he felt the hollow pit in his stomach, all that longing rushing through his blood.

She smiled. He couldn't move.

"Hi, Nate," she said.

"Hi."

"You okay?"

"Yeah."

She walked past him towards the table, the smell of Hawaiian Tropic—coconut, papaya, guava, and sex—trailing behind her, giving him a contact-high.

He sat down slowly on the lounger next to Jess, watching Suki walk away.

Jess turned her head, her black cat-eye sunglasses facing him. "Words, Nate."

Cam climbed out of the pool, nodded at Nate, and settled himself on the other side of Jess.

"Genesis or Phil Collins solo?" Jess asked them.

"Genesis," Nate said.

"Phil Collins solo," Suki called back, laughing.

"'In the Air Tonight.'" Jess nodded. "So good."

"So good," Suki said.

"You know," Jess said, "Phil Collins actually wrote it about a guy he saw who let a kid drown in a lake and didn't do anything."

"Come on," Nate said.

"He did. Then he invites the guy to one of his concerts and puts the spotlight on him and sings the song to him."

Nate laughed.

"Don't laugh, the guy killed himself," Jess said.

"I heard he was in a boat with a friend and it capsized," Suki said, lying down next to Nate. "And there was a guy onshore, who didn't help, and then his friend drowned."

"No, it was definitely a kid," Jess said.

"Okay, so why didn't he just save the kid himself?" Nate said.

Jess shrugged. "He was too far away."

"But close enough to know who the guy was?" Nate said. "That doesn't make any sense."

"So, Cam," Jess said, ignoring him. "This is it. Our last official day as high school students. For the rest of our goddamn lives."

Cam kept his eyes closed.

"How do you feel?" Jess asked.

"Fine."

152

"I feel amazing," Jess said. "Freedom. Finally."

Suki sat up and started rubbing lotion into her skin, then lit a cigarette.

"The only thing that would make it even better would be my parents giving me a car," Jess said, waving her hand at Suki for a cigarette. "It seems like half the graduating class at Annie Oakley is getting a car. My parents are savages."

"Bastards," Cam said.

Jess eyed him. "Don't tell me your dad is giving you a car, too."

"Oh, yeah," Cam said. "He's giving me his old Chevy Caprice. Real hot ride."

"That's almost worse than no car at all," Jess said.

"Hey," Nate said. "Don't knock the Woody Wagon. It's a classic."

"Sure," Jess said. "If you're into vinyl wood detailing."

"Don't listen to her," Nate said, reclining the lounger all the way back. "I love that car."

He closed his eyes and a memory flashed through his mind. A night spent at the rectory house, when he Cam were eleven or twelve. Reverend Cross must have been out, and Nate and Cam were in the garage, sitting in the Woody Wagon, pretending to drive the car. Nate had been at the wheel.

The garage had an undeveloped room above it, accessed by an outdoor staircase, but the door was always locked, and they never went up there. But that night, while they were messing around with Reverend Cross's car, they'd heard noises above them. Footsteps.

"There's someone living up there," Cam had whispered. "Don't tell my dad."

"Who's living up there?" Nate had asked, feeling suddenly really scared, aware that they were alone in the house.

They'd heard the footsteps moving across the ceiling of the garage, and then sounds like someone descending the outside stairs.

After it had been quiet for a while, Cam'd said: "Come on. I'll show you."

Nate hadn't wanted to go, but he also hadn't wanted to admit he was afraid. When Cam opened the door, Nate saw empty tins of food, a couple of blankets, old beer cans scattered around the floor. These signs of life, but not a life like his own, filled him with a dark, unnamable dread.

"Let's get out of here," Nate had said, but Cam had wanted to stay.

"It's my mom," he'd told Nate. "My mom's come back. And she's living up here."

Nate hadn't been able to imagine Cam's mom living on beer and baked beans, but then Cam had seemed so sure.

"I put some things up here for her," Cam'd said. "I think she's watching over me. Waiting for the right time to come back to the house."

"What's the gun for?" Nate had asked. Leaning up against the wall was a small shotgun. Nate had never seen a gun before. "Is it your dad's?"

Cam shrugged. "Dunno. Maybe she's been hiding all this time? Maybe there're people after her."

"Maybe."

Over the years, they'd played a kind of game, imagining all the things that might have happened to Cam's mom: she'd become a famous actress who'd had surgery on her face to make it in the movies; she was a nurse helping the poor in India; a stowaway on a boat who'd been marooned on a desert island. But this felt different.

"Promise you won't tell my dad," Cam had said again.

"I promise," Nate'd said.

And they'd gone back downstairs, and played in the car for a bit and then gone and read comics in Cam's bedroom. They didn't talk about it, that night or ever again, and Nate had forgotten about it completely.

"Hey, Cam," Nate said, "do you remember when you showed me that place above your garage?"

Cam didn't answer.

"With all the cans and stuff?" Nate sat up a little, looked at his friend. "I was just remembering that."

Cam seemed to be asleep.

"Cam? I was just thinking . . ."

"You know, sometimes you think too fucking much," Cam said, not moving, not even opening his eyes.

Nate kept looking at him, expecting him to smile, or do something to signal that he was joking. But Cam remained still. Nate looked at the girls, but they lay motionless too, seemingly unsurprised by it, like maybe they'd heard that tone before, like maybe that's just the way it was around here.

The four of them lay in a row on the loungers as the minutes, the hours ticked by. Music came and went, hovered around them: The Cars, Tom Petty, Rick Springfield. The sweet, lemony smell of the privet hedge in the heat mingled with the perfume of cigarettes, skin, suntan oil, and the slick, rich, plasticy odor of magazine paper.

Nate must have fallen asleep and when he opened his eyes, the pool, the color of a Caribbean sea, greeted him. He rose and dove in, chlorine sliding over his skin. Surfacing, he could hear the lilt and jangle of Bob Marley, saw Suki get up and head inside the house. He completed a lap and pulled himself out. Wrapping a towel around his waist, he followed her.

The Pfeiffers' house was quiet. He stopped and listened. He could hear the sound of running water from the downstairs bathroom. He walked through the enormous split-level kitchen out into the entry way. The door to the bathroom—a small lavatory under the stairs, its walls painted with exotic birds—was open and Suki stood there, drying her face.

She turned and looked at him. He walked to her. He had no words—no good words, no fucking great words—so instead he reached out his hand and ran it down the curve of her shoulder, her bicep, her forearm. She was warm, her skin a little slick. He couldn't look at her face, so he concentrated all his efforts on the dips and shallows of that shoulder, that arm.

He could feel her inch closer to him, catch his hand in hers. In one swift move, he took the towel still in her hand and threw it into the sink and closed the door behind him so that they were standing, their bodies almost pressed together in the small room.

Fleetingly, he wondered if Cam and Jess had noticed their absence, and as this thought ran through his head, a loud bang came from the entryway outside, then he heard the front door slamming and the sound of Suki's father's voice roaring through the house. He was yelling for—or at—Suki's mom, it was hard to tell which. And in an instant, Suki pushed past Nate, almost knocking him over to get out of the bathroom, shutting the door hard behind her, leaving him stranded in the small space, almost panting, staring at the golden taps, the monogrammed hand towels.

Nate waited until it sounded like the coast was clear, then made his way back through the kitchen to the pool.

Cam and Jess were gathering their things while Suki stood, white-faced.

"Sorry," she said, turning to him. "But my dad's home."

"Sure," Nate said.

Suki's dad was rarely in Wonderland during the week; like Nate's dad, he commuted from the city. And when he was home, the Pfeiffers stayed in, friends weren't allowed over. It was an unspoken rule, but one that they all knew, and had never really questioned. "He needs his rest," had been the common refrain about Dutch Pfeiffer.

The three of them—Cam, Nate, and Jess—trooped through the house on tip-toe, and out the front door.

"He's such an asshole," Jess said, when they reached the sidewalk.

He and Cam just looked at her, silent. Nate wanted to ask her what she meant, exactly, but something stopped him.

"See you guys," Jess said, setting off.

"You want to come over?" Nate asked Cam.

"I should get home," Cam said, coldly.

Nate watched Cam walk down Church Street. "Right," he said to nobody. "Good times."

He walked into his house, the screen door snapping behind him. He looked around, at nothing. Best thing to do, he decided, would be to smoke a joint, maybe watch a movie.

Instead, he stood at the kitchen table and he thought about the small lavatory in the Pfeiffers' house, trying to remember every detail. The feel of her under his fingertip, the sound of his heart beating. The smell of the chlorine on her skin, her breath sweet with grape bubblegum. She'd had earrings in her ears—glittering chips pressed hard into small holes that looked red, tender at the edges.

He thought about what Jess had said. Then he thought that if he couldn't use his own fucking great words, he'd use someone else's: that's what mix tapes were for.

The church bell was chiming three o'clock. As he passed the dining room, he could hear the murmur of his father's voice through the semi-open door.

Ash stared out of the window of the small, stuffy dining room, which he had commandeered as his office. It was a blindingly bright day, warm, clear blue sky. Inside it was darker, cooler. He could hear the sound of music coming from the Pfeiffers' pool next door—Nate and his friends. He shuffled some papers around the mahogany surface listlessly.

He hadn't spoken with Candice in almost a week, and he owed her a call. Maybe he should go back to the city, just for a few days. The office would be pleased. In fact, he thought they might be getting to the end of their tether with his telecommuting. The Democratic primary was less than a month away and while their guy, Mondale, had decisively seen off Gary Hart after a particularly tight and bitter contest, there was still a lot of work to be done. They'd done well with the "Red Phone" ad, but Hart had a young campaign, aimed at the anti-Establishment baby boomers, and they needed to look beyond the primary now, to how to get some of that youthful glow to stick to their guy.

Despite all this, though, Ash felt rooted to the spot, to this house.

He'd found he wasn't sleeping well lately. He'd wake in the middle of the night unable to settle, and then he'd go down to the kitchen and fire up the crock pot.

His thoughts often wandered to Miller. She seemed full of secrets these days. Only this afternoon, for example, she'd come home while Ash was making a sandwich in the kitchen, and when she'd walked past him he'd seen a grass stain running down the back of her tank top and shorts like she'd been painted with one large stroke of a brush. When he'd asked where she'd been, all she would say was, "*At the Little Forest.*"

What was she doing there, he wondered. It was a place for children. Children, and secret canoodling.

Of course, there was no danger that Miller was having some kind of affair now, he knew that. He knew what someone having an affair looked like, and it wasn't her. She'd never been overtly fashionable or glossy, but she had a kind of—*indolence* was the word that sprang to his mind—that had made her irresistible: bracelets jangling on her wrists, shirt opened a little low, no bra. But now her clothes looked distracted, arbitrary, undone. And not in a good way. It was as if she'd forgotten what they were for.

What bothered him most of all, though, was the writing—he'd seen it on her arms, imagined it was in other places he was no longer allowed to look. He'd never liked it; even when they were young it had disturbed him.

There had been times in their marriage when he'd wondered if Miller was actually unstable, if what he'd first accepted as dreaminess, as idiosyncrasies left over from childhood, was actually a kind of illness. But then he'd think that, no, she was just a girl who'd grown up in the weirdness of Wonderland. And he'd try to put himself in her position, to catch the feeling of it, of how it'd been—their unnatural closeness, the three of them, how they'd lived in a kind of secret, closed-off world in this small town, indoctrinated by all the hocus-pocus of the meeting house—but it always eluded him.

Because really, who needed make-believe? And that's what it was—Olly's colors in his head, Miller's body art, the Quaker notion of hearing God's voice speak to you. The real world was more than enough, at least it was for him.

It might not be for Miller, and it certainly never had been for Olly. Fucking Olly.

There was no doubt that even after he'd won Miller, he'd been jealous, suspicious even, of Olly. That was one of the primary reasons they'd moved back east from L.A.

After Nate was born, they'd stayed on for a couple of years; they'd been stunned by the upheaval of suddenly having a child and a marriage, and were too exhausted to think about moving, looking for new jobs, a new life. But Ash couldn't ever fully get rid of the idea that Olly was mocking him, that he knew something Ash didn't, that maybe he was visiting Miller and Nate behind his back.

So, to preserve their sanity, they'd moved. First to New York, but with the power outages and the rising crime and the municipal bankruptcy, Ash had convinced Miller that it was an unhealthy place for Nate, that they should move away from the chaos, back to where they came from. Back to Wonderland. They kept a place in New York, and Ash commuted.

It was funny, ironic, he could admit, that he was now the one carrying on. He hadn't been looking for it; Candice had just happened to him. Candice *was* the fashionable, glossy type, but that wasn't the primary attraction. She was exciting mainly because she had all these other things going on, these dramas unconnected to him or his failures. She made him feel alive; he was a cliché, he knew, but as Ash had always said, clichés are clichés for a reason.

As for Miller, her *raison d'être* had been creating their home, creating some kind of *atmosphere*, as if she were a theater designer setting up for a very important play. Over time, though, he'd begun to feel like he should never have been cast in that particular production. In so many ways and for so long, he'd been so grateful and so surprised that he'd won her, that she'd chosen *him*, that he hadn't really thought about whether he fit into her vision of what life should look like.

But now he could see, with all the swimming, the writing, the secrecy, that his wife clearly had some idea she was puzzling out— one she wasn't going to share with him. So, he had two choices: go along blindly with her and let the chips fall where they may, or come up with his own plan.

Coming up with his own plan was an extremely unattractive proposition to him, but he also felt exposed, vulnerable. And that wasn't something he found appealing, either. Because the place he was most vulnerable was the one thing he couldn't lose: Nate.

Ash picked up the cream touch-tone phone and dialed Candice's number.

"Hey, it's me," he said, when she answered. "I'm sorry I didn't call sooner," though he knew she probably didn't mind or maybe hadn't even noticed.

Silence.

"It's Ash."

"Mmmm-hmmm."

"How are you?"

"I'm fine."

Maybe she did mind. "Sorry. I've been thinking about you, it's just been a little crazy here."

"Really." Somehow she managed to sound both bored and incredulous at the same time. "How has it been crazy?"

He waved his hand, as if she could see him. "Oh, family stuff, old stuff. I don't want to bore you with domestic drama."

"Please," she said, flatly, "bore me."

"Really? Okay . . ." Ash got up and leaned against the window frame. From outside, he could hear splashing, the tinkle of voices over the hedge. "My old business partner—our old business partner, I should say—has come back to town and . . ."

"I thought you said it was a domestic drama."

"Well, it is. He's more than an old business partner. It's complicated. We're—*I'm*—in a bit of a situation . . ."

"Oh, Jesus, Ash, just get on with it or I'm hanging up."

"Right . . ." Ash tinkered with the cord of the window blind, tapping it gently against the glass. He could hear the church bells chiming three. "No, it's just . . . I've never said this out loud to someone other than . . ."

Silence.

God, the woman was good at silences. He dropped the cord, took a breath. "Olly . . . You know how he and Miller were together first, in high school, they were boyfriend and girlfriend. And when we first went to L.A. Then, later, she left him and we got together. But, the thing is, there was a bit of overlap, if you see what I mean . . ."

"I see," Candice said. "This sheds a new light on things."

"What do you mean? What new light?"

"I don't know. The way you've always described her, she sounded like a little, lost housewife."

"Really?"

"Yes."

"Oh, well." Ash knew he was on dangerous territory here. "I mean, she is—lost. And a housewife."

"Okay," Candice said, seemingly letting that one pass. "So, she had an affair with this Olly guy, and then what?"

"No, it was more like . . . well, she wanted to leave him, and I helped her. Or she wanted to be with me. But then she didn't actually leave him right away."

"*Right* . . ."

"What?"

"Nothing. Go on."

"Right. The thing is, so during this time, she got pregnant with Nate. And, well, he's never said anything, we've never talked about it with him, with Olly I mean, or Nate for that matter, but it's just . . ."

"Jesus, *what*, Ash?

"Olly might think Nate's his. His son."

"Is he?" Candice didn't sound shocked, just curious.

"No, of course not," Ash said, turning away from the window. "The dates don't add up," he lied. "But, you know, people get ideas. And he's never gotten over being furious about Miller choosing me over him. So . . . it's just, well, now he's come back, and he isn't leaving, and I think he might have come back for them. Well, for him."

"I see. That *is* tricky."

"It is, isn't it?"

"Clearly you have to confront him," Candice said. "Just tell him to fuck off, that the kid's not his, and he needs to crawl back under whatever rock he crawled out from."

"Well," Ash said, nodding his head side to side, the phone pressed to his ear. "That's one idea."

"Oh, Ash. Christ."

"I know, I know. I should be more . . . more of a man. You deserve . . ."

"Oh, never mind that," she said, impatiently. "Honestly, what use are men? Okay. So what was your idea?"

"Oh, I don't know. Do nothing. See what happens?"

"Do you really want him to take your kid away?"

"No, of course not. No. But Nate's almost an adult. It's not like he can kidnap him. Can he?"

"Well, he can certainly mess things up. Put ideas in his head."

Ideas *were* a dangerous thing, he knew that well. "You're right." Ash suddenly saw the danger clearly. This wasn't hypothetical, it wasn't an exercise in his abilities. This was something that had to be dealt with, and quickly. Before it got out of hand. "No. You're absolutely right. I have to go talk to him."

"Yes, you do," Candice said.

And Ash continued to feel the urgency for about five minutes after he'd hung up with Candice. And then, as he sat and thought, it deflated, little by little. Until he'd convinced himself that maybe he hadn't *quite* reached the critical juncture just yet.

When he'd decided this, he felt relieved. It was fine. It would all work out. And it was only then that he realized that he could no longer hear the laughing, the music from the Pfeiffers' next door. That he'd left the door to the dining room ajar. He rose and closed it gently.

1980

Ash hadn't really known where he was going until about three hours into his journey, when he began to see the signs for Leighton, Addisonville, Clarktown (100 miles). It was then that he realized he was going to see his son.

Nate had been at Leighton Hall two months, but each time Ash returned to Wonderland from the city, he missed his child's presence more. The house felt quiet, empty. Miller was there of course, but without Nate it all seemed less, she seemed less, somehow.

She'd started writing since Nate had gone away, and when Ash had returned yesterday from the city for a long weekend, she'd wanted to show him some story she written. She'd brought it to him, almost shyly, he'd thought, but he hadn't really been able to focus on it. It was something about a day, and a woman making a cake, and seeing her husband and son, and . . . feeling happy? Something.

Anyway, she'd hovered over him while he read it, making him feel anxious. Afterwards, she'd asked him what he thought.

"I'm not sure I get it," he'd said, truthfully. "What's it for?"

"What do you mean, what's it for?" she'd said, frowning at him. "Did you think it was good?"

"I . . . I don't know. I guess that I don't know about this stuff. You should probably ask somebody else."

She'd snatched it away, angry. And she hadn't spoken to him for several hours. Ash had spent the time in his son's room, lying on his bed, smelling his pillowcase.

When he'd woken up this morning under the depressing October sky, he'd wanted to leave again immediately. So, he'd gotten into the car, telling Miller he was going for a drive, and now he found himself two hours away from Nate's boarding school.

They'd received a couple of letters from Nate since he'd been gone, and while Miller seemed to find nothing unusual about them, Ash was certain he could sense a kind of sadness in them. A lostness to them. It wasn't like Nate to be unsure of anything, and his heart ached for his son.

It had been Miller and Nate who had been fixed on Leighton Hall. Ash hadn't understood it. At thirteen, Nate would be younger than all his classmates. "Why did we have a child just to send him away?" he'd argued with his wife. But he'd been outnumbered, once again, so he'd just given in and made the best of it.

Except, it seemed, he wasn't making the best of it, after all. Parents weren't supposed to visit for the first term, to let the kids get used to living away from home. So when Ash finally arrived at the school, he went to Nate's dorm and explained to his dorm master that there was a family emergency and he had to take Nate out of class for the afternoon.

The dorm master went off and retrieved his son from whatever class he'd been in, and when Ash saw Nate walking across the quad towards him, his heart filled with relief at being in such close physical proximity.

"What's up?" Nate asked, a worried expression his face.

"Get in the car," Ash said. "I'll explain it to you on the way."

Once they were alone, Ash leaned over and pulled Nate to him, holding him tight, breathing in his boy smell, sweat and shampoo and cold air.

"Dad."

"Sorry," Ash said. "There's nothing wrong, don't worry. I've come to break you out."

Nate had laughed, pushed his blond hair away from his face. "What are you talking about?"

"If you hate it here, you don't have to stay. I can explain it to Mom."

"Dad," Nate said. "I'm fine. It's all good."

164

Ash's heart sank. "Really?"

"Really," Nate said.

He looked at his boy: he looked too small, too young to be in this big, red-bricked place. "Do you want to go back to class?"

"No way," Nate said.

Ash laughed. "Well, what do you say—lunch and a movie?"

They ate at a Denny's in town and went to see *Private Benjamin*, the only thing playing they hadn't seen before. As they sat in the darkened theater Ash watched his son, laughing, eating popcorn, and he felt better than he had in months.

After the movie ended, though, the dread of returning to Wonderland began to creep back over him. They walked a bit, but Nate said he was getting cold, and Ash knew his time was up.

He drove Nate back to his dorm. As they sat there, the heater blasting in the Volvo, Nate leaned over and hugged him. Ash felt his shoulder blades, so sharp through his shirt and sweater, inhaled him one last time.

He suddenly remembered holding Nate for the first time in the hospital when he was born. Miller had been unwell and those first couple of days, it had just been him and his boy. His boy.

"I love you," Ash said.

"I know, Dad," Nate said. He let go and got out of the car.

"Well," Ash said, trying to think of something else to say.

Nate leaned in and said: "I have really missed you, Dad." Then he waved goodbye and disappeared into the cold, formal building.

Ash made it about a mile before he had to pull over. With the engine running, he put his head down on the wheel and wept, as cars passed by on the road, their headlights sweeping across him.

WEDNESDAY

It was hot in the Little Forest, at least ten degrees hotter than the rest of town. Miller's tank top was soaked through at her armpits, in between her breasts, in the wet V spreading down her back. She used the edge of the fabric to wipe the beads of moisture that had gathered on her upper lip.

The Little Forest was a miniature wood in the middle of Wonderland, designed and planted in the '20s, paid for by one of the town's prominent Quakers at the time, Jonas Hillier. The size of about seven or eight backyards, it was dense with pine and oak and willow and birch. When they were children they used to build ghost traps in there; in spring, they'd catch tadpoles in the small pond, the little bodies soft and slippery in their hands; in winter, they ate icicles off the tree branches.

She'd been coming here every day for the last couple of weeks. She'd bought herself a composition book from the corner store, and what she'd begun in that small notebook she'd found in the glove compartment of the Volvo had taken on a shape, a purpose all of its own—like a trapdoor in a locked room.

She wrote quickly, the words slipping across the page, because she knew it was only a matter of time before someone else told the story, before it all exploded in her face.

She'd found herself digging out her old journal—the one that she'd kept on their road trip across America—reading through it, staring at the faded photographs of herself and Olly and Ash, surprised to find strangers staring back at her. *This is the story of us.*

Miller's hand began to ache. She put down her pen and notebook and lay back on the mossy, leafy, slightly fermented ground.

She could feel pine needles against the back of her shoulders, her bare legs, the tender bite of mosquitoes flickering over her skin.

She ran her hand over her collar bone, down over her left breast, the dip of her rib cage. She pulled off her tank top, and slid out of her bra. She unbuttoned her shorts and slid her hand down, inside.

Something in her was coming undone, like the world was slipping off its axis incrementally. She didn't know when exactly it had begun—when Olly had returned, when she'd started writing, when she'd read the journal, when Ash made it clear he wasn't giving up his mistress—but in the words of Aunt Tassie, *Something was happening*. When she looked in the mirror now, instead of wondering what the point of all that flesh was, she could see that it took up space, space that was hers to do with whatever she wished. Like everything that had been on the inside was coming to the surface now. She was all reaction, like some unstable chemical. She was all lit up.

On her way home, Miller was surprised to see the streets full of kids in their caps and gowns: Annie Oakley High graduation day. She felt like she'd stepped out of a dream, as if days had passed and lives had changed and everyone had grown up and left and been replaced by a whole new generation. She felt like an animal coming out of hibernation into a blinding spring day.

She didn't want to go home. What would she do there? Sit in the den pretending Ash wasn't working in the next room? Scrabble through Nate's things to find clues as to what was going on in his secret inner life? Drink a Tab, eat some almonds?

She followed the stream of people, the black tasseled caps bobbing along in front of her. It was four o'clock, hours after the ceremony would have finished, but these kids were unable and unwilling to relinquish their ceremonial garb, to forsake their big moment, their rite of passage. They would make it last as long as they could. Who could blame them, really?

When she reached the town hall, a poster for *Footloose* occupied the glass-covered marquee box outside. *Next showing: 5 p.m.* And she thought: Yes, I could do that. Why not?

She had an hour to kill so she decided to walk to the Dairy Queen at the other end of town, near the bridge. It was still warm and her flip-flops slapped the concrete as she walked the distance, down Main Street, past the shops and the library, past the gas station, her rubber soles sticking from time to time to chewing gum wantonly discarded on the pavement.

When she got to the DQ, bikes were piled up outside, leaning against the clapboard building; inside, the air smelled like syrup and vanilla and sugar cone. She was the only customer over the age of eighteen. Above the steel counter, the menu gleamed with promises of a Mr. Misty or a Dixie Belle Sundae or a banana split or a Jack 'n Jill. In the end, Miller chose a cherry dipped vanilla cone, which came out hard and silky with a curl at the top.

She ate it slowly, her teeth gently cracking the thin shell and sinking into the criminally sweet softness beneath, as she made her way back to the town hall.

Upstairs, Matt McCauliff was leaning against the counter chatting to the ticket girl behind the window.

"Hey, Miller," Matt said.

"Hey, Matt." She turned to the girl. "One ticket, please. And a box of popcorn."

The girl tore a ticket off the loop. "So," the girl was saying to Matt, "what's the latest on the whale?"

"I don't know," Matt said. "Everyone keeps asking me that."

"That'll be four dollars," the girl said to Miller.

"Oh, hang on," Miller said, and crouched down to get a full view of the candy selection beneath the counter.

"Tssss. You hang out with those guys every day. Come on."

Miller ran her hands over the bars and boxes: Whoppers, Milk Duds, stopping briefly at the Dots.

"I'm telling you, like I tell everyone else: no one knows," Matt was saying. "I don't even know if *he* knows."

"The director guy?"

"Yeah. I mean, whenever anyone asks him he kinda freaks out."

She continued on past the Raisinets and Sno-Caps, the Big League Chew, Smarties.

"I bet it's really big. Right? I mean it's got to be pretty frickin' big."

"I guess."

"I bet you, we just look out for a big truck comin'. That's how we'll know."

Jujyfruits. She picked up the bright yellow box.

"And these," Miller said, putting them on the counter.

"I like these, too," the girl said, tapping her nail against the box of Jujyfruits. "But they stick in your teeth."

Miller smiled. "Thanks," she said, putting down her money. "See you, Matt."

She sat in the half-empty theater in a seat close to the front. In the great debate of first-row, last-row, Miller was a first-row person.

The lights went down and the images flickered over her face. It was pure joy, this silly cinematic distortion of small-town life, these bored kids whose circumscribed life made them long for a dance. The drama! But their bodies were the main event: radiating youth and health, and just twitching to get out of those pesky clothes.

When the lights went up, she stood, and the box of Jujyfruits fell to the ground. She'd forgotten about them. She picked them up and put them in her purse.

On her way out, she saw Cam and Dick Cross leaving ahead of her, Cam's gown slung over his arm and cap in hand. She tried to catch up to congratulate him, but when she finally did manage to get through the crowd, they seemed deep in conversation so she abandoned the idea.

As she made her way home in the almost-dark, Miller passed by Aunt Tassie's house. She saw Olly disappearing through the side gate, a slice of white shirt in a tangle of vine. She followed him, watched him as he crossed the lawn and climbed up to the old tree house. A match flared and a moment later the space was illuminated. She watched him undress until he stood naked, glowing like a jewel in a box. She wondered how different her life would have been if it had been Olly she'd ended up with, instead of Ash.

She stood there, eating the Jujyfruits one by one.

The girl was right: they did stick in your teeth.

THURSDAY

In the early hours of Thursday morning, a 35-foot, unmarked big-rig rumbled over the bridge and into Wonderland. It drove slowly, as soundlessly as possible, and pulled up behind the boathouse, after some painful maneuvering. The rig was detached and four padlocks were put in place by Rodrigo himself, who then crept back to his fisherman's shack and lay down for a few hours' sleep.

Miller was working on her menu for the dinner party, basically plundering the *Silver Palate Cookbook*. A salmon mousse as an hors d'oeuvre, Chicken Marbella—with prunes and capers and olives—and wild rice for the main course. She'd need a salad to go with it, and some bread, though there was no really good bread to be had in Wonderland. She could always toast some Pepperidge Farm, maybe?

It was all a bit too much, especially given that she'd have to go to the A&P and buy absolutely everything, since there was no uncooked food to speak of in the house. In his mania, Ash had left no jar, no vegetable, no ingredient of any kind, unturned, and he was now living off the spoils of his crock pot.

He'd gone off early that morning to the city: "Just for a day, maybe just the afternoon," he'd said. "Have to put out a few fires at the office." Miller didn't believe him—she knew he was probably going to see *her*—but she was also relieved he was gone. She'd gone to the Little Forest earlier, to do some writing. And after that, she'd thrown herself into reading all the cookbooks lining the shelf over the stove in the kitchen.

She'd just started perusing dessert options when the phone rang.

"Hello?" Miller waited. Silence. "Hello?" She took a risk: "Olly?" No answer. So then quickly: "Ash?"

She was about to hang up when a woman's measured voice came through. "Hello, I'm looking for Ash."

Miller knew immediately who it was, and she felt the adrenaline rush through her.

"He's not in," she said.

"Right," the voice said. "Do you know when he's expected back?"

The nerve, the absolute fucking nerve of this woman. "No, I fucking don't," she replied.

"It's Miller, right?" The voice was calm, drawing out its words.

Jesus. "Yes, this is his wife." *This is his wife?* She sounded like a pinched school marm. But then, how was she supposed to sound? Cool? Like, *Hey, affair lady, so glad you rang?*

"This is Candice Cressman."

Miller stayed silent.

"I assume you know who I am."

"Yes, I know," Miller said. How had this conversation gotten so off track? How had she lost the righteous indignation she was entitled to? *Bitch.*

"Great. He was supposed to meet me, but he never showed up. If you hear from him, can you have him return my call?"

Miller slammed the phone down. But that wasn't enough, so using both her hands she ripped it out of the wall and threw it on the ground, where it clattered abjectly.

She looked around the kitchen, then headed upstairs to Nate's room and began opening his drawers, looking under socks and shirts until she found his pot stash in, predictably, a carved wooden box at the bottom of his closet. What was it with pot and carved wooden boxes?

She rolled a joint and sat on her son's bed smoking it.

The way Miller had found out about the affair had been both extraordinary and utterly banal. She'd flown to the city to do some Christmas shopping, and she thought she would justify the trip by also surprising Ash, who was spending the week working there. He'd sounded tired and down on the phone, and she'd thought she could both cheer him up and cheer herself up with a trip to New York to see the Christmas lights, maybe do some ice skating at Rockefeller Center, pick up some presents for Nate.

Later, she'd think that if probability had played any part, she would have caught them at the pied-à-terre, or at least coming out of it, but that's not how it had gone. It had been bitterly cold, so after fighting the crowds at Saks, she'd walked up Fifth Avenue, past all the Salvation Army Santas and panhandlers, to the Oak Bar to have a drink before heading to their apartment on East 71st.

She'd settled at one of the tables with her exorbitantly priced $4 Old Fashioned and was admiring the murals of snowy New York amid the beautiful wood paneling, when they'd walked in.

It had clearly started snowing outside because Miller saw Candice Cressman, laughing, brushing snowflakes off her blonde television hair, while Ash dusted it off the shoulders of her mink coat with a black-gloved hand.

Miller's own coat was wool, navy, and practical for Wonderland's winters.

When he'd leaned in to press his lips to the woman's white neck, Miller's heart had started beating so fast, and her only thought was to get out of there before they caught her. Caught *her*. As they ordered at the bar, their backs turned, she'd grabbed her coat and purse, trying to keep her shopping bags from rustling, and had hurried out.

She'd flown back to Wonderland that evening.

Afterwards, of course, there'd been Christmas to get through with Nate, and then that grim meeting in New York, when she'd effectively banished Ash from the house and gone home to fall apart.

Miller stubbed the joint out on the rim of a can of Fresca sitting on Nate's desk, and went downstairs.

She made her shopping list and decided to head to the super-market. As she backed out of the driveway, though, she almost ran over Cricket Pfeiffer, who quickly turned a sun-glassed face away from her and hurried across the road.

Miller rolled down the window. "Sorry, Cricket," she yelled after her, but Cricket only waved her hand behind her in a gesture Miller, stoned, found difficult to decipher.

Nate was standing outside the slaughterhouse on the small farm just on the edge of Cuttersville, waiting. Through the door, he could see some of the animals, hanging upside down, thick like tree trunks, their flesh white as the moon, their skin hanging off of them like a bride's veil. Cows mainly, he guessed, from the size of them, but there were some smaller carcasses, as well. The smell, which he'd always imagined would be kind of rotten, was actually humid, like the inside of a greenhouse, but thick with iron and a little sweet. From where he stood, what he could see of it was clean, very clean actually, not what he'd imagined when Rodrigo had sent him there to pick up three barrels of blood.

Nate had always assumed they used fake blood in the movies—dyed syrup or something—but Rodrigo'd insisted that, in this case, it had to be real.

He hadn't been overly psyched to be sent on another errand; he'd have rather been on set where the action was, but they were filming on the square-rigger anchored in the causeway today and he wasn't allowed on board. Insurance, or so Rodrigo had said.

It had actually been a rough couple of days for the cast and crew of *Moby-Dick*. They'd been filming out on the ship since Tuesday, but choppy water and uncooperative tides had meant the

178

camera work had come out too shaky, the ship kept moving so that the bridge was in view in the shots, and some small pieces of lighting equipment had fallen overboard and been lost.

There also seemed, from what Nate could gather from the grumbling on set, to be a growing unease among the cast that they weren't being kept in the loop about anything, and a feeling that the production might be spiraling out of control. The whereabouts of Moby-Dick himself were either so religiously guarded or so completely unknown—nothing was shot in order, and no one seemed to have seen the full script—that every time Nate had asked someone about it they'd shrugged or mumbled some unintelligible answer.

And today, a new entry into the production schedule had added more confusion to the whole business: entitled "Whale," it called for Rodrigo and his director of photography, along with a couple of engineers no one had ever heard of, to shoot a scene away from Wonderland, in deep water off the shore of the mainland.

The cast had conferred and sent an emissary to confront Rodrigo. But all he'd said was "Are you a whale? No? Then you're not needed."

If things were getting complicated on the set of *Moby-Dick*, things were getting even weirder at home. Events seemed to be moving pretty fast there, and he wondered what, if anything, he should or could do about them.

"Okay." The farmer owner was standing at the entrance to the slaughterhouse. "They're ready," she said. "The boys will bring them out. But you'll have to get them refrigerated pretty quickly, or it will stink."

"We're using it right away," Nate said.

"This is definitely the strangest request I've ever gotten," she said, taking the wad of bills Nate handed over.

"Yeah, pretty weird one for me, too," he said.

The "boys"—actually two very big men with corded arms—carried out the barrels and loaded them into the flatbed. Nate climbed in front and put his hand out of the window in a kind of salute, before driving back down the track to the main road.

He drove slowly, the barrels bouncing in back. As he neared the bridge, the radio station cut, and he adjusted the dial, until Steve Perry's plaintive voice floated out of the speakers.

A car was idling at the entrance to the underpass, and he slowed to a crawl to see if it planned to pull out. It was only a few seconds before he'd rolled by them, but that was all it took: Cam's dad looking at Suki's mom, touching her face, just the tips of his fingers on her cheekbone before he leaned in and kissed her. Then he was past.

Nate watched them disappear in his rearview mirror, the sounds of "Oh, Sherrie" trailing out behind him into the hot air, like fumes.

After he'd dropped off the barrels at the marina, Nate had headed home. In his room, he thought he could still smell the sweet, rich odor of the slaughterhouse, that maybe it had gotten into his clothes, his skin, until he realized what he was actually smelling was dope—it had a deceptively similar register—and he wondered if he'd forgotten to air it out that morning when he'd done a wake-and-bake. He opened the windows as wide as they would go, stripped off his clothes, and got in the shower to clean off the stink of blood, of pot and sweat.

Afterwards, he found his mom in the kitchen unpacking groceries. She was wearing an old T-shirt and cut-offs and her sunglasses.

"Hi, honey," she said, absently.

"Hi, Mom."

"Just getting ready for my dinner party." She glanced up at him. Her gold and blue rimmed sunglasses reflected his own image back to him. "Did I mention that I'm having some people over tomorrow?"

Nate looked at the counter where a pile of Jello-O Pudding Pops, Oreos, Goldfish, and Pepperidge Farm Gingermen lay heaped next to the fridge.

"Are you having a dinner party for ten-year-olds?" he asked, picking up a pack of Nilla wafers.

"Don't be fresh," his mom said. "Have you tried these pudding pops?"

"Yeah, I've tried them, Mom," he said.

"They're amazing. Would you like one, honey?" His mom held one out of a pack, which had clearly already been opened.

"No, I'm good."

"Okey doke," she said, cheerfully.

"Where's Dad?"

"Who knows? Your dad is a mystery wrapped in an enigma in a . . . whatever."

He looked at his mom. Her mouth looked sad, he thought. He didn't like it.

"Do you need any help?"

"Oh, that's kind, baby. But no. You go have fun. I'm fine here."

"Sure, Mom," he said, and gave her a kiss before heading out the door.

Olly was in the parlor watching some street dancers called the Kangol Kid and Doctor Ice on *The Phil Donahue Show*. They were finishing up a pretty impressive performance to the sound of just one steady beat, a simple percussion. Listening to the stripped-back, unchanging line, he wondered, if he hadn't lost his ear, what it would be like to stand in the landscape of that particular piece of music. Monochrome, maybe.

"So is this . . . break-dancing?" Phil Donahue was asking the boys.

"Nah, we call it popping. Or electric boogie," the Kangol Kid said.

Olly heard a knock at the window and turned to see Nate standing on his porch. "Hey," Olly said, and went out to meet him.

Nate was leaning against the house, and he turned his head and smiled wanly at Olly.

"What's up?" Olly said.

"Not much," Nate said. "Just having a weird day. Wondering what you were up to."

Olly smiled. "Come on, let's go for a walk. There's something I want to show you."

They began walking down Foster Street towards the Ring Road.

Earlier in the day, Olly had gone looking for Rodrigo and when he couldn't find him on set, he'd gone looking for him at the boathouse. When he'd arrived, there'd been a Teamster at the entrance to the track, sitting on a metal folding chair reading the newspaper.

"Can't go in there," the Teamster had said, without looking up.

"I'm a friend of Rodrigo's," Olly had said.

"Not here," the Teamster said.

Olly squinted down the track, and that's when he'd seen it.

"The boathouse?" Nate said now, as the large octagonal building came into sight.

It was a fanciful structure—with its unusual shape and wrap-around galleries—for something whose purpose was to store racing shells and to over-winter sailboats.

They headed down the wide track that wound from the street to the back of the building, built to allow the passage of boat trailers. On the other side of the track was a dense pocket of tree and scrub, which over the years had been left to its own devices. And there, nestled against the underbrush, sat an enormous, white trailer. It was partially covered in a few black tarps, as if a half-hearted attempt to conceal it had been made.

"Is that—?" Nate looked at Olly.

Olly shrugged. "What else could it be?"

Nate walked the ten feet across the stretch of track and weed, and inspected it. He turned back. "It must be, right?" Olly could hear the excitement in his voice. "It definitely wasn't here two days ago." Nate pulled the tarp away a little from the back doors as Olly strolled over and stood next to him. Nate rattled the padlocks.

"Ahhh," Nate said, grinning at Olly. "I really want to know what's in there."

Olly smiled. "I thought you'd like it."

"Yeah," Nate said. Then he sat down on the ramp that led up to the trailer doors. He blew out his cheeks.

Olly sat down next to him. "You okay?"

"Yeah," Nate said, shaking his head. "There's just a lot to keep up with at the moment." He leaned back, resting his palms against the ramp. "Do you get the feeling that things are getting a little weird around here? Because I'm beginning to pick up some very strange vibes."

Olly laughed. "It's always been weird here."

Nate didn't say anything, just scuffed his sneaker in the dirt.

"Hey, it's hot," Olly said. "Let's go for a swim."

"Yeah," Nate said, a little cheered up. "Yeah, okay. A swim."

Pebble Beach was empty except for an old couple set up on plastic beach chairs close to the shoreline peering at the distance through binoculars. Everyone else was probably either at Dune Beach or Shell Beach; the rocky carpet covering Pebble Beach made it a last resort for townspeople and tourists alike. Olly and Nate both stripped down to their boxers and made their way gingerly over the smooth stones before diving in.

The cold, tangy saltwater washed away the heat and sweat of the day, stinging Olly's face where the skin was only just beginning to heal. He'd missed living by an ocean you could swim in bare-skinned. The Pacific was beautiful, but the water was too cold for anything but wetsuits.

They raced each other, before getting winded and treading water, the sun making hard, sharp diamonds across the surface.

"Is it that girl? The one you like?" Olly asked.

Nate shrugged, and Olly let it drop.

Nate looked out into the distance, an unbroken line. "You know," he said, "sometimes I wish that I could capture with my camera what I can see with my eye. All the detail, just the way I see it. But it doesn't translate like that, somehow."

The sun was beginning to dip towards the horizon and the light was getting weaker, more diffuse. They began to swim back. Nate pulled ahead of Olly, and Olly stopped for a moment and watched him, his brown arms slicing through the water in a continuous, smooth motion, his legs barely kicking up any wake. Then Olly put his own head down and tried to catch up.

Back on shore, the old couple had packed up and moved on. Nate and Olly toweled off with their T-shirts, Nate using his to dry his hair, as well. "I guess, everything just feels . . . sideways at the moment. Like, off-kilter or something. And I'm not sure what I should do about it," Nate said. "If I should do anything about it."

Olly thought for a moment. "I guess it's just like that sometimes," he said. "You just have to remember . . ."

"I know, I know," Nate said, pulling on his shorts. "*Fortune favors the bold.*"

Olly looked at him, laughing a little. "What is that supposed to mean?"

"That's what you always said about starting up your label."

"Jesus, did I?"

"Yeah, in *Rolling Stone*. And *Variety*. And *Vanity Fair*." Nate pushed his hair back, dropped down on the sand and stretched his legs out. "That's what you said. About your gift for . . . being you, I guess."

"Christ," Olly said, sitting down next to him.

Nate smiled. "I've read everything about you."

"I'm clearly a real, modern-day Aristotle," Olly said.

Nate shrugged.

"Look," Olly said, "what I said, that's not true. Not entirely. Sometimes shit just . . . happens. And there's nothing you can do about it."

Nate looked at him, a strange, intent expression on his face. "Like what shit just happens?"

"Well, for example," Olly said slowly, "in my case, my gift—or whatever you want to call it—the music, it turns out it's gone. I can't hear it. I mean, I can *hear* it. But I don't know it anymore, I can't distinguish one thing from another." Olly lit a cigarette. He hadn't meant to talk about this now, or maybe ever. He took a long drag, then another. "You know, I used to have this system, this way of categorizing the things I heard. It had to do with the colors I saw and flavors I could taste when I listened to music. And then I could put them into these categories: Songs To Dance To, Songs To Drink To, Songs To Drive To, Songs To Smoke To, and

Songs To . . . you know . . . Fuck To. And if it moved me and I could put it in one of those categories, I knew I had a hit on my hands."

"Colors?" Nate asked.

Olly blew out smoke, blue-gray. "Yeah, for me, it was like entering a whole other sort of other dimension when I listen to music. Like my brain kind of lit up. There's a name for it, synesthesia. It's a kind of condition. I saw a doctor about it once." He crushed out the cigarette. "He said it's not unusual, you know, it's something some people have, where their brains are wired differently." He shook his head. "A lot of musicians have it. It's hereditary, apparently. And, as it turns out, you can lose it, too."

Nate was quiet.

"Look, the thing is, I had this thing my whole life and then it was just gone. And every day afterward was a little bit worse than the day before. And then things got really bad. And . . . I don't know. So bad, that I wanted to die. And I gave it a good try." He laughed a harsh little laugh. "I guess what I'm trying to say is that sometimes it's just about being able to cope with all the shit, just kind of sit with it when there isn't a damn thing you can do about it. I think . . ." He stopped, thought. "I think you have to have a certain kind of bravery, a certain kind of appetite for life to survive it." He looked at Nate. "And you are definitely brave enough, Nate. You are just as you should be."

Nate looked at him. "And are you better now? I mean, are you fixed?"

"I'm . . . yeah, I'm better now." Because what could he say? That he didn't know if people ever really got fixed?

Nate didn't ask him anything else; he just reached into his sneaker and pulled out a flattened joint and matches. Olly watched as he bent the cardboard flap back, pinning the match between the flap and the strike, and lit it, the acrid smell of sulfur hitting him.

He lit the joint and offered it to Olly, who shook his head. "I don't use drugs."

"Really?" Nate asked, inhaling.

Olly looked at him and then back at the joint. He shrugged. "Fuck it. Pass it over."

Nate took another quick drag, exhaled, then passed it to Olly.

"It's weird," Nate said after a while. "You know, how things go in, like, a chain reaction. Like one event sets off a whole series of shit. Like an earthquake."

They just sat, smoked in silence until early evening fell and the mosquitoes began to emerge. Nate slapped his leg, turning his palm over to expose a flattened mosquito, blood spreading underneath it. He inspected it.

"We should go," Olly said, standing and brushing himself off. "I'll walk you home."

When they arrived at the house on Church Street, Nate said: "You want to get something to eat? I just have to take a quick shower."

"Sure," Olly said, but he stayed out on the sidewalk as Nate went up the front steps.

Nate turned to him. "You coming?"

"I'll wait here," he said.

"Come on," Nate said, laughing, and pushed the door open.

Olly felt somehow foolish—childish, really, so he followed Nate up the steps and inside the Everleys' house.

Nate headed up the stairs. "I'll be quick," he said, and left Olly there in the foyer.

The first time Olly'd been here, the day he'd arrived back in Wonderland, he'd been too hyped up to take notice of anything. Now, he looked around. It was strange being in *their* house, the home that his two ex-best friends had built together, the outward manifestation of their hope, their complicity, their ambition, their love. *This is us, this is us.* He realized that he'd built it up in his mind, what it would look like and how it would make him feel. Now, however, all he saw was a small polished curving staircase opposite the front door, a ragged seagrass rug, a half-moon table covered in framed family photographs and other knick-knacks. Just a house.

On the wall next to the staircase he saw the Betty Tompkins "Fuck" painting, a large-scale photorealistic painting of a penis entering a vagina, the edges of the woman's white buttocks spreading out against the man's darker, more mottled, open thighs. The scale and detail made it look at first glance like a black and white aerial shot of the earth—of a darkening river or canyon where water once flowed, perhaps. He smiled. He remembered being at a cocktail party in New York in '72 with Miller and Ash. They'd stopped speaking to each other by that point, their only communication centered around the operation of Lay Down. But they'd found themselves thrown together by accident at this out-of-town party. The host, a wealthy SoHo landlord who'd amassed a formidable collection by taking art in trade for rent from his tenants, had one of these paintings on his wall and Miller had admired it. Olly'd looked over at Ash, who'd rolled his eyes. It was a rare and surprising moment of complicity—the last one— between the two of them. She must have tracked down the artist and bought one. Looking at it now, he saw she was right to have done it; they were wrong to have laughed.

Nate reappeared a few minutes later, freshly showered. "Sorry," he said, descending the stairs, two at a time. He used his hand to rake his hair away from his forehead in a gesture that was both familiar and arresting. For a moment, Olly had the impression that he was looking at a pre-Raphaelite painting, he was so pretty—a little raffish, his self-assurance sparkling a little too bright, a little painful to look at.

"Ready?" Olly said.

"You know, I just remembered I have to meet someone, actually. Sorry."

"Okay," Olly said, confused.

"But you should stay here," Nate said, pushing open a swinging door that Olly now saw led to the kitchen.

Through it, he could see Miller sitting at the kitchen table, reading, oblivious.

"Nate . . ."

"You guys should talk to each other," Nate said, his blue eyes darkening a little. He pushed Olly gently in the direction of the kitchen. "Seriously." And then he opened the front door and walked out, shutting it after him with a bang.

Miller was sitting at the kitchen table, legs propped up, drinking a glass of Chardonnay and reading *Heartburn*, when she heard the front door slam.

"Hello?" she called out.

She turned toward the door that led into the foyer and there he was. She had a fleeting image of him at her window, late at night, all those years ago. Just a small flash, so quick it only left the impression of a memory, rather than the memory itself.

"Hi," Miller said.

Olly shifted his weight. "Hi," he said. "Sorry. Nate thought it would be a good idea . . . and then he just left . . ."

"I know you don't have a lot of experience with this." Miller swung her legs off the table. "But teenagers are generally the worst people to take advice from." She took a sip of her wine. "Mercurial."

"Sorry. I'm leaving."

"No," she said. "Stay." She tapped her glass slowly with the edge of her nail. "So, you two have been seeing each other."

"Would that be a problem?"

They looked at each other a moment. Then she stood. "Wine?"

Olly shrugged. "I mean, why not? In for a penny, in for a pound."

Miller laughed, a small laugh. She rose and poured him a glass. It was pale yellow, like straw, in the kitchen light and very cold in her hand. She wiped her palm on her shorts after she handed it to him, feeling the chill of it clinging to her skin.

"How's Aunt Tassie doing?" she asked.

"Fine."

She watched Olly as he drank it, in big gulps, as if he'd never been so thirsty for anything. It was odd watching him—he'd been teetotal since they were twenty-one. She wondered how damaged he actually was.

He seemed to feel her gaze, and stopped. He placed the wine glass carefully on the table, and sat down next to her at the end of the table. She could feel him casting around for something to say.

"Where's Ash?"

"He went to the city this morning. He's not back yet."

Olly nodded. Then: "I walked by the meeting house today. It looks smaller."

Miller continued to watch him.

"Not just smaller, but, I don't know . . . dingier." Olly looked at her. "What?"

"Do you miss it?"

"What, the meeting house?"

"All of it. The Way."

She could see him relax a little. "No," he said.

"Me, either."

"Really?" He seemed genuinely surprised. "I always got the impression that you felt like I took you away from that. I thought that's why you came back here."

Miller smiled. "No. That's definitely not the problem I have with you." She finished her glass. "But I don't hate it. I don't know . . . I'm not sorry I was raised that way. It just feels like somehow it's part of the past, the way this place used to be."

Olly nodded slowly. "Yeah, I know what you mean. It's like milk: you drink it every day when you're a kid and it makes your bones strong. But that doesn't mean you want to drink it as an adult."

She laughed. "Mmm."

"What?"

"Nothing. Pithy."

"It's strange, though," Olly said, "how Nate—and his friends, too, I guess—know nothing about that Wonderland. The one we knew growing up. The Way. The meetings. The light, hearing God's voice. Like it's lost in the mists of time or something." He laughed. "A Bermuda Triangle of Quaker life."

"You know, when I was little, I thought all those words in my head were God speaking to me. The inner light."

"And now?"

"I think they're mine," Miller said, smiling.

"Nate said something to me today, about things setting off a chain reaction. And it got me thinking about what it was that set all of us off on our path—what was the one thing that started it all, got us here, to this place in our lives. Made us change."

Miller raised an eyebrow. "What, like in the movies? *And with that, their whole world was turned upside down and they would never be the same again*," she intoned.

"Fine, laugh." Olly shook his head. "Wine?"

"Sure," she said.

He stood and walked to the fridge.

He looked better, at least his face did. The bruises had turned from dark purple to yellow, his eye was unbandaged and the swelling had gone down.

"How are you feeling?" she asked, as he filled her glass.

He tipped the rest of the bottle into his own. "Great. Better than I've felt in a long time."

"All right then."

"Why? How are you feeling?" he asked.

"I really, really don't want to talk about it."

She could see his mouth do an impression of a faint smile.

"Anyway," she said, "that's my new thing at the moment. Not talking about it."

"Hunh. My new thing *is* talking about it, apparently. I can't seem to stop."

"That is new for you," she said.

Olly laughed. "Was I really that bad?"

Miller just arched an eyebrow at him.

"Okay, I guess I was." He was quiet for a moment, then he reached across the table and gently removed her sunglasses. "I can't see you like that."

They looked at each other.

"Well, anyway, I'm having a dinner party. On Friday." She flashed him a winning smile. "We'd be delighted if you could come."

Olly laughed again. "Oh, would you?"

Miller nodded. "We would."

"Well, how can I say no?"

"You can't," she said.

"It's a date," he said.

Miller clinked her wine glass against his.

She felt his gaze on her naked face, steady, watching. Miller could feel the worn linoleum beneath her bare feet, the cool smoothness of the glass in her hand, the back of her thighs sticking to the wooden chair, the air on her skin. Everything.

"I should go," Olly said, finally.

"Yes."

He got up and put his glass in the sink. "Thanks for the wine."

"Anytime," she said. "And Friday."

"Friday," he said, nodding.

After the screen door had shut behind him, Miller rose and went over to it. She didn't know why, perhaps to watch him go, just to watch him walk away under a Wonderland streetlamp, like she had so many times before.

When she got to the door, he was there on the other side.

They both reached for the handle at the same time, and she stepped aside and let him open it, and then he was inside.

She couldn't say who kissed who first, whose move it was. She was sure he couldn't say either. That neither one would ever be able to say.

But when her mouth met his, she was struck with an overwhelming fear that he would pull away, that it would stop. And every millisecond that passed, the fear grew until she realized that he had no intention of stopping, and then she could feel her desire, real and completely overwhelming.

Headlights flashed behind Olly, catching them like a spotlight on a stage kiss. As they broke apart, Ash got out of a taxi. He stood there in the driveway, over Olly's shoulder, like an actor waiting in the wings for his cue.

1966

Ash watched Miller rise in the morning light of his Malibu bedroom, the sun hitting her bare shoulders, the curve of her spine, as she stood turned away from him. He had been waiting years for her. And she was finally here.

The night before, when she'd come over crying, telling him it was over with Olly, that she'd ended it, that he didn't even look at her anymore, Ash had known his time had come. Olly had had his chance. And he'd blown it.

Ash knew Miller could love him, that he could make her love him. And he'd told her so last night, as she sat on his sagging sofa.

She'd stopped crying and looked at him, obviously surprised by his declaration.

"Oh, Ash," she'd said.

"No. Don't say anything," he'd told her. "Just listen: I've loved you forever. For as long as I can remember. And I never would have said anything, as long as you and Olly were happy. But you're not happy anymore. And you deserve it, Miller. You deserve to be happy more than anyone I know. You are the most beautiful girl— woman—I've ever seen. And I will love you 'till my dying day and make it my mission to make you happy. Let me make you happy."

"Ash . . ."

And then he'd kissed her. She'd been hesitant. And then she wasn't and they'd fallen into bed, and Ash had never been happier in his whole life.

Now, he watched her dress, quietly slipping on her white underpants, the sides skimming her lovely ass, the curve of her hip bone. All the places he'd been allowed to touch last night.

"Hi," he said.

She turned, as if she'd been caught at something.

"Oh, hi," she said, smiling. She tried to smooth her disheveled hair with the palm of her hand.

"Coffee?"

"Umm, I don't know." She pulled her Indian print dress on over her head, her breasts moving beneath the fabric, the nipples showing slightly. She came and sat next to him on his low bed. "Look, Ash. Last night . . ."

He sat up. "Miller. I know this is strange. But you have to trust me. This is going to work."

"It's just all a little . . . close, you know?"

"I'm your best friend," he said. "I know you better than anyone."

Neither of them mentioned Olly.

"Look, we can take things slowly, or quickly, or however you want," he continued, trying not to sound breathless. "I only ask one thing: just don't think too much. Just let it happen. See if it feels right. Please. You can change your mind, throw me overboard whenever you want. But just . . . turn off your mind. For a little while."

She bit her lip. Looked at him, nodded. "Okay," she said. "I just don't want to break your heart."

"You're not going to break my heart, Miller."

FRIDAY

Until you know who you want to be, be a queen.

That's what Blue had said on Letterman.

Suki was sitting cross-legged on her floor in front of the full-length mirror. On her stereo, the mix tape Nate had left for her in the mailbox—*For Suki*—played loudly, but not loud enough to entirely blot out her parents. The song—something by Prince that she'd never heard before, a live recording that he'd marked as "The Beautiful Ones" in the handwritten track listing—came to an end.

Do you think I'm stupid, Cricket? Do you?

Do you think I don't notice you sneaking around?

Who are you fucking? Who are you fucking? Who are you fucking?

Suki could hear the blows, more like thuds followed by grunts, mass hitting mass: *A body in motion stays in motion.* Then her mother's screams, high but short, like she was trying to stop herself. She could imagine her mother's body, where it was taking the blows. Never in the face.

She'd learned long ago that there was no point trying to help. It only made things worse. This time, though, it seemed to have been going for days: on/off, on/off, on/off.

Who are you fucking? Who are you fucking? Who are you fucking?

The next song, "Good Feeling" by the Violent Femmes, started up. Suki rose and turned the volume as high as it would go, before resettling herself in front of the mirror. She'd always been fascinated by Nefertiti, the Egyptian queen who worshipped the sun god, Aten; Great of Praises, Lady of Two Lands, Lady of All Women. And since she didn't know who she was yet, she was going to be Queen Nefertiti.

They'd said in school that underneath her crown, Nefertiti's hair was shorn. Black and inky. Suki picked up the scissors and started cutting. First slowly, tentatively, then carving away at it in great hunks, her red hair falling around her, clinging to her skin, her clothes, like a multitude of sticky, silky spider webs.

When she'd done all she could with the scissors, she picked up the electric shaver she'd stolen from her dad's medicine cabinet and carefully trimmed it all the same length. She dusted off the top of her head, her neck, her shoulders and inspected her work. It was short, very short, but not a complete buzz cut like an army boy would have. She could see the shape of her skull, and her cheek bones, like her skeleton revealed. It was beautiful. But she wasn't done yet.

In her bathroom, she covered her hair and the sides of her face and neck in some of her Finesse conditioner. She found the rich, fruity smell comforting.

Downstairs, she could hear a chair overturning and the crash of some kind of china—a vase, a cup? And another thud, then silence. *A body at rest stays at rest.*

She picked up the jar of Manic Panic that Jess had given her as a joke, brought back from some famous shop in the Village on her tour of AADA. The color was Raven—black like a moonless night, an endless night, a punk black—and she applied it to her new hair, combing it through, the teeth biting into her scalp, before covering her head in Saran wrap.

She waited. She was good at waiting.

Through the door to her bedroom, the tape clicked over. A fast, twangy guitar. Tom Petty's "American Girl."

It was time. She rinsed her hair and looked at herself in the mirror.

There she was, a queen.

Queen Suki, Lady of Two Lands.

*   *   *

It might turn out to be the world's worst dinner party. Miller reflected on this as she chopped the capers and olives, the colors blending into one through her tinted lenses. Still, she supposed, maybe it was like playing Hearts: it was better to be either the absolute best or the absolute worst, than anything in between.

Rickie Lee Jones was playing on the record player in the kitchen. The track ended, and in the silence she could hear the shower running upstairs.

When Ash had stepped out of the taxi the night before, he'd just stared a moment, his overnight bag on his shoulder, before turning on his heel and, without a word, walking down the street away from them. She and Olly had stood frozen for a moment, then Miller had gone back inside, alone.

To her surprise, though, Ash had returned to the house that morning.

"Still having your dinner party?" he'd asked, standing in the doorway, holding his suitcase.

Miller had nodded, biting her lip. She didn't ask where he'd spent the night.

"What time?" He'd asked politely, like they didn't know each other.

"Seven."

"Okay. Let me know if you need any help."

"Thanks," she'd said.

And that was the only interaction they'd had for the rest of the day. What was there to say?

Now she was showered and dressed, an apron over the old Indian print dress she'd had for years. She'd had trouble with her closet: realizing that she'd stopped looking at her clothes for ages, she hadn't been sure what on earth was in there, and what would look good. So she'd grabbed the dress: pinks, reds, yellows, shot through with silver thread, it sort of floated around her. Anyway, it was a safe choice.

She'd put on some gold bangles and perfume and checked her reflection in the mirror in their bedroom. Then she'd put on her sunglasses and gone downstairs to finish up the cooking.

Ash came downstairs, his hair wet. "I picked up some wine," he said, putting a few bottles in the fridge.

"Oh, great," Miller said, pretending to be very fixated on the capers.

Ash sat down at the kitchen table. "So, who's coming to this shindig?"

"Ummm, well, Dick Cross, and Olly, of course—" She turned, waving the knife around in an overly cheerful gesture. "And, uh . . . Cricket and Dutch Pfeiffer and . . . you and me."

"Really?"

Miller turned back to the counter, measuring out the prunes with excruciating care. "Mmm, hmm."

It was definitely going to be a disaster, and not in a good way.

Originally, it was supposed to be the Baxters, and Roy Baxter's father who was a painter, and his girlfriend. But then Roy's father had had a fall and ended up in the hospital, so they'd canceled. She'd called the Woods, but they were going on an evening booze cruise with some friends, and the Gunthersons hadn't answered the phone. So in a panic—because it most certainly couldn't be her and Ash and Olly eating Chicken Marbella alone together— she'd called Cricket and invited her and Dutch. Then, at the A&P she'd run into Reverend Cross, and on a crazy impulse had invited him, as well.

"I don't think I want Dutch in our house," Ash said.

"No, I know," Miller said. "But I ran into Cricket and she seemed so upset. I didn't think he'd come too, but . . ." She knew this was a particularly flimsy lie. Honestly, she didn't want Dutch in their house, either. She regretted everything. She had thought about canceling, but it had just gone too far and gotten out of control and, as usual, she'd done nothing to stop it.

Ash sighed.

"Could you pour me some of that nice wine?" she asked.

"Do you think you should start so early?"

"Jesus, Ash. People will be here any minute." She slammed the chicken into the oven. "It's not exactly early."

"Sorry," he said, getting up.

"That's okay." She didn't want to fight either. Or at least she didn't think she did. "Sorry about the guest list." She was nervous; she hadn't spoken with Olly since the kiss and she wasn't even sure he would come. Wasn't sure whether she wanted him to or not. She needed Ash to be her ally in this; as perverse as that was, she didn't want to face it alone.

Ash handed her a glass of wine and slid his hand down her back. "I remember this dress," he said.

Miller willed herself not to pull away from his touch. She handed him a bowl of Blue Diamond almonds. "Can you put these on the table outside?"

They'd have drinks in the backyard on the old rattan furniture, then dinner in the kitchen with the French doors open, and the hurricane lamps lit outside. She'd always hated the dining room in their house—poky, with just one small window. Anyway, it was Ash's office now.

Ash came back in and, fearing another intimacy, Miller immediately handed him the salmon mousse.

"Knock knock." Cricket was standing at the kitchen door wearing a long-sleeved navy dress down to her ankles with a white Peter Pan collar and her nurse-y shoes with their thick, soft soles. She looked like an Amish lady. "I hope I'm not too early."

"No, of course not," Miller said. "Come in."

"I'm so sorry, but Dutch can't make it. I would have called, but I just found out myself. He had some kind of work emergency."

"Shame," Ash said, giving Miller a sideways glance. "Hope everything's okay up in the sky?"

"Oh, I'm sure it is," Cricket said, quickly. "He doesn't really tell me much about it." She fiddled with her collar. "It was very nice of you to invite me. Us, I mean."

"We really should do it more often," Miller lied.

"What's your poison, Cricket?" Ash stood ready at the bar in the corner of the kitchen near the doors.

"Oh, just water for me, thanks," she said.

"Maybe just a small, sweet sherry?" Ash had already poured it.

Cricket smiled, a charming, shy kind of smile. "Okay, just one."

"Hello?" Dick Cross tentatively pushed the screen door open.

He really was a handsome man, Miller thought, looking at him standing in her doorway like some Greek god in a blue button-down shirt. Maybe too handsome, she thought idly.

"Oh," he said, when he saw Cricket.

"Oh," Cricket said.

Miller laughed. "Come in, Dick. I know you two know each other. It can't be that much of a surprise." She felt a little guilty that they were so surprised to be invited, like she was using them. Which, of course, she was.

Ash handed Miller a fresh glass of wine, and a Scotch for Dick.

"Shall we go outside?" Miller led the way out the doors.

Cricket sat next to Miller on the wicker love seat, looked at her face, then whispered: "Are you okay?"

"What?"

Cricket nodded at her sunglasses.

"Oh, these? No. I don't know why . . . I'll just take them off," Miller said. She immediately regretted it, though she had to admit that the soft, deep blue of the evening sky without the tint of the lenses was lovelier than she remembered. "We're just waiting for one more, so please help yourself to the salmon mousse," she said.

"Dutch?" Dick asked.

"No, Dutch isn't coming," Cricket said, quickly, then stopped. "I mean, I don't know who else is coming. But not Dutch, he's not coming."

"It's an old friend of ours. Olly Lane." Miller sipped her wine, eyeing Ash covertly over the rim.

He crossed his legs and smiled genially. "We had a record company together. In the bad old days."

"Oh," Cricket said. "That's so exciting. I can see now where Nate gets his creativity from."

Miller laughed. "I think that's his own special gift. Ash and I were the less creative ones."

"I'm sure that's not true," Cricket said.

A silence descended. Miller looked at Dick. For a minister, he wasn't exactly holding up his end of the conversation.

"I don't know what you're cooking, Miller, but it really smells good," Cricket said, finally.

"It's Chicken Marbella."

"Oh, *Silver Palate*?" Cricket said brightly, nodding. "I love that dish."

"Me too," Miller said.

More silence.

Finally, Dick cleared his throat. "What's the *Silver Palate*?"

"Oh, Dick," Cricket said, laughing a little. "Do you live under a rock?"

He smiled a gorgeous smile. "I must," he said. "I definitely need help with my domestic skills."

"Have you thought about getting someone in to help?" Miller asked. She didn't know why she said that.

"No," Dick said.

"Oh," Miller said.

"More drinks?" Ash was already on his feet.

Before anyone had a chance to reply, they heard a strong, accented voice call out: "*Hello, house.*"

Miller turned and looked through the open French doors towards the kitchen.

Olly was standing there with a bear of a man: curly dark hair, big features, large Adam's apple. This was an interesting turn of events for the World's Worst Dinner Party.

Ash stood still. Cricket and Dick stared. Miller rose.

"Hello back," she said, walking towards them.

"This is Rodrigo Rodrigo," Olly said. "A friend. He was at loose ends for dinner, so . . ."

Miller glanced at Olly. The subtext was plain: he hadn't wanted to come unarmed. "Welcome, Rodrigo. We're delighted you could come."

"They're delighted," Olly said. "I told you."

Rodrigo took Miller's outstretched hand and shook it hard. "I've always liked shaking hands," he said. "It's good, direct. All the kissing can get too much. Once, I was at a party in Mexico City and by the time I'd kissed everyone hello, I had to kiss them all goodbye." He laughed.

"Well," Dick said. "It's the American way."

"Actually, it was the Greeks," Rodrigo said. "It was their way of proving they didn't have any weapons in their hands." He smiled at Miller.

She smiled back at him. She felt an unexpected rush of genuine warmth for this stranger.

"What can I get you?" Ash asked.

"Wine," Rodrigo said. "Red wine. Strong. Please."

"Red," Ash said, looking back at the bar. "I think we have some floating around."

"I'll have one, too," Olly said. "Thanks."

If Ash heard him, he made no sign.

Miller cleared her throat. "Well, follow me. I made a salmon mousse," she added, pointlessly.

"You're the director of the movie," Dick said, after Miller had made the introductions.

"I am." Rodrigo clapped Dick on the back, as if congratulating him.

"Oh, my goodness," said Cricket.

"I didn't realize," Miller said, looking at Olly.

He was inscrutable. "Yeah, we know each other from L.A."

"Olly was the first one to believe in my idea for the film." Rodrigo settled himself into one of chairs, making it look very small.

"I've never been to Hollywood, so this might sound silly," Cricket said, "but do all of you famous people know each other?"

"Olly's not famous." Rodrigo smiled broadly.

Olly smiled, sat down. "I was his producer."

"Oh, I thought they said you had a record company."

"Not anymore," Olly said. "I did have a small stake . . ."

Ash looked up sharply, looked at Miller, who looked at Olly, who shrugged. "Had to sell it when I got fired."

"Oh," Cricket said, nodding, as if she understood completely.

Miller took a long drink from her wine glass and put her sunglasses back on.

"Prescription?" Rodrigo said, indicating the lenses.

"No, it's not that," Miller said.

"She just likes wearing them," Ash said, curtly.

"The spotlight has always been too bright for Miller," Olly said.

"What spotlight?" Rodrigo asked, seemingly bemused.

"The spotlight of life." Olly leaned back in his chair, running his fingers through his hair. Miller remembered that gesture, it was one of Olly's I-just-scored-a-point attitudes.

"I feel like I'm in a comedy and I don't know the lines," Rodrigo said, turning to Dick and Cricket. "So." He slapped his knees. "You two are married?"

"Nooo," Cricket said, downing her sherry.

Dick laughed. "No."

"Dick is the minister of First Presbyterian," Miller said. "The big white church down the road? And Cricket is our neighbor. Her husband couldn't make it."

"Could I possibly have another sherry?" Cricket held her glass out to Ash.

"How are you liking it in Wonderland?" Dick asked, crossing his legs.

Rodrigo shrugged. "It's a very strange town."

"Why strange?" Miller asked.

"Come on," Rodrigo said.

Miller laughed. "No, really, why strange? I mean, it's a small town. But no weirder than other small towns, I don't think."

"Who names a town Wonderland?" Rodrigo shook his head. "*Dios mio.*"

"Well," Ash began, "actually, it comes from a misunderstanding of the name used by the Wampanoag tribe . . ."

Rodrigo looked at Ash like he must be putting him on. "It's crazy. No sane person, no sane *town*, keeps this name."

"I think you're giving us too much credit," Miller said. "We're not that interesting."

"He's right," Olly said. "Everyone here is a train wreck."

"I don't think he's right," Dick said. "We're all just people. Making some mistakes, living our lives, hoping for forgiveness. For His grace. Like everyone else."

There was a silence.

"I'm going to be honest," Miller said, finally. "I'm not hoping for His grace. You know, honestly, I'm not. I feel like, what I learned was that I was born into grace. I don't need to be forgiven." Then she said brightly: "I think the chicken's ready."

When Nate and Cam got to Pebble Beach, the party was already in full swing. It was dark and the moon hung over the ocean, casting a silvery glow over the small, round stones that lined the shore. The bonfire itself was at a peak; Nate could feel the heat of it even from the entrance to the beach. As they picked their way toward the center of the party, they passed couples, already drunk, making out noisily, sloppily, around the path.

The boom box set up on one of the rocks was blasting Corey Hart's "Sunglasses at Night," and a group of guys was strutting around wearing their own shades, posturing to the song, the beer in their red Solo cups spilling over the edges and splashing the ground.

Nate kept his eye out for Suki, scanning the crowd, looking for red hair, or a body that moved like hers. When he and Cam had walked by her house on the way over, all the lights had been off, and Nate wondered if maybe she was waiting to sneak out.

He hadn't heard from her since he'd left the mix tape in her mailbox, something he was beginning to regret. Maybe she didn't understand what he was trying to say? Or maybe she did, and thought he was some crazy-intense guy?

When he and Cam reached the keg, which Cam had picked up from over the bridge earlier that day, they stood for a moment watching the guys making their moves to the music, peacocking, singing in unison.

"This song just doesn't make any sense," Nate said. "I mean, what does that even mean, masquerading with a guy in shades? Can you masquerade *with* someone? Is that a thing?"

"I don't think you're supposed to think that deeply about it," Cam said.

"I guess," Nate said. "But seriously . . ."

"Jesus, why do you even care about this stuff?" Cam snapped. "Can't believe I'm the one going to community college."

"All right, all right. Take it easy," Nate said. "Let's get a beer." But he realized that this was the stuff that used to make Cam laugh. Cam wasn't laughing anymore.

Nate was refilling their beers for the third time when he felt someone bump him from behind, almost knocking him into the folding table next to the keg.

"You need to watch your back, Everley." Chris Stodges, drunk and already slurring, was behind him, the creamy Naugahyde arms of his letter jacket glistening in the moonlight.

"All right, Chris," Nate said.

He got in Nate's face, pointing a finger. "I'm telling you, man."

"What's your problem?" Chris had always been an asshole, even in elementary school.

"Your friend, man—Cross—he's un-fucking-hinged. He's cuckoo for Coco Puffs."

Out of the corner of his eye he could see Cam talking to some girl, his arms folded across his chest, stretching his yellow and white baseball shirt tight around his muscles.

Nate looked back at Chris: "What are you talking about?"

"Ask anyone, Everley. He's gonna hurt someone. I'm telling you, man."

"Okay, okay," Nate said, backing up slowly, trying to extricate himself from Stodges' bulky mass. "Just take it easy. It's a party."

"Fuck, yeah, it's a party." Chris raised his cup, staggering slightly.

Nate left him there and walked over to Cam.

". . . Longfellow Community College forever," the girl was saying to Cam, going in for a cheers, but only managing to spill her beer.

"Sure," Cam said.

"It's going to be out of hand," she said. "Fuck the Ivy Leagues."

"Right," Cam said.

"Stodges is already feeling it," Nate said to Cam, handing him one of the cups.

"Stodges is here?" The girl said. "*Stodges! You asshole.*" She walked away, yelling Chris's name.

Nate tapped his cup against Cam's. "So, this is officially your last bonfire."

"That's fine by me," Cam said.

Nate laughed. "No nostalgia for the good ol' days, then?"

Cam was quiet, surveying the crowd. "You know," he said, finally. "I hate these people."

Nate looked at the cold, hard expression on Cam's face. "You okay? You can talk to me, you know . . ."

Then Cam did laugh. "Right, right." He nodded. "You have no idea, do you?" Cam said. "You think you do, but you don't. You . . ."

But Cam didn't finish that thought; he was staring hard at some point in the distance. Nate followed his gaze to the edge of the bonfire. Jess was there, in her usual Madonna-inspired attire—off the shoulder crop-top with newsprint on it, a blazer and leopard shorts—and next to her was a girl with shorn, jet-black hair, dark eyeliner, drawn in an Egyptian style. She was wearing a white cotton dress, tight to the waist, with Converse high-tops. Something about her, the shape of her shoulders, the movement of her head.

They both stared at her. Nate was absolutely riveted. He'd never seen someone do that before. Change, transform, like a chameleon or a magic trick.

And all that red hair. Gone.

"Borderline" came on the boom box and they watched as she turned her sleek, otter-like head and smiled widely at Jess, the muscles in her jaw fully pronounced. Like she had all new lines. Jess smiled back, the both of them laughing at some joke.

Nate started toward her, Cam behind him. Nate could feel his nerves jangling as he got closer, and he made a conscious effort to relax his limbs, his gait.

"Hey," he said, when he reached them.

"Hey, Nate," Jess said. "You're looking very . . . I don't know, *something*." She fingered his Neil Diamond T-shirt. "Hot shirt."

"Yeah," he said. "Scorching."

Suki smiled, reflexively touching her hair, the back of her skull. Nate wondered what it felt like under her hands. He couldn't stop looking at her. The heat from the bonfire made his cheeks sting, and cast a glow over Suki's skin, orange and gold.

"Hey, Cam," Jess said.

"Hey."

"I've collected from most of these idiots," Jess said, indicating the keg. "I'll divvy it up after."

Cam ignored Jess, instead staring at Suki. "What happened to your hair?"

Suki laughed. "Don't you like it?"

"I mean . . . I guess."

"Do you want a beer?" Nate asked her.

"Jesus, Nate," Jess said.

"Beers," Nate corrected himself. "Would you both like a beer?"

"Forget it," Jess said. "I don't trust you to remember mine. Let's all go together."

They left the warmth of the fire, traveling down into the darker, cooler parts of the party, their feet crunching over the pebbles, moving towards the sound of the waves sliding up and down the shore. They passed a girl Nate recognized, Pam somebody.

"Nice look, Suki," he heard her say as they walked by. "What is that, Concentration-Camp Chic?" Then to her pack next to her: "Jesus, did you see her?"

Suki looked down.

"Fuck Pam Spamface," Jess said, tightening an arm around Suki. "She smells like Designer Imposters and will probably die in a jazzercise class. You look totally rad, Sukes."

"Sympathy for the Devil" was playing as they waited for their turn by the folding table, and some kids, looked like Longwell kids, were doing karate kicks to the songs, a group of girls standing by, egging them on. Jess was laughing, doing some karate moves of her own.

"Wax on, wax off," she said, moving her hands around Cam's face, her cropped shirt moving up and down over her exposed stomach.

They'd all seen the trailer for *Karate Kid*. Nate laughed. Cam's face remained impassive.

"Come on, Cam," Jess said. "You know you want to see it. We could smoke a joint and laugh our asses off."

"Sure," Cam said, but he wasn't looking at her.

"So it's a date?" Jess said.

"What?"

"Oh, Cam," Jess said, pursing her lips.

They were inching their way towards the keg, when Chris Stodges' face loomed large again over Nate's shoulder.

"James," Chris said, looking at Jess. "You're looking hot this evening. What do you say we find somewhere a little more private and I'll let you sit on my face?"

Jess held up her middle finger.

"I'm just saying, James, this face leaves here at ten o'clock. You better be on it."

Nate groaned. "Stodges, man . . ."

"Hey, Everley. It's natural." He turned to Cam. "What are you looking at, you freak?"

Cam looked away.

"Cool it, Stodges," Nate said.

"What?" Chris said. "I'm just saying, he's a freak. I mean, a guy says one little thing about his mom fucking the mailman . . ."

It happened suddenly. So suddenly that it took a moment for Nate's brain to catch up with it. Cam advanced one step, his arm shot out, and he felled Chris with one blow. Nate heard the crunch as Cam's knuckles connected with Chris's face. Chris stayed down, and the look in his eyes. He was scared of Cam.

Cam said nothing, just stood over him; Stodges made no move to get up.

"Fuck," Nate said. He'd never actually seen someone get hit before—he'd seen guys trying to go at it, punches not landing, and fights that just ended in head-locks and wrestling matches on the ground, like animals scrapping. But something that silent, that fast, that brutal. He'd never seen that. It had intent, it had precision. Chris was meant to get hurt.

Cam looked at Suki, looked like he wanted to say something, but it wouldn't come out. "Why did you do that to your hair?" he said finally, in a low voice.

She just stared at him, silent.

And then Cam was gone, pushing his way out of the line and disappearing up past the bonfire toward the road.

"I'm going after him," Jess said, leaving Nate and Suki standing there.

A group of Stodges' friends had gathered around them, and some of the girls, too.

"Your friend's a psycho," the girl, Pam, said.

"Yeah, yeah. Your friend's a massive dick, so there's that," Nate said. He turned to Suki. "I think we should leave."

She nodded.

When they reached the Ring Road, Nate turned to her. "Where do you want to go?"

"Let's go to my house," she said.

"What about your parents?"

"They're not home," she said. "I think they're at your place."

"So why *Moby-Dick*?"

They were on their second helpings of chicken and rice, and their millionth helpings of wine, when Ash asked what Miller thought most of them had been wondering ever since the movie had come to town.

"Ah." Rodrigo smiled. "That's a question whose answer has many parts," he said.

"Okay," Ash said, carving another sliver off a drumstick.

"The more interesting question for me," Rodrigo said, "is *What does this story mean?*"

Miller laughed; he really was a director, never passing up the opportunity to reframe the narrative to his liking.

Ash waved his fork impatiently. "It's a tale of madness and revenge."

"No," Rodrigo said. "Not to me. To me, it is a like a fairy tale. Ahab has been cursed. He thinks his only way to lift this curse is to destroy the white whale. There are many stories like this, yes? Like the German Brothers Grimm—you know, the prince is turned into a bear and the spell can only be broken when he kills the midget who cursed him."

"The dwarf," Olly said.

"Yes, the dwarf," Rodrigo said, nodding.

" 'Snow-White and Rose-Red,' " Miller said.

"That one," Rodrigo said.

"So," Miller said, "Moby-Dick is like an evil, magical being. Like the dwarf."

"No," Rodrigo said. "Because it's not Moby-Dick who's cursed him. The white whale is everything and nothing. He's a vessel, a symbol. No, it's Ahab's mind that's cursed him. Because Ahab can't believe in accident, in bad fortune: there has to be a reason. And because there is no reason, he goes mad and creates the devil."

"Right," Ash said. "So it's a tale of madness and revenge."

"Or of a world without God," Dick said.

"Yes, without God. The Christian god. It's like a myth, you see? The myths are about the human things, you know—jealousy, and death, ambition. But there's also magic and ghosts and crazy creatures, right? And they are as real as you and I. *Moby-Dick* is the same." Rodrigo tapped the table with his index finger. "He's also real. This enormous, fantastic white whale. And the interesting thing is what happens not when Ahab meets this everything, this nothing, but when he meets the real whale."

"Well, we know what happens," Miller said. "He dies."

"Maybe." Rodrigo cocked an eyebrow. "Myths are open to all sorts of crazy interpretations."

"Well," Ash said. "You're the director, I guess."

"I've always found those *Grimms' Fairy Tales* very frightening," Cricket said. "I wouldn't read them to Suki when she was a child."

"I read them to Nate," Miller said. "But some of them were just, I don't know, depressing."

"I hated 'The Frog Prince,'" Cricket said.

"Yes, me too," Miller said, nodding vigorously.

"It was somehow awful and sad," Cricket said.

"I know. I think it's because somehow we're supposed to feel that the princess is a bad person because she doesn't want to kiss the frog. But really, why should she? She's not attracted to him, that's not her fault. And he's basically withholding her property in exchange for sexual favors. I mean, it's extortion."

"No," Ash said, "that's not the situation there. She's made a promise and then she thinks she can get away with not keeping it."

"No, that's not it," Olly said. "It's true she makes a promise and changes her mind. Okay. But then she gives in quite easily when he shows up at her door and says, 'You have to be with me.'" Olly shrugged. "It's obvious: she's fickle."

"Well," Cricket said, "I don't know. But wouldn't you promise someone like that whatever they asked, in hopes you could get away from them? So they wouldn't hurt you or follow you to the ends of the earth? I mean, it's clear he's never, ever going to leave her alone."

Something about the way she said it made them all look at her.

"It could go like that," she said, looking down at her plate.

"You know," Dick broke in quickly, "I think it's interesting what you said, Miller, before, about not needing His forgiveness."

"Dick . . ." Cricket said, looking down her plate.

"No, I do," he said, looking only at Miller.

"Well, I'll tell you, Dick." Miller could feel the wine and indignation running through her veins. "I was taught, in my religion, that God is in all of us. I might be confused, as a person, but I'm not so evil, so bad, that I don't have His grace. That was the way I was brought up, anyway. Though, honestly, I don't know that I believe in God anymore. Sorry. But I think I'm agnostic."

"Always hedging your bets," Olly said.

Miller shrugged. "I admit, I don't know everything."

"No, he's right," Ash said. "You've never met a fence you didn't want to sit on."

"Oh, that's rich, coming from you," Miller said.

Cricket got up, started clearing plates.

"I learned from the master," Ash said, finishing his drink.

"Seriously, Ash? You want to compete?"

"You don't want to compete with her, Ash," Olly said. "Trust me."

"Thanks, Olly. But you can fuck right off. I don't need lessons about my wife from you."

"Sorry," Dick said. "I didn't mean to start a fight."

They ignored him.

"From where I'm sitting, it looks like you might need some lessons." Olly smiled at Ash.

"Okay, I see," Ash said, nodding, looking between Olly and Miller. "That's fine. I can see what's going on here."

"What do you see, Ash?" Miller was furious. "By the way, your girlfriend called here looking for you. She left a message."

"I think we should go," Dick said, standing and going to Cricket, who was frantically rinsing dishes in the sink.

"What was the message?" Ash asked.

"That *you* can fuck right off."

"What?" Ash looked confused, like maybe that was the actual message.

Now it was Olly's turn to look surprised. "You have a girlfriend?"

"Shut up, Olly," Ash said, staring hard at Miller. "What did she say?"

"Seriously?"

"You obviously want to tell me," he said.

Miller stood and threw her napkin on the table. "I don't want to talk about it."

"Bye." They turned to see Dick pulling Cricket out the door. "Thanks for the lovely dinner," she said.

Miller felt the anger leave her as quickly as it had come on. "Nothing." She shook her head. "Nothing. She wants you to call her."

"You have a girlfriend?" Olly said again.

Miller went to the bar and poured herself another drink. "Candice Cressman."

"The morning TV host? Jesus."

"I don't want to be here," Ash said, rising. "I can't deal with this."

Miller turned her back on him, but she could feel him leaving, heard the snap of the screen behind him.

"This has been a good party," Rodrigo called in through the French doors.

Miller had almost forgotten about him. He must have slipped outside without her noticing. She could smell the smoke from his cigarillo: thick, rich. She raised her glass to him. "Thanks, I try."

"I'd like to stay," Rodrigo said. "But I think my exit is required for the next scene." He crushed out his smoke and came in. He took Miller's hand and kissed it. "I know what I said, but kissing when you leave is nice." He looked at Olly. "Good night, my friend." And then he, too, made his escape.

"So, that's why," Olly said, looking down at his hands. "That's why it happened."

"What?" Miller leaned against the wall next to the bar. She felt exhausted.

"Miller." He shook his head. "After all this time. You just can't, can you? You can't tell the truth." He rose from the table. "I don't want to be here, either."

She followed him to the door, like there was a string attaching her body to his, like he couldn't move without her moving, couldn't breathe without her involuntarily taking a breath also. She watched him walk through it. This time he didn't turn around.

She saw Nate and Suki walking towards the Pfeiffers' house, passing Olly on the drive.

He turned on them, suddenly. "You think it's all fine now," he said to them. "But you have no idea what you're going to do to each other."

She watched them watch him walk away, a kind of wonderment on their lovely, unetched young faces.

Nate sat by the edge of Suki's pool, looking at her in the half-darkness. Her bare shoulders were smooth, her feet ghostly pale under the chlorinated water.

"What do you think he meant?" Suki asked.

"Olly? Who knows," Nate said. He didn't care about Olly right now. He was looking at her hair, the shape of her head, so changed, so different now. "Can I touch it?"

Suki looked at him and nodded.

He ran the flat of his palm over it, from the crown of her head down to the nape of her neck. Then back, feeling the short hair ruffle up beneath his fingertips, like a soft brush.

"Why did you do it?" he asked.

"I wanted to be someone else."

"Why?"

"Because I'm not myself. Or that wasn't me."

He rolled up the cuffs of his jeans and put his feet into the water—silky, warm on top, cooler underneath. Under the water, Suki made circles with her foot. He could feel the pull and swell of the small tide against his own foot, his ankle, as if they were touching each other.

"I like it," he said, finally, feeling his voice catching in his throat.

She laughed. "You might be the only one. Cam clearly had strong feelings about it."

"Yeah, well," Nate said. "Cam." He shook his head. "That was some crazy shit."

Suki shrugged.

"What?" Nate said.

She bit her lip. "I don't know. He's been different this past year."

"In what way?"

"Just more intense, I guess. Darker." She pulled her feet up from the water and hugged her knees. "And the thing with Chris . . ."

Nate watched her.

"I don't know what happened, exactly," Suki said. "Only that Chris was making fun of him in the locker room, said something about his mom, and Cam went ballistic and just started smashing stuff up. He had some kind of breakdown. That's what they said. He was out of school for a couple of weeks."

"When was this?"

"Spring, I guess? Ever since then, Chris has been telling people he's crazy."

"Hunh," Nate said. "Do you think he's crazy?"

"No," Suki said.

"I don't either." He didn't, but he also didn't want to think about Cam anymore now. He wanted Suki to look at him, instead of the water or the hedge or the moon. He wanted her to look at him so that he could see if she felt the same way. He wanted to kiss her again, like he had that winter night in the square, ice crackling in the tree branches above them, the air sharp as a paring knife.

But she didn't look at him. Instead, she said: "I used to be friends with her, you know. Pam. We had a joint birthday party together. When we were twelve. At Cola Roller Rink." She bit her lip. "I don't know how that happens. How one day you love someone and then, the next, they hate you."

"I don't know," Nate said.

They sat in silence. Then Suki said: "Thanks for the tape, by the way."

"Of course," he said. "I wasn't sure you'd like it."

"I did. All the songs were really . . ."

He felt a kind of shame coming over him, waiting for the word she would use. "Sorry if it was too much," he said.

218

Then she did look at him. "No, it wasn't too much. It's just weird, listening to songs like that—the kind that make you feel a certain way . . ."

He thought it might be now or never. The way she looked at him, her large eyes like dark pools reflecting the water below them. The close, humid air, the night.

"Because"—she leaned back, resting on her palms—"they don't feel like they're about me. It's like I'm hearing a story that's supposed to be about me, but really it's about someone else. It's about how someone else sees me."

And just like that, the moment was over, gone.

The small airplane shook and shuddered, and Blue gripped the armrest of her seat to steady herself.

Blue had gotten her name, her mother said, because "I'd just been so blue when I was pregnant with you. I thought it must mean something."

Her parents were normal people, who lived in a small town in northern California. They lived in a nice, clean house in this nice, small town. There was a drug store with a soda fountain, and a high school and well-tended, if small, front lawns, and a hardware store and a movie theater. And Blue probably would have grown up to be a nice woman who lived in a nice, clean house in this same small town if a few surprising things hadn't happened to her. These surprising things had collected over time and given the impression of a plan, of fate.

The first happened when she was fourteen. She was hit by a car crossing the street. The man was drunk, a man from out of town, and he'd just mowed her down, crushing her leg. She'd developed gangrene and they'd amputated her left leg below the knee.

One night, after her surgery, she'd woken up in the hospital with the distinct impression that her leg had grown back. Or not grown back as much as it had floated back to her, somehow, from where it had been. It was so real that she could feel it, its molecular density. From that night onwards, the phantom limb taunted, tortured her with its there-not-thereness.

When she got home, while she was recuperating in bed, she'd spent all her time reading *Archie* comics and listening to the radio, and trying not to think about her leg. She'd sing all the billboard hits, pitching her voice to theirs. She was particularly good at the torch songs and the Burt Bacharach-type stuff. Dionne Warwick was her favorite: "Do You Know the Way to San Jose", "(There's) Always Something There to Remind Me", "I'll Never Fall in Love Again."

One day, she found an advertisement in the back of one of the comic books, hidden among the temptations of mail-order good-luck charms, Davy Crockett flashlights and promises to turn a 97-pound weakling into the perfect man. It had caught her eye because of the rhinestones: an ad for a life-sized doll, constructed of plastic, made-to-measure. The picture showed a doll, about the size of a six-year-old girl, with rhinestones on her arms and legs, and long dark hair like hers. It guaranteed "full radial movement."

She'd written a letter to the address provided and included her name and address: *I have no leg. A man ran over it. But it wants to come back. I'd like it to come back with rhinestones, like your doll. Please could you tell me how much it might cost? I'm only fourteen, but I have saved all my allowance.*

And that's when the next surprising thing that was going to happen happened to her: she met Trucky Lansome.

Trucky was small and neat, an engineer who'd studied prosthetics. He made the life-sized dolls as a sideline, he explained to her parents when he called the house, to earn extra money.

"Your daughter wrote me a letter," he said. "I'm interested in making a special prosthetic for her."

Trucky went on to say that he'd have to measure her and it might take a while to fit, but if they'd bring her to his clinic in Los Angeles, he could get started right away. It had seemed like providence, he said, that their little girl had written to him for his help.

And he couldn't ignore providence, or at least that's what his wife had told him.

"She said, 'Trucky, it's your duty to help this poor girl and her poor leg. God has brought her to you, and now it's your turn to do something for God.' Mrs. Trucky is a very determined woman," he'd told them.

Her parents had been bemused, but Blue had been ecstatic, and so, of course, they acquiesced. A few months—and several fittings and adjustments and trials—later, Blue had a leg with rhinestones running down the sides. It was the beginning of a new life.

Of course, it had not been without pain—the fittings and alignment tests could be agony before the prosthetic was perfected, and there was always the threat of infection. But when she donned Trucky's first prosthetic it had been a revelation. While the new leg gave her ghost leg back its corporeal body, gave it peace, she also realized that the real Blue was the girl who'd lost her leg below the knee. The other Blue, with the flesh and blood leg, had been a temporary aberration, an incomplete version. In short, destiny had transformed her into a higher being.

Over time, she and Trucky began experimenting with more unorthodox designs. Some were inspired by aesthetics: they were intricately painted, or deconstructed, or embellished with different materials—bits of hardware, ceramics, fake flowers. Some had a dream-like quality, like her corkscrew rhinestone leg—her Ahab leg, she called it, due to its white bone color and the way it tapered to a peg—a leg that could really only be used for a static function: standing still under a spotlight, for example. And yet others were developed with a specific purpose in mind, like dancing or going up and down hills or swimming (there had been an unfortunate foray into fins for swimming, which had been nothing short of a disaster at a pool party with Slade.)

Blue's first husband called Trucky "Svengali"; Slade hated him, hated the relationship he couldn't get in between. But Trucky wasn't like that. In fact, they rarely talked about personal things, or anything really, except their vision for Blue's leg, their vision for the various transformations that she required.

Part of what had bugged Slade so much was the way she and Trucky spoke to each other, their "secret bullshit language," he called it. It was true, they did have a private dialect. But that was because there was no language for this, none that she knew—one that included words like "torque" and "dorsiflexing," but that was also comprised of silence: of Trucky watching Blue's body language, her gait, her facial expressions when something hurt or wasn't right.

The surprising things that had happened to her in her life had made Blue believe in signs: The comic book advertisement that had led her to Trucky, Olly's unexpected appearance backstage after the Eidolon Lounge, the tour with Felix—all signs. Granted, many of the signs seemed to lead to a man. But, really, the only free agents in this world were men, anyway, and they were every-where, inescapable, so better to see them as a force of change, of surprise, of destiny, than as something worse.

However, signs were only as good, as powerful, as the ability to interpret them. You just had to know what to look for. Like a medium interpreting the spirit world. Blue believed in things like that. She was a California girl, after all; if a desert could be turned into an oasis, all manner of things were possible.

In her case, she'd found through experience that when a sign presented itself, it gave a kind of glow, it radiated some sort of signal, like a doorbell ringing. You never knew what would be behind the door, never knew where it would lead, or what its ulti-mate purpose was—it could mean fortune, fame, heartbreak—but it always meant change, and it had to be answered.

Yes, Blue believed in signs. And she believed that Rodrigo Rodrigo's phone call had been one of them.

The small plane touched down, bouncing as it hit the runway, and then finally came to a full stop. Blue descended slowly from the coolness of the cabin into the warmth of the summer night, adjusting her gate to the tarmac. The pilot carried her bag himself, smiling shyly.

They made their way through the small airport, out to the parking lot and Patty Tithe's waiting car.

"So," Blue said, when she settled herself in the front seat. "This is Wonderland."

Olly lay in the grass underneath the tree house, smoking, looking up at the moon.

He heard her footsteps moving softly across the damp lawn.

Then she was standing over him, barefoot, grass stuck to the tender arches.

He looked up at her. No sunglasses now.

He put out his cigarette and stood up.

"I'm scared," she said.

"I'm not doing this anymore," he said. "I'm not going to be a place holder for your real life."

"Don't say that," she said. "Don't ever say you're not going to do this again. I couldn't bear it, if I thought that."

He knew it was true. His heart felt tired, bruised, but she was right: it was now, and had always been, open to her. He'd always had a stupid heart.

"Okay," he said. "I won't say it."

She put her hand to his face.

"I remember this dress," he said. "I remember taking it off."

She lifted her arms. He bent down, and took the hem in both hands, pulling the dress over her head. She was naked underneath, the body he knew so well, the one that lit at his touch, that had moved underneath him and above him so many times. He knew all its muscle, all its delicate spots, its lengths and breadths. He knew what places to touch to make her come, to keep her from coming. And the sweetness, the aching fucking sweetness in all that knowledge.

"I'm scared," she said again.

"I don't want to talk anymore."

"Okay," she said. "No more talking."

PART IV

YOU MUST BE, OR YOU WOULDN'T HAVE COME HERE

BEGINNING OF JULY, 1984

WEEK 1

It was only six o'clock in the morning, but the ad hoc editing room they'd set up in the boathouse was already stuffy and Rodrigo was sweating as he rewatched the previous day's dailies on the flatbed Moviola.

He'd woken early again, with a feeling inside of him like his guts had been scooped out. It was becoming familiar, this feeling. It would only get worse, he knew, as things got more and more complicated, as it became necessary to deceive more and more people around him.

It was his habit to run through the dailies with his director of photography and his editor at the end of each day's shooting, but something in them, something that kept appearing in them, made him watch the scenes again this morning, as if to be sure.

He had the strange sense that while the movie was acting on the town, the town was also acting on his movie; the excitement of the townspeople here, their mania for the whale, their constant questions—Where was it? When would they see it? How big would it be?—like a pack of hungry wolves. He could see it in the film in front of him now—scenes from the Spouter-Inn—which had an eerie quality, tension flitting across the actors' faces, a haunted look about them. Looking at the rushes was like looking at people going mad. But then, maybe he was the one going mad.

He'd been pleased with his idea of bringing the whale over — he'd figured if the people of Wonderland knew it had had arrived, it would quiet them down. But it had seemed to have had the opposite effect. It was now a bigger mystery for them, and there had even been a headline, beneath a grainy photo of the trailer, in the town's weekly newspaper: *Is This Our Whale?* So he'd been forced to set up a Teamster out front, in case anyone had the idea of taking matters into their own hands and breaking in.

Even his cast had been questioning him, especially after seeing the "Whale" scene on the shooting schedule. He'd even had to go so far as to hire outside people for those deep-sea shots; he couldn't have anyone along for that who couldn't keep their mouth shut.

When Rodrigo had first seen Wonderland, he'd known that this weird, tidal island was the perfect location for what might be his greatest work; no, his greatest rebellion, to date: *Moby-Dick*. It was Olly's stories about his hometown that had first intrigued him about the place, and had led him to scout it in October.

And now here they were: the cast and crew had taken up camp in some old fishermen's shacks the studio had rented for them; they'd commandeered the large boathouse to store equipment, set pieces, and costumes, and to act as their improvised editing room; the Teamsters had been hired, the extras cast, the square-rigged ship moored out in the bay; shooting was well underway.

But Rodrigo, who had been so sure of his vision, of his abilities, had begun to doubt himself. Or, really, he was doubting Faramundo—Faramundo who had set this whole thing in motion; Faramundo's words whispered to him over and over that'd put him on this path to either potential triumph or potential disaster.

It was hard for Rodrigo to describe how exactly it was that he "heard" Faramundo: it wasn't like an actual voice in his head, like lunacy or a possession; it was more of a sense of him. A very slight phantom, maybe, like seeing your shadow. Anyway, he didn't talk about it often, so he wasn't called upon to explain himself articulately.

If anything, it was the story of Faramundo's death that he told, rather than the fact that his twin had kept on living after he'd come out of their mother's womb a tiny, flattened mummy. Rodrigo, on the other hand, had been fine, blooming, in fact: an extraordinarily healthy, fat, loud baby boy.

But despite that, or maybe because of it, their mother had been awash in grief, unable to understand what had happened, where she'd gone wrong. In order to provide some reassurance, to find some solid facts to help her deal with her sorrow, their father, an obstetrician in Mexico City who'd delivered his own children, had written to his colleagues on the subject and found that Faramundo was what had then only recently been termed a "vanishing twin." The theory was that one twin ate the other twin in the womb. Sometimes, the dominant twin would almost completely absorb the other; while in other cases, like that of Rodrigo and Faramundo, the dominant twin would only partially absorb his fluids and nutrients, compressing and draining his rival as he went, until the other became practically mummified, pressed thin, like a piece of papyrus.

Living in a doctor's house, these medical facts were explained to Rodrigo at an early age, their father believing that dispelling any mystery or secrecy would help Rodrigo not dwell on it, or develop superstitions. But what their father had not counted on was that once absorbed, Faramundo had gone on living in Rodrigo.

Rodrigo had never really questioned it, how Faramundo had guided and influenced his work. But now he was beginning to wonder if maybe, after all, he was just fucking crazy.

And even if he wasn't, what would the studio do, what would Seymour Geist do, when he saw what he'd created? Would Rodrigo's picture ever see the light of day? Did it matter?

It was Olly who'd been his champion at Obscura Pictures, Olly who'd convinced Geist that Rodrigo could deliver him something that the studio head desperately wanted—his very own *Jaws*. Or, to be exact, his very own rip-off of *Jaws*.

Geist, a practical man, had agreed to *Moby-Dick* as the vehicle for this because he didn't need to pay for the rights, and the story's fame was its own kind of publicity. This was a specialty of his: taking literary stories out of copyright and butchering them into gore and sex romps. He'd given Rodrigo a $5 million budget and agreed to shooting a good part of it on location. *Just don't make it too fucking depressing*, Geist had told Rodrigo. *This is a*

creature feature, not some literary bullshit. And I want to see tits.
Rodrigo had pointed out that most of the story took place on a
boat where there were no women aboard. *Well, they're on land for
the first fucking hundred pages, aren't they? Tits on land. And
maybe flashbacks to more tits.*

Also, Geist wanted a whale—a big, scary mechanical whale.
Rodrigo had been all too happy to go along with this fiction.

But then Olly had been fired—pushed out over a disagreement,
something about a *Doctor Zhivago II*—and Rodrigo was on his
own. It was only by chance—his phone call to Blue three weeks
ago—that he'd learned about Olly, what'd happened to him in
L.A., and about his return to Wonderland.

And when Olly had finally turned up at the Spouter-Inn,
Rodrigo could sense something had shifted in his friend. He
seemed softer, somehow, more still.

He couldn't deny that it was a sign, Olly washing up on the set
of *Moby-Dick*. Though a sign of what, he could not yet say.

He thought about Faramundo's words to him: *A conjurer's trick.*
Yes, yes, brother, a conjurer's trick.

"Are you talking to yourself now? That can't be a good sign."

Rodrigo turned to see Blue standing in the doorway of the
dusty boathouse in a floaty zebra-print thing, her dark hair parted
in the middle.

He smiled.

"You called?" she said.

Rodrigo rose, walked to her, took her hands in his.

"What's with the Teamster guarding the front?" she said, hooking
her thumb behind her. "Has someone put a bounty on your life?"

"To keep nosy villagers away from my whale."

"Funny, I didn't see anyone with pitchforks."

He shrugged.

"So," she said, "let me get this straight: You call me down here
for some top-secret, last-minute soundtrack recording, and I find
you in an old—what is this, a warehouse? Boat store?—under
guard, talking to yourself." She raised an eyebrow. "What in the
Sam Hill is really going on here, Rodrigo?"

He held her away from him. "Beautiful, as always," he said.

She snorted. "Right." She disentangled herself and walked into the center of the boathouse, looked up towards the ceiling of the octagonal building, at the gallery that wound around it. "If all I needed was flattery, I wouldn't have to fly so far to get it." She looked back at him.

"Okay, okay," he said. "It's true. It's a little more . . . complicated than that."

"I'm all ears," Blue said. She walked over to the Moviola, and began running the film forward, shifting her weight, resting her palms on the table. The sounds of Beethoven's Ninth Symphony roaring out. She raised a groomed eyebrow at him.

"I know. They all look fucking crazy, don't they?"

Blue stopped it. "The 'Ode to Joy'?"

"Well, the work of a madman, a genius. Right? A song of love, of freedom. It's the fucking 'Marseillaise of humanity.'" He smiled at her. "It was also Hitler's birthday song, and they made them sing it at the camps. And, in World War I, German prisoners of war sang it to the Japanese. And they played it for their kamikazes in World War II." He shrugged. "It is, as they say, an empty vessel, meaning nothing and everything."

"Oh, boy," Blue said.

"*Oh, boy,*" Rodrigo said, nodding.

"Well, it's your style." She sat down in the swivel chair Rodrigo had had shipped from California, and rotated a few times. "So," she said, "does he know I'm here?"

"Does it matter?"

"Well, it might to him."

Rodrigo turned away. "Oh, we're all adults here," he lied. "Anyway," he said more brightly, "have you seen your sound booth?" He pointed to the wooden box standing in a corner of the boathouse. "I had it built just for you."

Blue walked over, opened the door, looked inside. "Fancy."

"Listen, some poor kid had to spend his whole day finding that shit, and some poor bastard Teamster had to put it together."

"It's everything a girl could dream of."

Rodrigo smiled. "Good. So, where are you staying?"

"I'm staying with Patty. In one of those *lovely* shacks of yours."

"Oh, well, Patty," Rodrigo said, waving his hand. "She wouldn't be satisfied until she'd kicked some poor old fisherman out of his home so she could be right in the middle of the action."

"Actually, I think the place was being used for storage. She's paying a fortune to some guy for the privilege of sleeping in a glorified lean-to."

"My story's better," Rodrigo said. "Anyway, it wasn't a shack for long. I think she got the whole fucking Sears catalogue delivered there."

"It *is* quite a glamorous lean-to," Blue said. "Anyway, enough about my accommodations. Where's this whale of yours?"

Rodrigo looked at her, smiled. "Right here."

Blue looked around the boathouse, confused. "Where?"

"Come," he said, and walked across the room and out the door.

He led Blue to the large trailer parked under the trees out back and up the ramp, offering her a hand. She shook her head no.

Rodrigo pulled aside part of the tarp covering the locks. Reaching into his pocket, he took out the key chain with the four keys, which he always kept on him. He unlocked the padlocks and removed them. He pushed up the bolt. "Ready?"

"I mean . . . sure," Blue said, standing back a bit.

He took a door in each hand and pulled hard until they parted. Blue moved forward, squinting into the darkness. He waited while she looked.

"Oh," she said, finally. "Oh, I see."

After the dinner party, after that first time out in the cool night, grasping, hurried, against a tree, they'd agreed to a motel over the bridge. Not in Longwell, but further out, off the two-lane highway.

Olly drove them in Aunt Tassie's old Oldsmobile. He drove carefully, it seemed, just above the speed limit. They didn't look at each other as they passed over the bridge, the water sparkling below. They didn't look at each other as they rolled past the banks of pine and oak and tangled vines wending between the branches, past a strawberry stand, a hand-printed sign for wool, past lumber yards and boat yards. The sun drew triangles on the dashboard in the silence. A hot breeze blew through the car, the occasional odor of a dead skunk pressing up, oily and rich, through the open windows.

When they arrived at the Moonrise Inn—a semi-circle of one-story bungalows next to a gas station—Olly parked and they walked through the glass doors into the reception area: threadbare green and red paisley carpet, beadboard walls. She hated it. But one of them had suggested it and the other had agreed—she couldn't remember which now—so they were both complicit. The bored young man behind the counter gave them a key to room 238. Miller tried to find significance in the number and came up with nothing.

She kept her sunglasses on until they entered the room and Olly shut the door, enveloping them in a semi-gloom. The bedspread was clean—yellow chenille—and she sat down on the edge. Olly was busying himself with removing things from the back pocket of his madras shorts—wallet, keys.

She noticed how clean and crisp his white button-down shirt was. "I'm just going to take a quick shower," she said, standing up and heading toward the door to the bathroom.

"Oh." Olly looked up, confused. "Okay."

She flipped the switch and shut the door behind her. The fluorescent tube light cast the small white bathroom almost blue. It was the saddest place she'd ever seen. It made her feel empty and inhuman and like she wasn't in real time, somehow. She couldn't bear to take a shower in it, though now it would look strange if she didn't. So she stripped out of her cut-offs and tank top and turned the taps on. She wet her hands under the spray and patted them over her body. Then she wrapped herself in the small white towel that smelled of bleach, and turned the shower off again.

She opened the door, and suddenly the gloomy, boxy room felt like a relief.

"Now I feel like I should take one, too," Olly said.

So she sat back down on the bed wrapped in the towel and looked at her feet, which looked long and white against the dark carpet.

After a few minutes, Olly emerged, stood in the doorway illuminated, towel around his waist, his dark hair wet and slicked back off his forehead.

She looked up at him. "I don't want to do this again."

His eyes, dark, liquid, watched her.

"I mean, in a place like this," she said.

He ran his hand through his hair. They stared at each other across the room. She tucked the corner of the towel tighter around her breasts.

"Me, either," he said, finally. "Come on. We're leaving."

And in a rush of dressing, and fumbling with zippers, and clothes sticking to damp skin, they were out the door and into the sunshine, Olly grabbing her hand and running with her toward the reception, where he threw down some bills and the key, and then they were in the car and driving fast away from there, back towards Wonderland.

Miller laughed out loud, the air whipping her blonde hair across her face, stinging her top lip, sticking in the corner of her mouth. Olly looked at her and smiled. She put her feet up on the dashboard and reached for the radio dial. He caught her hand, stayed it. Then he held it and drove them home.

He parked the car outside the entrance to the Little Forest and took a blanket out from the trunk. Neither of them talked or looked around as they walked the path into the heart of the small woodland. Off a side path, past the frog pond, they ducked into a circle of shrubs, one they used to play hide-and-seek in when they were children, and Olly spread out the blanket.

Miller got undressed, this time in the hot July sun, and reflexively made a mental catalogue of all the ways her body had changed since he'd last seen her, shrank from them.

But then he stared so hard at her and said: "My god, you're beautiful." And after that she didn't care about anything except the way he saw her: standing there glowing and perfectly formed.

She sank to her knees on the blanket and pulled him down next to her and they lay facing each other, their legs entangled. She ran her hand over his body—his chest, his forearms, his thigh—and she'd forgotten about his skin, so tight across him, across his bones and muscle and sinew, holding him in place, supple and smooth. He reached down between her legs and she reached between his, felt him, and she tasted his mouth, salty, cigarette smoke clinging to it. He was watching her, fixated on her—her mouth, her brow. She closed her eyes, but she could still feel his gaze, like a drill. When she opened them again, she saw his expression, lashes lowered: concentrated, insistent, almost ruthless; she could feel him willing her to come, feel him wanting it, wanting only that, consumed himself by her desire.

Later, they lay on the blanket half-dressed and Olly smoked. Idly, he ran his hand down the center of her throat, down her clavicle, tracing the curve and dip of her breast over her tank top.

She lay back. "I don't want this to be a secret." She turned away from him so she could think clearly. "I mean . . . that's not what I mean, exactly," she said. "I don't want Nate to know."

"No," he agreed.

"But I don't want to pretend, either," she said.

"I'm not sure how that works," Olly said.

"Me, either," she said.

They were silent for a while.

"Would you like to go out to dinner? Tomorrow night? Somewhere in town? Is that how it works?"

"Maybe," she said. "Maybe that's how it works. I don't know. Let's see."

"I'm worried about him," Jess said. "Something's not right."

"What's not right?" Nate said, looking up. "I mean besides the Stodges thing . . ."

Jess had paid him a surprise visit on set, and he was listening to her as he set out Styrofoam coffee cups for the crew's break.

"I don't know," Jess said, leaning against the folding table, making the cups shiver. "He's just acting weird. Weirder than usual."

"You're gonna have to give me a little more than that, Jess." He righted some of the cups that had fallen over.

"Okay, well, he's talking about his mom a lot."

"What's he saying?"

Jess made way for the catering lady carrying the coffee urn. Nate took it from her and positioned it on the table.

"I don't know, it doesn't really make sense. Something about his mom coming back?"

"When?" Nate turned to face Jess, shading his eyes with his hand. "Recently?"

"No, no." Jess waved him away. "A long time ago, I think. When he was a kid?"

"Oh, that," Nate said.

"What's 'Oh, that'?"

"Nothing. Don't worry about it. Is that it?"

"I don't know, he just keeps talking about how she came back for him, and how now he has to find her, so they can be together. He's just become obsessed with it, like it's a real plan, like she's going to save him or something. And also he's been weird about you and Suki."

"What about me and Suki?"

"I don't know, it's not exactly coherent stuff. Anyway, you know Cam—it's not like he's great at expressing his emotions. But I'm worried, after what happened this spring, that he's flipping out. Maybe permanently."

Nate thought about a nature program he and Cam had watched once, about how disfigured animals coped in packs. It had talked about wild dogs who'd lost their tails. One of two things happened to those dogs: either they learned new ways to compensate— moving their whole bodies like a tail to communicate pleasure, fear, hostility; or they ended up dead, through expulsion and then

238

starvation, or pack aggression. He remembered how Cam had been completely absorbed in it, and then afterwards had said quietly: *That's me.*

"Hello? Earth to Nate?" Jess said

Nate shrugged. "I don't know."

"Well, it's weird, Nate," she said, positioning her newspaper print shirt so that it hung off one small, round shoulder. "And you're his friend, so you should talk to him."

"Okay, okay," he said. "I'll talk to him." The crew had begun to swarm the table and Nate and Jess walked over to the boardwalk, leaving them to it. "Have you seen Suki?"

"Yes." Jess smiled at him. "I've seen her."

"How is she?" He hadn't seen her since he'd left her at her pool.

"You know, you can always ask her yourself."

Nate was silent.

Jess eyed him, and he found himself shifting uncomfortably. She folded her arms across her chest. "It's really hard for you, isn't it?"

"What?"

"Having to actually work for something."

"Jesus, Jess. That's harsh." He picked up a loose cable apparently forgotten by the crew and started coiling it.

"All I'm saying is—you're a guy." She pointed her finger at him. "A very specific, lucky kind of guy." She smiled. "But I like you, Nate, and I'm sure you'll be able to figure this one out."

He laughed.

Jess laughed, too, and sat down on the edge of the boardwalk, her bare legs dangling above the harbor.

Nate sat down next to her.

She nudged him with her shoulder. "So, where's your new boyfriend? Thought you guys were always together these days."

"Olly? I don't know," Nate said. "Haven't seen him for a couple of days." The last time he'd seen him was the night of the bonfire, coming from his parents' house, yelling something crazy at him and Suki. The next day, Nate's dad had left for the city. He'd wondered if perhaps he'd gone too far, trying to help his parents. But then he'd thought that, no, sometimes you needed to shake things up.

"I can't wait to get out of this fucked-up town," Jess said.

"I don't know. I don't think I realized how interesting it is here, you know? I always thought of it as kind of boring."

Jess shook her head, rose. She started to walk away then turned back. "You know, Nate, just because you think it's so *interesting* doesn't mean people aren't going to get hurt for real."

"I don't even know what that means," he called after her.

"That's because you don't know anything," she called back.

Olly was getting ready to take Miller out. They'd decided—over the phone—on Acapella, the one Italian restaurant in town, owned and run by the decidedly Swedish-sounding Lundgrens. There really wasn't a whole lot to choose from in Wonderland's food scene, and while Acapella wasn't great, it did have a nice view of the harbor off its deck.

Olly knew what he was doing was dangerous. Not just because it could jeopardize his relationship with Nate, but also because he couldn't stop thinking about her, wanting her. And wanting Miller had always proved to be a dangerous pastime.

By letting this thing go on, he was skating recklessly close to the past. And he knew, from painful experience, that the past was a black hole whose gravitational force was so strong that it might crush him if he ventured too close.

And yet, here he was showering, combing his hair, putting on his red Izod shirt and khakis, slipping into his old espadrilles and setting out to meet her. Because even if he knew all that, he still couldn't stop.

They'd agreed to meet at the restaurant, the way friends would. Olly had called ahead and booked a table and by the time he arrived, she was already seated outside, close to the edge of the deck overlooking the southern limit of the harbor. He saw her before she saw him, and he thought she looked lovely in a white tunic kind of dress and gold hoops, her sunglasses pushed up on top of her damp hair. She was fiddling with her napkin, smoothing it, pulling one corner down. The table was decked out in a red and white check cloth, with one of those ridiculous wax-covered wine bottles sporting a worn-down candle. The sound of Domenico Modugno—the instrumental versions—wafted through from the main dining room, though luckily it was almost inaudible once Olly reached the table.

When she saw him, Miller started to stand and then sat down again abruptly.

"Hi," he said, smiling, taking the chair opposite.

"Hi." She spoke in a nervous, breathy sort of way, like she was trying to get the words out quickly.

Olly looked out at the harbor and around at the other tables, mostly empty. "Guess I didn't need to reserve."

"I think it starts to fill up around eight?" she offered.

"Oh, right." Then: "What time is it?"

"Seven."

"Oh, right. I knew that."

Miller smiled.

The waitress came with some menus. Miller ordered a glass of Chianti and Olly followed suit.

"So," he said, once the waitress had departed, "this is nice."

"Yes." Miller fidgeted with her hoop earring.

They sat in silence until the waitress returned with their drinks. Miller picked up her glass and took a big, long gulp, then set it carefully back down. She looked at him, smiled, took a deep breath. "Sorry," she said. "This is just . . ."

"Weird?"

"Yes. Very weird. Deeply weird."

He laughed, relaxed a little. "Yeah. Maybe this isn't how it works, after all."

"Let's try to be normal," she said, straightening her back,

arranging herself in her chair. "What do normal people talk about?"

"Their jobs, their families, their children."

"Right." She nodded, grimaced. "Anything else?"

Olly shrugged. She really did look lovely.

"And how's Aunt Tassie?"

"She's, you know . . . Billy Budd." He lit a cigarette. "I took her to see Dr. Cleves. He said it's probably a form of dementia, not uncommon at her age, I guess. And that I should keep an eye on her, watch for signs that it's getting worse."

"You two are getting along."

"What do you mean?" He narrowed his eyes. "Why wouldn't we?"

Miller laughed. "Oh, Olly."

"What?"

"You left Wonderland twenty-five years ago because you were angry with her. And you never came back. What do you think I mean?"

He shrugged.

"Is it weird being in the house again?"

"Look," he said, "let's drop it."

She nodded. "Anyway . . ." she said. Her hair was drying in the breeze, curling up around her face.

They both looked out at the harbor and then back towards each other. Miller smiled again, brushed an imaginary crumb off her dress.

"More wine?" Olly suggested.

"Oh, my god, yes," she said. "A lot more wine."

He signaled the waitress who was guiding another couple to a table.

"So," he said after the second round of drinks had been delivered. "Have you heard from Ash?"

"Oh, so straight in," she said. "I didn't know we were playing that game."

"I think you started this game."

Now it was her turn to shrug. "Ash. Well, I haven't heard from him, really. He called—you know, the morning after the party—to say he was staying on in the city for a while. And he'd be in touch. And to give Nate his love. And . . . that's it."

"Do you think Nate knows what's going on? With you two, I mean."

"No," she said. "I don't know. Maybe." She sighed. "But marriage is hard." She paused. "Ours has been hard lately, anyway. So that's nothing new in our house, I guess."

"Sorry."

"Oh, come on, give me a break."

"No, I'm sorry it's hard, not sorry it's . . . fuck, I don't know, Miller."

"Well, it seems that Nate talks more to you than he does to me at the moment."

"Really?"

"Don't sound so smug," she said.

"Well, he doesn't talk to me about that, if it makes you feel any better."

"It does," she said, curtly. She took her sunglasses off her head, folded them and put them in her handbag.

A sharp silence lay between them; this wasn't going at all as he'd planned.

"You look so lovely," he said, finally. "I've been meaning to tell you that since I came in. I don't know why I haven't. I'm an idiot. I'm sorry."

She kept her eyes on her handbag, but he could see the corners of her lips curl up in a smile. "Thank you."

"We should order," he said. "And then I want to go somewhere I can take that clean white dress off you."

She laughed, a throaty sort of laugh, and he knew then that she wanted him, too; that it was going to be okay.

The waitress returned with their bottle of wine and then again a little later with the food they'd ordered.

"Penne alla vodka?" Olly said, looking at her plate. "Is that even Italian?"

"Who cares?" Miller said. "It's delicious."

"You need to get out of Wonderland more often."

"I do," she agreed, taking a big mouthful of the pasta.

And he felt good—the food, the flush of the wine, the smell of her perfume. Then Miller said: "Don't look up."

And because of the way she said it, and because it was her, he didn't. He kept his eyes focused on his slightly gelatinous-looking Chicken Piccata.

"It's Blue."

Then of course he did look up. Blue was being led to a table on the other side of the deck, followed by Patty Tithe.

The last time Olly had seen Patty had been the day he'd been fired from Obscura Pictures. The day before he'd swallowed a handful of Seconal next to his swimming pool in a pair of salmon-colored Ralph Lauren swim shorts.

Patty had been on the lot, ostensibly doing reshoots for *Crawling to Babylon*, the second picture by Billy Kent, a former Western star from the '60s and '70s whose recent directorial debut, *Slick Bodies*, had been a surprise critical hit for the studio and had transformed him into that special sort of movie monster: the *auteur*. And Olly remembered that he and Patty, white teeth and laugh lines, all freckles and golden skin, had chatted about Blue, about Blue's tour with Felix Farrow, from which she was returning that afternoon. And the reason he remembered it so well was because that day was also the last time he'd seen Blue.

"Are you okay?" Miller reached out her hand, grabbed his. "You look . . ."

"Yeah," Olly said. "It's just . . ."

"Did you know she was here?"

"No."

"Oh, god. Should we go?"

"Yeah," he said. "Yes."

"Okay," Miller said. "You just go. I'll pay and meet you outside."

Olly took another look at Blue. Her long, dark hair was parted in the middle, pulled back in a ponytail and she had on some silky jumpsuit. She looked like a million bucks. Olly looked back at

Miller. "No," he said. "It's fine. We'll walk out together."

Olly didn't bother asking for the check, just threw some bills on the table to cover it—he was doing a lot of that lately—and stood, holding his arm out to Miller. She took it, and they walked across the deck toward the main dining room. He had to exert a certain amount of willpower not to look to see if Blue had clocked him, but he managed.

They passed through the restaurant and were almost away, when a woman stopped Miller.

"Miller, fancy meeting you here," she said, kissing Miller's cheek.

"Hi, Mary," Miller said, then stood awkwardly for a moment. When the woman didn't move, or give the slightest indication that she meant to, Miller said: "Do you know Olly Lane? Olly, this is Mary Guntherson."

"I don't believe I've had the pleasure," Mary said. She smiled at them both. "Well," she said, finally, "enjoy your evening." Before they could make their escape, though, Mary leaned in close, her lips almost touching Miller's ear, and stage-whispered: "Good for you."

Olly watched Miller's face in profile, saw her features harden and set into unhappy lines.

Then they left, and quickly, outside into the fresh air, safe for the moment, anyway.

"Well, that went well," Olly said, and smiled.

Miller looked at him and began to laugh, and she laughed until she shook. Olly started to laugh too, and soon they were both doubled over, tears streaming down their faces. They leaned against the clapboard building collecting themselves.

"Oh, my god," Miller said. "That was the worst date in history."

"No, really. Jesus," Olly said, wiping his eyes.

They began to walk. The sun had set, but it had left some of its glow behind. The purple-blue of the sky cast a haze across the brightly colored houses, muting their tones as they walked, down the narrow streets, past the well-tended roses, the willow and cherry trees muscling their way through the sidewalks. Miller's shoe caught on an uneven brick and Olly reached out to steady her, her fingers sliding through his. A couple of kids on bikes rode by, their hands behind their heads, cool as cucumbers, legs pedaling smoothly. Dishes clanked through open windows. All these things, this small, profuse life, closed in on them.

Their path led them to Foster Street, through the side gate, across the lawn and to Olly's tree house, where he did what he had promised and got Miller out of her clean white dress.

Afterwards, they lay on the pile of wool blankets on the floor, Olly smoking and Miller staring at the ceiling.

"She's very beautiful," Miller said. "Even more beautiful in person."

"She is."

"Was it hard to see her?"

"Straight in, hunh?"

"Not exactly straight in." She gave him a cracked half-smile.

Olly, cigarette between his lips, shifted onto his back, put his hands behind his head. "It was a surprise . . ."

"Right."

". . . but it wasn't hard to see her, not in the way I think you're implying." He crushed out his cigarette. He looked at her. He brushed a small curl away from her skin with the tip of his finger.

She watched him as if she were waiting for something, something bad, maybe.

"Miller, I never loved anyone the way I loved you. Not her, not anyone. How could I? We're all tangled up together."

Her eyes on him, a deep blue, dark, almost violet, in the evening light. "Me, either."

"Seeing Blue . . . reminds me . . . Just something I'd rather forget."

"It's hard to forget," she said, looking back at the ceiling.

"Yes, it is."

After Olly had seen Patty on the lot that day, things had unraveled quickly. He'd been called to Seymour Geist's office, and in an instant, his job—his career, really—was finished. What had made getting fired from Obscura particularly devastating was that he'd known there was no going back to what he'd had before; it wasn't just that Geist would keep control of Lay Down, but that music itself had left him.

By the time Olly had arrived back at The Bower, his life was fraying dangerously.

The house had been quiet inside and he could remember heading out to the terrace, down to the pool. He could remember thinking it was the color of heaven. And he'd thought maybe if he just jumped in, and held his breath and then inhaled it, and died, maybe he wouldn't have to worry about all the hours between that moment and whenever it was going to get better.

But instead, he'd turned away and gone back inside. He'd found Blue in the bedroom moving between the closet and the Spanish Revival bed, where an open suitcase sat, half-empty. She'd just returned that afternoon from her tour with Felix Farrow and The Forgotten, and he could remember her turning, holding several dresses over her arm, and how she'd stopped what she was doing and taken a deep breath.

He could see her dark hair spilling over her left shoulder, one long brown leg and her cheetah-painted prosthetic extending beneath a pair of short shorts. He could smell her perfume, Shalimar, filling the bedroom.

"Blue." He had that feeling that he was going to cry despite himself, like when he'd been a small child and he'd held some grievance in until he got home to his mother, when he would cry passionately, almost uncontrollably, soaking her blouse.

"Olly, I'm sorry," Blue had said, standing still, stricken.

Someone must have called her, Olly had thought at the time, to warn her he'd been fired. Maybe Gloria? "It's all such a goddamn mess. I don't know what I'm going to do." And then he was crying.

"It's not your fault. God, Olly. It's all mine. I'm so, so sorry. I . . . I've been a coward. I didn't mean for this to happen. It just did . . ."

And that's when it'd begun to dawn on Olly that they were talking at cross purposes. "What's your fault?" Then he'd looked at the suitcase and he realized that she wasn't unpacking it, she was packing it. She was taking her stuff. Blue was leaving him.

He'd stopped crying. "Blue?"

"Olly?" The concern for him had drained from her face, a different kind of worry replacing it, as she, too, understood they hadn't been talking about the same thing.

"Are you fucking leaving me?"

"Oh, Olly." Blue had put the dresses in the suitcase, and sat down on the edge of the bed. "Yes, I'm leaving you. I've fallen in love with Felix."

"I'm sorry, what? Felix Farrow? That smackhead?"

"Yes," she said. "That smackhead Felix Farrow."

"Have you lost your mind?"

"Maybe," she said, shaking her head, as if she'd already interrogated herself on this point and hadn't come up with a satisfactory answer. "I don't know."

"Don't you love me anymore?" He knew this was a pathetic question, a groveling, weak question. And he was disgusted with himself for asking it.

"I don't know." She looked at him straight, those dark, dark eyes. "If I do, I can't feel it. And that happened before Felix. Olly . . ." She held out her hand, but he just backed away. "Right. Well, the truth, then. You saved me, Olly. And we fell in love. But god, you have to control everything. Not like Slade, you're not bad, or a bully. But you don't really *live*, Olly. You know, it's all perfect, our life is perfect. But it's like being in a painting or a photograph. There's no room for anything other than what you've decided in advance can be there. There's no *feeling*."

Olly stumbled back, as if he'd been hit. "That," he said, "is the most bullshit thing I have ever heard, Blue. I mean, what the hell does that even mean? I love you, I've loved you since I first saw you—that's not some fucking photograph. Those *are* feelings. My goddamn feelings."

"Do you love me? Really? I mean, in the way you know you should?" She shook her head. "I'm sorry, Olly. What do you want me to say? I'm obviously not as good a person as you are; in fact, I'm probably a really bad person. I'm imperfect and I have messy emotions and I can't toe the line and I do disagreeable things sometimes. Awful things, like fall out of love and hurt good people." She got up and started closing the suitcase.

It was then he noticed that she was wearing one of his old Lay Down Records T-shirts, and rage overtook his panic.

"You can't take these things. You can't just leave me. You can't have that fucking shirt. Or that suitcase. Or anything in this house." He yanked the suitcase off the bed, Blue's clothes tumbling to the ground. "It all belongs to me: I'm the one who got you out of your marriage, got your money back, got you sorted out. Fuck you."

Blue let the dress she was holding fall from her hand and she backed away from the bed, shrugged. "Okay, I don't need these things, Olly. I've started over before, I can do it again." She shook her head, pity in her eyes. "I don't care. Those things don't matter. But whatever I've done to you, however horrible I'm being, you *do* matter to me." She walked over to him and lay her hand against his cheek. He wanted her to stop, to never stop. "I don't know what's going on with you. But, whatever it is, maybe it's not such a bad thing." She looked at him. "Olly, my love, sometimes you just have to mess up your life to live it."

Then she kissed him full on the mouth and walked out of the room, down the hall, out the front door, off the property, into Felix's waiting car. And with her went the last shred of anything that had held him tethered to his life.

Miller was getting dressed. She pulled the tunic over her head and looked around her. "It's nice here," she said.

He watched her, her long, graceful shape, long fingers covered in rings, bangles on her slim wrists. He could see Nate in her. Or the other way around, he supposed.

"You're welcome to move in," Olly said.

249

"Tempting." She slid her sandals on. "Run away from my life. Live in a tree house."

"It's not running from life," he said. "It's about keeping things clear. Keeping them simple."

"I see," she said. "God forbid things get complicated."

"Exactly. There be dragons." He smiled, though he knew that he'd already landed on perilous shores. He just hoped that Blue had been right, and that he would end up living his life, not just messing it up. Because while, in many ways, he felt far away from the man who had made such a dangerous and desperate and stupid choice, there was always the undeniable possibility that what he'd allowed himself to do once, he might do again.

"So, you're just here for the simple life, then." Miller laughed.

"I'd like for things to be simple." He propped himself on his elbow. "But that's not why I came back."

"Oh?" she said, lightly—falsely, he thought. "Why did you come back?"

He didn't move his gaze from her. "I think you know."

She checked her earrings, and patted down her hair, which was disarranged from their lovemaking. Finally, she looked at him. "Do I?"

Then she walked over, bent down, and kissed him on the mouth. And before he could answer, she disappeared down the ladder.

"Is this place really called Wonderland?" Gordon, the executive producer at *Morning? Morning!*, was sitting across from Candice in his office on the 32nd floor in midtown Manhattan, looking skeptical.

"It is, Gordon. And it's perfect. This little, hokey, one-horse pueblo, that's been practically cut off from civilization, has a big studio movie come to town. It's the perfect segment for us. And I want to do it."

250

"Do our viewers want to see movie stars swanning around, drinking champagne at eight o'clock in the morning?" Gordon said, tapping his pencil eraser against his desk.

"It's not about the movie stars." Candice leaned forward, projecting professional intimacy, or at least that's what her coach said it did. "It's about the real folks, how their lives have been transformed by movie magic. You know—a shot of Marge and Ben at the pancake house, Pretty Penny on the beach, Mayor Mudville looking proud. Are the stars just like you and me? Are they scared the whale is going to eat them? Whatever." She leaned back. "It's cute. It's fun. It's *summer*." It'll also get me the hell away from Clark Dennis, she did not add.

"Okay," Gordon said, also leaning back. "But let's send a field reporter. We need you here."

"No, Gordon, listen. This is a chance for America to get to know me, out and about, relaxed. Engaging with the average Joe. It'll be great for the show."

Gordon inclined his head. But before he could answer, the office door opened and there stood none other than Dickweed Dennis. *Fuck.*

"A little bird told me that you're pitching a hometown-meets-tinseltown story. Naughty." Clark waggled his finger at her. "But seriously, my feelings are hurt, Candice."

"Oh, Clark," she said, making a moue of disappointment at his accusation. "*I'm* hurt. No, I'm more than hurt, I'm mortified you'd think I'd keep *you* out of the loop. It's just that it's such an itty, bitty segment, I didn't think you'd be interested." She widened her eyes. "I mean, after all, you're the gold standard of serious morning reporting."

"Well, true," he said, seating himself very close to Candice on the producer's small blue, nubbly couch. "But that can get exhausting, honey, always being the grown-up in the room."

"Of course," Candice said, sympathetically. "But it might be a tad grim for you—it's so short notice. And over a weekend."

"No, I think this sounds fun. I'd like to let my hair down a little. What do you say, Gordon?"

"Guys," Gordon began, "we really don't need both of you to do this. We don't need either of you to do this, actually."

Candice could feel Dickweed's finger sliding up the side of her skirt. She didn't move an inch. Through Gordon's big office window, Candice could see into the high-rise across the street—the office workers, like tiny ants moving from room to room while outside the June sunshine bleached the pavement. She had a sudden fantasy that one of those ants would pry open their window and shoot Dennis Clark right in the head.

"Gordon," Clark said, in the cajoling tone he was so fond of, "come on. When do I ever ask you for a favor?"

"Well, actually, Clark . . ."

As she vaguely felt Clark's hand make its way over her thigh towards the top of her L'eggs pantyhose, Candice realized that this was now just one more thing she would have to handle.

She'd come up with the idea of doing the segment a few days after Ash had explained how things stood with his wife and his ex-best friend. But it was no good Dickweed Dennis coming to Wonderland, too, when she had to help Ash take care of his situation. She couldn't be fighting off the pervert every ten minutes, and be on her game.

It was the same with Ash, really. She liked fucking Ash, she liked being with Ash. But Ash needed handling. He'd be eaten alive, from what she could gather, by the wishy-washy, ethereal yet ruthless Miller, and the victim-playing, savvy Olly. The man simply couldn't make a decision to save his life. Which was fine. Candice was good at handling things and she liked doing it. This, she knew, made them perfect for each other.

And maybe, she thought now, it was high time she began handling Dickweed, too.

"He's right, Gordon," she said. "It'll help cement our chemistry with the viewers. I mean, I know some of them were upset when Susan left." The finger stopped in its tracks. Candice gave Clark an "aw-shucks" look. "They were so good together, even I can admit that, though it stings a little." She looked down sadly, but not too sadly.

"Fine," Gordon said, putting down his pencil. "I don't want to hear about it anymore. You do it over a weekend, you stay somewhere budget and you drive there."

"*Gordon*," Clark said.

"Okay, you fly. But no extracurricular expenses."

"Deal," Clark said, smiling, withdrawing his hand from Candice's skirt.

"Deal," Candice said, giving her most *Morning? Morning!* smile.

It was early evening and Miller had been writing all day. She was sitting in the chintz chair, the French doors open allowing the sharp, sugary scent of privet and hot grass to blow in, her pen moving across the lined page at speed. There was a new urgency to her words now; she felt the danger of Olly's presence and of Ash's absence like a portent, and she knew she would have to work quickly to outrun the impending collision.

"What are you writing?"

She hadn't heard Nate come in. He bent down, resting his head on her shoulder. She had to will herself not to shut the book with a sudden snap. "Just some thoughts," she said, closing it slowly, carefully. She rose. "Did you just get off work?"

"Un-hunh." Nate ambled over and buried his head in the refrigerator.

"You hungry?"

"Starving."

"I think there's some of that stew left in the freezer. The one your dad made." She shuffled Nate to the side a little and took the stew out—a gray, grainy frozen cube interred in Tupperware. "Honey, would you pour me a glass of wine?"

Nate walked to the bar while she banged out the stew into a saucepan on the stove, returning with a glass of wine for her and one for himself.

"What are your plans tonight?" she asked. "Are you going to see Cam?"

"Nah," Nate said.

The way he said it—almost too casually—made her look at him. "Everything okay?"

Nate shrugged. "I don't know."

Miller stirred the stew, breaking up frozen chunks of carrot and meat. "Well," she said. "It can be a hard time for some people your age—you know: what to do next. Dick said Cam was going to Longwell Community College? Maybe it's making him anxious, all the change."

"Maybe," Nate said. "I don't think he's going to go, though."

"Really? What's he going to do?" She turned the burner down low.

"I don't know, Mom. I don't think I really know him anymore."

"I wouldn't worry," Miller said. "Friendships go in cycles."

"Like you and Olly?"

Miller turned off the heat. "Can you get a bowl out of the cupboard?"

Nate held out the bowl and she spooned some of the stew in, then they both went and sat down at the table: he with his food, she with her wine.

She watched him, the little animal way he ate, his tanned, muscled forearms spooning in the food, his hair falling in his eyes. She could remember when he was small, his hair blond and fuzzy like a baby duck or a chick's head, always mashed up in the back, and the way he ate fruit—blueberries, raspberries, chunks of pears—greedily, plopping them in his mouth one by one, chewing nosily. It was strange, unnerving, to see this young man in his place, but still with the same mannerisms.

"You want to watch a movie?" Nate said, when he'd finished.

It moved her that it never occurred to him to ask if she might have plans. To him, she was the same as she'd always been—immutable, boring, safe. Part of her wanted to stay like that in his eyes forever, though she knew this was impossible. "Sure," she said. "What were you thinking about?"

254

Nate got up and disappeared into the den. When he returned, he held up a VHS tape: *Une Femme Est Une Femme*.

She smiled. "I haven't seen that in twenty years," she said. "We all wanted to look like Anna Karina."

"Godard is a genius," Nate said.

"You get it set up," Miller said. "I'll make popcorn."

Miller popped the corn, added melted butter and salt into a brown bowl they'd had since forever, and brought it into the den. Nate had cued up the tape and was sitting on the hunter-green sofa. She sat next to him and when he leaned back to rest against her, she put her hand on his neck, like she'd done so many times before, and Nate pressed play on the remote.

The film was a bright, quirky little comedy about a woman, played by Anna Karina, who wanted a baby. When her husband refused her, she slept with his best friend, played by Jean-Paul Belmondo. Of course, she ended up sleeping with her husband, too. So, somehow, in the world of French New Wave, everything was all right in the end.

From time to time, Nate would sit up, and say excitedly, "This is the best part"—when the husband and wife brushed off the soles of their feet before they got in bed, presumably to clean off the dust and dirt from the floor; or the silent argument they conducted through pointing at book titles: *Monster*, *Executioner*, *Peruvian Mummy*.

When it was finished, Miller said: "I'd forgotten what it was about."

"Is there any more popcorn?"

She looked in the bowl. "No."

Nate got off the couch and lay down on the rug, stretching out. "Do you think all women want kids?" he asked.

"No, I do not," she said.

"Did you always know you wanted kids?"

She shrugged. "I was really young when I had you. I was only twenty-four, you know."

"But is that really that young? I feel like that's normal."

Miller laughed. "Well, it felt young to me. Wait until you're twenty-four," she said.

Nate rolled over and looked at her. "So . . . what is going on with you and Dad?"

"What do you mean?"

Nate snorted. "I'm not blind, Mom."

Miller smiled. "No, you're not, though it would be nice if you were, sometimes." She brushed some popcorn off the sofa back into the bowl.

"So you're not going to answer?"

She sighed, and slid down to sit next to him on the floor. She looked at him, her son, her lovely, lovely boy. She put her hand back on his neck, curled a piece of his blond hair between her fingers. "Your dad and I have been together for a very long time, and that's not always easy. Things get complicated. But we both love you very, very much."

"Mom, you can skip all the after-school special stuff . . ."

"Don't be a smart-ass, Nate," she said.

"Do you still love him?"

This, of course, was the trickiest question of all, the one she'd rather not try to answer.

"Mom," he looked at her, his blue eyes, steady and intense. "Be honest."

"Sweetheart, your dad is my family. He always has been, and that's never going to change. There are things . . ." She stopped. ". . . things I want to explain to you, but now isn't really the right moment . . . Not yet."

He stared at her a while, and she wondered if he was waiting for her to go on. But then he just nodded, as if he accepted this as enough. Miller was relieved. She didn't want to lie to her son, but she also didn't want to have a conversation that risked being muddled, and causing more pain. The story, *her* story, had to be laid out carefully, fully, truthfully. Nate deserved that. And she didn't want anyone else to be the one to do it.

"I think we should watch another," she said.

"A double feature? Daring, Mom."

She laughed. And as they sat together in the evening, the lamps lit in the den with its familiar pictures of hunting dogs, and the sounds of the town outside the screened-in windows, images flickering across the convex glass of the television, she wondered how much of her love for Olly, for Ash, was wrapped up in the body of the young man sitting next to her. And she wondered how she would feel if Olly were there with them, if Ash were there.

WEEK 2

Billy Budd set off on her daily walk. She'd had breakfast—porridge and cream—and she'd pressed her suit, tied a gay silk handkerchief around her neck, and she felt jaunty and light as she walked, arms swinging, in the warm summer air. The body of Billy Budd, its strength and beauty, its fluid, nimble lines, like quicksilver, was an extraordinary one to walk about in and she never tired of it. Billy made sure to change the hour of her walks from one day to the next, so as not to always see the same thing. Variety, as the man said, was the spice of life.

Today, she was heading first to the marina; it was a favorite spot of hers—she loved watching the sailors, a wonderful assortment of men in all shapes and sizes. They hailed from ports ranging from Iceland to the South Seas: some in beaver hats and sealskin, some with gold hoops quivering in their ears, or turbans on their head; some naked to the waist, with skins of all shades and hues, some heavily tattooed from top to bottom—the glory of the sun, the glory of the moon, the glory of the stars. Billy liked to watch them as they lounged, or swayed together in a group, liked to listen to them tell their stories to each other. And she particularly liked talking to the man in charge of them all, Rodrigo. And looking at the old ship. She envied them that ship: she'd like to board the *Pequod*, to smell the air from the deck, stand in the Flemish horse in a strong wind, float in fair weather in the mild, enchanted pools of tropical waters. To set sail, to remain Billy Budd forever.

She'd gotten into the habit of taking trinkets with her from the places they gathered—the Spouter-Inn, the marina. They were small things: bits of scrimshaw and such. Billy felt so strongly that they belonged to her, were part of her, that it didn't even feel like stealing. God would understand.

The last time she'd visited the marina—when was it? A few days ago? Weeks? Time had started to unspool for Billy—she'd spoken to Rodrigo. He was used to seeing Billy, now, and always stopped to chat if he was able. Their last conversation had stuck in Billy's mind.

They'd spoken at first about inconsequential things—the beautiful plumage on one of the hats, some questions about the plain speech of the Quakers—and then Billy had asked: "What are you hunting on your ship?"

"Oh, so you're curious about the whale, too?"

Billy had laughed. "You're hunting whales? I don't think you'll find many of them in such shallow water."

He'd paused a moment, looked around. "I'll tell you a secret," he'd said, in almost a whisper. "I'm not hunting whales. I'm hunting love, I'm hunting brotherhood." He'd winked. "But I'm not sure the world is ready for it."

"A great poet once wrote that nothing is greater than the quality of robust love—it leads the rest."

"Hmmm." He nodded. "Well, I'm not sure if my producer will agree with that poet."

"Never you mind. God continues to speak to us, through poetry, through art." She'd smiled.

Rodrigo had straightened up, looked towards his band of sailors. "God's voice, is it?"

"Well," Billy had said, "I think everything will become clear. Seasoning. That's all it needs." She'd patted his shoulder. "I'll hold you in the light."

These were Tassie's words, she knew, for Billy was illiterate and not prone to speechmaking. And it continued to be a mystery to her how she could be both one and the other. Like a piece of cloth, mended with another newer, brighter thread. Or perhaps, it was more that the two were blending together faster and faster, water circling a drain.

262

Today, when Billy reached the marina, Rodrigo was directing his people into boats. They would be heading to the *Pequod*. She studied him from a distance. *Mind the light.*

She saw the boy, Nate, tidying up after them. There was no doubt that boy was Miller's boy—he was his mother through and through. She watched him a while, considering him, then continued on her way.

She walked back down the Ring Road and turned right onto Main Street. She passed the theater—in Tassie's day it had just been the plain old town hall, where the elder statesmen of Wonderland met to decide the small disputes that arose from time to time: who had built a fence on who's property line; how should the education funds donated by Annie Oakley (sharpshooter, Quaker, philanthropist) be distributed among the elementary and the high school; how much tax would need to be levied to pay to tar the roads. She passed the thrift store and saw Miller and Ash's neighbor, the lady with the dark cap of hair and the sad face, arranging pairs of used shoes out on a table in the sunshine. There was a glow around her today. Signs, Billy thought. Signs everywhere.

The day was fine, the clouds like small puffs of pipe smoke dotting the blue sky as Billy walked, swinging her arms. Turning onto Meeting House Way, Billy could see the Ring Road at the end and across it, the meeting house, surrounded by a bit of open land where switchgrass and wildflowers grew. Further up the road was the high school and behind, on the outer edge of Dune Beach, was the old cemetery.

Billy crossed the Ring Road and passed into the small field, her hands touching the tops of the swaying stalks, not yet browned out by the sun, their seed heads like clusters of fur. She'd only gone a few paces when she spied him, lying up ahead, just outside the cemetery gates. He was on his back almost completely hidden by the tall grass, looking up at the sky, the child who couldn't cry. For a minute she thought he was dead, then she saw a leg move.

She could hear music playing. Bach, canon in D Major. Tassie's mother had loved Bach. She'd loved all music, really. And after much pestering and pleading her mother had convinced Tassie's father to buy a phonograph. Her father had been skeptical of that sort of entertainment, but he was very partial to her mother. And from then on, music had filled the house on Foster Street.

Billy watched the boy—young man, really—from a distance. She'd seen him before on her walks, most recently on her nocturnal forays. Like Billy, he seemed to like to wander; he appeared to have no purpose except putting one foot in front of the other, and at first she'd wondered if he were sleep-walking. But from time to time, he'd sit down and clutch his head, as if it hurt, keening lowly. At those moments, he seemed very much awake. Billy sighed. There was so much that was connected to itself that Billy sometimes had a hard time keeping it all straight in her mind.

She began walking toward the meeting house. A girl rode past on a bicycle, turning off ahead of her to cut through the small field. Billy stopped to watch her, shading her eyes from the sun. The girl, short black hair cropped to her head, rode so close to where the young man was lying that Billy thought she might run right over him. But the girl didn't seem to notice, her face staring straight ahead, riding toward the beach.

After she'd passed him, the boy stood up and watched her cycle away. And then they were in a kind of tableau—Billy watching the boy watching the girl—a half-remembered painting. Once the girl had disappeared out of sight, Billy turned away and continued on to the meeting house.

The meeting house hadn't been used for years, its white shutters closed against the outside world, though the town was careful to keep it from falling into complete disrepair. If she closed her eyes she could see it, feel it, the way it used to be: dust motes dotting the luminescent air, the silence like a bell in its clarity, in its sharp, tangy quality.

All her life, Tassie had believed in the Society of Friends, in the inward light, in the direct and unmediated experience of God. As had her sister and her parents, and their parents before them. They practiced waiting worship, coming together in silence, listening for the still, small voice to speak to them. As a young woman she never could have believed that one day Wonderland would no longer be seen as a Quaker stronghold, that it would shut its place of worship for lack of congregation.

It had happened little by little, as time slipped by. Tassie's sister, Eleanor, died, leaving Tassie to raise the fifteen-year-old Gweny herself; Gweny's father had already been taken in the Great War, before his daughter was even born.

And by the time Gweny had grown, the population of Friends had narrowed to less than half of the tidal island. Even Gweny herself by that point had given up attending worship. This had disappointed Tassie at the time, but when she'd interrogated herself, Tassie realized that she'd been foolish to think it could have been otherwise: her niece had always been a slip of a thing, unsubstantial in some intangible way. So when, two years later, Gweny fell for a feckless traveling salesman who proceeded to die on them in less than eighteen months, Tassie had just accepted that it came with the territory, the delible geography of the life of Gwendolyn Lane, née Curtis. By the time Gweny took her own life, it had come to seem inevitable. This was not to say that Tassie didn't love her dearly, only that Gweny had always been like smoke—forever on the way to disappearing.

Olly had been different: more intense, more high-strung, more invested in this world than his mother. So Tassie had made sure to take him to worship at the meeting house, to talk to him about the practice of faith, believing strongly that this would not only ground him, but would give him peace in his heart. *Mind the light*, she would say to him when he would pass into fits of rage and despair. And, just as she had hoped, God had spoken to him there. She knew he wouldn't describe it that way now, but to Tassie, the music in his head was the particular form in which God's truth had been revealed to Olly.

Billy looked at the meeting house, stark, alone in the grass in unrelenting sunshine. Like a ship on a too-bright sea. There was another over the bridge, and Wonderland's few remaining Quakers now met there for worship. Just as Tassie had done before she'd gone to Starry Acres.

She could still see him, Claggart, watching her—watching her every hour from the first day she'd arrived at the retirement home. Whispering about her to the others, his false smile drawing across his teeth. She hadn't realized right away what he was, but when he began accusing her of things she hadn't done—petty grievances at first, then more serious transgressions—she'd understood that he was preparing the ground so that no one would believe her. The staff at Starry Acres started searching Tassie's room regularly, convincingly informed that she was stealing things: medication, trinkets, things Claggart had likely taken himself.

She began to have nightmares, and to fear turning a corner, or walking down one of the empty paths on the grounds. But then she remembered something her father had always said—*There's no use being frightened, but there is profit in being prepared.* So she did steal something: a paring knife from the kitchen. The smooth black handle had given her comfort. And when he finally came for her, at night in her bed, as she knew he would, one hand covering her mouth, the other tearing at the bottom of her nightdress, his intent so clear, she was ready for him. Just a few quick stabs of the knife had been all it had taken to get him to roll off her bed, crying out in surprise and pain.

Of course, he'd told the staff that *she'd* come to *his* room, that *she'd* attacked *him*, unprovoked. And they'd believed him. They already thought she was trouble. And besides, no one wants to think that the kind, grandfatherly man you see everyday could be your neighborhood rapist.

And when she'd been rescued by Ash, and was finally somewhere safe, Billy Budd had come for her.

Billy sat down in the switchgrass, leaning her back against the soft gray clapboard of the building, and took a pear and a piece of cheese out of her pocket. She took a bite of the pear—sweet, almost sugared—then a bite of the salty cheese. She alternated between the two until they were both finished. Then she lay herself down, and watched the clouds puff along in the sky. She felt she could almost sleep, and smiled to herself. The last time Billy had come this way she had fallen asleep, farther out in the field. It had been late afternoon, and when she'd awoken she'd seen them, up against the back of the meeting house, Olly and Miller, entwined around each other, Miller's dress bunched around her waist, Olly's trousers around his ankles. She hadn't been able to hear what they said to one another, though the words were perhaps unimportant. The act itself was the thing, and it seemed both sacred and profane.

She'd been moved by it, and after they'd left, each in a different direction, Billy had lain there and thought about love. Billy knew nothing about it, but Tassie had been in love once, when she was a young girl. Barbara Vere had been her best friend. Beautiful—she could still remember the green-ribboned stockings she tripped around town in, the ones her grandfather, a Wonderland bigwig, had brought back from Paris. Those stockings did cause some talk among the other Friends. But Tassie thought they were glorious. And she and Barbara had vowed never to part—to set up a house together, and live together in silks and satins and music and flowers until a ripe old age. She could remember the feel of Barbara's lips upon hers, the smell of her: the rose water and lavender oil that her clothes were ironed with. Barbara had been crazy about astrology. She'd surreptitiously cut the horoscopes from her father's newspapers and bring them to the Little Forest, where she'd read them to Tassie as she rested her head in Barbara's fragrant lap.

When they were nineteen, Barbara had agreed to marry some third cousin of hers who lived in Washington State. She'd announced it with a bright, creamy smile on her lovely lips, the words slicing through Tassie's heart like a hot knife through butter.

Barbara turned out to be a very silly woman, in the end; astrology had only been the tip of the iceberg. Tassie knew this through letters Barbara would write to her throughout their lives. It got to the point where Tassie began just dropping them in the wastebasket unopened rather than read another missive on her masseuse or the shaman she consulted or the movement of the planets and what that might mean for Barbara's next electronic purchase.

Still, no one had ever compared with Barbara—not with the ribboned stockings, and the bow mouth, and the smell of roses and warm linen. The sacred and profane.

It was clear that Miller and Olly felt the same—nothing had ever lived up to what they experienced when they were together. It was a curse in some ways, to have your first love be your biggest, to be the most profound. It ruined a person, bound and trapped them. Those two seemed destined to continuously circle each other throughout their whole lives without being able to find a way to untangle the knot.

As for Ash, Billy had seen him a few times outside his house, breathing deeply and walking barefoot on the front lawn. But Ash was a pragmatist and there was a great strength in that, in being able to walk away, to see clearly when something was truly over. The way Tassie had been able to see Barbara clearly in the end. Anyway, it was neither Miller nor Ash that she worried about: it was Olly.

Olly, the little orphan boy, so distraught after Gweny's death. Whose hand she held until he no longer wanted to hold hands, who grew up and fell in love and then became angry and left. How she'd missed him while he'd been away. How glad she was he was back. There were so many of these lost, orphaned children in Wonderland, like a fairy tale—Gweny, Olly, the boy in the field. And Nate, in his own way.

But Olly was hers. It was toward Olly that Billy Budd strode. Olly was Billy's destiny.

WEEK 3

In the dim light of Jess's curtained bedroom, Cam rose and pulled on his jeans, stuffed his underwear in his back pocket. Jess lay in bed smoking a joint and drinking a Fresca. She watched him, but said nothing.

He was relieved, and wondered if he might make it out of there without having to say anything at all. It made him feel worse each time they did it. He kept thinking it might do something for him, hollow him out, take away all the dark feelings, cool his brain, but afterwards, the hollowness he felt was a bad kind, bottomless.

Each time, he'd swear he wasn't going to do it again.

He pulled his T-shirt over his head, and pushed his feet into his flip-flops. Now came the moment when he'd have to turn and look at her, think of some way to get out.

"That was nice," she said.

He tried to smile. "Yeah," he said. When she was quiet, he continued: "Right, well, thanks, for . . ." He inclined his head.

"Jesus, Cam," she said. "You really know how to make me feel like shit."

"Sorry," he said. "Sorry. Do you want me to stay?"

She sighed, tapped out the joint. "No. Forget it. It's fine. Just . . ." She looked at him, shook her head. "See you later."

"Yeah," he said. "Later." And then he hurried from her bedroom, down the stairs and out of her house before anything else could happen.

When he reached his car, he realized that he didn't have his keys; they must have dropped out in Jess's room. He wasn't going back up there, so he stuffed his hands in his pockets and started walking home. It wasn't like it was far. The only reason it was parked there was because Jess had wanted to go to the Denny's in Longwell—she said she was craving Moons Over My Hammy. He'd watched her eat the eggy, gooey sandwich, cheese sticking to her lips, then afterwards, they'd driven back to her place.

When Cam got back to the rectory house, his father was waiting for him.

"Oh, good, you're back," he said. "I need to borrow your car."

"It's not here," Cam said.

"Where is it?"

"What's happened?"

"I lent my car to Mrs. Cuthbert, and I . . . the police have called from Longwell. They have some things that they believe belong to the rectory that they want me to look at." His dad stopped, ran his hand through his hair. "But where's your car?"

"I'll go get it," Cam said. "I just left it at Jess's."

His father raised his eyebrow.

"I'll go get it," he repeated, and went out the door and started walking down the drive.

From down Church Street, he could see Jess walking towards him, dangling the car keys between her fingers.

She met him at the end of the drive. "Forget something?"

"Thanks," he said, reaching for the keys. "I was just coming to get them."

Jess pulled them away. "Really? Because it seemed like you couldn't get out of there fast enough—didn't even have time for your underwear."

Cam felt his cheeks go hot. "I just need the keys."

"Hey, Jess."

Cam turned to see that his father had followed him down the drive. He looked down at his feet.

"Hey, Reverend Cross," Jess said. "Cam left his keys at my house."

"Did he?" He looked from one of them to the other. "Well, thanks for bringing them back. It seems I've found myself in an automotive pickle, so to speak."

Jess gave his dad a sort of laugh, probably out of pity. "Glad I could be of service," she said, still holding the keys. "What's going on?"

"Ah," his dad said, "some poor soul—a vagrant, it seems—has died, and the police found some things in his possession that I'd reported stolen, a while ago now. Ten years, maybe? But it would be nice to have them back, if they're what I think they are. So I just need to pop on over to the Longwell station and confirm it for them. And wouldn't you know it, I've lent my car to a parishioner."

Jess reached around Cam and handed his dad the keys. Cam tried to control his temper.

"Well, see you later, Cam," Jess said, putting her hand gently on his bicep.

He could feel his father's eyes on him.

"You know," his dad said. "It would be nice to have some company. Why don't you two come with me? You can tell me what you've been up to. It's been a while since we've had a chat."

"I don't think . . ." Cam began.

"Great, I'd love to," Jess said, waggling her eyebrows at Cam.

Cam switched on the radio, WNDR, as they drove through town, hoping it might discourage his dad from asking too many questions, or Jess from saying, well, anything. After an ad for the local market came the sound of a synthesizer and clock-ticking percussion followed by Cyndi Lauper's sad, longing voice, and all at once, Cam was no longer in the car.

Lyin' in my bed, I hear the clock tick and think of you . . .

He was with Suki, he was with her in his bed at night; in a field, her bare legs pedaling past him, yellow skirt fanning away from her white underpants, damp around the edge of the elastic; he was watching her on the tennis court, her long red ponytail swinging from shoulder to shoulder as she hit the backboard— tick-tock, tick-tock. He was with her when she went to the movies—*Sixteen Candles*—watching her from a couple of rows behind as she ate Junior Mints and drank a Tab; with her in the halls of Annie Oakley High as the boys slung their arms carelessly against the lockers above their heads when she passed by. Full of all the longing he had endured, in silence, for years.

His dad turned the radio down as they crossed the bridge. "Seems a little morose," he said, smiling.

"Oh, Cyndi Lauper's totally rad, Reverend Cross," Jess said. "She writes a lot of her own songs, and she worked at an IHOP, and left home at seventeen to study art, and lived in the woods with her dog in Canada. I mean, she's basically my hero."

His dad laughed. "Well, I didn't know all that, Jess. She sounds . . . spirited."

"She's white-hot."

"White-hot, hunh?"

Cam wanted to disappear into the seat, but instead he looked out the window. They passed the Denny's he and Jess had eaten at hours earlier, a Chinese restaurant, and a laundromat, before his dad turned the car into the gray parking lot of the Longwell Police Station.

"You guys can wait in the car," his dad said.

"Can I come with you?" Jess asked. "I've never been inside a police station."

"Well, thank God for small mercies," his dad said. "All right, no harm in it, I guess."

Cam didn't want to leave Jess alone with his father so he got out with them and they walked across the hot asphalt and into the squat, gray, stone building.

A young policeman led them into a room where there were numerous items spread out on a large table.

"We found this silver cup, that has your church's name inscribed on it, and we figured we better give you a call."

Cam's father picked it up, turned it around in his hand. "Yes," he said. "This belongs to our church. A gift to us from our sister congregation in Scotland when First Presbyterian of Wonderland was founded. It's very dear to me. Thank you for returning it."

"Yeah, sure thing," the policeman said. "Take a look, see if there's anything else. Seems this guy had been robbing local churches for years."

Cam's father raised an eyebrow. "But he didn't sell any of it," his father said. "Perhaps he was just a lost soul seeking God's comfort."

"I don't know, Reverend. When I seek God's comfort, I go to church, I don't take stuff."

" 'The Lord redeems the life of his servants; none of those who take refuge in him will be condemned.' " His father looked over the things on the table. "This Bible," he said, touching a black calf-skin Bible. "It was a gift from my wife. A real minister's Bible. I wondered what had happened to it." He picked it up and opened a page. A photo fell out—a small laminated school picture of Cam in the sixth grade. His father picked it up, looked at him. "Odd," he said, turning the photo over.

Cam felt sick. He realized that he was, in fact, going to be sick right then, and hurried out of the room, down the hall and out to the parking lot where he vomited on the pavement, then sat down, abruptly. He put his head in his hands to stop the spinning.

Jess came out and sat next to him. "You okay?" She rubbed his shoulder. Her touch made him scream inside.

"Yeah," he said. "Must have been the Denny's." But he couldn't look at her.

"You didn't eat anything."

A few minutes later, his dad appeared.

"Something I ate, I think," Cam said, standing up.

"All right, well, let's get you home. I've just got to sign some paperwork and we'll get going."

On the drive home, Cam hung his head out the car window. Like a dog.

"That poor man," his father was saying. "To die alone, like that. I hope he found God. I hope he knew God. It's very possible, you know, that he felt too wretched to be in society and took those things to be close to Him." His father sighed. "I'll pray for him."

Cam closed his eyes. His father just talked and talked and talked and said nothing. And, Christ, did he ever shut up?

Jess was quiet in the back.

When they got back to the rectory, Cam hurtled out of the car and up the stairs, into the silence of his own room. He lay on his bed and for the first time in many, many years he made the crying face, the one he had learned to hide so well. The ugly one, the one full of rage and pain and hate. But he didn't care, there was no one to see him. There was no one at all.

All these years he'd believed she'd come back to check on him, to watch over him; he'd convinced himself that the only reason she'd left again was because she was just biding her time, because maybe she was afraid.

One day, all those years ago, he'd taken that black calf-skin Bible and left it outside the door of the room over the garage, because he thought she might need comfort. Inside, he'd tucked a picture of himself and a note that said: *For you, Love Cam*.

A few weeks later, though, the food he'd been leaving began going untouched. When he'd checked inside the room, the Bible and the picture were gone. And he'd thought: She'll be back. She loves me. She'll come back for me one day.

But none of that had ever been true. It had only been some homeless guy looking for a place to crash.

Cam stood outside the church, staring at its white Greek revival columns, blinding in the sun. Through his shirt he scratched at his shoulder, tender from exposure. After lifeguarding, his peeling skin seemed to slide right off in the shower, rolling up into little gray balls, leaving raw, stinging patches.

He walked slowly up the steps and into the cool stillness of First Presbyterian. The stained-glass windows, bought and paid for by a congregant years ago, cast a blue light across the wood floor, and the familiar smell, faintly dusty, faintly sweet— lemon Pledge and Murphy's Oil and leather Bibles—engulfed him.

276

His father sat praying in a middle pew. Cam walked over to him. But his father stayed quiet.

"Where is she, Dad?"

His father looked up, surprised. "Who?"

"My mother."

His father sighed, put his hands in his lap. "Do you really want to talk about this, Cam?"

Cam looked at him, then straight ahead towards the lectern and the chancel. "Yes." Everything was a mess, everything was shit and dark, but he knew in his heart that if he could find his mother, there would be a path out of this for him.

"The truth is," his father said, then stopped. "You know, your mom, when I met her, she said she had no family, that they were all gone. So there was no one to track down . . . afterwards."

"Her parents were dead?"

"That's what she told me."

"You think she was lying?"

"She was a sad person, Cam, and I didn't want to make her sadder by prying or . . . making her feel distrusted, I guess."

He'd heard this before, or variants of it. But today, he hated his father for talking about her that way, like she was flawed or at fault somehow. He knew now, because of his own unhappiness, that it was his father who was to blame, his father was the common denominator.

"I'm going to find her, whether you help me or not."

"Look, son . . ." He felt his father's hand on his shoulder, knew he was looking at him, but Cam couldn't turn his head, couldn't take his eyes off the rose window behind the communion table. Blue and green, over and over again. "When she left, she did it so that she wouldn't . . . do something bad to you, hurt you. She loved you. She was doing what she had to do for our family. I respected that. There was no point dragging her back into a situation that would have been dangerous and unhappy for everyone."

"So, you don't know. You don't know what happened to her." He would have to start somewhere else.

His dad paused. "There was a letter."

Now Cam did look at his father. "She sent you a letter?" The thought of reading his mother's words, of seeing her handwriting, feeling her . . .

"No, not exactly."

"No, not exactly?" He wanted to take his father's mouth in his hands and make it move to say the words he needed to hear.

"She didn't *send* me a letter. A cousin of hers sent it on to me, after . . ."

"After what, Dad?"

His father looked at him, his eyes soft and patient, the look he used on his elderly parishioners. "She's dead, Cam. She took her own life. Years ago. And she wrote me a letter. A kind of good-bye letter."

Cam could feel his face cramping, his eyes squinting, he could feel the ugliness, the aloneness inside of him. He didn't want to believe his father, but he knew it was true. It was the truest thing he'd ever heard; he'd always been abandoned, he'd always felt it.

"It was years ago, not long after she left. I didn't see the point in telling you, in making you think about her that way."

"You didn't *see the point*?" His breath felt hot.

"Sometimes, we have to make decisions for our children . . ."

"What did it say?"

"It was . . . she was trying to explain why she'd left, I guess . . . She talked about her love for me—for you, too, of course . . ."

"Where is it? I want to read it."

"I . . . destroyed it. I didn't want you to have to read it. It was to me, Cam. It was private."

"What about me?" Cam said. "Dad?"

His father was quiet.

"Dad, what about me? What about what I . . ." He couldn't articulate exactly what he meant: what about what he needed? Or wanted? What about him and his mother, and what was between them?

But his father remained silent. He just looked at Cam, with an expression of sadness, and forbearance.

He could have smashed his father's face into a million tiny pieces. Instead, Cam stood up and left his father sitting alone, in his dusty-sweet church, with all his righteousness and privacy and power.

Nate was alone in the house when the phone rang. It was past eight o'clock in the evening and he'd been running through his short film in the den. It needed more—more something, or more some*one*. He just couldn't put his finger on what it was. He leaned over the side of the couch and picked up the receiver.

"Hey, Nate."

"Hey, Dad," he said, "hang on." He rose and pressed pause on the camcorder sitting on the tripod next to the TV, before returning to the phone. "What's up? Mom's not here."

"That's fine—I called to talk to you," his dad said. "How are you?"

"I'm good," Nate said, sitting down on the couch. "Just looking at my film."

"Great," his dad said. He sounded distracted or hazy or something. "Everything good?"

"Yup," Nate laughed. "Still good. You in the city?"

"Still in the city," his dad said.

There was dead air down the line. His dad had never been a great phone conversationalist.

"So what's new?" his dad asked.

"Not much. Or, well, you know, a lot, but probably the same new stuff that was going on when you left."

His dad cleared his throat.

"When are you coming back?"

"Yeah, about that . . . soon, I think."

"Cool," Nate said.

"So," his dad said, "who have you been seeing? Cam?"

"Not really," Nate said, not wanting to go into it all with his dad. "Just been working a lot."

"What about Suki Pfeiffer? I got the impression from her mom that you guys were close."

"I don't know," Nate said. "I can't figure her out, or something. I don't know what she wants."

His dad laughed. "Have you tried asking her?"

"I don't think you can just ask that."

"Why not?"

When Nate didn't respond, his dad said: "Look, I've never been very good at taking the bull by the horns, so to speak. Never been my thing, really. But I do think, when it comes to love, that bravery is required."

Nate laughed. "Fortune favors the bold."

"Something like that," his dad said. His dad was quiet for a minute, then he said: "Nate . . ."

"Yeah, Dad?"

"I just wanted to say that everything's going to be okay."

"I know."

"And I'm really proud to be your dad. It's been one of the greatest joys of my life."

Nate laughed. "You going somewhere?"

"No, not at all," his dad said, kind of defensively, Nate thought. "I just wanted to say . . . well, that I love you."

"I love you, too, Dad."

"Okay, then. Do you need anything? Any money?"

"I'm good."

"Okay. I'll let you go. Don't work too hard."

"I won't."

"I'll let you know when I'm heading back."

"All right . . ."

"Okay, then."

"Bye, Dad." Nate hung up and shook his head, smiled to himself.

He loved his dad. He loved his mom. And he liked Olly a lot. But they were making things way more complicated than they needed to be, in his opinion. Then again, who was he to talk?

He knew his parents would be disappointed when they found out that he'd agreed to go with Olly to California. But it had just seemed right, a road trip. Getting to know Olly better, seeing some of America. He'd tell them when his dad got back.

Nate pressed play on the camcorder and stood back, but his mind felt unfocused now so he paused it again. A cool air was blowing in through the windows, there was a shift in the weather.

He left the den and headed upstairs to look for some extra blankets in the guest room with the butterfly wallpaper. Through one of the windows he could see across into Suki's bedroom. Her light was on and she passed in front of her window. She looked at him.

He hadn't spoken to her since the night of the bonfire. He waved.

Suki reached up and slowly pulled down her shade.

By the end of the week a nor'easter blew into town. Miller was supposed to meet Olly, but because production had halted on the film, she'd found herself waiting all morning for Nate to get fed up moping and go to the arcade or the movies or see his friends or something so she could go out without having to give an explanation. But by the afternoon, when it became clear that Nate had no intention of going anywhere, she gave up the pretense.

She told Nate she was going to buy milk. She slipped her yellow slicker on over her shorts and old gray fisherman's sweater, and hurried out into the dark, wet storm. The nor'easter had turned the town silent, private. The wet streets glistened, the trees bending in the wind looked an even deeper, lusher green against the pewter-colored sky.

The rain, blowing at an angle, made her face slick, and she kept her eyes down on the pavement, as she hurried—practically ran—down Church Street, crossing at Vere Road, and turning onto Foster, her feet tripping now and again on the uneven brick sidewalks. She felt light.

A crack of thunder rolled out as she found the side gate to Aunt Tassie's house and pulled the latch, brushing past the wet, drooping hydrangea overgrown there.

He was there, waiting. Without a word, he took her hand and led her across the wet grass, pulling her as she followed on the balls of her feet, through the backdoor and into the kitchen. Never once looking back, he led her down the hallway and up the stairs into his childhood bedroom.

Once inside, he kicked the door shut behind him, and only then did he turn and look at her. Still he said nothing. But his eyes—his eyes held a kind of pleading look in them, as if he wanted her to interpret his desires, to articulate what he needed, what he couldn't say himself.

Miller looked around the room. It was the same, though faded with time: the green leaf-patterned William Morris wallpaper, the posters tacked up on the wall: The Byrds playing at Ciro's; Ike and Tina Turner; Miles Davis; The Beach Boys. She saw the familiar green plaid quilt covering the bed and the matching curtains; the record player and the neat stack of albums next to it; the hand-painted globe Olly used to spin with his eyes closed and see where his finger landed.

She could feel Olly watching her every tiny movement, like she was some unpredictable animal he'd just come face-to-face with. Miller walked over to the closet and opened it. Standing there, her back to him, she began to strip. First, her wet slicker, then her sweater, her shirt. She unbuttoned her shorts and let them drop, then stepped out of her underwear.

She ran her hand over the clothes hanging in the closet, and then she pulled out Olly's old Annie Oakley letter jacket. Still without turning, she slipped it on over her naked body. She could smell the odor of old mothballs, wool, and leather. Olly swallowed visibly as she turned, walked across the room and picked out a record. Carefully, she placed it on the turntable, put the needle to the vinyl, a tiny scratch.

The honey, syrup voice of João Gilberto, singing "The Girl from Ipanema" in Portuguese, filled the bedroom. Miller started dancing slowly, her feet making small circles across the room, her breasts moving under the jacket.

"Turn that off," Olly said.

Miller kept on dancing. She could feel his eyes boring into her. When she reached where he was standing, she swayed a moment before him.

Then she gently pulled his shirt up over his head. She hooked her fingers into the waist of his jeans; with a small tug she pulled the button open and unzipped his fly. Bending down, she removed first his pants then his boxers.

"I said turn it off." But he said it more softly this time.

Miller looked at him, rested her palms flat against his chest. Then she pushed him back onto the bed. She climbed on top, her strong legs straddling him. He put his hands on her breasts, her nipples. She bent forward and dipped her tongue into the small depression above his clavicle, licked the drops of sweat there.

Raising her head, their eyes locked a moment, before he rolled her over and was on top of her, her legs twined around his thighs. She placed her palms against the wallpaper behind her, and as he pushed into her, as he dissolved into her bones, she dug her fingers in, tearing the paper away from the wall, bits of green leaf and plaster lodging under her nails.

They lay on the bed, listening to the storm, to the lightning, like the crack of a bat, punctuating the rhythm of the downpour. She let her mind be empty. She looked over at Olly. He was staring at the ceiling.

"I always feel like maybe you're not coming back this time," he said.

She sat up, reached for her purse, dropped haphazardly by the bed earlier. She rummaged around until she found a pen. Then she turned over, ran her index finger over his pelvic bone, put the tip against his skin.

"What are you doing?"

"I'm marking you," she said.

"For what?"

"For later."

"You're bookmarking me."

She smiled. "I'm bookmarking you."

Sometimes she'd see him on the street or in a store, by chance, and they'd smile at each other, perhaps a little longer than they should, and she knew they were both thinking about it, about how they felt, and about what it would be like the next time, what it had been like the last time. His face, his hair slicked back, his grin like a fucking wolf.

They'd meet at the tree house, or at Dune Beach at night; once they'd even gone to the meeting house. Sometimes they'd eat or drink wine, or read propped up against each other. Other times, it was just sex. And she thought about it—thought about him—all the time: his hands on her, his mouth on her. The words he spoke to her, as they moved together.

"Sometimes I can't believe this is actually real," she said.

"It's real," he said.

"Yes, but still . . . it *feels* like it's kind of a dream. Like we're going to wake up soon and go back to our real lives."

He looked at her, his face grim. "This is my real life," he said. "Unlike you, I don't have another one."

"No, sorry," she said. "I don't know why I said that. Sorry. Please come here."

As evening fell, and the storm had finally quieted to a misty drizzle, Miller said she was hungry so they went down to the kitchen. Aunt Tassie was out on one of her walks. But even if she hadn't been, Olly wouldn't have cared; he didn't feel like he needed to hide anything from her.

Wearing one of Olly's old bathrobes, Miller sat on the counter while he made peanut butter and jelly sandwiches.

He handed her one on a plate. "Sorry about the limited menu."

"At least it's not from a crock pot," she said, laughing.

He liked it when she made fun of Ash, and it also made him uneasy, like he was being disloyal, and he wondered at that feeling. So instead, he slid his hand up her thigh, exposed where the plaid robe fell away slightly.

284

Miller took a bite of the sandwich. He watched her pushing her tongue backwards; the peanut butter presumably sticking to the roof of her mouth. "So," she said. "What actually happened in L.A.? In your *previous* real life, I mean, with your job . . . And what's happened to your house?"

Olly hopped up next to her on the countertop. "Well, the house—I'm waiting on insurance. The job, that's as dead as a doornail. My boss got fed up with me. It all came to a head over a film I refused to get involved with—it was called, if you can believe it, fucking *Doctor Zhivago II: Doctors Zhivago*."

Miller almost choked on her sandwich. "What the hell is *Doctors Zhivago*?"

"You see what I had to deal with?" Olly laughed. "Yeah, there were these guys, the Frick brothers, from Brooklyn. They looked exactly alike—short, both squat, they had these horrible toupees. And they were always pitching the worst shit. Anyway, they pitched this film: *Olly, it's modern Russia, you know, all KGB and ballet and shit. And we're with Lara and the doctor's kid now, who's also a doctor. Right? Like her dad. And one day an American fighter pilot on a secret mission . . .*"

Miller was laughing so hard that she was making coughing noises. "Wait, but so what happens? Why are there two doctors?"

"Oh, you're interested, are you? Maybe I made a mistake turning it down." Olly shook his head. "I don't know. The daughter of Lara and Dr. Zhivago—also a doctor, so they're two, if you missed that—falls in love with the pilot and hides him, and there's some barn sex, I was reliably informed. And then she ends up defecting, I guess? Anyway, it was all very jingoistic, which was right up my boss's alley."

"So he fired you?"

"It was a clash of personalities, you might say."

"Right. Right," Miller said, finishing her sandwich. She wiped her hands on a paper towel, eyed him. "And Lay Down?"

"Well, I lost control of Lay Down. I mean, I have my stake, but no job, so . . ."

"But you could start again," Miller said. "You always said that."

And for some reason, he just couldn't tell her—couldn't tell her about what had happened to his gift, what had happened that evening by the swimming pool, couldn't tell her how weak he really was. So, he said: "I'm sorry."

"I don't care about that anymore. Honestly, I really don't. It's in the past."

"Well, you did curse me."

"What are you talking about?" Miller started to laugh. "I didn't curse you. I'm not a witch, Olly."

"No, but you said . . . things, and that's when it all . . ." He stopped. Had he really believed that all this time? That what she'd said that night at the Eidolon Lounge was what'd made the music stop, had begun the disintegration?

"Well, I was angry. But I'm not anymore. Anyway, if we were all being honest, it was you—your talent—that made Lay Down."

"That's not entirely true." Olly got up and poured two glasses of milk from the old ice box, handed one to Miller. He saw his hand was shaking.

"No, not entirely. But pretty true," she said, taking a sip.

"I have to tell you something," he said. "Nate and I have been talking about a road trip to California. The two of us."

"Sorry?" The glass in Miller's hand stopped mid-way to her lips, suspended in air.

"I'm taking him to college. Like a kind of road trip," he said, trying to make it sound light, knowing he was failing.

She was quiet for a moment, and he wondered how she planned to handle the next part. How she planned to handle him. "Well, that's really . . . kind. But I'll need to talk it over with Ash first," she said. "I just don't want you to . . . make plans, I guess, that can't be undone."

"Well, I asked and he said yes. I think he wants to."

Miller bit her lip. "Yes, but he's our son."

They stared at each other, the silence in the kitchen like gunpowder.

"Look," she said, "I don't what you're hoping for, or angling for . . ."

"I'm not angling," he said, his voice hard.

"Okay." She looked at him, then hopped down from the counter. "So let me be clear. I'm not exactly sure what's going on with you, what's been going on with you all these years . . ."

"You know me."

"Do I?"

He was getting angry now, but he really didn't want to. "What are you saying? That I'm good enough to fuck you, but I'm not good enough to know Nate?"

"Don't be disingenuous, Olly. Don't play the victim. How do I know you're not going to disappear on him? How do I know"— she waved her hand—"that one day, you won't just get bored— he'll call you on the phone, and you'll be too busy?"

"What are you talking about?"

"I'm talking about being a parent, Olly. About being stable."

"I just want to get to know him." He reached for her hand; she let him take it.

"Yes, but to what end? Have you thought about what happens after? You want to get to know him, but that's the whole thing, Olly—it's not about you. That sounds simple, but actually it's a really hard lesson to learn, and it takes years of becoming an expert at erasing yourself to learn it."

"It's not like that," he said. "I know I don't have your experience, or Ash's experience, but . . . Miller, I just want to be a part of it. Of his life."

He could see her soften a little. "If you promise me . . ." she began.

"I promise."

"If you promise me," she said looking at him, hard, "that there's nothing in your life that I don't know about, nothing that could affect Nate. No reason that this is selfish . . ."

"I promise."

"And one more thing. You won't say anything to Nate about . . . anything else, either. Not yet."

He stared at her. He'd have to trust her. He nodded.

"Okay, then," she said.

"Okay?"

"Okay." She nodded.

"And California?"

Miller backed away from him a little. "Just let me talk to Ash. All right?"

"Okay." He knew she was probably lying to him, but what could he say? It wouldn't make Nate love him more if he alienated the only parents he'd ever known.

"Olly," she said, "don't worry. We'll figure it out."

As Miller walked home in the storm, the gray sky made her shiver and the town looked dull. She pulled her slicker tighter, her damp sneakers sloshing against her bare feet. She thought about what Olly had said. She wanted to trust him, she did trust him. But she needed to be the one who told the story, in her way, in her own words. And what Olly didn't know was that while his name might be written on her thigh, Nate's name was written all over her heart. She started to hurry. She needed to get back to finish the story. She was almost there.

WEEK 4

Ash couldn't sleep. He'd really done it now. He'd made promises, said yes to things, things that would be very difficult to take back. Was this what he wanted? This doorman apartment he was wandering around in now, in the middle of a Monday night? The glass-topped tables displaying crystal bowls full of Starlight peppermints and After Eights? The overstuffed couches and swag curtains?

He walked to the kitchen and opened the fridge: cottage cheese, pineapple, grapefruit, Tab and Chardonnay. A freezer full of Lean Cuisine.

All his adult life, he'd been led to believe—by his wife, mainly—that tiny sticks of straight-backed furniture, that edgy art, and elaborate home-cooked meals were the mark of true taste; that basically anything difficult to maintain was the only thing worth having. That everything should be hard and look easy.

But he really liked Lean Cuisine, as it turned out. And over-stuffed couches; they were comfortable. And After Eights were a nice thing to have around.

He'd been staying with Candice since he returned to New York, the pretense of sleeping at the pied-à-terre no longer necessary. Plus, living in the same place had been the only way of ensuring they saw each other, given their current schedules: Candice got up in the middle of the night to go to the studio to get ready for *Morning? Morning!*, while Ash had been staying late at the office in the run-up to the Democratic Convention last week. Thankfully, their man had won, and now they would be getting down to the real business of trying to get Mondale to the White House.

After that high, Ash had asked for a few days off—a death in the family, he'd told them, which didn't feel entirely untrue—and in a handful of days, he'd be leaving the city again. He could barely imagine what lay ahead. In fact, even contemplating it was entirely distasteful. But Candice had made a good case, and even if she hadn't, she was very hard to say no to.

When he'd left Wonderland, Ash had been furious. He'd felt like someone who'd found out that a terrible recurring nightmare was, in fact, happening: that you *were* naked in front of the college exam board, that the psycho *was* actually chasing you in a dilapidated house, that your child *had* actually disappeared in a shopping mall. He'd felt like he was seventeen all over again, and he'd lost his best friend and the girl he pined for. Oh, he'd been angry, all right. Worse, he'd felt invisible, obliterated.

He'd talked all these things over with Candice, and it had surprised him how understanding she'd been. He'd never really shared any of his emotional life with her before, but he'd been unable to contain himself and she'd listened and comforted him. And made the point that now was the time to make his stand: Olly and Miller were in cahoots and if he didn't do something himself, he'd lose Nate. Ash had been so grateful and he'd agreed to everything she said.

It had seemed so obvious, so sensible when she'd put it to him—children, of all people, she'd argued, needed to be told the truth or they'd never trust you again, and that he, as a father, needed to be the one to take that stand. (The stand being that he tell Nate that Olly was a manipulative psycho who wrongly thought Nate was his child, that Miller had fallen prey to Olly's machinations, and that Ash, despite himself, had fallen in love with someone else.) And most concerning of all, that she should be with him when he did it. But now . . . well, with a little distance, he wondered if he was making the right choice. Candice's methods, after all, her version of truth-telling, did seem a tad extreme.

Ash had been hemming and hawing over it for the last week or so. He'd even phoned Nate, thinking that perhaps he should warn his son, prepare him in some way. But he hadn't been able to go through with it; he'd only been able to tell him he loved him, which was the truth.

And, of course, he couldn't talk to Candice about his reservations. So here he was, hurtling towards his future, one he wasn't sure he actually wanted, or what it would even look like when he got there.

Ash pulled a Lean Cuisine out of the freezer—Filet of Fish Divan (270 calories)—and turned on the oven. He laid a placemat at Candice's sleek black counter, a fork and knife, and poured himself a Chardonnay. Then he sat down to wait.

As he was pulling the fish out of the oven, Candice walked in, dressed in a striped top and a red mini skirt. She came up behind him, leaned over his shoulder, kissed him on the neck.

"Morning," she said.

"What time is it?"

"Three thirty."

"You look nice," Ash said, as he brought his food over and sat down at the counter.

Candice sat next to him, took a sip of his wine. "Thanks. I have that meeting with my producer today. To go over the details of our trip."

"Oh, right," Ash said, trying not to look at her.

She eyed him keenly. "You look tired."

"I'm fine," he said.

Candice sighed. "Ash, if you're getting cold feet, you don't have to make these insulting attempts to hide it. Ugh." She took another sip of his Chardonnay.

"Should you be doing that?" he asked.

She waved him away. "Everyone on morning television is drunk or high on something." Then she touched him gently on his shoulder. "Look, you don't have to do it, if you don't want to. And you sure as shit shouldn't do it for me. It's not my fantasy to have some guy moping around, feeling like he's made a bad deal."

"It's not that . . ."

"But if you don't do something, Ash—anything, for heaven's sakes—you are going to be the one who suffers."

Ash was quiet.

"Anyway." She got up. "Back to the salt mines. You've got to keep moving forward in life."

When Ash returned from work on Wednesday evening, he was surprised to find Candice still awake. She was in the kitchen, leaning over a white box, *Patisserie Bonte* written in black scrolling on the lid. He came around and watched her while she pushed something into the bottom of one of six perfect cream puffs, a buff colored nail gently piercing the delicate pastry.

"What are you doing?" he asked.

"It seems Clark Dennis won't be able to join us in Wonderland this weekend," she said, not looking up. She squeezed the tiny hole closed between two fingers, then tapped it out smooth.

"What are you putting in there?"

Candice smiled at him sweetly, and kissed him on the cheek. "It's just a laxative."

"Are you serious?"

"Oh, Ash," she said, "it's for children. He'll be fine."

"But what if he . . . shares them, or something?"

"Dickweed doesn't share," Candice said, gingerly taking another small pink pill out of a brown bottle.

"Well, I mean . . . he's going to know you made him sick."

"I'm not going to give them to him myself." She began operating on another cream puff. "I'm having them delivered. From some non-existent woman he's slept with."

"Who? What woman?"

"'*Thanks for an incredible night. See you soon?*' That woman." She looked up.

Ash shook his head.

"Oh, for heaven's sakes, you're such a worrier."

"No," he said. "No . . ."

"What?"

He felt overwhelmed by her—her beauty, her power. Her resolve. She would take him in hand and he'd never have to make a real decision for himself ever again. It came to him then that this was it, what he'd been looking for his whole life, this was his kink. "You're just . . ." he said, shaking his head. "You're the most exciting woman I've ever met."

Blue had just finished off a couple of hours of recording in Rodrigo's makeshift studio—a far cry from what she was used to working with—and was standing in the checkout line at the A&P when she noticed the *People* cover was out. A picture of Blue and Felix wrapped around each other, with that nauseating tagline: *Making Beautiful Music Together: She keeps him clean, and he keeps making hits*. It had been organized by the label, intended as a plug for their album.

They were funny things, those signs. It was almost four weeks to the day that Rodrigo had called her with his request, one she'd rejected at the time. Three weeks to the day that the *People* photographer had come to shoot them at their house in Macon.

Felix had bought the house east of Macon, Georgia as a surprise wedding gift. The redwood ranch backed up to a ravine so steep that all they could see from their windows were the top branches of the beech trees growing from deep below. It was like living in an enchanted wood.

"It's our tree house," he'd said. "We belong up high."

Blue had loved it, loved being out of L.A. She loved Macon. It was a music town, home to soul and country music and Southern rock and Little Richard and Otis Redding. Any night of the week you could pop into Grant's Lounge, Adam's Lounge, The Cottage, or Nashville South and see someone you knew—or knew about— playing. They had a cherry blossom festival and a state fair.

If only Felix hadn't grown up a few miles away, it might have been perfect. There were the sweet things about it, of course. The cemetery where he and the boys would hang out, where he'd taken girls in high school, fumbling with their bras, lips pressed

295

hotly together. Or Mama Louise at the H&H, who'd fed The Forgotten fried pork chops, smothered chicken, black-eyed peas when they were broke and trying to make music. But it also meant that they were far from alone in their enchanted wood: there were always other people—people dropping by, hanging out, legs draped over the sofa; people helping themselves to anything and everything in the kitchen, sitting cross-legged on the floor smoking pot, their paraphernalia spread out before them. And there were lots of girls—young girls, lost girls. Some just taking a ride, having an adventure, but there were also the sadder ones—the drifters—no home, no roots, who worshipped these guys who could barely take care of themselves, let alone someone else.

It had started again the morning after the *People* shoot, when Randy, the drummer from The Forgotten, had shown up at their place with a couple of girls in halter tops and cut-offs, a case of Pabst tucked under his arm. Blue had gotten in her MG and headed for the Hilton.

They were supposed to be in the studio that day, but that wasn't going to happen. In fact, they'd only made it in a few times, and the album was far from being ready; it was still just a jumble of ideas, though the label was already hyping it in the press.

The album was meant to be a symbol of them, of their particular mixture, their scent. They'd started it while they were on tour together. Well, they'd started everything on that tour.

Ironically, it had been Olly's idea, the tour: Felix Farrow and The Forgotten were also signed to Lay Down—in fact, Olly had discovered them. Their music wasn't from the same planet, or even the same universe, and their fans would have cut each other dead on the street. But Olly had said that there were really only two types of music: good music and bad music.

Things had been falling apart with Olly for some time by that point. When they first got involved, it had been almost a sacred act: they had both been on the precipice of unhappiness, and he saved her and she saved him. They wrapped each other up like little babies and tended to each other. But, over time, she had begun to feel that something wasn't right. Like she was just treading water, and some other purpose awaited her around the corner. So, the tour had come at exactly the right moment, and she'd thought that it would do her good to get away, to think. She hadn't counted on Felix.

Unsurprisingly, Olly had been right about the tour. The fans had loved it, and the tour had turned into a rolling carnival of cool rock 'n' roll kids, blue-grass hippies—all tanned arms, cowboy hats and tight jeans and beads—and the sequined, Mardi Gras, rainbow people who were her people.

Fans followed them from gig to gig, hailing each other like long-lost friends reunited at each stop. They played in bright, bright sunshine, and under the stars, people's bodies swaying in a semi-darkness punctuated by lighters held aloft. They played in small intimate lounges, and in huge open fields.

And, in between, there were miles and miles of road, flat fields, and industrial towns and neon cities. And she'd look out the window and think: *I don't want to go home.*

Felix had just gotten out of a program and he was clean, and determined to stay that way. So the bus had a no-drinks, no-drugs policy, giving it a very different flavor to any tour bus she'd ever been on. All there was to do was sleep, write, read, play some music and talk to pass the hours. Which, as it turned out, had been enough to change their lives.

One evening, Blue watched him from the wings. It was a beautiful, soft, Southern summer evening and Felix was up there in the center of the stage and there was a breeze and they had a fan going and his hair was blown back, his throat exposed, and he was singing with his eyes closed, cupping the mic, he was singing his heart out, and she thought: *Jesus Christ.* And she had to catch her breath before she could go on.

She'd suggested a duet. "Maybe something country, something sad."

"All right," he said. "Let's try it."

" 'Help Me Make it Through the Night.' "

"The Kris Kristofferson?"

"We'll make it a little bigger. Put some pop into that fucker," she said.

Felix laughed. He had a laugh like walking into warm water. "All right, lady, whatever you say."

On stage, together, standing so close, his face inches from hers, they watched each other.

He started soft, and low: "*Take that ribbon from your hair. Shake it loose and let it fall . . .*"

So close she could feel his breath on her cheek, on her lips.

She could feel her moment coming and when it did, she let it rip, all her torch-singer training kicking in, reaching up: "*I don't care who's right or wrong, I don't try to understand . . .*"

Then back down together, their voices mingling, swooping in and out of each other: "*And it's sad to be alone, help me make it through the night.*"

And the whole time, he never took his eyes off her. He needed her; she needed him.

They'd been married before the tour was finished. In secret, of course.

They'd been determined to try to have as normal a life as possible, that's what they'd both said: make their music, raise a family. Felix had bought the house, sight unseen, while they were on the road, and they'd moved to Macon.

And now it was ten o'clock in the morning and she was writing by herself in a bar at the Hilton. It had been no easy feat covering for Felix, especially since the label executives were on to him, given his past; she'd even been forced to send the label some rough cuts of what they'd already laid down.

The thing was, it seemed Felix might not be able to stay clean. He wasn't using again, but she could see the slippage. *It's just a beer. It's practically water.* With a wink. Then, quietly, more seriously: *No, really, sweetheart, it's fine. I'm fine.*

So, as she waited in the Hilton, she realized that once again what she was really waiting for was a sign. It would be unmistakable, she had no doubt. And would tell her what she had to do next.

She hadn't had to wait long: that evening Blue returned home from the studio to find everyone flapping about the house, flustered and ineffectual. She put her satchel down on the floor and shut the door behind her. "What's wrong?"

Randy was fidgeting with his hands. He nodded towards the closed bedroom door.

Blue's body felt heavy, stiff, as she made her way across the living room towards the room she shared with Felix, and turned the knob. Inside, the curtains were half-closed and tree-dappled light filtered in. Felix lay on the bed, his kit next to him. His eyes were half-closed and his hair spread out on the pillow like a merman's.

She lay down next to him, curling around him. His body, lithe and long. She loved that body. She started singing to him, a song he'd written for her.

He opened his eyes. "That's sweet, so sweet," he said. He reached and touched her face. "Who are you, angel?"

Blue got up and left the room. She could hear him calling: "Come back, angel-woman . . ."

An hour later, the phone on the lowboy in the living room rang.

Blue picked it up.

"Blue?" It was Kurt from the label. "We've had a listen to the tapes."

"Un-hunh."

"Sweetheart . . . this is a bad album. I mean, it's bad already. And it's barely begun. You know we love you."

"I know, Kurt."

"So, you know how much I hate telling you this."

"Right." Blue sat down in the chair next to the phone.

"Your voices . . . they just don't . . . you just don't mesh, sweetheart."

That very evening she'd called Rodrigo. Then she'd called Patty and booked herself a flight to Wonderland. It was time to move on.

She picked up a copy of the magazine—a time capsule now—and put it in the basket with her shopping. That's when she saw Miller, standing at the end of the checkout, staring straight at her. There was something diffuse about her, something muffled. And something familiar, too—an animal in a trap, which only needed to have the courage to chew off its own leg to be free. And that's when she sensed it, like a doorbell ringing.

It was early evening when she got back to Patty's digs carrying her paper grocery bag full of plonk, with a jar of Planters peanuts and a pack of bologna thrown in for good measure. She had to put the bag down in order to open the door.

Patty was sitting on her bed, her hair wrapped in a towel, painting her toenails. She didn't even move to help Blue. This was one of the reasons Blue loved her so much. There was never an ounce of pity, not even concealed, from her friend.

Blue put the bag down on the small card table.

"How was the A&P?" Patty asked, placing the brush back into the polish bottle and screwing it tight. "As glamorous as ever?"

"Well, this is out," Blue said, throwing down the *People* magazine.

"Oh, boy. Have you spoken with him?"

"I spoke to Randy. They're trying to get him into another program, but so far he's refusing to go." Blue shrugged. "Maybe that was all the time we were supposed to have together."

"Easy come, easy go."

"I don't know about easy," Blue said.

Patty looked at the cover, sighed. "But, my god, he's a good-looking man."

Blue smiled. "Yes, he is." She sat down in one of the striped armchairs Patty had ordered. "Also, I ran into Miller," Blue said.

"Who's that?" Patty squinted at her. "Oh, Olly's old high-school flame?"

"Mmm," Blue said.

"Did she set upon you and try to claw your eyes out?"

"No, but she looked at me."

"Heaven's, no," Patty said, clutching her bosom.

Blue laughed. "No, I mean she gave me *a* look."

"Oh." Patty blew on her toes. "And what did it say, this look?"

"I don't know, I just got this feeling. It felt like a sign."

"Oh, you and your signs." Patty rolled her eyes. "Listen, are you going to open one of those bottles, or do I have to risk my polish?"

"I think," Blue said, picking out a corkscrew from a box of kitchen utensils, "I think I'm going to go talk to her. Miller, I mean."

"Oh, brother," Patty said.

Nate lay on his bed, restless and bored, staring at the antique trains that wound around a high shelf near the ceiling of his bedroom.

After the storm, the sun had returned but the high winds had remained, blowing now around the eaves of the house, making his bedroom creak. He could remember when he was little, how noises like these had scared him. Because his room was at the top of the house, under the peaked roof, it had all sorts of secret places built around it.

He and Cam used to take provisions—snacks, *Archie* comics, a flashlight, a canteen and a couple of those extendable aluminum camping cups—and crawl into the space in the back of the closet, shutting the small door behind them, waiting for the apocalypse. Nate hadn't known what that was, but because Cam's dad was a minister, he'd told Nate things about the destruction of Babylon the Great Whore, the Supper of the Lamb, about four crazed horses and battles with dragons and angels—weird, incomprehensible stories that gave him nightmares.

He could go into town, maybe see *Ghostbusters*, or drive to the Dairy Queen, or go to the beach and smoke a joint. But he didn't want to do any of those things.

He looked at the digital clock-radio next to his bed: it was flashing 12:00 on and off. The electricity had gone out during the nor'easter and he hadn't bothered to set it again, but he guessed it was around eight o'clock. He switched it on.

The DJ at the college radio station in Mistic was reading an ad for the midnight showing of *The Rocky Horror Picture Show* at the local theater there. Then "Avalon" came on, and Nate tried to listen to Roxy Music's smooth and dreamy track, but all it did was make him feel more restless.

It suddenly felt unbearable to lie there any longer. He got up and walked out of his room. The door to his parents' bedroom was closed; his mother was probably still in there writing in her secret diary or whatever it was she was always scribbling in these days.

He walked downstairs and out into the backyard. He could hear a rhythmic thudding coming from Suki's place. He walked over to the hedge and pushed aside some of the branches. At the far end of their yard, beyond the swimming pool, was a freestanding backboard. Suki was standing there, barefoot in a tight, high-collared green ribbed dress, whipping a ball against it with such force he was surprised that the felt hadn't shredded.

It was such a different sight from the one he was used to: the girl in the pristine tennis whites, long, red ponytail swaying. It was hard to believe that this one, with her black shorn hair and tough dress, was the same girl. But the arm that held the racket, corded with muscle, was the same arm. The expression, intense, contrary, was the same expression.

"Hey," he called.

Suki didn't respond.

"Hey," he called again, louder this time.

She continued to hit the ball. "I can hear you," she said.

"Can I talk to you?"

She stopped the ball with her racket, and turned to him. "What is it, Nate?"

"What are you doing tonight?"

Suki laughed, shrugged her shoulders. "I mean . . ."

"I was just wondering . . . *The Rocky Horror*'s playing in Mistic tonight. I thought maybe we could go."

She squinted at him, as if it were a trap or something. "You want to see *The Rocky Horror Picture Show*? In Mistic?"

"Yeah," he said.

"That's, like, three hours away." She started hitting the ball again. Thump, thump, thump.

Nate watched her. "I'll drive. If we leave now, we can grab something to eat and still make it by midnight."

She didn't answer, didn't look at him.

"I think you'll like it," he said. "It's about change. And being yourself. You know, no flies stuck in amber."

Thump, thump.

"Look, I want to take you out," he said.

This time she let the ball go past her. She looked at him again, a long, clear, hard look. "Yeah," she said finally. "Yeah, okay."

The wind began to die down and the night turned muggy as they drove inland. They passed through Longwell, through Cuttersville. On the stretch between High Hill and Vernontown, the road became narrow and the darkness closed around them like a hood. All they could see was the intermittent glow of headlights on the road ahead.

The radio was on and Suki's brown legs, just visible in the darkness, were propped up on the dash. They had rolled down their windows, but he could still feel the heat coming off her body and sense her bare skin so close to him. He gripped the wheel tighter.

The thrum of Phil Collins's "In the Air Tonight" filled the car. He thought about the day they'd spent at Suki's pool, all of them together; it seemed so far away now.

"Have you seen Cam lately?" Her voice startled him.

He shook his head. "No. I think something's . . . off between us. Not sure why."

She said nothing.

He looked at her. "Actually, I'm beginning to think it's because of you. Because he's into you."

She looked back at him, laughed. "No, he isn't. He's with Jess now."

"I'm not sure that's really a thing," Nate said.

"Oh." She went quiet again.

Nate stared at the road ahead. Then he looked at her. "Suki," he said, "I feel . . . look, I really like you. A lot."

She was looking out the window, her expression impassive, except for a slight curve of her lip, an almost-smile. "I know."

Blue had gotten Miller's address through directory assistance. Even though it wasn't far from the fisherman's shack, Patty had dropped her off in the car—the heat and humidity of the tidal island had given her a rash where her prosthetic met her skin, and walking too much inflamed it.

Blue stood outside, looking at the odd little house, painted the color of a cantaloupe with white shutters, big bushy hydrangeas with stage-blue flowers in front. It looked like it had dropped out of a 1950s movie set, though a lot of the houses in this town had that vibe.

From the street, Blue could see that the front door was closed tight. But she spied another door along the side that looked more promising. So, she walked slowly down the uneven shell driveway and up the steps to the screen door, where she knocked on the aluminum siding.

She didn't know exactly what she was going to say, or what the eventual purpose of this visit was going to turn out to be, but she'd had to come. She was beginning to suspect that Rodrigo's phone call, all those weeks ago, had been the sign that was meant to bring her to this moment.

Miller appeared at the door, carrying a bottle of wine in her hand. She was wearing a kind of hippy dress with gold thread shot through it, and hoop earrings and bangles. She looked a little like a pale gypsy. She was pretty, Blue thought, examining her more closely now. In a kind of careless way that some women had. Miller looked shocked to see her standing there, which made Blue smile.

"Oh, hello," Miller said.

"Hi," Blue said. "I saw you at the supermarket."

Miller just stood there.

"Can I come in?" Blue asked, gesturing at the screen door.

"Sorry, yes. Of course."

It was one of those damn doors that opened outwards, so when Miller pushed it open slightly, Blue had to step down to maneuver out of its way.

"Oh, sorry," Miller said again.

"Don't be sorry," Blue said, catching the door and stepping up and into the kitchen.

Miller continued to stare at her as Blue looked around the kitchen, taking in the strangely hideous yellow fridge, and a green phone that was hanging off the wall by its wires.

"Would you like a drink?" Miller said, finally. "There's some wine here . . ." She looked at the bottle in her hand, as if she wasn't sure what it was actually for.

"Were you going out?" Blue asked.

"I was supposed to meet someone, but it's fine. I've got time."

"Good, I'm glad," Blue said, smiling her best pop-star smile. "Do you have any vodka?"

"Ummm, I think so." Miller went over to a bar in the corner and filled a glass from one of the decanters. She turned. "On the rocks? Soda, tonic?"

"On the rocks." Blue walked over to some photographs on the wall. She stared at one, a large black and white photograph of Joni Mitchell standing next to a woman who looked like Miller, but much younger.

"This is you?" Blue took the drink Miller handed her. "Thanks."

"Yes, a lifetime ago."

"The Lay Down days." Olly used to talk it about it, on rare occasions: how happy they'd been, before Ash and Miller had betrayed him. She'd always wondered, though, what the other side of the story was. There were at least two sides to every story, sometimes many more.

"Mmm. The Lay Down days." Miller moved toward the chintz chairs near the French doors. "Would you like to sit down? I mean, is this all right . . . ?"

"Thanks," Blue said, and braced herself as she sat down in the unfortunately low chair, arranging her cheetah-print gown around her matching prosthetic. Miller sat next to her.

Blue smiled at her again. "So," she said, "you're probably wondering why I'm here."

Miller rose. "I just realized I didn't get myself anything."

Blue sighed. She was beginning to understand that Miller had that kind of East Coast formality that kept any real conversations from happening, at least while anyone was sober. She was clearly going to have to just jump straight in if they were going to get anywhere.

Miller opened the bottle of wine she'd left on the counter and poured herself a large tumbler-full, then returned.

"So, sorry—you were saying why you'd come."

Blue nodded. "You know, I've heard about you for so long. And I think maybe you've heard about me?"

Miller laughed, as if the question were ridiculous.

Blue tilted her head, acknowledging that it probably went without saying. "Anyway, I saw you today and I just felt like it was time we met. Like it was meant be."

Miller just looked at her.

"I get these . . . feelings sometimes, about things," Blue said. "Does that ever happen to you?"

"Not really," Miller said, in a clipped kind of way. "But I'm pleased you've come."

"You know, you're very polite," Blue said.

"Am I?"

"It's not a bad thing. I just imagined you more . . . I don't know, actually."

"Oh." Miller said. "Well, Olly probably described the person I was years ago."

"Hunh," Blue said. She honestly couldn't remember now if Olly had actually described Miller at any great length, only his feelings about her.

"Well, you're exactly how I imagined you," Miller said.

"And how's that?"

"Very sure of yourself." She smiled at her. "That's not a bad thing, by the way."

Blue let out a laugh. "Touché."

Miller took a small sip of her wine. "What *are* you doing in Wonderland, if you don't mind my asking?"

"The movie. Rodrigo and I are old friends, and he needed a favor." She took a drink. "And I said to myself: Blue, it's a sign." She smiled again. "But then when I saw you at the supermarket, I wondered if I was supposed to come here because I was supposed to meet you."

"You've got to be kidding," Miller said.

"I'm not kidding." Blue looked her dead in the eye.

She watched Miller watch her, take another drink from her glass. Blue wondered what she was like when she let it all go. She had good energy, in there somewhere, and a toughness Blue could relate to. She just needed to chew off her own damn leg.

"Are you very unhappy?"

"I'm sorry?"

Blue laughed; Miller sounded so offended. "It's a reasonable question," she said. "Lots of people are unhappy." She surveyed her a little longer. "Look," she said, "all I'm trying to say is that I think I've been brought to you for some purpose, and we might find out quicker if you could tell me what was making you unhappy, or holding you back. Because I can feel something's going on here."

Miller didn't say anything.

"You know," Blue said. "All my life, people assumed that *I* assumed that I was less than I should've been, not whole. Because of my leg." She caught an ice cube and cracked it between her teeth. "But actually, I knew I was more whole, because I had freed myself from the trap of other people's expectations. My difference made me powerful. I think everyone has that thing in them that's different, that the world assumes is a liability. The trick is not to hide it away, like it's ugly, but to let it out. Let it shine." Blue finished her drink.

They looked at each other a while. Finally, Miller shrugged. "What the hell," she said. "I'd like to show you something."

Blue waited as Miller left the kitchen and returned a little while later carrying a journal— the black and white ones kids used in school. She handed it to Blue, who opened the cover and began to read.

An hour later, Blue looked up. The wind had died down and there was a humidity creeping into the air in the kitchen. The temperature was rising after the storm. Miller was flipping through an old issue of *McCall's*: "He Comes Home But He's Not Here—how to turn on a turned-off man."

"Well," Blue said, closing the composition book. "This is extraordinary. It's beautiful. And so, so sad." It was, and Blue knew her instincts had been right: this was why she was here.

Miller smiled. "Thanks."

"What are you planning to do with it?"

"Well, it's a letter to my son, really."

"Yes, I got that. But it's more than that . . . It's art."

Miller frowned.

"Listen, I know a guy at *Rolling Stone*. He would love this kind of thing—you know, all the things about the music scene at the time, and all the people. And the way you describe it, it's a whole world. I mean, I know you could probably do so much better, but it's a start."

"Umm . . . no."

"No?"

"That's not why I did it," Miller said. "It's meant to be private."

Blue eyed her, then poured them both a generous serving of wine. "Is that why you showed it to me? Because it was private?"

"So, I got carried away," Miller said, arching an eyebrow.

"See, I think," Blue said, "you know how good are, or you suspect it. And you want me to free you or, more specifically, you want me to give you permission to free yourself."

Miller narrowed her eyes. "I don't know. No, it feels wrong, to profit off of that, off of those private relationships, really."

Blue laughed. "Everyone profits from their experience. Ash and Olly helped themselves to it, why shouldn't you? Just talk to my guy at *Rolling Stone*. All you need is for the right person to read it." She smiled. "This could be the beginning of the rest of your life, Miller Everley."

Miller bit her lip, a small smile creeping across her face, her skin beginning to light up. "Well," she said, "it just so happens that I am in the market for a new life." Then she laughed, which made Blue laugh, too.

Miller raised her glass. "To the signs."

"Blessed be the signs," Blue said.

When they reached Mistic, Nate and Suki stopped at a snack shack for a burger, then walked back to Nate's car. He pulled a six-pack of beer from behind the front seat.

"Can we put this in your bag?" he asked, indicating the dyed African basket—the kind all the girls seemed to have—which hung off her shoulder from two leather straps.

She handed it to him, and he put the beers in it, then chucked in a bag of uncooked rice, and a newspaper.

Suki looked at him. She was so close to him he could have brushed his knuckles over the tops of her breasts, pushing out from her tight dress. He stared at her and he could feel it, between them, the electricity. He smiled, she smiled. He exhaled.

They walked slowly to the theater—the Paradise—and stood in line to buy tickets. Mistic was a small college town, but the crowd was dressed like they were auditioning to get into a New York City nightclub—imitation drag queens, and punks, people with dark glam-rock wigs and ripped fish-nets, fruit charm jewelry, and an array of neon-colored plastic bracelets all the way up the girls' arms.

One girl ahead of them, in a French-maid costume and bronze, curly wig, stared at Suki. Then she leaned forward and grabbed Suki's wrist. "I'd die for your look," she said. "Your hair's amazing."

Nate looked at Suki. Her eyes seemed so big, rimmed with Egyptian black eyeliner, and her hair shone a bit under the marquee lights.

Suki smiled. "Thanks, I really like your look, too."

"Yeah. I'm Magenta tonight," the girl said, and winked. When Suki didn't say anything, the girl said: "You've never been to *The Rocky Horror*, have you?"

Suki shook her head.

"A virgin," she said. "Cool."

Suki leaned in close to Nate. "I love it already," she said, little puffs of breath pushing into his ear. He swallowed.

Inside the theater, the air was thick with the smell of pot smoke, stale popcorn and warm bodies.

"This is one experience where closer is better," Nate said, leading her down the aisle until they found a couple of seats in the third row.

The lights in the theater dimmed, but the projector hadn't yet been turned on. A guy dressed like Dr. Frank-N-Furter—fish-net stockings, high heels, black corset ending just under his nipples—got on stage in front of the big screen.

"Good evening. Before we start tonight's festivities, we just have one question . . . how many virgins are out there?"

The crowd cheered.

Suki looked at Nate, about to say something, when the French Maid from the ticket line appeared next to them. She reached into a small handbag tied to her wrist and pulled out a lipstick, twisted it. Then she took Suki's face in her hands and drew a bright red "V" on her forehead. "You're too cool to stay down here," she said. "Come with me."

Suki smiled at Nate and followed Magenta up the stairs onto the stage, joining the others who'd made their way from the audience.

The MC lined them up, girl-boy. "Now, I want you to raise your middle finger and repeat after me:

I pledge allegiance to the lips

Of *The Rocky Horror Picture Show*.

And to the decadence for which it stands,
One movie under Richard O'Brien,
With Sensuous Daydreams, Erotic Nightmares,
And Sins of the flesh for all."

Nate looked at Suki. She looked willowy and fine, the glossy red lipstick marking her skin. She looked completely at ease. She was so fucking cool.

The MC looked around. "Very good. Now, normally, things get a little kinkier for our virgins, but someone"—he turned and looked with mock outrage at Magenta—"forgot the Hostess cupcakes tonight."

"*Booooooo . . .*"

"So, off you go, my virgins. This will be a night you won't forget."

By the time Suki returned to her seat, the lights had gone all the way down in the theater and Nate couldn't see her expression. But when the film began to play—a pair of disembodied, glistening red lips singing in a twanging falsetto—he could see she was completely focused.

Nate got the rice out of Suki's bag and opened it. "Take a handful," he whispered.

Without taking her eyes off the screen, she felt her way to the bag and scooped some out.

The self-appointed live cast stood small against the large moving images, their tinsel wigs shimmering and shifting as they acted out their own demented version of the film. The movie had taken on a life of its own, beyond the celluloid. As if the story had come full circle: from camp theater to big-budget movie, back to camp theater.

When the wedding scene arrived, rice hailed down all around them. Suki, in her surprise and excitement, threw hers straight up in the air, laughing as it scattered down into her own hair, on her clothes, pooled between her legs. In the light of the screen, the delicate grains glowed bright white against the brown of her inner thigh.

As the audience played along with their props—snapping newspapers atop their heads, shooting water pistols into the crowd to mimic rain, flicking lighters dangerously close—Suki kept twisting around in her seat to see what people were doing. And by the time they got to "The Time Warp," she was up and dancing with the rest of them.

She reached out and pulled Nate up with her. "Come on." And then they had their arms around each other, knocking against each other in the small space between the seats, as they did the dance steps. His hand slid along the smoothness of her back, her hip, her waist, slid just underneath the hem of her dress. He could see sweat along her collar bone in the light of the reflected images, and wanted to taste it with his tongue.

In the final act, when Dr. Frank-N-Furter began to sing his ballad, "I'm Going Home," Suki slipped her hand into Nate's. The image of Tim Curry's face loomed, his iridescent blue eye make-up running down his face, as he sang: "Everywhere it's been the same, like I'm outside in the rain," and he heard Suki breathe in sharply. He looked over and saw her face and he held her hand tighter, as the remains of hot dogs and toast flew through the air around them.

Miller and Blue were in the kitchen of Miller's house trying on all the old evening gowns she kept stored in the cedar closet in the basement. They were very drunk.

"I can't remember the last time I put one of these on," Miller said.

"See? You need to get out more," Blue said.

"You're not the first person to have mentioned that," Miller replied, dryly. She looked over at Blue who was wearing a black faille number she'd worn to a political fundraiser ten years ago, now. "That looks good on you." Blue was actually the most gorgeous creature she had ever seen, even more so up close, in person. Bewitching, Miller thought.

Blue did a twirl, took a swig from a newly opened bottle of

vodka and passed it to Miller. "I like that one," she said, gesturing to Miller. "I'd like it for the stage."

Miller took the bottle and drank, before looking down at her white, one-shouldered dress. It still fit like a glove, though it certainly wasn't the same person wearing it. "I had it made for the Grammys. In the '60s. When I was still with Olly. God."

"So you and Olly. What's going on there? I saw you at that restaurant. I'm not prying, but"—she laughed, shot Miller that 1000-watt smile— "Well, I guess I am."

"Oh, that," Miller said. "It's complicated. It sort of happened by accident . . ." She shrugged.

"I doubt it's an accident," Blue said. "I bet some part of him was always here, with you guys. That's what it felt like to me, anyway. When we were together." Blue stopped. "Don't get me wrong, we loved each other, Olly and I. But it was the kind that passes."

Miller nodded. "Olly's always been good at that: making you feel like he wants to be somewhere else."

"Don't be too hard on Olly. He's had a rough time."

Miller snorted, took another swig. "Olly's always known how to take care of himself." She handed Blue the bottle of vodka. "I'm not criticizing: it's a good skill."

"If you say so." But she said it in a certain tone, an obvious one, the kind where you know.

"What? What is it?"

Blue sighed. "Well, you'd probably find out at some point, anyway. Olly took some pills. On purpose. He ended up in the hospital."

"I thought he was in the hospital because of his house, the earthquake . . ."

"Mmm, seems he took a fistful of barbiturates. At the same time as the goddamn earthquake, as luck would have it. Only Olly." She laughed. "I suppose it's not funny. Anyway, I only found out because I was his emergency contact and he didn't show up for his outpatient therapy."

Miller felt sick. She felt the vodka churning in her stomach and her head felt slow, like there were a million different puzzle pieces that she was trying to make a coherent picture out of, and had no idea where to start.

"It really shocks you." Blue seemed surprised. "Olly's not as strong as he likes to pretend."

"No," Miller said, darkly. She thought about Nate; she found she was suddenly furious. She absolutely couldn't think about that now. "Enough about Olly," she said.

"You're right," Blue said. "This isn't about him. It's about you."

"And you," Miller gestured to Blue.

Blue nodded her head, vigorously. "I think this historic meeting needs to be documented."

"I think I have a camera somewhere," Miller said. "I'll get it."

"Great," Blue said, slapping her hand against the kitchen table. She swayed slightly from the effort. "I think I have to sit down for a minute."

"Okay, you rest," Miller shouted over her shoulder. "I'll be right back."

After locating the camera in the back of her bedroom closet, Miller returned downstairs. "I think it has some film in it," she called out as she came through the door to the kitchen.

When Blue didn't answer, she looked up from the camera, and standing there next to Blue was Olly.

His expression looked stunned, pained. And it took Miller a minute to realize he was looking at the dress. She stood there, silent.

"We had a date. I just came over to see if you were okay," he said, flatly. "I guess I shouldn't have worried."

"I'm just dandy," Miller said, narrowing her eyes at him. "It seems you're the one we should be worried about."

Olly looked at Blue and then back at Miller. "What are you talking about?"

Blue raised her eyebrows, took a not-very-discreet sip from the vodka bottle.

Miller covered the distance between the doorway and the table, surprised to find herself so steady on her feet. "Oh, I don't know. What did you really come back here for, Olly?"

"You're drunk," he said.

"Blah blah blah," Miller said, waving her hand. "Don't change the subject. Did you come to assuage your guilt? To . . . what? Claim Nate as a way to make up for the hole in your life? Do you want my son so you don't try to kill yourself again? You're such a liar."

Olly looked like he'd been slapped, hard, cheeks reddening. "Who told you that?"

"I did," Blue said. "Emergency contact. Your doctor called when you didn't show up for your appointments with the shrink."

Olly turned on Blue, now. "What the fuck?"

Blue stood up. "Oh, grow up, Olly. It's called giving a shit."

"Really? That's what it's called?" He looked at Blue. "You know, I was going to come and thank you, for leaving me. Because you were right—sometimes you do need to fuck up your life to live it. But now I see you just like to fuck things up for the fun of it." He turned back to Miller. "And so what? I didn't tell you. Is it suddenly your right to know everything that goes on in my life?"

"Are you serious?" Miller said. "I mean, are you? We're having some sort of . . . affair, or whatever. You're trying to build a relationship with my son and it's not my business what goes on in your life? Don't use Nate to try to fix yourself, Olly."

"Okay, I was really fucking sad. It's not like you're the poster girl for happy living."

"I think I'm going to call a taxi, or something," Blue said. "Are there any taxis here?"

"Oh, that's perfect," Olly said to her. "Just make a mess and run away, as usual."

"I'll call Patty," Blue said, to no one in particular.

"Phone's over there," Miller said, nodding at the pea-green phone hanging precariously from the wall. "It still works," she said, then she sat down at the table. Her head had begun to throb.

Olly crossed his arms. "What are we fighting about here?"

"We're fighting about trust. And secrets. And all the bullshit, Olly, that we've been fighting about for twenty years."

"Patty's coming," Blue said, putting the receiver down. "Miller, I'll get in touch with my guy at *Rolling Stone*, and get back to you," she said.

Miller got up and hugged Blue hard. "Thank you," she said. "For everything."

"I'm so glad I finally met you," Blue said. Then she walked over to Olly, put her hand on his cheek, winked. "And you're welcome, by the way." And, flashing her extraordinary smile one more time at them, she headed out the door.

"What guy from *Rolling Stone*?"

"I mean . . ." Miller shook her head. "A guy she knows."

"Yes, I get that, but for what?"

"I might be writing something about Lay Down. About that time in our lives."

"What about it? About us?"

"Yes, about us—you and me and Ash. Maybe."

Olly laughed. "And Nate?"

"I've already written something for him. To explain . . . all of it."

"Oh, I get it. You're the one who gets to control the story."

"I think it's best if it comes from me," Miller said.

"No, right. Of course." Olly shook his head. "Talk about secrets. You're the one who's been keeping the biggest one of all. Who's fucking kid is he, Miller?"

"He's mine."

They both turned to see Ash standing in the doorway. He put his bag down and went to the bar. They watched him in silence as he lifted one of the decanters and found it empty. Seeing the vodka bottle on the table, he walked over and poured a generous portion into a lowball. "Been dispensing with the glassware, Miller?" he asked.

She shrugged.

"I can see not much has changed since I left," he said.

"Oh, god, Ash, get off your high horse."

He eyed the dress she was wearing. "Nice dress."

"Thanks."

"Are you drunk?"

"Yes, she is drunk."

"What are you doing here, Ash?" Miller said, ignoring Olly.

"Well, I didn't come here tonight to get into it. I came to tell you that I'm back. Candice has come with me, she's at the hotel." Miller could tell he was starting to get nervous; it made her want to die laughing. "And we want . . . um . . . I want to have a talk with Nate. About everything that's going on."

"And what's going on?" Miller said.

"Look, you and I should talk first, of course. But it's time we got all this crap out in the open."

"Oh, really?"

"Yeah, I think so. I think it's the right thing to do."

Miller laughed and lay her head down on the table. "Oh, my god."

Ash sat down, and took Miller's hand. "Look, I'm sorry. You know, Candice says . . ."

"Oh, shut up," Miller said.

"Well . . ." Ash said.

"I will never understand," Olly said, "how you left me for this guy."

"You . . . stopped . . . looking . . . at . . . me," Miller shouted.

"You *were* a complete asshole," Ash said. "All I had to do was not be a complete asshole."

"Oh, my god," Olly said, his eyes on Miller. "I stopped looking at you for ten fucking seconds. Is your world going to collapse? The fucking gall of me."

Miller shook her head. "Oh, give me a break. Try a year . . ."

"I'm going to the hotel. This is pointless," Ash said, turning to leave.

"Good," Olly said.

"Actually," Ash said, turning back, "I fucking live here. This is my fucking wife. I can stay or I can leave as I like."

"I'd think again, pal, about all three of those statements," Olly said.

"You're like two dueling cocks," Miller said, feeling disgusted and drunk and tired. "Look at the two of you. Neither one of you knows shit. At least *I* know he's my son."

"She's written about it, you know," Olly said, looking at Ash. "About us and Nate. She's written the story—her story, anyway—and she's going to give it to him."

"What do you mean?" Ash said, looking from Olly to Miller.

"She's planned it out. She's going to tell him."

"Tell him what?" Ash said.

"Yeah, Miller, tell him what?" Olly said, his face hard.

Miller got up, smoothed down her beautiful dress. "You know what? You can go both go to hell. I'm going to bed."

When Nate and Suki left the theater they were silent. Only when they'd been in the car for a few minutes did Suki begin to speak.

"I want to do something like that."

Nate looked over at her.

"I want to do something with people like that, with those beautiful, shiny people, with the freaks. Because I think . . . because the thing is . . . I'm a freak."

He laughed.

Suki laughed, too. She rolled her window down all the way and stuck her head out. The deep inland night was muggy, the remnants of the storm coupled with an incoming heat cast a misty gloom over the road. "It was so . . . I just . . . *loved* it."

"You look happy," he said.

"I am happy." She switched on the radio.

"If You Leave Me Now" was playing, with all its shakers and wind chimes and conga drums. Chicago grooving out to those French horns. The mournful sound of Pete Cetera's pleading lyrics.

318

"No, don't," Suki said, as Nate reached to change the dial. "I love this song."

"You *are* a freak."

"What can I say? Pete Cetera's white-hot."

"Oh, god," Nate groaned.

Suki laughed. "Don't be a snob," she said. "Listen to those horns."

"I am not a snob," Nate said.

"Oh, yes, you are."

"Jess told me I was a particular type of very lucky guy."

"Mmmm. She meant snob."

"Ha." Nate was quiet for minute, listening to the song. "The lyrics, though. They're just saying the same thing over and over."

But Suki wasn't listening to him. She had her eyes closed.

That was Chicago with "If You Leave Me Now." Such a lovely song. If you're listening to this out there, and you're feeling sad, just remember there's a difference between loneliness and being alone.

This is Bedtime Magic *with David Allen Boucher. Thanks for listening, and thanks for just being you.*

"Amen," said Suki.

Nate drove on through the night.

It was four-thirty in the morning when they hit Longwell.

"I don't want to go home," Suki said.

"Me, either," Nate said.

"We still have those beers," she said. "Let's go to the beach."

"Dune Beach?"

"No. The one here."

Nate parked under the bridge next to the anchorage, facing out towards the water and Wonderland beyond. The ocean was still stirred up from the days of stormy weather, and choppy little waves threw themselves against the breakwater, sending up small squalls of white spray.

The windshield quickly became sticky, almost opaque. The radio was on, playing "King of Pain." Nate and Suki rolled back the car seats and lay there, looking at the blurred view in front of them, drinking from the warm cans of beer.

"Do you think this song's about suicide?"

"Do you always do that?" Suki asked. "Pick songs apart?"

Nate laughed. "I think I do. Cam is always giving me shit about that."

She was quiet for a moment, then she said: "Did you know Synchronicity is actually a theory that certain things that happen in life are all connected? You know, coincidences that aren't coincidences, and signs, and dreams. All that stuff that people try to tell you isn't real, but you just know it is. Cam taught me that."

The water roiled before them.

"Anyway," Suki said, putting her feet up on the dashboard, delicate light hairs rising on her legs. "I don't feel like it's about suicide; I'm pretty sure it's a break-up song."

Nate looked up at the curved roof of the VW. "I think my parents are getting a divorce."

"My mom is having an affair with Reverend Cross. But it's not her fault. My dad hits her."

They were quiet.

"I don't want to end up like them," he said.

"Me, either."

Nate sat up. "Come on," he said, opening the car door and getting out.

Suki followed him as he walked to the edge of the breakwater, the music from the open car lost in the sound of the waves.

He stood there, his face, his hair dampening, his jeans turning dark. "*Fuck it*," he yelled into the ocean. "*Fuck it*."

Suki laughed. "*Fuck it*," she yelled.

"*Fuck it*," they yelled together, screaming into the wind.

Then Suki turned and looked at him. She stood on her tiptoes and pressed her mouth against his. He pushed his tongue in between her lips, then a little deeper into her wet mouth, running one hand down over her legs and ass, the other up over the dark, shorn hair.

In the front seat, she was on top, her body slick, her mouth open, her hands cupping his shoulders, moving against him, her legs gripping him. He watched her above him, rising up, up, up, the sharp outline of her chin, the round of her cheek, the slope of her breasts, pressing forward. And he, lying beneath, trying to hold her, hold her fast, hold her to him.

PART V

'TIS LOVE, 'TIS LOVE THAT MAKES THE WORLD GO ROUND

AUGUST, 1984

Olly woke up late. When he'd left Miller and Ash's house the night before, he'd proceeded to get very drunk, and now he had a terrible hangover. He put on a bathrobe and went off to the big house in search of some aspirin. He found Aunt Tassie sitting in the parlor on the Sheraton sofa, staring straight ahead, unmoving.

"Aunt Tassie?" When she didn't respond, he said: "Billy?"

She turned her head slowly and looked at him. "Who are you?"

"It's Olly," he said, going over and sitting down next to her. "Are you okay?" Looking at her, he noticed that her body was so light that it barely made an indent in the feather sofa cushion.

"Oh, Olly." She nodded slowly. "Of course."

"Are you feeling all right? Should I call Dr. Cleves?"

She shook her head. "I think I must have been dreaming," she said.

"A good dream, I hope," he said, gently taking her hand. His head throbbed. Olly pressed his fingers to his temple. The sunshine was streaming through the front windows, and the room was hot and stuffy.

"A ship on the water. Execution at dawn." She smiled at him.

"I think you're tired," he said.

"I am tired."

Olly put his arm around her. "Let's get you upstairs."

On the landing in front of her room, she turned to him. "There are some things we should say to each other while I can still remember them."

"Okay . . ." He could smell his sweat, the odor of booze, leaking through his pores. He led her to her bed, helped her under the covers.

"The boy," she said, lying back against the pillows. "The boy's the important thing now."

He stared at her a minute. She knew. She must have known all along.

"It's all connected. All the love is connected. Through all of you. Through all of it." She raised her hands, her fingers tracing mysterious lines that only she could see. "You must all mind the light, now." Her pale blue eyes turned back to him.

He squeezed her hand. "Yes, of course." He closed the curtains and then returned to her bedside. "Can I get you anything?"

She put her hand to his face. "You know, Olly my dear, I told your mother I'd protect you with my life, and that's what I've done. You were such a small boy when you lost her. But now you have to take responsibility for the man you've become."

"I know."

"You must not despair again."

He nodded.

"Promise me."

"I promise."

She closed her eyes, and after a minute or two her breathing became deep and even, her hands folded neatly across her stomach.

Olly looked around the room. In all the years they'd lived there, her room had never changed: the big four-poster bed and heavy green silk curtains, the dressing table with its silver dressing set. It was hard to imagine her as anything but old, but she must have been around the age he was now when Olly was born. She must have sat at that table, brushing her hair, applying her creams and make-up. She must have pulled aside those heavy curtains in the morning, and when she did, what did she think of? Love? Desire? Had she ever been allowed any of those things, or had she always had to think of everyone else, of his mother, of him?

On her bedside table, next to a lamp with a creamy silk shade, he saw a collection of what looked like scrimshaw. He picked one up and realized it was plastic.

It was engraved with a picture of a large ship, the words *The Pequod* carved into it. He picked up another, and turned it over in his hand. On the back, Aunt Tassie had clearly made her own, cruder scratching—the name of Billy Budd's ship. On the shelf below, he saw there was more: a collection of shrunken heads—presumably from the set of the Spouter-Inn—and a couple of silver grog mugs. Aunt Tassie must have been stealing these little treasures from the movie set.

Underneath was a leather-bound notebook. Olly slid it out and opened it. Inside were pages of writing in Aunt Tassie's curving, spidery hand, and he sat down on the floor, his back against the bed and began to read: disconnected sentences, paragraphs, many of them references to *Billy Budd* and her murky connection to it: *Billy is the sacrificial lamb, he must die to restore order. Claggart must die because he is evil. But Billy must go, too.*

Olly's heart contracted. Of course. He'd forgotten, or he hadn't paid attention: Claggart was the villain in *Billy Budd*, that symbol of inexplicable evil. Who torments and tries to trap Billy Budd, who envies and desires him, who lies about him in order to see him hanged, only to have the young sailor strike Claggart down in an unthinking act of self-defense. Claggart was also the name of the man that Aunt Tassie had stabbed at Starry Acres.

Jesus, he thought, what the fuck happened to her there?

He read on, wanting and not wanting to know what he'd see next: *"Pale ire, envy and despair . . ." These are the entwined evils that will lead to the tragedy. For as the book says, in a nature like that, "what recourse is left to it but to recoil on itself and like the scorpion . . . act out to the end the part allotted to it."*

The last entry read: *"The light shines in the darkness, and the darkness comprehends it and suffers."*

Olly closed the journal. God, what a fool he'd been. He'd squandered so much: time, joy, light. Miller was right: what the fuck did he know about effacing himself, about taking care of someone else? About being a man? What did he know about love, in the end?

He knew nothing. But it wasn't too late to learn.

Olly found Rodrigo in the boathouse, editing on the Moviola. He raised his arms when he saw Olly, like he'd scored a goal, and stopped what he was doing.

"You always show up just when I need you."

Olly gave him a flat look.

"What have you got there?" Rodrigo nodded his chin towards the shoebox he was carrying.

"It seems," he said, walking over to the desk, "Billy Budd made off with some of your props."

Olly had put the scrimshaw and the other film props in the box. He'd left one piece for Aunt Tassie—the one she'd carved "H.M.S. *Belliport*" on—and of course, her journal.

Rodrigo flicked the top off the box with his finger and looked inside. He smiled. He closed it again. "Not that important, but we might need them for continuity."

"I figured," Olly said. "Anyway. You've been avoiding me."

"I knew you'd be angry. You know, about Blue." Rodrigo smiled as if that would be the most ridiculous thing in the world.

Olly shrugged. "Well, you haven't exactly made my life easier."

"Easy. Who ever said easy was good? Anyway, listen, I'm glad you're here."

Olly waved him away. "I'm not sure I can deal with any more high drama at the moment. I've got my own stuff going on."

"Come on, you know you're just a little curious." He patted an empty chair next to him.

Olly sighed. "Fine." He sat down and folded his arms. "What?"

"So, one of the things I agreed to, you know, with the town, to get the permits, was to give them a screening of the rough cut. At the town hall. You know, for the people. Before we left Wonderland."

"You agreed to that?"

"Mmmm." Rodrigo nodded, thoughtfully.

"And Geist was okay with that?"

"Well . . . Geist. He doesn't need to know everything."

"Jesus, Rodrigo." Olly rubbed his eyes. "You'd better hope this doesn't get back to him."

"It might not be too bad."

"I don't know," Olly said. "It's a rough cut. For the public? That's a big risk."

"What does the song say? Accentuate the positive. Right? Get rid of the negative." He made a slicing motion with his hand "And don't mess with Mr. In Between."

"Johnny Mercer?"

"Johnny Mercer."

They looked at each other

"All right," Olly said. "So, what do you want from me?"

"Have a look at it. Tell me how much of a shit storm I'm in for."

Then he started at the beginning.

Following her evening with Blue, Miller had spent the whole of the next day in bed, in a hazy, hung-over slumber. But on the second day she awoke refreshed and clear-headed. She felt much better than she had in a long time; she felt like a million bucks.

She called Blue's friend at *Rolling Stone*. They had a long talk—at her expense, naturally—about her, about what she wanted to write, about what he wanted her to write, and they'd come to an initial understanding.

Afterwards, she got in the car and drove over the bridge to the only decent store in a twenty-mile radius where she bought herself a white silk dress, cut in a low, draped V at her breasts, and a pair of Ray-Bans. She left her Ted Lapidus sunglasses on the counter.

"I don't need these anymore," she said, tapping them. "They're nice, though—Ted Lapidus."

From there, she stopped at a gas station and bought a pack of Parliaments. She lit one, then started the car and drove fast and barefoot to the beach in Longwell, where she walked into the water and, this time, swam all the way to the buoy.

On her way home, she turned the radio up full volume, her wet hair and suit drying in the hot air. As she turned off the Ring Road onto Church Street, "Rock 'n' Roll Suicide" came on the radio. She was so distracted by it—the sheer joy of hearing the right song at the right time, of the strumming guitar and David Bowie's quivering voice—that she almost missed the turn to her house, and ended up pulling so fast into the driveway that the tires kicked up a cloud of broken shells which pinged against the car and the windshield.

Slamming on the brakes and putting the car in neutral, she rolled the seat back, put her feet up on the wheel, waving her cigarette, and singing at the top of her lungs about cigarettes, rock 'n' roll, and aloneness. The Naugahyde seats began to heat up in the sun, the acrid, desert smell of the cigarette draping itself around her in the motionless air.

"Well, hey there."

Miller turned her head slowly and met the face of Mary Guntherson.

"I've been trying to reach you. You've been conspicuously absent from the party circuit in the last few weeks. Though I think I can guess why." Mary winked at her. When Miller didn't respond, Mary said: "Is this a bad time?"

"No," Miller said. "Not at all. I'm just really into this song."

"Oh," Mary said. "Okay." She straightened up a little "Well, listen, we're having our last cocktail party of the summer, and we'd love it if you could come. As I said, I've been trying to get a hold of you, but . . . anyway, it's tonight."

"I'd love to," Miller said, turning away. "In fact, I have the perfect dress."

When Miller arrived at the Gunthersons' house—a sprawling pink Victorian overlooking Pebble Beach—she could hear the sounds of Carly Simon's new album playing over a stereo system: a mingling of soft pop and reggae. The air was still hot, but there was a little breeze, and Miller could feel her dress clinging to her, sliding over her skin.

She took a whiskey soda from the bartender and let an oyster slide down her throat, briny and slick, before joining the crowd on the lawn. When Mary saw her, she hurried towards Miller, a slightly panicked expression on her face.

"Oh, god, I'm glad I caught you." She stopped. "Oh, you look great . . . different."

"Thanks."

"Anyway, goddamn Kip . . . I don't know what's wrong with him . . . I'm sorry . . ."

"What's the problem, Mary?"

"Kip ran into Ash in town, and he invited him and, oh . . ."— she waved her hands a little—"now he's here and he's brought *her*."

Miller looked around.

"They're over there." Mary indicated a group on the other side of the lawn from where they were standing. "I'm so sorry, Miller. Look, I totally understand if you don't feel you can stay."

"It's fine," Miller said, taking a sip of whiskey. "In fact, I think I'll go say hello."

Mary raised her eyebrows.

"Don't worry. It's all going to be okay." She squeezed her friend's arm and began walking towards them, leaving Mary rooted to the spot.

She moved through the small clusters of guests, through clouds of Bay Rum, L'Air du Temps and Opium, clouds of whiskey and Almaden Mountain Chablis-tinged breath—the remnants of her own hangover whistling back at her.

The music floated in snatches, carried away from time to time by the push of a breeze.

When she reached them, Ash was in animated conversation with Roy Baxter.

"He's been indicted now . . . insider trading," Roy was saying. "They're going to nail him to the wall."

"Dutch was always a grade-A asshole," Ash said.

"Well, he can say bye-bye to that house, and . . ." Roy stopped when he caught sight of Miller standing at the edge of their circle. "Oh, hello, Miller." His voice sounded a little strangled.

"Hi, Roy," Miller said. "Ash." She nodded at her husband before looking directly at his companion. "Candice, I presume?"

"I'm going to get a refill," Roy said. "Can I get anyone anything?"

"Sure," Miller said. "A whiskey."

But Roy was already hurrying away.

Ash looked at her, taking in the dress, the slicked-back hair, the red lipstick and Wayfarers. He arched his eyebrow. "New look?"

Miller laughed. "Something like that."

Candice reached out her hand.

Miller took it—it was warm and soft, which somehow surprised her. Up close, Candice was a small thing, with a helmet of blonde, shellacked hair. She was wearing a dress cut from some accordion-type material with big shoulder pads; a large, gold cuff gleamed on each wrist as she shook Miller's hand.

"Well, this is an interesting turn of events," Miller said.

"Don't start. Not here," Ash said.

"Oh," Miller waved him away, "we're way past that, Ash."

"She's right," Candice said.

Ash looked at Candice sharply, then into his drink.

"I suppose you and I better talk," Miller said to Candice, "because I don't think he's going to."

"Agreed," Candice said. She had a tight, bright way of speaking. Economical. "Ash wants a divorce."

"Well, Ash is going to get a divorce," Miller said. "But there are going to be some conditions. And I don't mean financial ones, though those are expected, as well."

Candice nodded. "Of course. Goes without saying."

"Nate," Miller said, looking from one to other.

Candice shrugged. "I'm not very maternal. You'll get no competition from me, if that's worrying you."

Miller looked at her. "It's not. You better be fucking kind to my

332

son. In all things, Nate comes first." She looked at Ash. "This is the part when you need to speak."

"Nate comes first," Ash agreed. "Always."

"Good," Miller said, finishing her whiskey. "And I want to decide when he's told."

"And when will that be?" Candice asked.

"That's part of my other condition, but that's something I need to tell Ash and Olly together."

Candice stared at her and then looked at Ash. "I'm happy with that. You?"

Ash shook his head. "Jesus," he said. "You both act like I'm not capable of making my own decisions."

"Goodnight, Ash," Miller said. "And good luck," she said to Candice.

"Don't worry about me," Candice said. "I make my own luck."

Suki and Nate had just been to see the 3 p.m. showing of *Ghostbusters,* and as they made their way down the stairs into the hot August afternoon, Suki stopped at the announcement board at the bottom of the steps.

"Have you seen this?" she asked.

Nate peered at a flyer pinned to the cork board. He nodded. "The screening. Yeah."

"It says it's this Friday. So it's already done? I mean the movie, it's finished?"

"It's just a rough cut. But they're done shooting here for now."

"Well, so . . . what about the whale?" Suki asked. Then she shook him by the shoulders in mock hysteria. "Where's our freakin' whale?"

Nate laughed, shrugged. "Rodrigo won't say anything, but they had some kind of, I don't know, secret shoot for it. Wouldn't let the cast or any of the regular crew along. I think he wants people to be really surprised. He's big into 'authenticity.'"

"Well, that's boring."

As they made their way down Main Street, they had to cross over to the other side of the road to avoid a television camera crew. A small lady with big blonde hair who Nate vaguely recognized from TV was interviewing the mayor of Wonderland.

"So," she was saying, "this must just be so exciting. To have a real Hollywood film immortalizing your charming town. I mean, I look around and I can just see the excitement on people's faces. So, tell me, Mayor Ridgewood, what about the whale?"

"Well, Candice, that one's a bit of a mystery. Even to me. And I'm the mayor."

Nate laughed under his breath.

They turned down Church Street. Neither had asked the other what they wanted to do next. Because they both already knew where they were going and what they wanted.

As they passed the rectory, Nate saw Cam standing in his driveway. Nate raised his hand, but Cam turned away.

When they reached Nate's house, she followed him in. Nate called out and when there was no answer they went upstairs to his bedroom.

He pulled her over the threshold and began kissing her, his hands sliding up under her shirt, over her breasts. He'd been hard since the theater.

He led her to the bed where they lay down and peeled their clothes off one by one. And there was the quiet of the room and the sweet smell of her body and the sense of secrecy and the feeling that he shouldn't be allowed to do this with someone like her and it made everything good.

Afterwards, they both lay facing each other in his single bed, the sheets bunched up at the end. He watched her. "Can I film you? For my short?"

"Right now?" She rolled over on her back. "It's so hot."

"I won't use it if you don't like it."

She looked back at him. "Can I just wear the sheet? I don't know if I can deal with getting dressed right now."

"Yes," he said, running his hand along her naked body. "Yes, you can."

Nate pulled on his boxers and began setting up the camera and tripod, the boom box. He placed a chair up against a blank space of wall, and looked through the lens. "Okay. Just sit there."

Suki sat up and rolled off the bed. She walked slowly to the chair and sat down, re-adjusting the sheet around her like a towel.

Nate looked through the lens again. "You look incredible like that," he said.

She smiled.

"Okay," he said. "I'm going to play you a piece of music and I want to get your reaction. So just go with whatever it is. I'm going to be filming your face."

"This feels like a test."

"It's not a test," he said, cueing up the tape. "Ready?"

"Ready."

He hit play.

'Cause I've seen, oh, blue skies through the tears in my eyes. And I realize, I'm going home . . .

He watched her through the lens. She smiled, a secret kind of smile. He zoomed in on her face, her beautiful bone structure, the way she turned her face slightly left as she thought, or remembered.

"What do you see when you hear this?"

She closed her eyes. "Mmmm . . . glitter, maybe, and . . . I don't know. I don't know how to answer that. I don't see anything."

"Okay, how does it make you feel?"

Her eyes opened again. She looked directly at the lens, and through it, at him. "It makes me feel . . . like anything's possible."

Suki left Nate's house around eight; she'd promised she'd be home for dinner. But when she opened her front door, the house had a strange quality to it. As if it were deserted. She called out to her mother, but there was no answer, so she made her way upstairs and walked across the landing to her parents' bedroom.

Inside, it was chaos. The doors to the walk-in were wide open, half the racks were empty and there were clothes and shoes strewn around the floor. She called for her mother again and when she got no answer, started back downstairs, a dark pool of fear collecting in her stomach.

She walked through the foyer past the sunken living room and into the kitchen, towards the pool. As she got to the sliding glass doors that led outside, she saw her mother and Reverend Cross sitting at the wrought-iron table at the end of yard.

She opened the door and hurried out. "Mom."

Suki's mother looked up. "Oh, honey," she said.

"Are you okay?"

Her mother rose and took Suki into her arms. "I'm fine, I'm fine."

Over her mother's shoulder she saw Reverend Cross watching them silently.

"What's happened?" Suki asked. "I saw your bedroom . . ."

"No, no. It's all right. Your father . . . he's in trouble. He's left."

"Is he coming back?"

"I don't think so," her mother said.

They looked at each other.

"Good," Suki said, finally.

Later, Suki was up in her room, lying on her bed. She stared at the phone on the table next to her. It was an ivory and gold plastic thing, meant to look like a fancy telephone from the olden days. She remembered how she'd begged her father to buy it for her. Suki turned over and stared at the ceiling.

She switched off the light. From time to time, the headlights of passing cars on Church Street illuminated the room. She closed her eyes and thought about the song Nate had played for her, the one from *Rocky Horror*. She heard a tapping sound. She rose and went to the window. Through the screen, she could see Cam, standing in the front garden below.

"Cam?" She tried to keep her voice low. She didn't want to wake her mother.

"Come down," he said.

"It's late," Suki said.

"Please."

Suki sighed. She tugged at her T-shirt, stretching it to make sure it covered her underpants and then went downstairs. She went out the front door, and shut it quietly behind her. Cam met her on the steps.

"What is it?"

He stared at her. He was a big guy, something she hadn't really understood about him until she was alone with him in the dark. "What is it, Cam?"

"Run away with me."

"Are you drunk?" She squinted at him, but his features, even in the half-shadow, looked normal.

"No. Run away with me. We could go to California. You could get away from your dad. And I could take care of us both. I could get a job."

"Cam," Suki said, folding her arms across her chest, "I'm not running away to California. Anyway, my dad's gone."

"You hate it here as much as I do," Cam said.

"I don't know if I hate it here. I don't know what I think about anything."

"I love you," he said.

"Oh, Cam. You don't love me. You don't even know me." She shrugged. "I don't even know me."

"I do."

"Cam, you know I'm seeing Nate, right?"

"Nate only cares about himself."

"Come on," she said, quietly. "Look, it's late . . ."

Cam grabbed her arm. "Run away with me. I promise I won't let you down."

Suki didn't know what to say to make this conversation end. But she really wanted it to be over. "Well, what about our parents?" she said finally, flailing for something to stop him talking about running away.

"What about them?"

"Well, you know they're together, right? And now that my dad's gone . . ."

Cam looked at her, his face close to hers. "What do you mean?"

"You didn't know?"

"What?"

"They're seeing each other, or whatever. You know, they're a couple."

Cam straightened up and started backing away from her.

"Cam . . ."

"No . . ." he said, his arms outstretched as if pushing her away. "Don't talk anymore."

"Cam . . . come on."

"Don't say another fucking word. You're all fakes, it's all bogus. All of it, all of you." He said this with such violence, a kind that Suki was well schooled in, that she backed away slowly until she could feel the door handle with her hand, then opened it and fled inside. She leaned against the door, her heart pounding, until she was sure he was gone.

Suki had gone to see Nate in the morning. She'd been pale and shaking when she'd told him about Cam, that he'd gone to her house, what he'd said. She couldn't really explain, though, why exactly it had been so frightening. But Nate knew then that he had to talk to Cam; he hadn't listened when Jess had warned him that something was off, but now it was clear she was right.

When he went by the rectory house, Reverend Cross had told him that Cam was finishing up his lifeguarding shift, so Nate took off quickly to catch him.

When he arrived at Dune Beach, it looked like something from a movie: the bright blue sky, high, domed and clear, the waves rolling in evenly. The dunes rising behind, and in front, the rough golden sand peaked and troughed, sloping downwards towards the ocean. Nate could see the beachgoers playing in the water: kids near the shore with buckets and shovels, dots of primary colors; teenagers farther out with their boogie boards, shouting to each other, their words indistinct.

In the last month or so, there'd been a noticeable change in the people on the beach. It was no longer just the usual locals—moms with their kids, shop workers on their day off, teenagers working on their tans—there was a new group, different. It seemed that the movie had attracted them—wannabe actors, singers, maybe—like it was emitting some ultrasonic signal. The bikinis were tiny, the bodies were beautiful, the hair glossy, the towels plusher. They had little bits of sheer fabrics they seemed to cover up in, gold jewelry winking in the sunlight. The guys were all impossibly brown, no hint of a farmer's tan, their stomachs smooth and muscled, their hair perfectly tousled.

Ahead, Nate could see the high, wooden lifeguard's chair. Cam, having clearly already finished his shift, was climbing down and beginning to walk towards the road in the opposite direction. Nate picked up his pace, called after him, but Cam neither turned nor answered. Nate broke into a run.

He caught up with him at Cam's car. It was obvious that Cam had heard him calling and just ignored him, because he turned with a kind of *What now?* expression on his face.

"Aren't you working today?" Cam asked, accusingly, as he looked for his car keys.

"Day off," Nate said. "Listen . . ."

Cam wasn't listening, though, he was unlocking the door, throwing his stuff in the back of the Woody Wagon.

"Cam, hold up," Nate said.

"What do you want?" Cam said, turning now to look at Nate.

His expression was one Nate had never seen on his friend's face before—hard, almost mask-like.

"What do I *want*?"

"You couldn't let me have her, could you?"

Nate was getting angry now. "What am I supposed to do, Cam? Back off so that you can pine for her in peace from the sidelines?"

They looked at each other, and something—something awful, something irreparable, maybe—rose up between them.

"It should've been me." Cam crossed his arms against his chest.

"I'm not sure Suki would agree with that statement," Nate said, coldly.

"You have no idea what it's like for people like us. In this place," Cam spat. "You have no idea what it's like to be a freak."

"Jesus, Cam."

"You just come in here, and you're my pal. Right? You're so good. Right? Such a loyal guy, *Nate*. And you want this job, and you get it. And you want this girl, and you whine about it, and you get her. But you have no idea who she really is. And you definitely don't know who I am."

"What do you want me to say, here, Cam? I thought we were friends. I was clearly mistaken."

"You're so full of shit." Cam laughed. "You know what, Nate? My eyes might be fucked up, but you're the one who's blind." Then he got into his car, slammed the door, and peeled out of the verge.

They'd all agreed to meet at Aunt Tassie's house, or rather Miller had decided that when she'd convened the meeting between the three of them. It was safer that way—there was no chance Nate would walk in on them.

It was evening, the sun blowing out of the sky. Olly opened the door when she knocked, his hair wet and pushed off his forehead, his eyes serious. She swallowed, and looked away quickly. She followed him into the kitchen.

"Drink?"

"No, thank you," she said, looking around, thinking about the last time she'd been here, eating a peanut butter and jelly sandwich on the counter, in Olly's bathrobe. "Where's Aunt Tassie?"

"Asleep," Olly said. "She turns in early these days."

They stood there, quiet. After a few minutes, they heard Ash call out from the hallway.

"In here," Miller said. She leaned back against the counter, bracing herself.

Olly watched Miller lean against the counter, crossing her long legs, as if she didn't have a care in the world. He'd never known how she did that: flatten her surface, like newly laid pavement, become sealed, impervious to the elements around her. He'd seen her do it over the years: the last time had been when they'd all met at the Eidolon Lounge, when he'd revealed his betrayal, his revenge. That hadn't ended well for him then. He swallowed and turned to watch Ash walk into the kitchen.

Ash could have really used a drink, but when he saw that neither Olly nor Miller had a glass on the go, he knew he couldn't ask for one. He looked at Olly, and thought: He looks as nervous as I feel. Ash'd been annoyed with Candice after the conversation at the Gunthersons' party; he knew he could be indecisive, but still, he'd told her, that had been ridiculous. However, now that he was here, he found himself wishing she could do this part, too.

"Well," Ash said, casting around for something, anything, to say. "This place looks exactly the same."

"Yup." Olly nodded.

Miller watched them, these two men who had consumed so much of her life. She sighed. "So," she said. "Nate." They looked at her. "Things can't go on this way. Firstly, we don't know—none of us—which one of you is actually his father."

"There're tests for that kind of thing," Olly said.

"Yes," Miller said, "but that's not how this is going to go. At least not yet."

Ash shook his head, the exasperated look he'd been giving her for years passing across his face.

"No," she said, sharply. "No more of that. We all have to be on the same page now. So, Olly—Ash wants a divorce so he can be with his girlfriend. And I've agreed. So that has to be the first thing we deal with."

Olly looked at Ash, raised his eyebrows.

Ash shrugged. "She's great. She's very strong-willed. Candice, I mean."

"Right, well, anyway, Nate is starting college in a month," Miller continued, "and I don't want to ruin something for him that's supposed to be exciting and wonderful. Having said that, we can't hide it, either. So we'll have to tell him before he goes."

Ash looked back at Miller, as if to say: *We do?*

"Then, after that, we can deal with this mess . . ." She waved her hand at the two of them. "Obviously, we have to tell him everything we know, which isn't much, but, to him, it will feel like a bomb going off."

Ash and Olly nodded—Ash vigorously, Olly warily.

"So, what does that mean?" Olly said. "When do we tell him about me? In six months? In another seventeen years? When you decide to publish your book on the subject?"

"Look," Miller said, "there's no use getting on your high horse about it, Olly. You pretended he didn't exist for the last seventeen years. Then, when you decide your life has no meaning, you sneak back here to try to claim him behind our back."

"Exactly," Ash said.

"And," Miller said, "we need to know you're emotionally stable if we're going down this path. I'm not letting my son believe someone might be his father who then goes and tries to kill himself again. Or succeeds, god forbid."

"Wait, what?" Ash said.

"It's been a tough few years for all of us," Miller said, softly, putting a hand on Olly's arm, then extending her other towards Ash. "Me included. But we have to be better now. Agreed?"

They looked at each other, like a bunch of high-stakes poker players trying to decide who might be bluffing.

Finally, Ash said: "Agreed."

"Agreed," said Olly.

"Good," Miller said. "So, here's what I propose. Ash—you and I will sit down with Nate next week and tell him what's going to happen. You'll have to tell him about Candice, too. No more secrets. Then all three of us are going to drive him cross country to L.A. This will be a show of unity for him between me and Ash—that we can get along and that we're still here for him—and it will give you, Olly, an opportunity to be there for him if he needs someone to talk to."

"Oh . . ." Ash said, "I don't know."

"I'm with Ash. I don't think this is a good idea."

"It is a good idea," Miller said, emphatically. "And you both need to agree to it, or I'm telling him everything myself. This is a trust exercise."

"So, what? I just get to stay the trusted family friend?" Olly asked.

"For now, yes. I'm going to stay out in L.A. for a bit, just to make sure Nate gets settled, and that he's okay. I also have some stuff to do out there. And unless a perfect time arises before then, we all agree to a deadline of telling him in one year. And if he wants to keep things as the status quo, we respect that. If he wants a test, we respect that. He might hate us, but we have to deal with that. We made this mess and now we have to clean it up."

"Fuck," Olly said. "I need a drink."

"Oh, thank god you said that. Where's the booze?" Ash started looking around the kitchen.

Olly found a bottle of whiskey and poured a glass for Ash and himself. He held the bottle over a third glass. "Miller?"

She looked at it, nodded. "So," she said. "You're both in?"

"I'm in," Olly said. "I think it's a fucking weird plan, but I'm in."

"Who are we kidding?" Ash asked. "I'm not going to come up with anything else. I'm in."

They clinked their glasses together. Then finished their drinks in silence. Olly poured a second round.

After a while, Ash said: "This is going to sound weird, though given everything Miller's just said, maybe not so weird . . . But I think we should do something, you know, to seal the pact."

Miller laughed. "I'm not sure that's necessary."

"It's hot." Olly wiped a sheen of sweat with his palm up his forehead into his hairline. "Let's go to the cove."

Ash shrugged. "Why not?"

"I don't know . . ."

"Oh, come on, Miller. Don't be a spoilsport," Olly said.

"Yeah, Miller," Ash said.

She tilted her head, eyed them both. "Fine. But I need to go get my suit."

"No suits necessary," Olly said. "It's dark out there."

"I think we can honestly say, it's nothing any of us haven't seen before," Ash said, smiling a little.

"Well—" Miller shrugged "—if you guys think you can handle it . . ."

"I'm taking this, too," said Ash, picking up the whiskey bottle.

They walked down Foster Street, turning onto Meeting House Way, and the evening, soft and hot, the fireflies dotting the recent darkness, the smell of burnt-out grass seething in the air—all these things seemed to conspire to create a reflection of how the three of them were feeling in that moment. They didn't speak, but they all felt it like a current running between them—a rightness, something light, something joyful, at last.

When they got to the little cove, it was empty but they could hear the sounds of music and laughter come from the direction of the high school, not far from where they stood. One of the last of the summer parties for Wonderland's teens, perhaps.

They each took a swig from the whiskey bottle then started peeling off their clothes, that feeling of illicit excitement, of sex, of possibility, running through them again, each marveling at how this act never seemed to lose its ability to thrill.

Then they ran into the water, forgetting of course, that they were much older now, and the water was much shallower here than they'd remembered; they were too big to just dive in. So instead, they slowed down and walked out until they were thigh-high, then eased themselves in, floating gingerly just above the sand.

Slowly, at first, with the sculling motion of their arms and gentle kicks of their feet, small flashes of light began to zigzag through the water. They smiled at each other, and Miller rolled over on her

344

stomach and began kicking furiously until that chain of blue-green stars, so long remembered, lit up all around them. Exploding, tiny universes of glowing light. They sat, the water around their necks, pulling their hands through the salty ocean and letting it drip from their fingertips, shaking their heads and laughing.

From the high school they could hear the Talking Heads playing, "Once in a Lifetime." Miller was thinking about the last time she'd heard it, in the car months ago now, what seemed like a lifetime ago, when everything—time, motion—was stopped and colored green. Ash was listening to the lyrics, thinking, *Yes, that's right, that's how it's been for so long.* And Olly, he was seeing something hovering just at the edge of his vision, hues of gold and mossy-green and red, wondering if he was imagining the taste of lake water in his mouth.

On Friday evening, everyone who was anyone in Wonderland was making their way to the town hall for the screening of the movie, *their* movie. For truly, it did belong to them. In the collective consciousness of the tidal island, *Moby-Dick* had become a master signifier, it had become *them*. And they were all coming to see themselves reflected up on that silver screen.

Miller went downstairs after her shower to find Ash in the den, standing facing the TV, his back to her, his light gray dress shirt smooth like a puddle.

"Nate'll be down in a minute," she said.

Ash had moved back into the house, but this time into the guest room; Candice had stayed at the hotel; they had decided to wait until after the whole film business had wrapped up to break the news to Nate.

Ash turned when she entered, the case for *Une Femme Est Une Femme* in his hand.

"Do you remember when the three of us saw this?" he asked, a half-smile on his lips. "In Venice Beach?"

"You were there?" It came out before she could stop it.

Ash laughed, a hollow sound in his throat, and put the case back next to the television. "You probably thought it was just you and Olly," he said. "But then, I guess, for you it always was."

"No," Miller said, though she didn't know which part she was saying no to.

"It doesn't matter," Ash said. He looked around the room. "It feels like no one actually lives here anymore. Or maybe it's just me." He turned back to Miller. "Maybe it's felt that way since Nate went off to school."

"Maybe," Miller said. Her hair was dripping at the ends, still damp from the shower, soaking the straps of her white tank top. She coiled it in her hand and squeezed the water onto the red and green rug, only then remembering that Ash hated it when she did that.

But he said nothing, and she supposed that didn't matter either, anymore.

"Do you think you'll want to keep it? The house?"

"I don't know," she said. She looked around at the hunting pictures, the green couches, the feather seat cushions indented with their bodily imprints made permanent over the years, and a heavy, gray sadness lay on her heart.

"Hey," Ash said, "we did okay, didn't we? I mean, are we—am I—a failure?"

"No," she said, crossing the floor towards him. "No. We just couldn't see the road ahead, I think."

"I'm sorry," he said. "I know things got pretty bad, but everything's going to be all right."

"*Everything's going to be all right*." She shrugged. "Well, either that, or it's all going to end in tears."

"Yeah," Ash said, nodding. "Or that."

As the three of them were leaving the house, Nate said he was going to pick up Suki, and when he came out of the Pfeiffers' place, Suki, Cricket, and Dick Cross followed. Miller watched Nate lean into Suki, his mouth close to her ear, the kind of gesture that could only be made when some physical barrier had been

346

broken down, some kind of intimacy had been achieved. And she thought: God, the good parts are so good. Even the bad parts can't make the good parts any less good.

The six of them walked companionably in the heat of the evening. All the once-glittering green lawns in the front of the candy-colored houses were now browned out, an air of sandpaper about them; the hostas were burnt at the edges; the rose bushes hung with their red hips drooping like rouged nipples. And while it still smelled of salt and of sweet, crumbling pine, the air also carried the scent of autumn, of imminent ending.

Ash watched Dick and Cricket walking side by side, and thought: *Well, well, well*. He'd heard, of course, about Dutch's precipitous flight from the law—the whole town knew about it. Some said Brazil or Mexico, with a stop by the Cayman Islands to collect his cash on the way. Others thought Europe—Andorra or France. Either way, Dutch was on the run. And in his absence, love had apparently blossomed. Ash smiled; there was a certain symmetry to it.

"Is Cam coming tonight?" he asked.

"I don't really know," Dick said. "Nate, did he say anything to you?"

Ash watched his son and Suki exchange a glance. "Haven't seen him today," Nate said—very carefully, Ash thought.

"I'm sure he'll come along," Dick said. "He wouldn't want to miss it."

"Who would?" Cricket smiled at Dick. "It's so exciting."

When they arrived at the town hall, Candice and her crew were set up outside, doing man-on-the-street interviews. Ash watched Miller walk briskly by her and up the steps. He caught Candice's eye and winked, then followed the rest of them up the stairs.

The theater was packed, and some of Wonderland's citizens had brought their own camp chairs and set them up in the aisles. Clearly, Ash thought, the fire department had decided to turn a blind eye to the overcrowding—he saw the fire chief chatting to the mayor in the corner near the stage, which was set up with a microphone. They managed to find some seats near the front, only unspoken for because they were close enough that you'd have to crane your neck to see the screen. At a certain point, it seemed to have gotten too much, and the doors were closed. The fire chief barked at the waiting crowd to move back onto the street.

Mayor Ridgewood took to the stage to make introductions and big-up the town's involvement in the production. Ash looked around and saw Olly a few rows back, next to Aunt Tassie, who was wearing naval whites for the occasion.

"Following the screening," Mayor Ridgewood was saying, "the director—sure all you folks know him by now—Rodrigo Rodrigo, will say a few words and take some questions from all of you. So don't be shy."

The lights went out and the audience started clapping.

The opening credits began to roll to the sounds of the end of the second movement of Beethoven's Ninth Symphony—a tripping, waltz-like music perhaps more at home in a costume drama than a creature feature. As the music built, it was punctuated by a thump-thump of drums, like a knocking at the door.

Knock went the drums, up went "MOBY-DICK" in black bold letters on the white screen. *Knock* went the drums, up went "CALL ME ISHMAEL" in the same stark black blocks. Then the music cut off abruptly, like the screech of tires.

A voice-over sounded out into the theater: *I love to sail forbidden seas, and land on barbarous coasts.* The shot opened with Ishmael standing with his carpet bag in front of the swinging sign for the Spouter-Inn, and the audience applauded loudly at the sight of *Matt's*, their *Matt's*, transformed and appearing before their very eyes.

A bawdy and strange scene at the Spouter-Inn ensued, which included a sexual encounter between Ishmael and his shipmate Queequeg, brown skin against white, tangled limbs and mouths on indistinct parts of the body.

The end of the scene was punctuated by a quick shot of a barmaid at the Spouter-Inn pulling her top down to expose her breasts, and looking directly at the camera, black block titles flashing: "TITS ON LAND."

The room began to fill with the sound of people shifting in their seats, the air laced with anxiety.

And yet on it went, sections of Beethoven's Ninth serving as the only soundtrack: scenes of the crew in their hammocks at night, rocking madly as the sound of Ahab pacing the deck above—his whale-bone leg banging like an unceasing drum—drove them slowly insane; strange, violent speeches made by the captain, punctuated with music rather than words emanating from his mouth; semi-operatic scenes between the sailors at midnight; pagan rituals.

When a sperm whale, unseen on screen but referred to, was cut up on deck with uncommonly malevolent tools, the only indication of its existence was the blood gushing in rivulets across the *Pequod*, dripping down the faces, the arms, the legs of the actors, who were covered in bits of gore and hacking away at meat on the deck.

The mood turned sour in the theater.

People started mumbling, talking amongst themselves— *Disgusting, What the . . .? Jesus.* Yet, still, for the most part, the citizens of Wonderland persevered. They wanted their whale.

Then the moment came: the crew of the *Pequod* cried that they had spied the white whale. The audience held its breath. There wasn't a sound in the theater.

The perspective shifted, and the audience found themselves beneath the surface of the ocean, following the eye of the camera as it moved through the water. But no whale appeared. Starting softly, and building, was the sound of Blue's voice singing a high, eerie, cooing marine ballad. The underwater shots became long and languorous, diving deep into the dark water, before turning and pushing upward, at speed. This was the whale's perspective, yet, still, no whale appeared on screen.

And little by little, it became clear that it wouldn't.

Captain Ahab, standing in his boat's bow, gazed down at where Moby-Dick was supposed to be, opened his mouth and all that came out was a symphony recording of the "Ode to Joy," in stereo sound.

"Oh, friends, no more of these sounds! Let us sing more cheerful songs, more songs full of joy!"

349

The camera cut again to Moby-Dick's perspective and Blue's song responded: "Uh-ooo. Woo woo. Oooo ooo oooo."

Above water: "Joy, lovely divine spark, Daughter of Elysium, with fiery rapture we approach your sanctuary!" went the "Ode to Joy," spooling from Ahab's mouth. "Your magic reunites, what stern custom separated; all men shall be brothers, under your gentle wings."

They went back and forth—Ahab and the invisible, non-existent whale—singing a deeply weird, perverse love song to each other. Then the whole crew of the *Pequod* burst into song, mouthing the rousing full choral section of the symphony, the music thundering on, like an opera of the damned.

And that was it. The crowd went berserk. They now knew what Rodrigo and Blue and Olly knew: it had been a ruse, all the talk of a whale, all the secrecy, the huge, empty trailer brought over in the middle of the night and guarded by plastic policemen. The people of Wonderland had waited all summer long for their *Jaws*, their whale, their movie moment of glory, and they had been tricked and used and they weren't gonna take it anymore.

People stood and started throwing popcorn and Cokes at the screen. Others were desperately trying to escape the projectiles, pushing and shoving to get past each other to the aisles, and to safety. The pushing and shoving devolved into fights between the audience members—men swinging at other men for pushing their wives, kids scrapping over perceived insults, women swinging their purses in an effort to get out to the aisles—and when camp chairs began to be thrown, full-out pandemonium ensued, as the final movement of Beethoven's Ninth Symphony crashed on, until someone had the good sense to turn off the projector.

"We have to get out of here," Ash said, grabbing Miller and Nate by their arms.

Miller looked behind her and saw Olly struggling to get Aunt Tassie out of her seat; she seemed to be refusing to budge.

"Ash," she said, "go help Olly. We'll be all right."

But it seemed impossible to move, until Ash finally vaulted over the last two seats to the aisle.

Meanwhile, Rodrigo took to the stage, shouting into the microphone: "Don't you see? The white whale is a conjurer's trick, the invention of a demagogue. The white whale does not exist. The white whale does not exist. Only love, brothers!"

A couple of men tried to storm the stage, but the fire chief blew his horn, which seemed to bring them to their senses. People were streaming out the doors by this point, and Miller and Nate had managed to get up the aisle to where Ash was trying to help Olly deal with Aunt Tassie, who seemed agitated.

Rodrigo was still standing on the stage, saying, "Ladies and gentlemen, I give you *Moby-Dick: A Love Story*."

"Is everyone okay?" Miller asked, looking around at each of them. She could barely hear Aunt Tassie whisper: "It's time."

"Jesus," Nate said. "That was amazing. He's a genius."

Olly, holding Aunt Tassie close to him, laughed. "You're a director, all right. You're all fucking crazy."

"My god," Ash said, and started laughing, too. "That's not something this town's going to forget anytime soon."

They stood together until crowd had thinned, and there were only a few stragglers left. Cricket and Dick Cross were walking towards them, a few feet from where they stood, Suki in their wake.

"Well," Dick said. "I wasn't expecting that."

And just as the words were leaving his mouth, the first shot rang out.

They all turned to see Cam standing at the back of the theater, a lonely Greek god with a sawed-off shotgun in his hand, plaster from the ceiling falling on him as softly as snow. He began walking down the aisle towards them, not quickly, not slowly, but methodically and with purpose. It seemed they were frozen to the spot, as if their brains couldn't catch up with their eyes and tell their bodies to move, to do something, to do anything. And when he was a few feet away, he stopped, looked at his father, his face a pantomime of desperate, broken weeping, placed the shotgun under his arm, aimed and said: "You first," and shot him.

Dick went down. It felt like chaos: they all looked to where he was lying, bleeding; they began to move towards Dick, as if by instinct, as if they knew he was still in danger.

But, gun still raised, Cam advanced toward Nate. "You next."

Standing just too far behind, too late, Miller turned, saw her son raise both his hands in supplication, saying: "Don't, don't."

Cam looked at him for a moment, his crumpled face breaking and smoothing. It was just a moment's hesitation, and before Miller or Ash could even move an arm, a leg, a finger, an eyelash, Olly had stepped in front of Nate, and in the split second it took for Cam to shake his head *no*, and take aim again, Aunt Tassie had sidestepped in front of Olly.

From where Miller and Ash stood, it appeared like a tableau, the three of them—their son, their friend and Aunt Tassie—suspended in time, the kind of time it takes for a teardrop of water to form and fall, before the shot left the barrel and flew straight into the heart of Billy Budd.

The next shot, the final shot, Cam had reserved for himself alone.

PART VI

AND NOW THE
TALE IS DONE

SEPTEMBER, 1984

Nate, Miller, Ash and Olly were packing up the Volvo in the drive of the house on Church Street. A few boxes stood stacked and labeled near the kitchen door, to be sent on later, when Nate was settled.

When they'd awoken that morning, there had been a cool undercurrent running through the air, which was now slowly dissipating in the early September sun.

Aunt Tassie's memorial service had taken place earlier in the week, and the whole town had turned out to wish her and Billy Budd well on their next journey. There would be no public send-off for Cam, though Dick, still recovering from the shot to his shoulder, had arranged to have him buried privately in a cemetery a few towns away to avoid any desecration of his son's grave.

Nate had gone to see Dick that morning to say goodbye. They shook hands, and smiled, and Nate had promised to write. He'd also wanted to give Dick the footage he had of Cam, in happier times, though looking at it now, Nate wondered if indeed they had been happier.

"I didn't see it," Dick had said.

"Me either," Nate had said. "I guess we were looking in the wrong direction."

"I don't know why . . ." Dick had stopped, taken a deep breath, his gray face lined deeply now. "I don't know why," he said, "God has made some pain invisible, so that we can't reach out our hand to help. I don't know why there is emptiness where there should be manifestation."

"I don't know," Nate had said, but he'd thought about it all the way home, thinking of Cam, thinking of Rodrigo's invisible whale.

The film crew had long since departed, leaving Wonderland to lick its wounds in peace. Olly had heard from Rodrigo, who'd told him that while Seymour Geist was incensed and was threatening to sue the director for breach of contract, there had been some excellent feedback on early screenings of the unedited cut in France, and Seymour was hoping to unload *Moby-Dick* on a foreign distributor.

"You have to ask: what the fuck is wrong with people when universal love isn't as fucking exciting as some mechanical monster," Rodrigo had told Olly over the phone, a shrug in his voice. "Anyway, the French have always been the first to see genius."

After the screening, Rodrigo and Blue had made a quick getaway, flying back to Los Angeles in order not to be burned at the stake, though Blue had stopped by the house the night she left to give Miller her address in L.A., where Miller would be staying while she worked on her piece for *Rolling Stone*.

"Just come straight over when you get there," Blue had said. "There's always somebody home."

Ash shoved the last suitcase into the way-back and stood up. "I think that's it," he said, wiping his hands on his jeans. "Who's taking the first shift?"

"I will," Olly said.

"I call the front," Nate said.

Miller and Ash exchanged a look.

"Do I need to put a pillow between you guys?" Nate asked.

"Don't be fresh," Miller said.

Of course they'd considered putting off telling him about the divorce, after everything that had happened, but had decided they couldn't go on lying. Though, in the end, they did leave Candice's name out of it.

When they *had* finally sat him down and told him, he'd just shrugged: "I figured." Then he'd looked at them both, hard, and said: "Just don't be assholes to each other."

In fact, he'd seemed more concerned with what would happen to the house. Afterwards, Ash had been relieved, but Miller had wondered if it was all just boiling away beneath the surface, worried it might erupt somewhere down the road, and she was glad to be going to L.A. to keep an eye on him.

"I'm going to do one last run through the house," Miller said. As she turned to go back inside, she saw Suki coming out of the Pfeiffers' place. "I think someone's here to see you," she told her son, smiling.

Nate grabbed something from his bag and jogged over to Suki. Out of their earshot, they watched as he spoke to her, and then handed her a video cassette. Then Nate leaned in and, taking Suki's face in his hands, he kissed her—that kind of passionate, young, shining, desirous kiss that they all remembered.

Miller and Olly and Ash looked at each other, a ribbon of experience and pain and joy running between them, a memory of the shining lights of a fairground so many years ago, of chains of stars in the water, of music and heat and youth and envy and God, and of small, small towns and big cities and heartbreak, and of a boy that connected them all.

Olly got into the car and started the engine. The radio switched on.

By the front gate, Nate squeezed Suki's hands one more time. "I've got to go," he said.

She nodded.

"I'll see you in a month," he said. "You're gonna love L.A. I'm going to make you love it and then you'll come for good."

"We'll see," she said.

He kept looking at her.

She looked back.

"Okay," he said. "Okay, I'm going."

"Go."

He walked backward, still holding her hand until they couldn't hold on any longer and their fingertips broke away from each other and the connection was severed. Then he turned and walked towards the car, the sound of Wang Chung's "Dance Hall Days" blaring from the radio.

And in Nate's head, an explosion of color—gold, bright green, purple, red—the colors of late summer, of his friend's blood and tissue splattered in the town hall, but also the colors of a song that told you it was time to get on the road, to travel on to what was waiting around the bend. The colors that were—that had always been—in his head when he heard music.

He got in the car, shut the door and looked at Olly.

"I'm ready," he said. "Let's go."